Nookietown

Nookietown

V. C. CHICKERING

ST. MARTIN'S GRIFFIN
NEW YORK

This is a work of fiction. All of the characters, organizations, and events portrayed in this novel are either products of the author's imagination or are used fictitiously. Except for one of you, and you know who you are. Just kidding.

www.stmartins.com

The Library of Congress Cataloging-in-Publication Data is available upon request.

ISBN 978-1-250-06481-3 (trade paperback)
ISBN 978-1-250-09131-4 (hardcover)
ISBN 978-1-4668-7115-1 (e-book)

Our books may be purchased in bulk for promotional, educational, or business use. Please contact your local bookseller or the Macmillan Corporate and Premium Sales Department at (800) 221-7945, extension 5442, or by e-mail at MacmillanSpecialMarkets @macmillan.com.

First Edition: February 2016

10 9 8 7 6 5 4 3 2 1

Dedicated to A. C. O.

Acknowledgments

In somewhat chronological order, I heartily thank:

My family; Beth and Tricia Davey for being there first; Wendy Shanker for being my wrock; Joanne for suggesting *No Plot? No Problem!*, Stephen King for *On Writing*, Anne Lamott for *Bird by Bird*; Robert and Scott for not kicking me off the porch; Amanda, Elizabeth, Lee, Christina, Meg, The Solid B Dancers, Jackie, and DBT; Robbie for the title; Rick Reiken for the invaluable chats; Ted, Betsy, and Bill for their unwavering support; Risha, Jessica, Trish, Sandye, Jude, and Dr. J for reminding me of what's what; Amy, Karen, and Lara; Rebecca for getting the ball rolling; Eileen Rothschild for adroitly pushing it along; Brendan Deneen for his mad skillz and panache; Jennifer Enderlin, Meryl Gross, Nicole Sohl, Seamus, and Paul; Michael for his contract chops; Sarah, Tina, Marcy, Kolette, Jenny, and the GONK; Carla for just knowing; Dave Curtis for nailing the cover; Jennifer for David and David M.

Tenzer for navigating with savoir faire; Clancy Collins White and Dave Brown; Sophia Dembling for stomaching the irony; Greg Collins, Brant Janeway, Jessica Preeg, and Angelique Giammarino; the heavens, The Montys, and anyone who ever asked, "How's your book coming along?" Thank you for asking.

Nookietown

Chapter 1

- - - - - - - - - - - - - - - - - -

I just. Want. To get. Laid," said Lucy. Her married friends hadn't
heard her put it quite that way before.

"There are lots of single men out there," said Nancy.

"No, there are *not*," Lucy shot back. Her voice squeaked with
the effort. She was so tired of hearing that phrase she wanted to
put a Nerf bullet in her head. She steadied herself then slipped into
her teacher voice—frank and authoritative. "There are *not* scads
of smart, attractive, disease-free men out there. That is a myth, my
friends, a myth I'm through subscribing to. There are, in fact, very
few. I just want sweaty sex with a killer orgasm and oxytocin cours-
ing through my body. I want to be out of my conscious mind and
feel alive and connected to another adult. I want my neurons high-
fiving each other. Then, after I get my rocks off, I want to walk away.
No laundry, or bitching about the gutters, or would you please turn
off the game and help me with whatsis. None of that. No strings
attached. I just want a nice roll in the hay—about once a week

would probably do it. Twice would be ideal. By someone kind. And hot. And ideally funny and smart. But I'll settle for kind. And smart. No, hot and funny. No, funny and fit. And smart. Just not a slob, please."

"You sound like a hormonal teenage boy," said Nancy.

"Exactly. But without the acne."

"You could have sex with Duncan," said Gina. "It would be nice to get a break once in a while." Nancy looked over at Gina incredulously. Gina was texting, totally blasé. She looked up. "What?" Gina said. "The incessant pawing in the morning gets old."

"You mean at like 6 A.M.?" said Nancy.

"Hate it. Poke, poke," said Gina. She looked over at Lucy. "Can I send Duncan over to you before work?"

"Sure," said Lucy, "how's about Thursdays?"

"Deal," said Gina.

"Sign Ted up, too," said Nancy. "I love the guy but it's nonstop, and by the end of the day I'm wiped. I can't take the guilt."

"Fine. I'll take Ted every other Wednesday night at 8:30, after Gus is in bed asleep."

"I'll pencil that in," said Nancy.

"What should I wear?" asked Lucy.

Gina said, "Something trashy. Duncan loves all that French boudoir bullcrap but won't admit it. Do you own garters?"

Lucy said, "No, but I bet that place in Penn Station has them."

Nancy looked aghast. "Okay, enough kidding around," she said in all earnestness, "this is making me uncomfortable."

"It's fine, Nance, we're just joking," said Lucy.

"I'm not," said Gina matter-of-factly, looking up from her phone. "When do we start?"

"I think it's wrong to be talking so flippantly about infidelity," said Nancy.

"It's not infidelity if the wife's in control," said Lucy.

"I still don't think it's anything to joke about, with 20 percent of husbands cheating—"

"And 20 percent of wives cheating," added Gina.

Nancy continued, "—and everyone prowling around Facebook, looking up old flames, not to mention the 50 percent divorce rate—"

"Actually," Gina said, "they say it's higher but the government doesn't want us to know, because a healthy economy depends on people getting married."

"I read that somewhere, too," said Lucy. "It's all wrapped up in real estate and home goods and services. Something about selling more wall paint and vacuum cleaners and keeping landscapers and furnace-repair guys employed."

Gina said, "Our whole economy is tied up in people thinking it's a good idea to get married and buy a house. The real estate industry subsists on it."

"You're wrong," said Nancy.

Gina said, "We're not saying people shouldn't fall in love and buy a house and a vacuum and have a family. We're just saying that they don't need to get married to do that."

Lucy added, "Yeah, maybe there should be a ten-year lease renewal program instead. Every ten years you get to decide whether to renew each other or move on."

"Are you shitting me?" railed Nancy. She ripped her bread in half, then in half again. "Marriage is *not a car-lease agreement*! And I don't think it's *anything* to joke about. It's *hard enough!*" With that the table fell silent. Forks were adjusted and wine was sipped. Sitting positions shifted. Lucy reached over to touch Nancy's arm, but Nancy moved it away before she could. Gina looked at Nancy and spoke evenly, so as not to come off as patronizing. "Everything okay with you and Ted?" she said.

"Everything's fine," Nancy shot back, then stopped herself. "We're in a rut, but we've had them before. We'll be fine." Lucy took notice of her change in tone.

"Okay, good," said Lucy. "You know you can always tell us if—"

"I know," said Nancy, "I know, thanks. Let's skip it."

The maitre d' asked if they wanted more white wine. An oblong lighting fixture hung beneath a hand-woven fishing net, and a red polyester napkin, which had been folded like a teepee, still sat untouched at Kit's place setting. This was a two-fork Italian joint, Lucy thought, so Gina must have chosen the restaurant. Gina Martell had married Duncan Cho—a corporate attorney—and she herself was in maritime law, one of many degrees. Lawyers marrying lawyers, Lucy thought, shouldn't work in theory, but their marriage was solid and Lucy considered theirs the gold standard. After fourteen years and two kids, Duncan was still mad about Gina's quick wit, slow smile and chunky glasses frames. She was a little odd, which Lucy valued in any woman, and was rarely fazed by anything, which was comforting in a friend. Duncan was so flabbergasted that he caught such a dish, he would tell anyone outright, "I'm the luckiest bastard," then shake his head in wonderment. Gina agreed and loved him right back. They rarely bickered, occasionally fought, and always made each other laugh.

Nancy's marriage to Ted was something else entirely.

"Well," began Lucy, "Kit is going to be late—"

Gina interrupted, "Again."

"Something about one of her kids finding a pack of bubble gum and a Sharpie."

"Yikes," said Nancy, and made an uh-oh face. She was quick to rebound in social situations.

Lucy said, "Gina, did I hear you got another lawyer promotion?"

"A lawyer promotion," said Nancy. "Is that like a teacher promotion?"

"I get a private plane with my name stenciled on the side," Gina said, texting.

"Yup, just like a teacher promotion," said Lucy.

"I should have gone to business school," said Nancy.

"It's the least they can do for those poor lawyers," said Lucy.

"To lawyers," Lucy and Nancy said, raising their glasses. Gina looked up.

Lucy said, "May God bless their sweet, generous, selfless souls—"

"That's enough, it's just a change in title," said Gina, and she went back to texting.

Nancy said, "When do I get a stay-at-home mom promotion?"

"Never," Lucy and Gina said simultaneously.

Lucy leaned towards Nancy and spoke with a singsong lilt, "Don't worry if your work is small and your rewards are few, remember that the mighty oak was once a nut like you."

"Thanks," Nancy said. "Emily Dickinson?"

"Sylvia Plath."

"Right," said Nancy, then she proceeded with the monthly update. "Kit apparently has bunions. Or hammertoe, maybe. We're still not sure. She'll clarify when she gets here."

Lucy said, "She may need minor surgery, according to Nurse Nancy." Nancy Brisbane had applied and been accepted to business school before switching to nursing to appease her parents' financial scenario. She was an ER nurse before quitting to have her three kids and the most seemingly responsible of the group—not that all nurses weren't a little batty, they were, and Nancy had stories to prove it. She'd met Ted right after nursing school in a summer group share at the Jersey Shore. Both tall and blond, they made a striking couple—Nordic stunners. Ted had skipped college to take over his dad's lucrative car dealership and was a good guy, and that's all anyone ever said about him. Their marriage always seemed status quo and Nancy rarely discussed it.

Nancy asked, "Lucy, how's your electrolysis coming along?"

"Oh, swimmingly, thanks for asking. I'm almost done."

"You're still not done, yet?!" said Gina.

"No," said Lucy, "I've been blessed with tenacious upper-thigh hair, but thanks for your concern."

"But you're so fair. Aren't you, like, Danish or something?" said Gina, looking up from her phone.

Lucy said, "Half Danish, half Italian. The Danes have pubic hair, too, you know."

"Viking pubic hair," said Gina. "I'm full *Italian* and *I* haven't had the electrolysis odyssey you've had."

"Some girls are just lucky," said Lucy. "What about you, Gina. What are your unmentionable health issues of late?"

"Same old herpes cold sore b.s.," said Gina. "And the damn dog ate my good underwear. Surgery was beyond expensive."

"You had surgery for your herpes?"

"No, the dog needed surgery to remove the underwear."

"You've got to get rid of that friggin' dog," said Nancy, half serious.

"I can't. Our kids' favorite babysitter died," Gina said, as if that explained everything. Lucy and Nancy looked at her blankly.

"How come you never see these conversations on TV?" Nancy said.

"You have to ask?" said Lucy.

"I'm just sayin' that in the movies women either have cancer or the flu. But nothing in between, nothing embarrassingly lame."

"At least we're not discussing our kids' sports schedules," said Gina.

Lucy said, "Yeah, kill me now. Is our pact still in effect?"

"Now and forever. No one's mentioned their kids yet, have they?"

"No, thank God," Nancy said, and exhaled, visibly relieved, "I couldn't take it."

Lucy said, "Nance, I mean it, are you okay?"

Before Nancy could answer, Kit arrived at the table breathless, and by way of greeting said, "Bunions."

Gina said, "That answers that."

"And hemorrhoids."

"Still?" Lucy said.

"No, they were gone and now they're back," said Kit as she hung her coat on her chair, put her napkin in her lap, and swigged from the glass of pinot grigio they'd ordered her. Then Kit sighed, looked around the table, and asked, "What'd I miss?"

In unison, the other three said, "Nothing."

Chapter 2

- - - - - - - - - - - - - - - - - - - -

The waiter arrived to take their order. As the women took turns asking him about various dressings, substitutions and sauces on the side, Lucy couldn't stop herself from fantasizing about him. It was reflexive now, since her divorce. Like a tic she had no control over. Life as a third-grade schoolteacher had its rewards, but adult-male connection was not among them. Nor was adult excitement, adult risk, or anything very adult for that matter. So, she fantasized. Plus she knew that ordering would take a while.

The waiter was not hot by most people's standards. In fact, he wasn't much of anything. But he had a nice ass and strong hands. Lucy didn't actually know if they were strong—they were only holding a pen and a pad of paper—but she liked to think they were. She liked his eyebrows and decided he was probably Slavic. He had piercing blue eyes that had possibly witnessed stuff she'd only watched on the History Chanel. He was probably in his late forties, but looking around at her other options on the waitstaff, she decided he would do. She asked him his name after she ordered. He smiled a lackluster smile and said, "Sergei."

Telling her friends she'd be right back, Lucy slid out of the banquette and edged between a chair and Sergei's butt, slowing down to gently graze up against him as she passed. When she cleared his body, she glanced back over her shoulder with the best Brazilian-model-in-an-aftershave-commercial look she could muster. Lucy caught his eye as he looked over at her. He was game, all right, so Lucy invited her imagination to take over.

While she peed, she looked at the sink and pictured Sergei hoisting her up onto it. She fantasized about him inching up her skirt—like she had done to her long ago in college-dorm bathrooms—and finding Sergei's cock bouncing erect under his white apron like a friendly ghost. She imagined him pulling her underpants to the side, licking his finger, and finding her swollen, wet and ready. She would clasp her hands behind his neck as he slipped inside her, filling her completely, flushing her body with radiant heat. Lucy's lower body tensed just thinking about the possibilities as she washed her hands. She imagined wrapping her legs around Sergei's waist, locking her ankles before pulling him in deeper. She closed her eyes to savor the fantasy, the hand soap sliding between her fingers. Maybe Sergei would grab her ass as they moved against the sink in slow, steady strokes. Maybe Lucy would break the sink and land in a pile of porcelain and broken bits of tile, then have to explain it to her horrified girlfriends, and reimburse management. Oh, Sergei. Oh, brother. "What a great penis," she'd say to herself later, and she'd tip him an extra five. Seems only fair.

Lucy made her way back to the table, half-disappointed that this little coin-operated joyride of hers was over. She wished she could masturbate but would settle for a hot meal. It ran a close second to a hot quickie.

"You fall in?" Kit said to Lucy.

"Hardy-har," answered Lucy. "What'd I miss?"

Nancy said, "Well, Gina, hasn't stopped texting during our wine course, which leads me to believe she's still—"

"Oh, c'mon, Nance," said Gina.

Lucy caught on. "You are *not* still texting that guy. I thought that was work-related."

"If you consider the dick-photo guy work," said Kit.

"His name is Carlos," said Gina.

"Oh, okay, excuse me, Carlos the Dick-Photo Guy."

"C'mon," said Gina, but even she knew it was absurd that she was still texting him. Six months ago she got a text of a guy's penis. He thought he was sending it to this girl he met in a bar the night before (he was twenty-two) but it accidentally ended up on Gina's phone. At first she reprimanded him, but he apologized right away and was so contrite and seemingly earnest that she continued texting him. She told him that the kind of girl who would enjoy a photo of a guy-she'd-just-met's dick isn't the right girl for him and that he should have higher standards. Gina's nurturing mother side had been activated, and now she felt it was incumbent upon her to fix this young man and cure him of his poor upbringing before releasing him back into the world at large. She counseled him on where to apply to community colleges and what classes to take. She patiently described what he should look for in a girlfriend and how he should behave. Who knows how many texts and how much time Gina had invested in this kid. Her own kids were younger and their problems were simpler. Carlos needed her mentorship. Gina was embarrassed but couldn't help it. She also thought it was harmless.

"You gonna send the kid to graduate school?" said Kit.

"I might," said Gina. "He wants to become a lawyer."

"Uhhhhh," they all groaned.

"I'm just kidding. Jeez, you guys, whaddaya take me for?"

"A compulsive fixer," said Nancy.

"What about you, Lucy? How's the scintillating singles life of dating?" said Gina.

"Well, as you all well know, there is no one out there to fix me up with, otherwise you would have all done it by now, right?"

"Right," they said.

Lucy had been nagging them to fix her up since she became separated. Apparently any guy never married by this point was damaged goods, or way beyond the acceptable limits of damaged.

"Unless you'd like to date some award-winning basket cases," Gina said. "'Cause I can put you in touch with the dregs.'"

"No thank you, but thanks for asking," Lucy said. "I just don't have the kind of time you need to devote to online dating. Sifting through all those inappropriate quotes and ellipses used to separate every thought is a friggin' buzzkill. Why does a guy write that he 'likes'"—Lucy used air quotes—"to go canoeing?"

"But, Lucy," said Kit, "you don't give a shit about canoeing."

"Well, I might if the guy didn't use 'inappropriate' quotes." Lucy used air quotes again.

Gina said, "Wait, you just—"

"I know. I did it on purpose. See how annoying it is? And then he spells 'canoeing' wrong. How does a guy misspell his favorite pastime?! Makes me nutty. I can't be bothered. Plus there's still a world of STDs out there. Herpes is on the rise—no offense, Gina."

"None taken. Plus the dangerous sickos," said Gina.

"Yes, let's not forget the dangerous sickos. And to be honest, I just want to get laid."

Gina turned to Kit.

"You missed her speech."

Kit rolled her eyes.

"Oh, I've heard it."

Lunch arrived and Lucy waited for Sergei to leave the table before continuing. "In my fantasies I'm a total sex addict—compulsive and indiscriminate. But in my real life I'm being picky because I don't want just any oaf muscling in on my new life. I'm finally in a good place. I know that sounds a little mixed-messagey."

"Ya think?" said Gina.

"I know you, and you're not a sex addict, my friend," said Nancy, "You have your urges under control, don't you? Unless there's something you're not telling us . . ."

"No, there's nothing. It's boring. Just years of fantasizing about consensual vanilla sex and the average amount of masturbating."

Kit looked at Nancy.

"What's the average amount of—"

Nancy said, "Later."

"Relax, ladies. I'm in control of my urges. I'm over the two-year just-divorced hump and I want to feel good again. I've got you, my wonderful married friends, my wild-ass divorced friends, plus there's cable. We're in a golden age of television writing, you know."

"You do love your stories," said Nancy.

"I love my stories and don't want another husband. I don't need a place to live and I don't need a father for my son."

"Or a pony," said Gina.

"Exactly, no ponies. So I e-mailed this guy, Peter, I used to run into at teachers' conventions. We always end up laughing together, and he's younger and kind of sexy and I totally could see myself sleeping with him every other week."

"Really?" said Kit.

"That's my dream schedge," said Gina.

"Yeah, but listen: He says he's in a serious relationship but is always interested in making new friends," said Lucy.

"Noooooooo," said Nancy, Gina and Kit. They shook their heads, then leaned forward as if gearing up for debate.

"You've got to cut it off right now," said Kit.

"She hasn't even met the guy for coffee yet," said Gina. "What does he teach?"

"What if he's married?!"

"Infidelity is not illegal," said Gina. "Just immoral."

"It's wrong," said Kit. Lucy knew that as much as Kit loved her, she also could be very opinionated and judge-y. A compact, no-nonsense, stay-at-home mom with a permanent ponytail, Kit Bajinski was the kind of person who knew how to get the results she wanted out of store managers. Lucy's friendship with Kit began on the lame-o maternity-ward hospital tour.

"You're having a boy," Kit proclaimed to Lucy before they'd even exchanged names.

"And you know this because . . ." Lucy had said.

"I just know," replied Kit. Lucy had given Kit a look that suggested she didn't buy it, so Kit added, "Because I'm a witch." She managed to say it with a totally straight face.

Love her, Lucy had thought. They were fast friends after that.

Gina gestured to Kit's empty wineglass. "Drinking and driving's also wrong, pal."

Nancy said, "Maybe this is just what Lucy was talking about— breezy sex."

"I haven't even seen him, yet," Lucy said. "It would just be nice to have a new friend. And he teaches high school physics."

"So he's smart," said Gina.

"And funny, and most likely disease-free, and not a sociopath."

Kit said, "Well, find out if he's married, because straight married guys are not allowed to make new straight female friends. It's practically the law."

"Unless you're gay," said Gina. "Or he's gay."

"Or working together. Then it's fine?" said Lucy. "You can be dating everyone in your office under the guise of 'work-related.' Cocktails and candlelit dinner, midnight strolls at exotic convention locales. That's dating. If we worked at the same school or in the same office, we could have coffee every friggin' day and it would be fine. But work under different rooftops and nooooo waaaaayy."

"That's America," said Nancy.

"Well, I work with this guy one weekend a year at the teachers' convention, so that counts. Work-related."

To be honest, Lucy didn't want to know if Peter was married. She hadn't asked in the e-mail because that would ruin everything. It had been ages since she'd had a guy friend. She missed male energy. She was tired of only going out on ladies' night and for ladies' lunches. She missed the sorts of things you discussed with men: global crisis and indie music, biographies and science. She was sure there were women out there who discussed these topics—or did before they had kids—but she hadn't met any since moving to the suburbs. She'd been craving that kind of exchange for so long, and here's this guy who's funny, smart and has good grammar. Lucy knew Peter was no dime-a-dozen. Gina raised an eyebrow at Kit. Kit put her hands up to her head, then looked at Lucy and leaned in. "Look—" was as far as she got before Lucy interrupted her.

"Okay!" she said, crestfallen. "I'll stop. Jeez."

"I just can't believe you would even consider a committed man after the way Matt treated you," said Kit. "Have you forgotten about Delphine? His 'work wife'?"

Gina said, "We still don't know that he actually cheated, physically."

"Oh, please," said Kit. Lucy rolled her eyes; she'd given up caring long ago. Kit continued, "What if this guy lies to you like Matt did? Physically or platonically, that man had affairs. He gave the best of himself to other women who were *not* his wife."

Lucy said, "You know it didn't make any difference in the long run. His philandering was the least of it, I promise. It's never just the cheating, you know."

"Just find out if the guy's married," Kit said.

"Or the wrath of Kit will rain down upon me."

"It's not wrath. I just care about you more than they do."

Nancy and Gina laughed. Gina said, "It's true, she does."

"Oh, please. I think she should go for it," said Nancy. "It's time you got out there again."

"Thank you," said Lucy.

"Let the woman live a little. Hasn't she suffered enough?"

"She's a big girl," said Gina, "and he's an adult. He makes his own decisions."

"You guys are dicks," Kit said. "Let's get the check." She looked around for Sergei. "I can never seem to get the waiter's attention. Drives me insane."

Lucy smiled then arched her back over the edge of the banquette. She reached out in a satisfying stretch the way she'd seen her sexy friend Audra do a thousand times to tremendous success. Then Lucy unfolded her arm in Sergei's direction like a sleepy ballet dancer and said, "I'll get his attention."

Chapter 3

-- -- -- -- -- -- -- -- -- -- --

Lucy heard footsteps behind her on the way to her car in the restaurant parking lot. She turned around and saw Nancy walking briskly towards her. "Unlock your passenger door, I'm getting in," Nancy said without waiting for permission. Lucy unlocked her car and they both climbed in. Nancy was quiet for a long time. She stared out the window. It was 2:15 P.M. and Lucy still had forty-five minutes before her son Gus would be dropped off after a play-date, so she figured she'd kill time with Nancy. Though time would move a lot faster if Nancy were talking. Finally she spoke in an unusually small voice. "Were you . . . serious back there?"

"About getting together with that guy?" Lucy said. "I don't know. I thought I was, but Kit's right. If he's married, it's nuts to even consider—"

"No, about sleeping with our husbands."

"That?! No! Oh, my God, no. I would never. Oh, my God, Nancy, is that what you think? That I would sleep with Ted? God, no. Oh, my goodness, never. I was just kid—"

"Because I want you to," said Nancy. Lucy couldn't have heard her correctly.

"What?" she said. Nancy was quiet. She just stared out the windshield of Lucy's fifteen-year old Volvo wagon and didn't move. Just stared. Sergei came out the back door of the restaurant, sat on milk crate and lit a cigarette.

"Excuse me?" said Lucy again. This time Nancy repeated herself more quietly, almost sweetly. Lucy remembered that voice from her own floundering marriage. *It's like no other*, she thought. *Small, cynical, hopeless. Anguish.*

"I want you to sleep with Ted," Nancy said, then she turned abruptly and met Lucy's gaze. All of a sudden there was energy in her voice, and her dark eyes brightened. "But you have to promise me that you won't fall in love with him or let him fall in love with you, because I just don't know what I would do if—"

"Whoa, whoa," Lucy said, "Nancy, are you *serious*?" Nancy leaned back in the front seat and rubbed her hands up and down over her face. Nancy and Ted had been together a long time— maybe sixteen years, which was twice as long as Lucy and her ex-husband Matt had lasted. But Nancy didn't just look her usual tired self today, she looked profoundly weary.

Nancy said, "I might be. Can we at least talk about it?"

"Nance—"

"Please? Say that you'll think about it."

"*Nancy*—"

"Please?" Nancy sputtered. "I'm worried— I'm afraid— I'm just so . . . ugh. I don't know what else to do." With those words Nancy looked at Lucy. Everything about her body, her posture, hands, her eyes, pleaded. Lucy watched as big, Keane-painting-sized teardrops rolled down Nancy's cheeks. Lucy could count on one hand the number of times she'd seen Nancy cry in all the years they'd known each other. She was one tough broad.

"Okay, we'll talk about it," Lucy said. "Follow me back to my house."

"Thank you," Nancy said.

"Don't thank me yet."

- - - - - - -

Nancy followed close all the way to Lucy's house. They were just heading in the front door when an SUV pulled up and Gus hopped out. He said, "Thanks for the ride," to the driver.

Nancy said, "Gus says 'thanks for the ride'? How did you get him to do that?"

"If he doesn't, I beat him," Lucy said, and leaned down to give Gus a big hug.

"Hi, Mom," said Gus.

"Hey, pal," said Lucy, "did you have fun?"

"Yes."

"Did they feed you?"

"Yes."

"Please look Mrs. Brisbane in the eye and say hello."

"Hello," said Gus, looking Nancy in the eye.

"Hi, Gus," said Nancy.

"Use her whole name, please," said Lucy.

"Hello, Mrs. Brisbane," said Gus, but this time he was looking down to extract a Pokémon card from his coat pocket.

"One more time, with feeling and without looking down."

Gus looked at Nancy with bug-eyed flippancy, "Hello. Mrs. Brisbane."

"Good enough," said Lucy, and they all headed inside.

"Coats off, on the hook, hat in the cubby" Lucy commanded, and Gus obeyed. He followed her into the dining room and asked her to bend down so that he could whisper something in her ear. With his hands up in front of him, he tapped his thumbs up and down on his loose fists—the international sign for playing video games. "Can I have thirty farts of poop time?" said Gus.

"Okay," whispered Lucy, "but down in the basement." She considered Nancy and the topic at hand. "Actually, take forty-five. And this will fill your fart quota for the day, got it?"

"Poop," said Gus, then gave her a brief hug around the neck and headed off to play Wii.

"He's so good with manners. Notwithstanding his unique vocabulary," said Nancy.

"Thanks," said Lucy. "It's been no trouble at all."

Nancy managed to squeak out a little "ha." Lucy busted her ass to stay on Gus while her world was crumbling. She knew society would blame his flaws on her broken marriage. "His parents are divorced, you know," she'd heard teachers say about their most difficult students. It seemed to explain everything. So Lucy read all the pamphlets and followed the free counseling she got from the National Council for Jewish Women's classes for parents and kids of divorce, and it paid off—gotta love Jewish women for helping to pick up the pieces. Gus was a happy, thriving eight-year-old who had very few nightmares and just enough friends. It took every fiber of her being to stop herself from unloading on him about what a shit his father had been, but she managed to squelch those impulses and hoped that one day he would appreciate her efforts. Or maybe he wouldn't, but she knew in her heart of hearts that it was the right thing to do. In the meantime, Lucy had unloaded on her friends. But that was then. She had little to say about Matt anymore. The point was moot. The subject closed. Today it was Lucy's turn to listen.

Lucy gestured to Nancy to sit on her couch and handed her a glass of wine. She put on Bebel Gilberto very low and sat down on the other end of the couch opposite her.

"Okay," Lucy said taking a deep breath. "Take a deep breath and tell me what's up."

"Uhhhh," said Nancy, then took a largish swig from her wine-glass. "I was just thinking about what you guys were saying in there, and it got me so upset, but then when everyone was set-tling the check, I started thinking about my sex life with Ted, and how grumpy he's been for some time now, which makes me feel guilty. And there's this distance, and sometimes he can't . . . you know. And I'm just always so tired and never in the mood, but I just was thinking . . . I don't know. I love him so much and sometimes I worry that he'll leave me just so that he can have sex more often, which is such a stupid reason to leave someone who you've loved since college, but it's really not a dumb reason, you know? Sometimes I think about it—having sex with someone else, but I have no time or energy and can't fathom the effort it would take, all that sneaking around and lying. Are you kidding me? But Ted thinks about sex all the time and I can sense he's tiptoeing around me, waiting for the right time to bring it up. I know it makes him feel pervy because he's told me—which he hates by the way—then he's pissed and I'm stressed. It's so hard for me to get in the mood. Then there's moping, then more guilt. I don't know if it's a phase or if it's permanent or if it's me or him or both of us, but it terrifies me because I love him so much and don't want to lose him. I know he would *never* see a sex counselor with me. I just thought if you're horny and he's horny and if you promised me you wouldn't fall in love with him and take him away from me . . ."

Lucy said, "Nancy, you really think that after the divorce I've been through that I would want your lazy, CNN-watching-when-he-should-be-helping-the-kids-with-their-homework Ted for my-self? I would rather stick needles in my eyes."

Nancy smiled and said, "I was hoping you'd say that."

Lucy said, "No offense."

Nancy smiled. "So you'll think about it? You said you just want to get laid. He's good in bed."

"Aw, Jesus. Really?" said Lucy. "This is so weird. How many times are we talking?"

"I don't know. I hadn't gotten that far." Nancy thought for a mo-ment. "Maybe we try just once and see if that does it, and then take it from there."

"You really think that sleeping with me once is gonna save your marriage? I'm not *that* good."

Nancy teared up and said, "I just don't know what else to do."

"Oh, honey, I was just kidding. Sorry, no jokes. This is no laugh-ing matter. Did Ted actually say that he would leave you if you didn't start having more sex with him?"

"No. I can just tell. I know him so well. God, I've been with him since college. High school! I know he loves me, but men are men and he's no different. I think that's where women go wrong. When they start to think that their husband's different—that they don't need sex."

There was a moment's pause. Nancy took a sip of wine. Lucy moved the mug on the coffee table so that they could both put their feet up. It read, "My mom's been to hell and back and all I got was this lousy mug." It was a divorce gift.

Nancy continued, "Please believe me when I tell you I tried. I tried sex twice a week with one blow job, which turned into once a week with one blow job, then just a blow job. Then I couldn't even deal with that. My jaw got tired and he could tell I wasn't into it. Maybe we shouldn't have had three kids. Scratch that. I know we shouldn't have had three kids. But, I wouldn't trade any of them."

"Not even Nicky?"

"Maybe Nicky. Shit, Luce. I still love the snuggling with Ted and we still sleep naked, except in the winter when I need pj's, and socks. And sometimes a sweater."

"Are the kids still sleeping with you in your bed?" asked Lucy.

"No, that was the first thing to go."

"Good. Smart. Well, at least you don't need a scarf. Right up until the sweater you are one sexy mama, don't get me wrong."

Nancy's mouth turned downward as if she were about to cry again.

"Oh, shit," said Lucy, "I'm doing it again. I'm so sorry. No jokes. It's just that this situation is so over the top I can't help it. Please don't cry. There's no crying in baseball—or whatever this is we're doing. It's just . . . bonkers, right? I mean, it's *bonkers*! Or maybe it's not. Maybe everybody's doing it but no one's talking about it. For all we know we could be the only people *not* doing it. Maybe we're the last on our block. Either way, no more jokes. I promise."

"Please sleep with Ted," said Nancy, and waited for the answer.

Lucy looked heavenward then back at Nancy. She hadn't had sex in two years. She felt she had little or no other prospects. She knew there was no chance of her falling for Ted. She also knew, after years of trying to get pregnant, what it was like to have detached, perfunctory sex. She felt it was a simple enough thing. Okay, not simple, but it didn't have to be complicated, either. As long as no one freaked out. It could be so much easier than online dating, and safer in more ways than one. It would be weird, no doubt, but it could be just what she was looking for. Easy, breezy sex. Not to mention it would be helping her friend, which had a nice altruistic ring to it. Sounded to Lucy like a win, win, win.

"Okay," Lucy said to Nancy, "I'll do it."

Chapter 4

Lucy grabbed a coat, walked Nancy to the door, then sat on the front stoop and waved as Nancy drove off down the quiet little tree-lined street of their previously predictable little hometown community. The sun was warm that day and it was the first time in months that Lucy couldn't see her breath. Life sure was odd, she thought. *What the hell did I agree to?* It struck Lucy that she used to know what was going to happen next. At least she thought she did. She'd always had a plan: Date some boys, settle on a rewarding career, date more seriously. Check. Get married, buy a house, enjoy my husband and career, have two kids, enjoy them. Check. Live a quiet life of the simple, yet exquisite, pleasures that make a mundane suburban existence enviable. Find joy and contentment as the Happiness Industrial Complex prescribes. Check. She did not factor in secondary infertility or divorce. She certainly didn't factor in sleeping with her friend's husband—permission or not. She did not imagine any of this.

Things started out normally enough. She and Matt set up their ideal life in the perfect town of Nohquee. A harmonious hodge-podge of diverse, open-minded families, Nohquee was the perfect feeder colony for New York City liberal-arts types. Soon after Gus was born and Lucy met Kit, they met Gina at a boisterous YMCA-sponsored weekly playgroup. Lucy, Kit and Gina initially bonded over the fact that they didn't cosleep with their children. Nancy joined the group a few months later. Soon these renegade new moms broke off from the group and started hanging out nearly every day, all day, just the four of them. They took their babies and toddlers to children's museums and parks, playgrounds and Ikea. They also swapped babysitting hours, carpooled and picked up each other's kids when issues arose. The four moms functioned as each other's work colleagues, before everyone went back to office life and put their kids in day care. Then Kit, Gina and Nancy got pregnant again right on cue, and Lucy didn't.

Lucy's fertility quest quickly devolved from exciting adventure to harrowing odyssey with every failed attempt. Months turned into a year, so she began charting her morning temperature and using ovulation kits as her friends had babies—effortlessly. Numerous efforts with Clomid and IUI snowballed into four heartbreaking rounds of IVF. During this dreadful stretch, Kit and Nancy were particularly generous with their time. (Gina did what she could via text, though her job was consuming.) They drove across town to give her hormone shots when Matt was golfing, at a Devils game, or calling from a boisterous restaurant to say he was going to be "working late." They bucked her up and talked her off ledges. They listened while she vented, and in turn, she listened to them vent, too. It was challenging for Lucy to be empathetic while they complained that their beautiful, healthy newborns were tough to juggle with toddlers, and isn't nursing a bitch, and wasn't Lucy lucky to have only one. She knew they were trying to put a positive spin on her predicament, so Lucy bit her tongue. She knew their hearts were in the right place and was grateful every time they walked through the door.

While Lucy suffered the repeated devastation of yet another zygote that simply "didn't take," she chased after and wrangled her girlfriends' toddlers for them at weekend picnics so they could relax and nurse, or change a diaper. "You'll do it for me when it's my turn," she said, but her turn never came again. She and Matt finally gave up trying. Lucy tried dragooning him into adoption, but Matt wouldn't consider it. Their marriage, by that point, was beyond repair, not because she couldn't get pregnant—lots of couples had run that gauntlet and survived with their marriages dented, perhaps, but intact—but because he had stopped wanting to be married, at least to Lucy, and had met Delphine.

Matt didn't cop to it; instead he drove Lucy to the breaking point with a thousand painful slights. When she walked out the back door to have dinner with Kit, he turned off the back stoop light so she'd return home in the dark. "Your tennis game has gotten worse," he'd say. "Your London broil isn't what it used to be." All the small kindnesses that Lucy had once cherished went away: the backyard grilling, Saturday morning pancakes, foot rubs and tickets to plays he knew she would enjoy. He stopped celebrating her birthday and started bringing his laptop with him to the dinner table. He regularly left the house without telling her where he was going and refused to spend time with other couples he once enjoyed. He played golf more and more and spoke to Lucy less and less. In short, Matt stopped participating in their life together.

Lucy was in denial that he could be sleeping with someone else because they were still having sex. Eventually she would see how obvious it had all been. She rarely caught glimpses anymore of the terrific guy she'd married, and above all, didn't want Gus growing up thinking that people who loved each other could treat one another with such overt disdain. Couples retreats, counseling and stalagmites of "How to Save Your Marriage" books were last-ditch attempts that Matt wanted no part of, so Lucy flipped the switch inside her, as women do when they finally give up. She stopped haranguing Matt and asked him to move out. Immediately, they were both happier. Now Lucy could live in peace and Matt could live alone—as far as she knew. Her friends had other theories.

Lucy's relief was short lived, however. Her divorce was stressful, depressing and all consuming, as most are, and she worried nonstop about Gus, her job and her rudderless future. Plus she mourned the loss of her hypothetical, longed-for second child—the sibling she would never be able to give Gus—and was so livid at her body for failing her, she deprived it of pleasure for a very long time. Thankfully, Nancy, Kit and Gina stepped up in astonishing ways. They understood that while her situation might have changed for the better, she would be mired in misery for a while—the business of mourning a marriage was messy and ugly. But they didn't abandon her, thank God. For a solid year before she made any new divorced friends, it seemed all Lucy could do was cry and her friends rocked her while she sobbed, but they also forced her to take showers and get dressed on the weekends. They took Gus for play dates when she'd been up all night, noticed she was losing weight and brought over meals. Lucy's neighbors offered to mow her lawn and rake when the leaves piled up, and her stalwart mom, Dottie—a no-nonsense, fiercely independent widow—stopped by twice a week to cook or fold laundry so Lucy could lie on the couch and continue crying. Even Loretta, Dottie's best friend, who'd been through a divorce, took her to lunch once a month to see how she was faring and remind her that she wouldn't feel this way forever.

Two years later, on the day Lucy's divorce was to be finalized in court, Nancy, Kit and Gina told their bosses they had dentist appointments and went with her—they insisted. The girls and Dottie sat behind Lucy in the courtroom the whole boring time, and even squealed a little when the divorce was pronounced. The judge admonished the peanut gallery, but their smiles were so bright that Lucy could feel their heat on her back from two rows away. Dottie welled up when she told Lucy how proud she was of her, then left to pick up Gus after school so that Lucy could celebrate with her girlfriends. They enjoyed a lingering group hug with copious tears of joy, then took Lucy to get a manicure so that her ringless ring finger would "look fiercely independent," they said. Afterwards, there was a dinner in Lucy's honor, and all her gal pals were there. They served "divorce food" as they called it: split pea soup and free-range chicken, and for dessert, key lime pie with meringue topping, because you have to separate the eggs. They presented Lucy with new return-address mailing labels with just her name on them, newly monogrammed bathroom towels, racy sleepwear and underthings, and a new vibrator with extra batteries.

The first day of the rest of her life would be tomorrow, but on that night, Lucy toasted her friends for their amazing show of support. They toasted her back and cried more tears of joy. It was a milestone event celebrated with humor and solemnity, love and respect. Some people in town had inched away from Lucy at the supermarket or at school pickup, as if divorce were something contagious one could catch and should be steered clear of, but her true friends had stuck by her without taking on her heartache or attaching it to their own marriages. She couldn't fathom having to get through divorce alone. Thank God she hadn't had to. She just hoped her friendships hadn't been too badly mangled along the way.

And now this—sleeping with Ted. No, she hadn't considered this as a possible trajectory. Lucy approached things differently now; she assumed nothing. Life was a crapshoot, she'd learned, and although she wouldn't have wished the last few years on her worst enemy, it was freeing to not have any grand expectations, to have no plan. *So this must be how trained assassins live, like* La Femme Nikita, she thought, *not knowing what the next month or minute will bring. Anything could happen.* Something was about to. The question was, who was she? A mother, teacher, friend—certainly. But she wanted to be more. And possibly not in relation to others but purely for herself. Maybe that meant being a little more ego-centric, more selfish—less superego, more id. Lucy closed her eyes and lifted her face to warm in the late afternoon sun. She could be or do anything now, but would that include sleeping with her friend's husband?

Chapter 5

Though Matt got engaged six months to the day after the divorce, he continued to make Lucy's life hell. They were still coparenting, raising Gus together, so unfortunately she couldn't be completely rid of him. It was a full-time job trying to slough off the prickly tension and viscous negativity that he slung at her every week. Sensing the toxic psychic buildup, Lucy often stopped what she was doing, took three deeps breaths, did thirty jumping jacks, then masturbated in the hopes of diffusing her relentless stress into a zillion specks of twinkling pixie dust. She relished the bright lights of her orgasms, which bounced and danced through her and out into the air around her, like old-school fairy animation. She got a kick out of the shuddering fits and starts and occasional whooping laughter that her body elicited naturally, and the ensuing restful calm of a thousand tingles.

Lucy reasoned that masturbating was sounder than gambling or hoarding. It was also healthier than eating a box of Mallomars every night while they were in season, Oreos otherwise. Or becoming an alcoholic. Most of the men and women she knew in crap-ass marriages drank their way through days and years of unflagging tension—defiantly pickling themselves against despair. Even after half of those marriages ended, the drinking rarely stopped. But Lucy had a scare in college which resulted in her roommate getting her stomach pumped at the ER one night, so she stopped after three glasses of white wine (four tops) and generally went home to bed before the women around her began to slur their words and slither off stools. Lucy knew that becoming a workout freak—using the quest for good health as a mask for an adrenaline addiction—was the most socially acceptable option, but then she'd have to work out. So she settled on the natural oxytocin release from getting off as her drug of choice.

It was Sunday morning and Lucy lay in bed considering her options. She would need to go for it right now because she had to wake Gus for church in ten minutes. As a laissez-faire Protestant, she could always blow off church, but was trying to give Gus a soupçon of religious bedrock. If she used her battery-operated, lipstick-sized Little Buddy thingy, it wouldn't take more than a minute or two to get a nice, restful orgasm out of the deal. Such a pleasing way to start the day. Surely God appreciated a relaxed congregation. At little more than a finger's length and width, the tiny vibrator didn't fill her up the way a penis did, it was something else—a shortcut. It wasn't really sex to her, it was this other activity, the JV version, the way Skee-Ball isn't bowling but its little cousin. Lucy grabbed her Magic Buddy or whatever asinine name they'd given this appliance to make it seem like her pal and thought, *Let's get this show on the road*.

Deftly slipping the tiny wand out of its case with one hand, Lucy loosened the tie on her pajama pants with the other. Her creaky morning legs fell open under the sheets, bent at the knees like butterfly wings. Darkness helped when she was responsible for her own imagery, so her arm went back for the lavender-scented eye pillow filled with lentils. She flopped it onto her eyes and took a deep breath. Usually it only took a few seconds for Lucy to decide which speed to use. She assessed her mood then factored in how much time she had. She used the lower speed if she was feeling on the aggressively sexy side and had time to luxuriate and enjoy the ride. She used the higher speed as an administrative accelerator when time was a factor and bigger fish needed to be fried elsewhere. Chop-chop, time is money, that sort of thing. This morning called for the latter.

The smooth point of the conical tip nosed around between the petal folds of her labia, which to Lucy always sounded like a synonym for "veranda." "Let's have our drinks out on the labia, shall we?" she might say to guests in a Noel Coward play. The first touch of the vibrator to her clitoris shot a little spark of greeting to Lucy's nether regions. A little "Hey, I'm here" with a welcoming wave. The second touch loosened her butterfly wings and her legs fell open a little wider, her infamous hula hooping hips disengaging. Usually by the third touch Lucy moaned, which was her body's way of saying, "Okay, now we're talkin'." Involuntarily smiling, she arched her back and her body swelled and moistened with the attention.

This was about the time Lucy invited fantasies to join her, to move things along a bit, make things more social. "Okay, fellas, c'mon in," her visual memory said as it opened the door to a basement rec room where they all sat casually, patiently waiting to participate at a moment's notice, like some perpetual Facebook reunion of all the people she'd ever found hot. "Lucy will see you now," her imagination said. Her colleague, Peter, was usually the first guy in line and the clearest image in her mind. Maybe it was his eyes, the color of a child's prized sky-blue marble, or his crooked smile with the tiny gap between his front teeth. He wasn't classically handsome, but the most appealing men rarely were to Lucy. He had thick, reddish-blond, Hollywood hair and good lips—his lower lip especially full, like Paul Newman's. But to be honest, it was Peter's sense of humor and easy smile that made a lasting impression. He was hilarious but dry, and thankfully not sarcastic— the lazy man's default to a sense of humor when one hasn't been cultivated. He taught high-school physics about forty-five minutes away. But none of that mattered at this moment. All that mattered was that he was hot, and she could reasonably recall his face.

Other men in her fantasy waiting room included old boyfriends, movie and television stars, unrequited loves from days gone by, and Jon Bon Jovi. Her fantasies could be young or old, dead or Canadian. Lucy didn't discriminate, except she never went down the fantasy road with her friends' husbands—that would feel disloyal. So Lucy conjured Peter's face and pictured him kissing her between her thighs. Instantly a few "mmms" and "ohhhs" escaped her. She tightened then loosened her lower muscles—the ones nestled deep inside, then exhaled and readied herself. Her mind drifted from her body, higher and higher, up towards the ceiling and hovered there, waiting. She turned her head away from the door and her breath quickened. The pulsing overtook her as just over the far ridge, there on the horizon, her orgasm cantered towards her as if it were outrunning something huge and inescapable. Closer and closer it rode, a speck growing brighter as her body and mind prepared for the deluge. "It's coming! Your orgasm is coming!" a faraway voice shouted excitedly from somewhere near the ceiling. *Here it comes*, Lucy thought, and welcomed her climax. *Helloooooo!*

"Ohhhhhh, yesssssssss," Lucy said under her breath. She twisted and writhed, having abandoned any propriety concerning her physical self. Her mind whirred in the sky amidst a white-hot cascade like the sparks off an arc welder's torch. Her body seized as her head came off the bed; her eye pillow slid off her face. *Yes, thank you,* Lucy thought, and laughed out loud. A scatter of convulsions washed over her as she turned her head and squealed into her pillow. Anything that felt that outrageously good was hilarious to her—like zooming down a pitch-black tunnel on a waterslide. She loved the abandon of it all and found the release incredibly freeing. An orgasm was a full-body guffaw to Lucy, so she liked to let it out with whoops and cackles. But this morning she had to be quiet. A ripple of muffled giggles accompanied her climax followed by a few shudders. Then deep, deep rest and quiet steady breathing. Tingles. Calm. Relaxed.

Seconds later Lucy heard the padding of small socks on creaking floorboards just outside her bedroom. Gus was usually a heavy sleeper and rarely, if ever, woke up before Lucy went into his room, turned off his radio alarm and coaxed him awake. But this morning he beat her to it; he was awake.

"Mom, what's so funny?" said Gus from very close by. This was not good.

"Oh, hi, sweetie. What?" Lucy said, palming her Little Buddy and checking on the covers—all clear. The eye pillow fell on the floor at his feet. She tried to act casual.

"What's so funny?" He was standing next to her bed in the March darkness.

"This joke I was thinking about," Lucy chirped in her best I-am-awake-and-present voice. "You're supposed to knock before you enter a room, you know. We've talked about that." She held the covers up to her ears.

Gus said, "Your door was open. What's the joke?" At the age of eight, very little escaped him, especially anything that had to do with a riddle or joke. Plus he was sharp, so she knew this could take a while. She said, "Um, I can't remember."

"Mom, you were *just* laughing."

"Oh, right. Uhh." Lucy groped for a joke. Like a dope, she hadn't muffled her laughter as much as she probably should have, and she'd left the door ajar, or it had swung open without her noticing, so she knew the joke had better be good.

"Okay," Lucy began, "two rabbis walk into a bar—"

Gus interrupted, "What's a rabbi?"

"Like a minister for Jewish people."

"Why is that funny?" he said.

"It's not, it's just the setup—"

"Then why were you laughing?" Gus said impatiently. He wanted to get the joke.

Lucy said, "I haven't told you the punch line yet. That was just the setup. Didn't I teach you about setups?"

Gus said, "Yeah. So what's the funny part? Is it the punching?"

"No, honey, the rabbis don't punch each other."

"I would like the joke better if they were punching."

"I would like this conversation better if you were getting dressed for church."

"Poop," Gus said by way of signing off, and left the room.

"Go brush your farts!" Lucy called after him in her I-mean-business voice. She'd gotten so used to his arbitrarily inserting the words "poop" or "fart" into every sentence as adjective, verb and/or noun that she'd started to do it, too. She knew it was a phase that he'd outgrow, so she took it in stride. The deal was that he couldn't say it in mixed company, outside of the mom-son collective. In return for his adhering to this rule, he could say it as much as he liked. Secretly Lucy knew she would miss this phase when it was over.

Chapter 6

- -

That afternoon Lucy called her friend Audra to tell her about her bizarre conversation with Nancy. She couldn't stop vacillating and needed some perspective. Should she really sleep with her friend's husband? It was too out of the box to digest on her own. Audra Davenport was one of Lucy's new crop of divorcée friends, and she liked her take on life. Audra had a movie-star smile and the body of a Vargas pinup girl—warheads for boobs and shapely long legs, up to here. People tried to take her for a fool but she'd lived a hardscrabble youth in a dodgy part of Detroit before ending up in Nohquee, New Jersey. Consequently, very little got by her. Lucy was first drawn to Audra at the free, nondenominational Rainbows classes for "Children of Separation and Divorce" offered by the NCJW. Lucy liked the frank questions Audra asked the social workers, which paved the way for a budding new relationship. The first time they met for drinks, Lucy told Audra she was way too fancy and impossibly glamorous to hang out with. Audra simply said, "That's a bag of bullshit," and their friendship was sealed.

When Audra answered her cell Lucy could tell she was on the car speakerphone. "I'm on the way to pick up my cousin at JFK, what can I do for you?" Audra said, right to the point. "Not much," Lucy said, "just called to catch up." She was second-guessing if she should tell Audra, so she let her go on about her cousin's flight delay. Since Lucy was folding laundry—a chore she particularly detested—she happily stayed on the phone while Audra waxed about her cousin, Missy, and the pill-popping, alcoholic side of her family; put her car in short-term parking; and strolled into one of the terminal's classier sports bars to kill time. Almost immediately after describing the décor of the bar to Lucy, Audra relayed that she had spotted an exceptionally attractive, blue-eyed businessman from Iceland who looked similarly bored.

"Isn't 'blue-eyed from Iceland' redundant?" asked Lucy, "And how the hell do you know he's from Iceland."

"The flag," Audra said. "It's on his luggage."

"You've memorized *all* the flags from *every* country?"

"No. Only the good ones."

"*Only the good ones?* What, flags or countries?"

"Please, dahling, I'm kidding. My last client was Icelandic. She had a sticker on the back of her car."

"Oh, good Lord. Okay. So, what's your game plan with this guy? You should take me through this step-by-step. I could learn a lot," said Lucy. Audra was like a guru when it came to men, and Lucy had at least five loads to fold. Gus was at the next-door neighbor's.

"Well," said Audra, "I plan to sit next to him, obviously. Then swivel my stool, bumping my bare knee against his—remember, it's paramount to show some bare skin somewhere on your body all year round, regardless of the chill."

"Well, you lost me there. I don't do chill well," said Lucy.

"You're priorities are way off, then," said Audra. "I'll dazzle him with my pearly whites, mention my cousin's flight delay and take it from there."

Lucy bolted upright. "Leave the phone on. I want to listen. Please. I'll put myself on mute so that you don't hear anything from my side, and you can darken your screen and set the phone on the bar between you.

"Hmm, sounds like fun," Audra said, "but one sound out of you and I shut it down. And if you blow my chances—"

"At one of the good countries? Don't worry, I won't," said Lucy.

Lucy pictured Audra easing down next to some chiseled guy on an upholstered bar stool. She imagined Audra's bare knee peeking out just above the three-inch black suede boots and wool crepe pencil skirt she'd seen Audra wearing at school drop-off this morning, and knew that her lilac silk blouse would be unbuttoned just low enough to reveal an inviting shadow between her perfectly full C-cup breasts. It always was. Lucy heard a funny buzz— must be a text coming through—then Audra telling Mr. Iceland that her cousin's luggage was lost. It would be arriving on the next plane due in about forty-five minutes. Then she heard Audra say, "Now I have forty-five minutes to kill. Whatever will I do?" Lucy chuckled and kept folding.

Mr. Iceland said, "Would you like a drink?"

Audra answered, "Merlot."

He said, "Do you have a name, Ms. Merlot?"

"Anna," Audra said, and Lucy froze. "Yours?" Audra asked.

"Gunnar," he replied.

They clinked their glasses and their conversation took off. *This*

is better than a daytime soap, Lucy thought. She heard them talk
about thermal heat and architecture, blacksmithing and Klimt.
Lucy imagined the touch of Audra's hand on the man's sleeve and
knew he must have felt like he was being rocket propelled into
space, then she heard her throaty laugh—broad and unapologetic.
Lucy let herself float into Audra's body as if she were there, touching his sleeve, his wrist, his arm, then letting her fingers linger
there. Lucy imagined Gunnar placing the back of his hand against
her thigh for a moment, then turning it over to gently squeeze her
knee. Heat lit up Lucy's body as she heard Audra purr. What if
Gunnar was sliding his hand down Audra's thigh right now and
hooking his finger under the hem of her skirt? He might be sweep-
ing it slowly back and forth then moving his hand northward,
steadily moving up, up her skirt as he watched Audra's eyes for
any sign of halt. Lucy's eyes shone brightly and her cheeks took on a
sheen. Guys masturbated twice in one day when the opportunity
arose, why shouldn't she? She put down the unfolded T-shirt,
slumped down onto her living room couch and closed her eyes.

Lucy listened as Audra maintained her side of the conversation,
cool as a cucumber. No doubt the crinkles around her sparkly eyes
had deepened with every sip of wine, and her toothy smile had impossibly whitened. Lucy slid her own hand down her jeans as she
imagined a beautiful blue-eyed blond stranger's middle finger
reaching Audra's black thong. She pictured him tapping it a little,
as if he were scratching the tiniest bit of frost off a window. Lucy
arched her back slightly as she heard Audra say, "Mmmm." Just
then Lucy heard that phone buzzing sound again. "Now they're
saying ninety minutes," Audra said to Gunnar. Lucy conjured the
shape of Gunnar's eyebrows and tortoiseshell glasses. She gave him
a film noir nose and a rugged jaw, which made her think of jewel
thieves driving sports cars in Monte Carlo. Lucy felt a dot of her

wetness seep through her underpants and onto her fingertip. She pictured Gunnar's hard cock straining against the fabric of his exceptionally well-tailored suit. Both were beautiful if only in her mind.

Audra asked Gunnar, "Have you got plans for the next thirty minutes?"

"No," Gunnar said. Lucy opened her eyes. Audra could not mean what Lucy was thinking, did she? Oh, come on. She must be teasing because she's got an audience. This didn't really happen. Lucy's heart quickened. Gunnar's must have been about to explode.

Audra answered her phone, or at least pretended to.

"Hi, Lucy. What's up?" Audra said to Lucy. Lucy shot up off the couch and groped for the mute button on her phone. To Gunnar, Audra said, "You. Follow me."

"Are you talking to me?" said Lucy.

"No," Audra said, "I'm talking to my friend Gunnar who is still sitting on his stool and not following me." To Gunnar she added, "You only get one chance at this."

Lucy said, "Why are you talking to me? I thought I was—where are you leading him?"

"Somewhere more intimate," said Audra. Lucy heard the quick-paced clack-clack of Audra's boots on the linoleum, imagined the shiny mane of hair flowing in the small breeze she stirred.

Lucy said, "Are you deranged? He could be a whacko!"

"Well, he isn't dressed like one—"

"That doesn't—"

Audra continued, "He's wearing a beautifully tailored Armani suit, a Thomas Pink chartreuse pinstriped shirt with an Hermès lilac silk tie printed with some sort of architectural repeat pattern, seven hundred dollar shoes and understated gold cufflinks. His Coach leather briefcase is the color of butterscotch.

"Gunnar," she said, "my friend Lucy would like to know if you're some kind of whacko."

"No," he said, "I'm an architect."

"Just as I thought. He's an architect," Audra said into the phone.

Lucy said, "Oh, well, now that that's cleared up. Just because his shoes cost more than my couch doesn't mean he isn't—Hey, where more intimate?"

"My car," said Audra.

"*Really?*" said Lucy.

"Really," said Audra. Lucy knew that there was no changing Audra's mind. She also realized that Audra had described Gunnar and her intimate plans to Lucy in front of Gunnar so that he wouldn't try anything squirrely.

Audra asked Lucy, "Why did you call me in the first place?"

"It's nothing. You're obviously preoccupied."

"It's fine, start talking and I'll stop you when things get interesting on my end."

Lucy shook her head. "I had lunch with The Marrieds yesterday."

"Fun. How are everyone's bunions?" Audra asked.

"I told them how horny I am always and they told me how their husbands want it more often than they do. Then they started asking me to have sex with their husbands for them—"

"You should," said Audra.

"Wait, I'm not—what do you mean I *should*?! Let me finish. I thought we were all joking. We *were* all joking, and then my friend Nancy approached me afterwards in the parking lot and asked me to sleep with her husband, Ted."

"No Fun Nancy?"

"Yes, No Fun Nancy, but she *is* fun, you just haven't—have you heard what I've said?"

Audra caught all of it. As a mother of three children, she had the ability to carry on multiple conversations while simultaneously making a meal for additional drop-in guests. Lucy had seen her do it. She never missed a beat. It was really quite astounding.

Lucy heard the peeping sound of Audra unlocking the door to her BMW SUV. She wondered if the phone call was going to end with her hanging up and calling 911, or having to hear her girlfriend come. She couldn't decide which was worse.

"What are you doing now?" Lucy said.

"Taking off my coat."

"How will you—"

"I folded down the seats earlier. Oh, look, he's loosening his tie. How sweet."

It dawned on Lucy that she was jealous. "Why do you get to have all the fun?"

"I *get* to have fun because I *make* my own fun. No one hands me fun on a silver platter."

Lucy made a mental note. *Must make more fun.* "Are you wearing your good underwear?"

"Always," said Audra. Her voice was getting breathier. Lucy did not take her underwear seriously. Audra's cost more than Lucy's entire clothing budget for a year.

"Mmmm," was all Audra said.

Lucy looked at her own Band-Aid colored bras and mismatched cotton Target underwear in the laundry basket. This was not the intimate wardrobe of a serious adventurer. Lucy would have to step it up. She imagined Gunnar diving between Audra's perfect little rosebud areolas as if he were a child putting his face into a plate of whipped cream. The text sound buzzed again.

"Is it your cousin?" Lucy said.

"She says: 'Still waiting. So sorry! Feel bad. Hope u r ok.'"

"Ha!"

"Maybe you should fuck him," Audra said, "I've got to go in about one minute. Things are getting interesting."

Lucy said, "Okay, real quick, real quick, you think I should? Please think this through with me. Put some time into it, mull it over and tell me what you—"

"It's not unheard of. Mormons have sister wives to satisfy excess unfulfilled desire. His wife's not sleeping with him as much as he wants it and you want the sex. Ted's an attractive guy, I've seen him at the pool. Good body. He'll be willing to please, which is always a plus, and you'll be familiar with him, which should work in your favor. He a nice guy?"

"Completely. Super sweet."

"Okay then. This could work out well. You'd have to compartmentalize, but you're good at that. You'd have to be discreet obviously; I won't tell a soul."

"Shoot me now."

"Trust me, dahling, no one is going to talk because each party has too much to lose. I'm thinking this through and I like the outside-the-box concept. Very European."

"Oh brother."

"Seriously, it could work. You've got little to lose because it's not infidelity—Nancy has given you permission, she's in control. Give him a blow job. Bet he hasn't had one of those in years. Then he'll work twice as hard to please you, trust me."

Lucy said, "But I—"

Audra said, "Look, do you want some clean, safe, convenient, no-strings sex or not?"

"I do, but—"

"Do you want him for yourself?"

"Hells no! He's Nancy's. I mean, he's perfect for Nancy. No, I do not want Ted."

"Could you be attracted to him? Have you ever considered sleeping with him?"

"Never. But . . ." Lucy gave it a moment's consideration. "I suppose if I shifted things around a little in my head, I guess I could get to that place where . . . it would be totally surreal, of course, I've known him a long time. It may take a shot of tequila. But yeah, he's cute enough."

"A shot for each of you. Excellent. You'll be doing her a favor, him a favor and yourself a favor. You should start a business. I've gotta go."

"A business!" said Lucy, but Audra had already hung up.

A moment later, Lucy's phone rang again and Audra's picture popped up. Lucy said hello but the reply came to her in a cascade of moans. Lucy planned to hang up Audra's butt-dial call, then thought better of it. She had a few spare minutes and knew Audra would approve, so she reclined, sinking back into the cushions of her couch, and grabbed a clean black sock to drape over her eyes. Then she leaned the phone against the laundry basket, closed her eyes, and picked up where she'd left off.

When they all finished, Lucy hung up the phone and thought, *Hell, I'm going to e-mail Peter.* She had his e-mail so why bother with Facebook? She knew there were others out there like her, Facebookers who only visited the site every so often, and she didn't want to take the chance that he would miss her message. So she composed an e-mail asking if he remembered her—she was sure he did but it had been at least a year since the last teachers' conference—and told him that she'd always enjoyed his company.

Lucy continued that she thought he'd mentioned he had a girlfriend the last time they spoke, but that things change and if in the future he ever wants to get together, well, then fine. She also said that she was recently divorced and occasionally dating an odd variety of miscreants, but in the meantime, maybe Peter would like to hang out. Then Lucy typed her name and sent it into the ether.

Chapter 7

- -

Lucy had become a lot hornier since the divorce was final. Prior to that, the administrative legal mire had been a daily buzzkill for the better part of two years. Now that her life was her own again, she was hitting a fresh new stride, which included the unbridled and often inexplicable inclination to have hot sex with just about every unmarried man she came into contact with. She felt as if she were trapped inside the body of an eighteen-year-old boy—no agenda, no goals, just fuck me, please, then go away. Her married friends couldn't understand, but her divorced friends totally got it. They were teaching Lucy that however distracting and compelling her own sexual longings were, they didn't hold a candle to her new divorced friends' antics. Hers paled in comparison.

This new group of divorcées gave her permission to be wilder and take more risks, something she used to do in college and the years before she got married, but hadn't explored in a long time. For now, she only took those risks in her imagination because, well, third-grade teachers aren't supposed to take risks—too much social responsibility. It sucked, frankly. So when Peter e-mailed her back that he would like to meet, Lucy's head almost popped off. She felt lit up inside with renewed hope and abuzz with expectation. Now she had two upcoming dates, both completely nutso in their own special way. She could feel herself inching closer to some sort of thrilling edge. Whether the edge was named Ted or Peter, she didn't care, she just knew she was jumping off.

At the divorcées' monthly dinner, Lucy, Audra and Dix from school, slouched forward on their elbows around Fran's kitchen island. Fran was a dishwater blonde with a wedge haircut and a squat body the shape of a fresh fig. What she lacked in subtlety, she made up for in fierce loyalty and could be counted on to speak her mind, if not the truth. Divorced three years with four boys under fourteen, Fran worked as a general contractor for a commercial building business and spent most of her life around construction workers. Lucy had met Fran at a kickboxing class soon after her separation, when they were paired up to spar. At first she was terrified by Fran's brute confidence and sweaty aggression, but then when Lucy tripped over her own feet and landed on her ass, Fran was the first to ask if she was okay. Her voice was so compassionate and her eyes so kind that Lucy started to cry and couldn't stop for a half hour. "Cry it out," Fran said to her, while down on one knee, "Cry that bastard right out of you. He sure as hell doesn't deserve to be taking up that much room inside you, rent free." They remained sparring partners until Lucy quit. Fran became certified to instruct.

Dix was a phys-ed teacher at the same elementary school where Lucy taught third grade. "Howdy, sucker," were the first words she spoke to Lucy on her first day. "Are you from the South?" Lucy asked. "Nope, Vermont," said Dix. "Want a clementine? You're gonna need your strength." "Sure," said Lucy, and that was that. Dix became a valued mentor, explaining who the cast of characters were at the school, who to avoid and who to suck up to. At five-foot-twelve as Dix liked to say, she had the fresh-scrubbed looks of a woman who grew up on the ski slopes, and wore her cherry-red hair in two long braids every day. The students adored her, and her biggest fans among them wore their hair in braids, too. She was always coercing Lucy to sneak off campus for lunch, and covered her class if Lucy needed a brief but necessary break.

Dix asked Fran, "Is your ex still stealing a book each time he comes over to your house to get the kids?"

Fran said, "Yeah, I've taken photos of the bookshelves so I know which ones. I'm waiting until he takes me to court again to show the judge the photos."

"Loser." They all shook their heads in disbelief.

Dinner was over and Audra untucked her blouse while Fran and Dix unbuttoned the top button of their pants. The table was littered with the detritus of Thai take-out dinner, two empty bottles of red wine and a couple of empty beer bottles. A single, Ikea-esque droplight hung from above the table; Lucy dimmed it halfway through the meal saying, "Can we turn down the blessed lights, please? We're adults having an intimate dinner in someone's home, for Pete's sake, not at Costco with our kids." Lunch dishes were still piled up in Fran's sink and stacks of mail and magazines blanketed the counter tops. A cookbook, shoelace and an opened pack of nine-volt batteries cluttered the far end of the counter along with four Lego guys, a dying houseplant and a broken Nerf gun. It was messy, but not out of control. Just relaxed.

None of the ladies judged Fran for her laissez-faire approach to housekeeping and Lucy welcomed it. She was certain that the combination of Fran's chill attitude and the lowered overhead lighting enticed everyone to be the most intimate at her house, divulge more secrets.

"What the hell else has the UPS guy got to look forward to in his day?" Dix said with mock defensiveness. "I mean," said Dix, "all those monotonous right turns."

"That's FedEx," corrected Audra.

"Are you fucking kidding me?" said Fran, nonplussed. "The UPS man?! You fucked the UPS man?! *The guy's got a job to do, for chrissake!*"

"Everybody deserves a break," countered Dix, grinning. She was a daredevil and there wasn't much she wouldn't try. Lucy loved and envied that about her.

"Is there nothing you won't do?" said Lucy. "I wish I had half your balls."

"You can have 'em all," said Dix.

"Aren't you worried about the cliché factor?"

"Aren't you worried about the crabs?" said Audra, the voice of reason. "What about the GPS thingy they hold in their hands?" They all looked at Dix who sipped her beer with that damn Cheshire grin and poked at the decimated remains of the mango and sticky rice. Audra continued, "Doesn't it record the location of every stop and how long he spends there?"

"So what if it does?" Lucy said. "She didn't grill him a sandwich. It was a quickie."

"I once asked the UPS man to help me move my couch," said Fran.

"Same difference, I suppose," said Lucy.

All eyes waited for comment. Dix's eyes grew sinister, then wide, but she kept mum. Audra said, "For fuck's sake, dahling," which made Dix chuckle, dribbling a little beer onto the kitchen table. Audra could deliver off-color comments with the delicacy of Grace Kelly, due to the soft *r* she picked up from her British boss as a buyer at Neiman's.

Fran said, "He could always say it was a big package and took more time to deliver." Clearly she seemed to be giving the conundrum earnest consideration. "Or, if the UPS people asked, he could say that you needed help opening your box." Dix shook her head as Lucy shot a look at Audra. Their eyebrows raised in unison. Apparently, neither Dix nor Mister UPS had needed any assistance opening anything. Lucy looked at Fran, and then swiveled on her elbows towards Dix.

"Well, Miss Dixie-Lula-Mae Kirnbaum, was it a . . . big . . . package?"

Audra added with a fake Southern accent, "Yeah, Dix, did it take . . . mowah tahm . . . to delivah?" They often teased Dix about being from the land of Dixie even though she grew up in Vermont.

"And dee-id you nee-yid hay-elp openin' iyit?" said Fran in a terrible Southern accent.

Everyone cracked up. Dix pointed with a piece of mango on the end of her fork, first to Lucy, then Audra, then Fran while saying, "Yes, no and yes." They shook their heads and giggled.

"Well, then. Service with a smile," said Lucy.

"Fuckin' UPS," said Fran, and held up her bottle of beer.

"Fuckin' UPS," the rest said in straight-faced unison, and clinked their glasses.

Fran said, "Audra, who's your latest conquest? How's your stable these days?"

"Well, Howard is fine, but he's fifty-two and can't keep it up. He refuses to use Viagra—thinks he's too young for it."

Fran said, "I had a guy in his late forties who couldn't keep it up. Totally limp."

Dix said, "I had that with a guy who was forty-four."

"Forty-one," said Audra, and sighed, then continued, "Anyway, besides not being able to stay hard, Howard keeps saying he wants to marry me."

The ladies reacted as if they'd just seen something disgusting pop out of a hollow log in a horror movie. "Ewwww!" "Noooooo!"

"I know. Gross, right? I tell him over and over that I will never marry again, but he doesn't listen. He just keeps offering to fly me places and buy me stuff."

"I hate it when that happens," said Lucy rolling her eyes.

"God, me, too," said Dix.

"I've seen him, he's hot," said Fran.

"You mean not completely out of shape?" said Dix.

"Yeah, I guess," said Fran, thinking about it for a sec. "I can handle a man with cushion, but a totally overweight dude doesn't do it for me." They nodded in agreement.

Dix said, "Though I love a Rubenesque woman with ample curves. I think that's sexy."

They continued to nod. Fran said, "Case in point," and turned sideways, hands on hips.

Dix said, "It's a double standard, I know, but I don't care. What I really wish is that younger guys would start using Viagra."

Audra said, "They need to cast younger actors in their ads."

Dix said to Audra, "Exactly. What about your personal trainer, the young one?"

"He's okay," Audra said.

"Just okay?" Dix asked.

"Well, he's got a big dick but he doesn't know how to use it. Plus he's so shy I have to throw myself on him. It's like trying to bed a really good-looking upscale store mannequin."

"With a big dick," said Lucy.

"And Tarrique texts me way too late. I'm sorry but Adonis bod or not, I have to get up in the morning. Midnight, 1 A.M. booty calls? Please. Forget it."

Dix said, "Doesn't sound like any of them will last."

"They won't. I wish there were more virile age-appropriate men out there who date women their own age, before 10 P.M., but won't fall in love with me. Within a six-mile radius. I'm very busy."

"That is one small list, my friend," said Fran.

Lucy said, "What about you, Fran?"

"Oh, I'm still putting on DVDs for the kids upstairs then letting Cliff in through the basement window. But he's so busy it doesn't happen very often. Sometimes weeks go by."

"I bet he's busy," said Dix, shooting a look at Audra.

"And you're doing it where? On the pool table?" asked Lucy.

"Only once," said Fran. "I got a felt burn so I bought a pullout couch." The women cracked up. Fran continued, "The pullout's not so bad."

"Eighty-eight minutes of heaven," said Dix.

"Plus twelve minutes of previews," said Fran, raising her eyebrows once.

Audra said, "Has he finished your cabinets yet?"

"What do you think?" said Lucy. Dix shook her head, no.

Dix said, "What about you, Luce?"

"I got nuthin'," Lucy said, and shot a look at Audra who knew implicitly that it meant to keep their conversation about Ted in the vault for now. Lucy liked that about these women: ironclad discretion.

"Aw, c'mon. Nuthin'?" said Fran, aghast.

Lucy shook her head, sighed, then began one of her rants. "I can't seem to meet anyone, and if I do it's when I'm out with you guys: Dix the Amazon Goddess; Fran the Man-eater."

"That's me," said Fran.

"And Audra, Queen Vagina Blocker. I only get scraps when she's in the room."

Audra concurred. "My beauty *is* problematic. You may kiss my ring."

"You may kiss my ass," said Dix.

Lucy said, "There's this guy I always run into at conferences, Peter. He's funny and we get along famously. But I think he may have a girlfriend."

"E-mail him," said Fran.

"I did, and we're going to meet up for coffee or dinner next week."

"Coffee or dinner, eh? Big difference. Good job, girl. Way to go after it."

"Yeah, until he's married, he's fair game," said Dix.

"Fabulous," said Lucy. "More hunting metaphors. Why don't you just tell me to stalk him like prey? I thought we banded together to bury the cougar metaphor?"

Dix said, "Right, sorry, I forgot."

Audra said, "The coffee thing sounds promising. What about on-line dating? You said you were going to update your profile and lie about your age."

"Please. What a useless time suck. Half of them look like ex-cons and the other half don't post photos for '*business reasons.*'"

All the women said, "Mar-ried," in unison.

Lucy said, "Then they say that they're funny but don't write anything even remotely funny. If they say they're sarcastic, that's code for 'I can be a real prick.' Hardly anyone smiles. How can I be sure they have teeth if they don't smile?"

"Good point. Teeth are key," said Fran.

Dix said, "You've got to dial it back, sister. You're coming off like a hater."

"Ugh, I know. But I don't hate men, I love them, I really do. I'm trying to love them. They're making it difficult for me, though. Their punctuation and grammar are beyond repair. Is proofreading some sort of Internet crime? JerseyGentleman writes, 'I have a sarcastic sense of humor'—fabulous, the lazy man's version of verbal abuse masquerading as humor—'a good listener and there's many things I like to hang around on the weekends.' That sentence is a train wreck, and 'there's' is a contraction of 'there' and 'is'. It's singular, not plural. You say 'there are many things.' No one says 'there are' anymore."

Dix said, "You're going to be singular forever with that attitude."

"Your standards are too high, Luce," said Audra. "You need to lower them."

"Yeah," said Dix, "you need to be open to dating illiterates."

"You could teach them grammar," said Fran.

"Now there's a turn-on," said Audra.

"I blame our public school system," said Dix without irony.

"Yeah, well," said Lucy, "our public school system is cock-blocking my sex life."

"It's a good thing you're a teacher then, isn't it," said Dix.

"A lot of good it's doing me now. Wasn't your mom an English teacher? I blame her. I blame your mom."

Dix said, "Fine, call my mom and tell her she's cock-blocking your sex life."

"Don't think I won't," said Lucy, then cut the last strip of mango in half and ate one half. Dix cut the other one in half and ate the resulting quarter. Audra was cutting the last quarter into eighths when Fran said, "Just eat it, for chrissake!" They all paused to watch Audra eat the teeny mango morsel. She could make the stupidest thing sexy.

Fran said, "All I know is I'm horny."

"So horny," said Lucy sighing.

"Batshit-horny," said Dix, looking at Lucy.

"Me, too," said Audra.

"I just want to be ravished voraciously, then left alone," said Lucy. "About once, maybe twice a week. But also have him on retainer for occasional dinner, movies and as a date for parties."

Audra said, "With a working cock."

Fran said, "And not married, and not fat."

Lucy said, "And smart and funny. And—"

"Stop." Dix cut her off. "Quit while you're ahead. Besides, you're sending mixed messages out into the universe. You're asking for something that doesn't exist."

"Right," Lucy said, then sighed and folded her napkin into triangles upon triangles. The women shared a moment of deflated resignation with her. Lucy truly didn't hate men at all. She adored their bodies and minds, their strength and smells, their humor, delivery and surprising tenderness. She loved their big hands and hairy chests, their pelvic bones and sweat. She loved that they approached life from a different perspective entirely, and thrilled to make them laugh. Of course she hoped to find a confidant to elbow when a bad toupee walked by, a lover and dance partner, banterer and best friend. But she also knew that was statistically rare. Really, Lucy was just exasperated with the whole circus, but life was long and she remained open to its possibilities—though she kept her optimism in check.

Lucy spoke first. "It's odd, really, to think that I might never have sex again."

"Buzzkill," said Fran.

Lucy laughed, "I'm not trying to bring down the room. It's just always possible. Isn't it? Statistically, I mean. I'm not suggesting you feel sorry for me, I'm just stating plainly that there's always the chance that the last time I had sex will be the *last time I have sex*. Ever."

Audra said, "When was the last—"

"Two, three years ago. Feels like a hundred."

Dix said, "But that's true with everyone for everything. The last time you do anything could be the last time."

Fran said, "It's ridiculous. Turn the ridiculous cart around, my friend." She held up her hands like a steering wheel and made a screeching sound.

Audra said, "Lucy, you sound pathetic. You need to cowboy up." Fran patted Lucy's arm. Lucy patted Fran's hand back.

Dix said, "Well, if anyone knows cowboys, Audra, it's you." Dix was going for levity.

"Yeah, ride 'em cowgirl, giddyup!" said Fran.

Dix began to sing, "She'll. Be. Comin' round the mountain when she comes . . ."

"Yee-haw!" hollered Fran.

Dix continued in a Southern accent, "She'll be comin' round the mountain when she comes."

Audra said, "Ooooh," and batted her eyes like a screen siren then fanned herself as if in the throes of passion.

Fran harmonized with Dix: "She'll be comin' round the mountain, she'll be comin' round the mountain—"

Audra heaved while running her hands through her hair. Lucy laughed and joined in for the big finale.

"She'll be comin' round the mountain when. She. Cooooom-mmes! Yeeee-hawww!"

Audra let out a big ol', "Yeeeesssss!"

The friends helped Fran clean up then hugged their good-byes. Lucy texted Nancy from Fran's driveway, *Okay. I'm in ;)* and giggled as she put her key in the ignition.

Chapter 8

I'm going to send Ted over straight from work," Nancy said under her breath. She and Lucy ended up in line together at the dry cleaner a few days before she was supposed to meet Ted. "I don't want him to see the kids. Might make things more difficult." Lucy wondered if by "things" Nancy meant Ted's dick getting hard, but decided not to press her on specifics.

Nancy said, "I think he still thinks it's all a big joke."

"I've no doubt." Lucy was nervous at first when she saw Nancy but realized quickly that her mood was upbeat. Thank goodness.

Nancy continued, "He got mad when I first told him, said I was being idiotic and mean to tease him. Took me a while to convince him I was serious. Then he finally believed me, and you should have seen him. It was like he'd been awarded the Nobel Prize. Floating through the house, giggling."

"Did you tell him it's me?"

"Yeah, but that doesn't matter. Could be anyone. As long as it isn't me."

Lucy let the comment slide.

"In the last week Ted's cleaned out the garage, fixed Nicky's headboard, which came away from his bed, like, four years ago, and restacked the firewood that slumped over on the side of the house. Then, for the last two days leading up to his 'appointment'—"

"Is that what you're calling it?"

"Well I sure as hell wasn't going to call it a date." They both chuckled.

"True. Very professional."

"Right? So Ted's been thinking for sure that I'm going to change my mind and take it all back. He told me that he told himself not to think about it, so that he wouldn't be disappointed when I change my mind."

At that moment the woman in line in front of them turned around and asked, "Are you talking about surprising your husband with a new car?"

Nancy and Lucy both said, "No," without explanation. The woman turned back around.

Nancy said, "I know he was trying not to think about it, but that was all he could think about, I could tell. He had a crappy week at work. He broke a glass in the kitchen. I bet he's been looking at his cell phone constantly, expecting me to text and call it off."

"I almost feel sorry for him."

"I know. It was kinda funny. He finally asked me point-blank if I was going to call it off. I mean, did I think about it a thousand times? Yes. But then I found myself getting excited about it, too. Our sex has been fantastic." Nancy mouthed this last sentence and they both advanced in line, smiling thinly at the woman who'd been in front of them, as she left.

"I'm thinking *I* might like a different guy sometime, too."

"Good luck with getting Ted on board with that." The proprietor signaled for the next customer in line. Lucy advanced to the counter.

Nancy said, "Yeah, I know. But I can't even fathom right now. No time." She laughed out loud.

Lucy whispered, "Yeah, one bizarre, sanctioned, extramarital roll in the hay at a time."

Nancy said, "Exactly."

Lucy had a million things on her mind, making the slog to Friday at 4:30 agonizing. She was wiped out from the long work week, but her date with Ted in a few hours gave her a renewed vim. Wups, appointment. That's what Nancy had called it. But so clinical. Fling? No. Tryst. Whatevs. *Goddamn, teaching is exhausting,* she thought. She tried in vain to nap for a half hour while Gus played Wii, knowing the rest would center her, calm her. *Screw it,* she thought after ten minutes, then hopped up and made herself some coffee, though she probably didn't need the caffeine; Lucy was amped. She had two dates that she couldn't really talk about and it was killing her. As much as she loved Kit, she was a little judgy on the topic of Peter, plus Lucy didn't want to hear anything that might stick in her head and fester. She was pretty sure Peter still had a girlfriend, and whatever this thing was with Ted was ludicrous on so many levels—but she was forging ahead. Nothing ventured, nothing gained. Reckless or not, after a two-plus-yearlong dry spell she felt entitled to some physical connection.

"How did I get here?" Lucy sang. "This is not my beautiful house. This is not my beautiful wife," and hustled Gus into the car. *My God, what have I done?*

Lucy drove Gus to their usual drop spot—the playground parking lot—where they waited for the weekend handoff to Matt. While

Gus drifted on a nearby swing on his stomach, Lucy assessed her face in the flip-down mirror. She tried to look at herself objectively, the way Ted and Peter would soon be seeing her. Errant eyebrow hairs needed plucking—not top priority, she'd get to that later this week. Her lashes seemed to be thinning but her hair was still holding on to its shape—when it wasn't humid, which it was from July through October. Her brownish-black corkscrew curls had gone completely gray in her early thirties, but no one had to know that thanks to her colorist. And her body was reasonably held together by Kundalini Yoga, short jogs around the track at school and a fairly decent diet of moderation—not workout fit, but not let-yourself-go, either. Lucy thought she looked pretty good for her age, but felt like an ass for thinking it. "For my age" was such a pathetic suffix to any thought.

Lucy checked her watch—Matt was late again—and continued her inventory. Her pale green eyes still had dark gray flecks around the rim that looked like pencil points—at least that's what Pauly Judson told her in tenth grade. Lucy smiled into the mirror and noted the laugh crinkles at the corners of her eyes, which she convinced herself were useful to have in her role as an elementary school teacher. They made her look friendly. Old, but friendly. Lucy's teeth were yellowing slightly—time for whitening strips—but had otherwise held out well enough even though she'd lost her retainer almost immediately after getting her braces off. *Good Lord, when do our teeth begin to fall out of our heads?* she wondered, then smoothed a hand over the brown spots on her left cheek that no one told her she might want to slather with sunscreen when she got her driver's license back in the late eighties. Lucy's phone rang. It was Kit. She knew she'd get the third degree later if she didn't answer it so she picked up and said, "Do you think that fortyish women in England have age spots on their right cheeks from driving on the other side of the car?"

Kit said, "Probably. Yes. So, now you're forty*ish*? Ha. That's a good one. What are you up to?"

"Nothing. Dropping Gus with Matt. What about you?" Lucy deflected the question.

"I have my brother's second trophy wedding this weekend."

"Good stuff."

"Kill me now."

Lucy said, "I've decided I skipped my first marriage. Think about it. I got married at thirty-two, which is closer to when people are getting remarried after their first marriage ends at thirty, the one that began when they first got married at twenty-four."

"Okay. So then," said Kit, "if you get remarried—"

"Not happening," said Lucy as Matt's black BMW pulled into the lot. Lucy held up one straight finger to Gus, which he knew meant to wait. She opened the car door to her used twelve-year-old Subaru—Matt had always been tight with money—then remembered to swipe on some lip gloss. On some stupid, pointless level, Lucy wanted to show Matt that he'd missed out on something, even though it was Lucy who'd told him to leave, even though she would never, ever want him again.

"Or I should say, *when* you get remarried," said Kit.

Lucy loved the way Kit always thought she knew what direction Lucy's life would take, as if merely uttering the words aloud was some sort of directive that destiny would surely heed. She felt a swell of deep guilt for not telling Kit about her weekend plans but knew it was the right choice. "Don't hold your breath," said Lucy as Matt parked in a spot at the far end of the lot.

"Is he still a dick? I mean, I know he's a dick-dick. But is he still a day-to-day dick?"

"What do you think?" Lucy thought about Matt's parents. Walter was a well-respected Main Line neurologist, and Constance was a tenured professor of adaptive microeconomics at Penn. They were both intellectuals, and according to Matt had been too busy to bother with the muss and fuss of actually raising their son. They supposedly had him as an afterthought because their friends were having children and their innate competitiveness finally got the better of them. This they admitted one night over port. They apparently never argued, but also rarely parented. Lucy recalled all the stories Matt told her over the years of being forgotten after sports games and having to walk home in the dark. He told of learning to live with broken promises and empty seats at violin recitals, when they never materialized—too busy, you know. Lucy knew that Matt was once a trusting child who had no reason in the world to think his parents might let him down, but they did, over and over. She didn't think she'd married a dick. No one had, but alas. Lucy wanted to punch Matt's parents almost as much as she wanted to punch him.

Lucy called to Gus, "Please wait for your daddy to get out of his car."

Gus said, "I know, Mom," and kept swinging. Gus loved his weekends with Daddy and he loved coming home to Mommy. That much had worked out for the best. Gus dutifully waited for his dad's grand entrance, which Matt would milk like a Borscht Belt comic. Lucy knew he was probably on the phone or texting someone, or just making them wait for the sheer joy of lording power over someone. He couldn't help himself. It was a pathological need for attention.

Kit said, "Is Frenchie with him?"

"No. She's probably on one, of her modeling assignments. Delphine's oh-so-busy."

"He really is living the cliché, isn't he. How does he look?"

Lucy looked at Matt's chiseled jaw and long, Grecian nose that she used to find so handsome and said, "Same." But the truth was that she didn't think he looked like a guy who was finally living his dream—unburdened at last by the trappings of the suburbs. Tall and tan, Matt was a private-wealth manager with a big ego and a small penis—a lethal combination. But he looked doughy and tired, still bitter and vaguely disappointed—even from the side. His bald spot had grown exponentially and his chin seemed to be weakening. For a while she wondered when Matt would get tired of being a colossal jerk so they could relax into a pleasant rhythm of amicable divorced-ness. (If Frenchie was such a sexpot in bed, why was he still so damn cranky?) Lately, though, Lucy was coming to the conclusion that although he'd won everything he wanted out of the divorce—a fat buyout check for their house; a brownstone in Harlem; an icy French trophy fiancée; and the freedom to drink, flirt, play golf and work as much as his workaholic heart desired—he would always be unhappy. Miserable Matt, she thought, tethered to her for life.

Kit said, "Text me if he's still a dick."

"Loveyabye," said Lucy, and slid her phone into her coat pocket.

Gus wandered over to wait with Lucy. He said, "Daddy's probably on an important business call." He said the words as if he had wanted to get them exactly right—they were words he heard often. "Of course," said Lucy who had stopped believing anything Matt said years ago. She knew that only about one out of ten calls were actually "important business calls." Matt was still texting as he got out of his car. Probably another woman: no doubt he was cheating on Frenchie, too. Gus shouted, "Hi, Daddy!" and Lucy let him run ahead. Matt patted Gus's head absentmindedly, his thumb still on the keypad. "Hi, Augs," he said without looking up. "Dad, don't call me that," said Gus. Matt ignored him and said to Lucy, "I have a business trip in two weeks so you have to take him," without saying "please" or looking up from his phone. Lucy knew it was just as likely a soccer or golf tournament, a steamy getaway or guys' fishing weekend. She ignored this comment for now. Lucy crouched down to get eye level with Gus, wrapped her arms around him and said, "Say good-bye and I love you to your mother."

Gus said, "Good-bye and I love you to your mother," and lifted his chin to invite a kiss.

"Good-poop, Fartypants. Have a superfun weekend," said Lucy and pecked him lightly on the lips. She assumed now that every kiss might be their last. One day without warning he would decide no more kisses from Mom. She knew it would also happen with hugs and hand-holding and all sorts of simple pleasures that had kept her from wanting to crawl into a hole the last few years. She told herself she was ready. She even braced herself for missing his clean smell after a bath when she towel dried his hair or his ankles rubbing her shins when he sat on her lap. He would eventually stop letting her get so close. Lucy hoped that when Gus grew hairy and smelly, his general stink would help her adjust to the physical wedge that puberty would lodge between them, but she didn't actually think it would deter her. She would still want to hug him and he would hate it. She sighed and decided to think about something else as she walked off, leaving Gus in a giddy one-sided conversation with his father, who was now talking on the phone while driving. Lucy texted Kit, *Yep, still a dick*, then started her car.

Lucy tried not to think about Matt ignoring Gus by using her Jedi mind training to exorcise him from her brain. Like an intermittent hangnail, he surfaced in Lucy's life weekly to annoy or try to hurt her, so she got lots of practice. The fact that she was tethered to this jerk for the rest of her life was something she hadn't considered when she agreed to marry him. *I can always divorce him*, crossed her mind during a big fight over buying a pullout couch while they were still engaged. But in her mind, the severance would be clean, like when you delete an ex-boyfriend's number from your phone and, *presto*, gone. Lucy hadn't figured what divorce really meant when kids were involved. She hadn't imagined the three-legged race that her life would become, tied to Matt. Divorce was a knot, too, she often thought, tighter and lasting longer than most marriages. There was no walking away.

Up in her bedroom, Lucy changed into a tight, deep teal cardigan sweater buttoned just to where the shadow of her décolletage began. She chose the red-and-pink bra she'd gotten for her divorce party, and for the first time simultaneously wore the matching panties. She put on a black miniskirt and the cheesy black vinyl boots that she'd bought at a secondhand shop to wear on dates. Her knees were cold but she remembered Audra's comment about leaving a bit of skin exposed, regardless of the temperature. She thought the outfit she'd chosen was a bit trashy, to be honest, but she figured they both knew why they were there, so, what the hell. She forewent any jewelry, because she knew she'd just be removing it. Then Lucy tousled her hair and went downtstairs to empty the dishwasher.

She tried not to think about Ted and really tried not to think about Nancy. She'd met them at the same time and knew them only as a couple, so it was odd to consider him as a separate entity, much less a sexual being. He was married therefore off-limits. But once she told Nancy "yes," she didn't look back. Lucy was thrilled at the possibility of sex, of being fused with someone, of being desired. So for the past week she had conjured Ted in a few different ways, in a few different outfits: on top of her, below her, in her bed and in his car. It was strange but titillating. She figured she'd be mentally warmed up for him when he arrived, like an athlete visualizing her victory before the big game. At least that was how Lucy decided to spin it to her inner critic. Her nonplussed inner critic, who stood with her hands on her hips, fuming, and looked suspiciously like her mother. She thought about her former self and what she would have said if someone had come at her with this proposition when she was still single. She was positive she would have said absolutely not, then laughed and moved on. A married man was off-limits. *O. F. F.*

Lucy's world was so set then, so clearly defined. Sleeping with anyone's husband—not to mention your pal's husband—as a favor to her was definitely not part of her moral program. She thought of it in terms of robbing a bank. If anyone had asked her to rob a bank as recently as two years ago, she would have said "Are you out of your mind?" But then Matt cleaned out their joint bank accounts one day and started stealing furniture out of their house. Lucy's imagination and paranoia teamed up to fuel an endless loop of devastating scenarios in her waking mind and sleeping subconscious. Those events triggered her outlaw thinking. What else was he capable of, the sweet man she'd married? And if he was capable of such behavior, what was *she* capable of? Robbing banks? Lucy wondered: If they were destitute and Gus needed an operation, would she do it? Maybe. Maybe if all of the wrong circumstances aligned to create a confluence of rationalization, maybe then, yes, she could see herself robbing a bank. But . . . really?

Lucy hadn't been lacking a moral compass up until now. Her parents had raised her to be a good person and society had reinforced it. In fact there was absolutely nothing in her upper-middle-class upbringing that would have led anyone to be able to explain away her behavior. She'd never run with a bad crowd or harbored bad habits, though there was that spate of kleptomania in junior high and the pot smoking in her best friend's tree house. And the time she cheated on her prom date with what's-her-name's cousin. And that time in college when she lied about . . . oh hell, didn't all kids do this stuff? No? Okay, maybe she was an occasional bad seed, but that was so long ago. She'd been very good for years and years and definitely for all of her marriage. She reasoned she was reacting to all the rejection from Matt, but that was just shifting the blame—unacceptable. And such a cliché American mind-set, the old gaping hole-in-my-soul bit, like a toddler having a tantrum and stomping her feet at the closed sign in a candy shop window.

Lucy hated herself for a split-second, then told the voices in her head to sit down and hush up. She poured herself a glass of wine and turned on some Astrud Gilberto. The stage was set. All Lucy needed was a willingness to step over a line in the sand—she'd even been given permission—and see what was on the other side. Maybe being a teacher had something to do with it, all that social expectation. She once heard a coworker say that he thought teachers were like modern-day castratos, neutered for the good of the community. (She'd thought that was a little extreme.) Maybe Lucy was rebelling against that. *I'm a damn good teacher and a sexual being, darn it, and the two aren't mutually exclusive*, she heard herself whine. Then she tired of trying to find an excuse for what was about to happen and wiped down the stovetop. Her personal, private, moral, seminal crossover moment was happening in about two minutes and she wanted the kitchen to look clean.

Ted would be at her front door and she would become an adulterer. Or complicit to adultery. Or was it adultery? She wasn't married. In any case, it was wrong and she reasoned her kitchen should reflect goodness. *Call it off, it's not too late*, she thought. *I'm just doing a friend a favor*, she reasoned. *Everyone leave me alone.* But she was alone. That was the problem. *Full circle*, she thought. What a mess. Would she be able to go through with it? *Shake it off.* This was just another activity. Like tennis. Lucy had to stop thinking and get out of her head. She needed a stiffer drink. For her whole life, Lucy had been on one side of the line, and in a moment she would be on the other. It was that simple. She knew she could stop at any point, call time out or apologize and beg off. But she also knew she wouldn't. She wanted the sex and she wanted it now. She wanted the uncertainty, the excitement and risk. Lucy wanted to shake up her new life and be bad and the moment had arrived. She threw her shoulders back and inhaled. She was ready to step over the line.

Lucy was about to rob a bank.

The doorbell rang at 7 P.M. on the dot, and Lucy looked out the window even though she knew damn well who it was. *Here we go*, she thought and swung open her front door as if she were about to take the stage at Carnegie Hall.

"Hello, sailor," she said, and backed up in order to give him a wide berth. The joke was lost on him. He looked a wreck. She hoped the breezy bossa nova music would work its magic quickly, or else the whole thing could go down in flames. Lucy had turned off most of her lamps. *The lighting is good*, she thought, *low and cozy*. She turned the music down. Ted stepped into the front hallway, tentatively, gripping his briefcase. He was still in his work suit.

"Hi," was all he said.

Poor Ted, thought Lucy. He was clearly undone by this whole thing. Ted glanced at Lucy then looked away. She pried his overcoat off him gingerly, as if peeling skin off a sunburn, and took his briefcase.

"How was your day?" Lucy asked as she led him down the hall and into the living room.

"Fine," he said, and didn't return the nicety. *Nervous as hell*, Lucy thought, then willed herself to get down to business. *Okay*, she thought, *what would a high-class prostitute do? W.W.H.C.P.D.?*

I should have Googled this. Probably would have found step-by-step instructions on YouTube. Lucy occasionally daydreamed about getting paid for her orgasms—everyone always says that you're supposed to love what you do for a living. But no, who was she kidding? She'd make a lousy prostitute. Most prostitutes make lousy prostitutes. Though it *was* recession proof. *Nah, too dangerous,* Lucy thought. *And illegal. Don't forget about illegal—duh. Focus. Make him comfortable.*

"Hey, Ted, would you like a beer?" she said, and walked away from him into the kitchen so that he could get a good look at her bare legs and nice ass. She wondered if the boots were working. He stayed in one spot, rooted to the floor and unable to speak. She changed her tack.

"Or bourbon?"

"Uh, sure," he said

"Fabulous," said Lucy. Then she thought, *Maybe he would relax if I gave him a task. Men like to have something to do.*

"Hey, Ted," Lucy called from the kitchen. "Would you mind taking a look at my stereo? There's a speaker out in the dining room and I've jiggled the thingee but I can't seem to figure out why it's not sending sound. It was working before Gus's birthday party. But I don't know what happened. There was a lot of searching-for-Nerf-pellets behind things, and maybe one of the kids . . ." She trailed off. *Oh God*, she thought, *don't mention Gus. Or Matt.* Then she wondered what Nancy was doing right now. Was she burning her kids' dinner? Furiously knitting? Maybe she was sobbing in the shower, drinking white wine out of a soggy box. *Now there was an unhelpful image.* She had to block Nancy from her mind.

Lucy handed Ted his drink, a Phillips-head screwdriver and a pair of pliers she found in the kitchen junk drawer. He said thanks, but still didn't look her in the eye. She showed him the stereo then stepped back to give him space. "Are you hungry?" she asked. She and Nancy had forgotten to sort out food. Was she supposed to feed him? She was pretty sure Nancy wouldn't want her having dinner with him. That would be too much like a date, and this was just supposed to be just a lay. A quick screw with perhaps a blow job thrown in, depending on her mood. She could eat later, but she figured he was probably hungry. *Men are always hungry.* "Uh, sure," he said, and looked at the school portrait of Gus on her mantel. Lucy thought of the least romantic meal she could think of and then—almost reflexively—got the peanut butter out of the cabinet. *Definitely not W.A.H.C.P. would D. Maybe I should have another drink, too,* she thought. She wasn't usually a boozer, but this was a special occasion. She poured another glass of wine for herself and then brought the peanut butter and jelly sandwich into the living room, stopping off at the mantel to set the portrait facedown. Then she sat down to watch Ted fix her stereo so she could get a better look at his bod.

What have we here? Not bad, not bad. Good shoulders for medium build. Thinning hair, clean cut, though, possibly a recent trim. Lucy thought back to the hours she and Matt had logged at the town pool with Nancy and Ted. She was pretty sure Ted had a nice chest and hadn't let himself go too far in the paunch department. Nice legs. Something about playing lacrosse in college she remembered Nancy saying once. Lucy flashed to him smiling in the deep end with his kids. Honest smile, decent guy. Not a very complex or sophisticated human being, but perfectly nice. She remembered him telling a story once at a barbeque and laughing at his delivery. Good storyteller. She also remembered him as friendly, well-mannered—the kind of guy who holds the door for strangers, even if it means giving up the better place in line. He was comfortable using the tools she'd just given him—*capable hands, so there's that.*

He'd been a good husband to Nancy and a pretty good father to his kids as far as she could tell. Lucy bet he was good in bed. Generous. Probably more than willing to please. Lucy could usually tell the selfish types and he didn't strike her as one of them. She hoped he'd be hungry. Voracious. "Let me take your jacket," Lucy said, and he stood up, took it off and handed it to her. *Nice ass*, she thought as she handed him half a sandwich. He took it without taking his eyes off the back of the speaker. His lips were thin, but in her experience that didn't matter. She didn't think she'd be making out with Ted, but who's to say? This was uncharted territory.

Ted was still tinkering when Lucy went over to him and rested her hand on his shoulder. He tensed. She moved her hand across his broad back once and down his arm, then took his hand and led him over to the couch. He was still holding the pliers. She sat him down and said, "Hand me the pliers and take off your tie," then she bent down to unlace his shoes.

Ted said, "I don't—"

"Eh, stop," Lucy said. "No point in talking. Unless it's important. Is it really important? Is my house on fire?"

"No."

"Okay, then. Unbuckle your pants."

Lucy leaned over him to put his tie on the end table while he unbuckled his pants. Leaning back, she moved her chest across his sightline so that he would have to look at her boobs. She thought they looked nice today and wanted to make sure he saw them. She also knew that boobs were like a kind of launch button for men and that she would need him hard. This was not a nuanced scenario; she was going for bold strokes. So to speak. She leaned in and rubbed her cheek against his, then bit his ear ever so slightly. He moaned and slumped down a little. Then, with the very tip of her tongue, she slowly licked his neck, near his ear—once. He rested his head on the back pillow of the couch as she took off his glasses and placed them next to his tie. Then she moved the coffee table out of the way and knelt between his legs.

This would have been about the time that Lucy would ask for a condom or take one out from behind the planter or from under the cushion or one of the three or four other places she'd hidden condoms around the house—wishful thinking. But she and Nancy had decided on no condom, owing to Lucy's diagnosed secondary infertility and the fact that they were both coming from monogamous relationships and disease free. Nancy also figured it would be a bonus for Ted in the sensitivity department, but ultimately left it up to Lucy. (Neither of them expected to be making this arrangement again.) For Lucy, using a condom after years of trying to get pregnant felt like a cruel mockery of her broken body. She didn't want the muscle memory of rolling it on dampening the mood by reminding her of her wasted years of fertility. The decision seemed risk free.

"Close your eyes," Lucy said, and ran one hand up from his knee and the other down from his chest. Her hands met at his fly. She unzipped it slowly and untucked his shirt. Ted lifted his hips a little so she could ease down his pants and reach into his boxers. She found his cock hard and yearning. *Excellent*, thought Lucy, and starting to swell herself, pulled it out with as much care as she would use to remove a bird's nest from under a nettle bush. She put one hand around the warm shaft—it wasn't particularly thick, but of average size and a decent length—and with the other cupped his balls. Gently kneading them, she touched her tongue to the base of the underside of his penis. Ted moaned. Slowly, Lucy licked up the vein of his appreciative cock as if she were chasing a drip from the bottom of an ice cream cone. Then she licked her right hand and in one smooth motion, ran it up and down the bulging shaft. She continued kneading his balls as if she were moving ripe plums around in her palm. He moaned opened mouthed this time and sunk even further into the couch. If there was one thing guys loved—besides the obvious—it was having their balls kneaded. So easy and yet so underused.

Leaning in again, she circumnavigated the rim of his cock's dark pink head with just the tip of her tongue, then flattened it out to gently cover the whole top. Ted let out a long, "Ohhhhhh." Lucy knew that if the frontal lobe of his brain hadn't switched off when she unzipped his zipper, it was firmly off now. Still kneading, she slowly moved her lips down onto him. Ted snapped his head up and opened his eyes. Lucy thought for possibly the first time that Ted was really seeing her, his wife's friend was looking right at him, his cock disappearing into her mouth.

Lucy went to town on him, as Ted twisted and moaned. She switched hands occasionally and gave her jaw a rest now and again, but she enjoyed the creative challenge. There were so many combinations of moves, so many different rhythms to try. *"For men, blow jobs are the equivalent of getting flowers,"* she'd read once on a greeting card. So simple and yet, so marginalized. "The blow job is always the first thing to go in a marriage," she heard a guy friend say once. Lucy believed there wasn't a man alive who didn't thrill from the feeling of someone other than himself touching his penis now and again, and any wife who thought her husband was somehow above it all or different in this regard was fooling herself. Smart men? Shy men? Older, erudite men with heads full of knowledge and theories? Damn straight they want a blow job. Stephen Hawking? Ask him.

After bringing Ted to the brink a few times, Lucy said, "So, Ted, how about we get busy?" She was pretty sure all he heard was "Mwah, muh-mwah, mwah, busy." He lifted his head just enough to meet her eyes, which she took as a yes, then she leaned back to unbutton her blouse. He was ready and she was already wet and more than ready and wanted to cut to the chase. In a daze, he took off his pants. He was too out of it to take off his socks. "Unbutton your shirt a little, then help me off with these boots" Lucy said moving over to the couch, and he did as he was told. She took off her skirt and matching undies and was about to lay on her back when she remembered, *Oh, right, the missionary position—probably the bane of every long-married husband's existence.* "Let's mix it up, shall we?" she said. With that she straddled him, and taking his cock in her hand, moved it back and forth across her folds to moisten and separate them. He explored her breasts then leaned in and put his mouth on her left nipple and sucked. His wet lips felt good on her, and as he bit down ever so slightly, an electrical charge shot down her chest and lit up her nether regions. He had a nice touch, old Ted. Lucy had taken him for more of a rough-and-tumble-fumbler type, but she was impressed and starting to find him downright sexy. He grabbed her buttocks and squeezed. Then she took his wanting cock into her hands and slowly, slowly moved down onto him, thrilling with every inch that brought her closer to the feeling of fullness, a sated hunger—and bliss.

This time is was Lucy's turn to moan. "Ohhhhhhh," she said. "Ohhh, yesssssss." *My God, this feels good*, she thought, *an actual man inside me.* She couldn't believe this was truly happening. She'd heard, "Don't be silly, of course you'll have sex again," but friends didn't get it, didn't understand that she couldn't envision it because her ego had been beaten down for so long. Who would possibly find her attractive? Matt had spared no thoughts in sharing with her the many reasons why she wasn't. And now she was having sex—without batteries! With a married man, subcontracted by his wife, but still. Amazing. Lucy sat him up, wrapped her arms around his neck and rocked harder. The angle of his full erection hitting the back wall deep inside of her gave her an almost rough pleasure. A zillion tingles rushed to her scalp and she shook her head—giddy. This was why she craved sex, to take her out of her mind and immerse her in levity and joy. To light up what had been snuffed out by Matt over the years. To unbind Lucy and set her free.

They tried a few more positions before Ted asked what he could do to make Lucy happy. "I'm glad you asked. I was just going to tell you," she said. "Get on top and do as I say." Lucy told him to grind into her slowly but evenly and fill her up with everything he had. With that he scooped her up with one arm and laid her down on her back. He moved into her again with the weight and power of his body. His rhythm echoed the arching of her back beautifully as she thrust herself towards him to meet the hard bones of his pelvis. *More, more,* she thought. *Deeper, dammit.*

"Yessssssss," she said, "here it comesssssss. Oh, myyyyyyyy, yessssssss!" And before she knew it, Lucy was laughing and screaming. Ted was shouting, too. He pounded the wall next to the couch with his fist and cried out with a low clenching groan, as if trying to lift a car. His eyes rolled into the back of his head and veins popped in his neck as Lucy's body exploded, shattering all the molecules in the room and sending her mind into deep space. Out there, all the particles in the universe were consumed by her orgasm. Out there, there was no Lucy. No job, no ex-husband, no bills or groceries, just the sweet, sweet tingles of precious nothing. She shuddered. Her leg kicked out reflexively as if she'd missed a step in a dream, then she lay still and listened to herself panting. Her cheeks and chest flushed, a satin sheen of sweat covered her skin.

Lucy had come with a man deep inside her. It was even better than she had remembered.

When they finished climaxing together, Ted pulled out of Lucy and backed away almost immediately. *Aw,* she thought, *but whatevs.* Ted reclined against the couch, breathing heavily. Lucy didn't move. She was going to lap up every morsel of this, so she remained still, floating on a cloud of pixie dust and tremors. When Ted started looking for his clothes, Lucy didn't feel angst or regret, she didn't feel personal affront or looming insecurity, nor did she feel the need to help. It was time for him to get dressed and go, she thought, without any accompanying complication. Then she thought, *This is perfect, no strings attached.* It's amazing how easy this can be when everyone knows where they stand and everyone knows the rules. *Good fences make good neighbors,* she thought as Ted finished dressing and reached for his coat. Lucy finally lifted her head, groped for her skirt on the floor and wedged it between her legs.

"Bye, Ted," she said. "Thanks. That was fun."

"Bye," he said, then turned and looked like he was trying to think of an appropriate exit line. Lucy chuckled.

"Please don't feel like you have to say anything, Ted," Lucy said from the couch, supine, "Really, you're good. We're done here."

He paused and said quietly, "Okay."

"Drive safely," she called from the couch.

"Okay," Ted said again as he showed himself out the front door. Just before she heard it close, Lucy thought she heard him say, "Uh, thanks."

Lucy was able to compartmentalize the entire episode remarkably well. She luxuriated on the couch for a while longer, then showered, slipped into comfy clothes, made a ham-and-Swiss sandwich, and hunkered down to watch TV. Not unlike what she would have done after returning from a tennis match. Check that box, what's next. The phone rang. It was Nancy. *Oh, shit,* Lucy thought. But she knew she had to answer it. *Pick up the phone.*

"Hi, how did it go?" said Nancy. She spoke quickly with hushed excitement, in the same tone one might ask a performer once they've come off stage.

"Uh, fine, I guess. Yeah, fine," Lucy said. She spoke brightly but without too much enthusiasm.

"Did you give him a blow job?"

"Yes."

"Oh, thank God. I hate those things." Lucy wanted to launch into a lecture about how Nancy should really turn that mind-set around but decided that now wasn't the time. A remarkable act of self-restraint on Lucy's part, and so unlike her.

Nancy asked, "And how was the sex?"

"Fine, good. It was just your garden-variety lay. Nothing special."

Nancy panicked. "Oh, no! I thought you said—"

"No! I mean—of course it was *special*! What am I saying, yes, it was very special, but not in a candlelight and satin sheets kind of way—"

"Good, because Ted would have hated that shit."

"It was just a lay. But a good one."

"Just good?"

"Okay, it was fantastic. It was the best sex of his life. Is that what you want me to say?"

There was a pause. Nancy said, "Um. No."

"I didn't think so."

There was a time-out in the conversation while they both reconsidered what they'd done and where this was going. The possibilities for this to turn into a complete and utter clusterfuck were just now dawning on both of them.

Lucy forged ahead. "How did Ted seem when he got home? Satisfied?" It was a funny question to ask with her ego at stake. She felt like Ted had been her client.

Hey! she realized. *This is what high-class prostitution must feel like. Huh.*

Nancy debriefed, "Yeah, I guess. He was pretty quiet. He just looked at me then went upstairs. He's in the shower now."

"Huh, not exactly a rave review."

"I'm sure you were fine. You're sure you sucked his dick?"

"Um, yeah-ah."

"Well, then, that about covers it."

"I guess so," Lucy said, then waited to see if they were done.

Nancy said, "I'm not going to ask you if you—"

"I get it. That's fine." Another pause.

"Do you know if the marching band is doing their fund-raiser in town tomorrow?"

"Not sure. I think so. Hey, I've got prep for tomorrow morning. Parents are coming in."

"Oh," said Nancy. "Right. Okay, well."

"Yeah. Keep me posted," said Lucy. This was now officially one of her top ten most awkward conversations. Ever.

"Okay, you, too," said Nancy.

"Okay, bye," said Lucy.

"Okay."

Yikes, Lucy thought. *Maybe top three.*

Chapter 9

One down, one to go. At 5 P.M. on Saturday, Kit came by to help Lucy pick out an outfit for her date with Peter. Lucy didn't say who her date was with, she just said it was with some Internet guy. Kit loved picking out clothes because her dream had been to become a fashion designer when she was little, and because she loved bossing people around. Lucy didn't always agree with Kit's choices but loved the girl time and, to be honest, the compliments. "That looks really cute," said Kit. Lucy was wearing a burgundy full skirt, a black cardigan sweater unbuttoned to her shadow and black, shiny flats.

"Hmm, cute," Lucy said. "Do I want to look 'cute'?"

"Doesn't everyone want to look cute?" said Kit.

"In my forties? Really?"

"Well, how do you want to look?"

Lucy looked in the mirror. "Alluring. Attractive."

"Nope," said Kit. "'Attractive' is not enough. How about 'pretty'? You never outgrow pretty. It's always age appropriate."

"Sounds too young to me. How about 'dazzling'? Too awards show-y?"

Kit shrugged. "Eh."

"I also want to look sexy without looking cougar-y."

"Well, what you're wearing is not sexy, exactly, unless the guy lost his virginity to his third-grade teacher."

Lucy said, "Oh my God. I *am* a third-grade teacher. I'm dressed for work! Shit."

"I'm just sayin'," said Kit.

"Right. Thank heavens you're here," said Lucy, then she looked back at the pile of clothes that blanketed her bed: about seven different outfits in all, plus various shoes and possible accessories to match.

Kit said, "You have too many clothes."

"I know, but I got them all on sale, so they were cheap. And I haven't gained any weight since grad school and I never throw anything away."

"Bitch."

"Which part? The steady weight or the hoarding?"

Kit laughed as Lucy pointed to a brown leather pencil skirt and open-collar silk blouse with shiny, wide belt and heels. "What about that? You never saw me in that."

"Too office vixen let's-do-it-on-the-conference-table-during-a-group-call-on-mute."

"What the . . . Where did you come up with that?" Lucy pointed to the pedal pushers with the navy-and-white striped boat neck crop top and espadrilles. "What about those together?"

Kit said, "Too Elvis Presley-movie-background-extra. And too summery. It's still cold out." Kit folded a few tops from the "no" pile with a straight face, all business.

"It's warming up," said Lucy. "Man, you're tough. But I appreciate your discerning eye."

"More like my no-bullshit mouth." Lucy laughed and threw the Elvis top at her.

"I'm just thinking that I want to look age-appropriately sophisticated, pretty and sexy. Because, after all, I like sex. And that's the goal. Eventually."

"How about a T-shirt that says, 'I Like Sex' bedazzled in script. Script is sophisticated."

Lucy said, "Okay, you're done here. You're just distracting me. Time to go."

Kit laughed and got up from the bed. She paused in the doorway and said, "Look, you're going to look terrific no matter what you wear. And you're not just pretty, you're beautiful."

"Easy for you to say, Miss Boobs-the-Size-of-Rhode-Island. All you ever had to do was walk into a room behind your boobs—who've already introduced themselves—and voilà. You never had to worry about this shit. Plus you've always had Fwank."

"Are you kidding? I spend thousands of dollars on scaffolding and chiropractors and have to dig holes in the ground if I want to lay on my stomach. Plus I'm stuck with Fwank."

"Boo-hoo," said Lucy.

"Yeah, yeah. Have fun. Text me the name of the place where you'll be and what you know about this clown. I don't want anything to happen to you, okay? It's scary out there."

"Yes, Mom. I've already given all the details to Audra."

"Fine. As long as someone knows where you are," Kit said. "And let me know how it goes." Kit leaned in for a kiss. Lucy made a "move aside" gesture with her hands as if having to move Kit's boobs off to the side and out of the way in order to reach her face. "Very funny," said Kit, and kissed Lucy before taking off, leaving Lucy still flummoxed by what to wear. Lucy felt guilty for lying to Kit about her date with Peter, but she had made her decision and didn't want to be lectured. Besides, nothing had happened yet, so there was nothing to tell.

Walking towards Peter, Lucy thought, *He's shorter than I remember him. And older, thank goodness.* She was worried that he'd be twenty-eight, but he was probably at least thirty-seven. Okay, maybe thirty-four. He was handsomer than she remembered. His hair had a bit of red tone to it. Maybe it was because they were outside in the sun. He was probably strawberry blonde as a kid. Still had those excellent shoulders. He looked trim, strong. Yes, indeed, he would definitely do. She hoped she made as good an impression on him. Lucy felt fabulous—comfortable and pretty and just a little flirty. She was glad it was unseasonably warm that night so she could wear the brown leather skirt with the black sweater and low-heeled black boots—a reasonable compromise. Her hair was behaving—miracle of miracles—and she was newly shaved and brand-spanking clean. *This is as good as it gets with me,* she thought.

It was Peter's idea to meet in front of Yum Café, two towns over and halfway between them. She immediately felt like she was doing something sneaky—meeting him outside of their usual teachers-convention setting—which made her giddy and excited about what might happen next. Peter hugged Lucy when he saw her. It was a friendly, familiar hug that ended perfunctorily. "Hello, friend," she said.

"Hey, good to see you. The restaurant's closed," he said, and gestured to the "Out Of Business" sign.

Lucy said, "Yikes. Not yum enough, apparently. Well, we could—" She began to shift into problem-solving mode when Peter jumped in. "I thought we might get takeout and eat down by the river. There's a bench, or there used to be, in a park. Unless you think it's too cold."

"No, no. Sounds lovely," Lucy said, and wanted to throw herself into his arms right then and there. A man of action! A man with a plan. This guy had taken the helm and found a creative solution. She could sit back and enjoy the ride. Major points.

Dinner was over-the-top romantic, more than any restaurant ever would have been. They sat on the bench by the river and ate on their laps as the water rambled by. The early spring forsythia had just bloomed in big, welcoming explosions of yellow, as white and purple crocuses faded along the embankment. Vertical ribbons of stratus clouds reflected salmon pink above a darkening fuchsia sunset, and squirrels rustled tree branches above. Lucy and Peter were the only people in the park. It was all so stupid perfect that she felt as if she were on a fake set in a Hollywood musical.

"It's not that I don't like Shark Week," Lucy began.

"It's that you love Shark Week," said Peter. He had a dry, steady, surefire delivery.

"So much so that I have a hard time watching—"

"—because the sharks aren't getting royalties."

"Or trailers. Or little green rooms off camera, with platters of chum."

Peter said, "Sounds like they need to unionize. Maybe you're just the gal to do it."

"'Gal'?"

"It's not meant to be pejorative. My grandfather said 'gal.' I think I got it from him."

"Did he die?"

"No. He's still alive. He's a shark."

"You mean, like, a lawyer?"

"No, an actual shark."

This was not the typical conversational pabulum she'd become used to on Internet dates. They talked about Mel Brooks movies and stand-up comedy, helium parade balloons and trepanning. "It's the ancient practice of drilling a hole in one's own head," said Peter when Lucy asked him to recall the weirdest thing he'd ever seen. "The documentary is not for the weak."

"I bet. To what purpose?" asked Lucy.

"Increase blood flow, cure epilepsy, relieve migraines."

"No kidding. Was this a popular method of, uh, relief?"

"Apparently. There's prehistoric evidence of it all the way up through the Middle Ages and the Renaissance. The Greeks and Incans were big into it."

"Those nutty Incans."

"That's my favorite candy bar. Then Christianity came along and stopped the practice."

"Killjoys," said Lucy.

"Yeah. Ruiners," said Peter. "Imagine all those poor cavemen with migraines. What's a Neanderthal to do?"

"Cut a hole in your head, I guess."

"I guess," Peter said, and forked his last heaping bite of pie. "You want my last bite?"

"No, but thanks for offering," said Lucy. She liked that he was curious and open to learning about oddball stuff, and really liked that he had manners—bonus points for both. Lucy slipped her feet out of her shoes and ran her toes through the cold grass. Peter put his napkin in his lap. They discussed favorite Halloween costumes and childhood card games, James Bond, string theory and jazz. They traded horrible teaching-moment stories and laughed themselves silly. Then the sun disappeared and the trees all turned black against a dark blue sky. Peter jumped up to grab the napkin that had escaped him and when he sat back down, he sat closer.

Lucy grew quiet and loosened her coat. How could it be so warm on an early April evening? How could everything be so perfect?

Was it a sign? Was it divine intervention? Did God want Lucy to kiss this man with a girlfriend? She found that hard to believe. But maybe Mother Nature did. Maybe they'd broken up. Lucy looked at the heavens and grinned at the stars. When she brought her eyes back to meet Peter's she decided not to avert his gaze. Her little game of chicken made him uneasy—and she dared him, without speaking, to not look away. He leaned in to kiss her and faintly brushed his lips against hers. A bolt of electricity shot up from deep inside Lucy, pulsed through her thighs then lit up her body like some sort of unleashed electric eel. This was nothing like her bolt with Ted. This was a much bigger bolt.

"Wow," Lucy said, and shuddered. Peter said nothing, then leaned forward to kiss her again. This time he reached up with one hand, ran it through her hair and held the back of her head. It was a slow kiss, tentative but inviting. His tongue swept hers. Then he pulled back and stared at her. One of his eyes had little flecks of sea green near the pupil.

"I've been wanting to do that for a very. Long. Time," he said.

"Really?" she said. "Why didn't you?" Then a little voice reminded her that he'd said he was in a serious relationship the last time they got together. Lucy'd been married then, so they hadn't discussed it—it wasn't relevant. Lucy was single now and decided she didn't want to know what his deal was. She liked Peter so much and had wanted him for so long, and here he was in front of her, kissing her, messing up her hair like they did in the movies. In that instant she decided she wouldn't ask Peter about his situation. She rationalized that it wasn't her business, and whatever his attachments were had nothing to do with her. She was a free woman responsible only for her own destiny. *She* wasn't cheating on anyone. *It's amazing what the mind can rationalize when it wants something—or more insidiously—when it thinks it deserves some-*

thing. "You know what?" said Lucy. "You don't have to go into it. In fact, let's skip it altogether. It's none of my business."

"Okay," Peter said, then Lucy's phone rang. She dug into her purse to make sure it wasn't Matt with a Gus emergency. Nancy's photo popped up. Lucy declined the call.

"Do you need to take that?" he asked.

"Nope."

"Everything okay?"

"Yup," Lucy said, and leaned in to kiss him again, this time letting her tongue explore the inside of his mouth with dips and turns. His lips were soft and his mouth opened just the right amount at the right time. They took turns caressing teeth and the warmth of each other's mouths with their tongues like old friends revisiting familiar terrain. They shared the same tension and rhythm, used their hands to measure and touch. Lucy explored Peter's face, ears and neck. She ran her fingers through his thick hair. Their bodies inched closer each time they kissed, and they only pulled their heads away to switch angles. Now their torsos faced one another. Their hands began to wander over each other's shoulders and backs, moving up and down arms and, finally, legs. Lucy bit his ear. Peter moved his hand down her neck and over across her chest. He squeezed her breast. The tingles that began with the mere brush of his lips grew into waves of energy radiating from her wellspring like pulsing cartoon animation. Their bodies were ablaze.

Lucy and Peter made out like fifteen-year-olds for the last two hours of their five-hour date. She was transported back to the memory of making out all night on the swing set in back of the house she grew up in, amazed that she could still feel this way. She relished the feeling of being back in high school, of not feeling tired even though it was late-late at night, the fury of hormones all surging at once, like a storm. She thought this feeling had been lost forever to her youth, but she was wrong. Her whole body was vibrating and she wrestled with restraint, with not throwing herself at him right then and there on the bench, aching to lift her skirt and straddle him. The feeling was unbelievably powerful, like some sort of heightened mania and she thought, *This is what compulsion must feel like.* It was exhausting to fight and Lucy was losing.

Suddenly, Peter jumped up and said, "I have to stop. I have to go," and sort of reeled, in a what-happened-where-am-I manner. He looked like someone who'd just been teleported to an unfamiliar planet in a science fiction movie and fumbled as he tucked in his shirt. Lucy took the opportunity to put some distance between them and helped him gather up and toss the dinner containers. She was grateful that he'd stopped them when he did and didn't question why. Wordlessly they wove their way towards her parking spot, stopping every twenty or so steps to grope each other then break apart. *Jeez,* Lucy thought, *we can't keep our hands off each other.* She willed herself away from him and walked ahead a bit, needing the space. When they reached her car, Lucy didn't ask when she would see him again. Instead, she looked into his eyes, said, "Thanks for dinner," and smiled slyly. Lucy climbed into her car without waiting for a response. Her eyes flashed at him one last time as she glanced back. He looked stunned.

She left him in the street, watching her as she drove away. She giggled at the thought that she might have a chin burn from his whiskers. *A chin burn at my age,* Lucy thought, then rolled down all the windows. She grinned madly as she welcomed the wind's rushing swirl into the car; papers fluttered in the back seat. Lucy turned the radio's volume way, way up and banged out the drumbeat to an old Kinks tune on her steering wheel. She sang every song—whether she knew the words or not—at the top of her lungs all the way home.

Chapter 10

- - - - - - - - - - - - - - - - -

The next morning, Lucy enjoyed a few minutes of lollygagging in bed, thinking about her night with Peter before reaching for her Magic Buddy in the middle drawer of the nightstand. Did it really happen? Would she see him again? None of that mattered now, she thought, coasting on the remnants of desire still clinging to her. Then she showered and prepared herself mentally and emotionally to listen to her voice-mail message from Nancy. (She hadn't listened to it yesterday. She'd been too afraid, in case Nancy was pissed or freaking out; she didn't want to ruin her good mood or her date with Peter.) Lucy braced herself for the worst.

"Lucy, ohmygod, this is Nancy. You are not going to believe this but Ted spent all day today trimming the branches from that dying chokecherry we have in our backyard and then repaired the lid on the garbage hutch. I've been on his case to do that for like *four years*! *Then*, he took us all out to lunch and asked me where I wanted to eat. Hel-lo! Then he suggested we go to the playground afterwards. *As a family!* And he left his phone in the car *on purpose*, and actually kicked a ball 'round with the kids. He even got on the damn seesaw. Do you know how long Sophie has been begging him to get on the damn seesaw? Then he asked me to get us a sitter so that we could go to the movies. It was that stupid new comic book action figure hero piece of overblown junk, but still, it was *his idea*! Can you believe it? Now I'm not saying it was all you, but maybe it *was* all you. Or hell, maybe it was a coincidence. And I'm not saying it was you in particular, but just the fact that it was someone that *wasn't me*. And I'm not saying that it's the magic bullet that's going to fix our marriage. But wouldn't it be amazing if it *were*? Do you think you would ever want to do it again? I'm not even kidding. And do you know he hasn't even said anything about it? Not one word, so I'm not saying anything either. Anyway, I just called to say thanks and I wanted to bring you over some chili that I made yesterday. You can freeze whatever you don't eat. And some cornbread, and I made cookies for Hugo's book fair, so I'm giving you some of those, too. Hope you like them. Oh, and Ted said that he could get you a new car at cost from his dealership. If you need one."

No frickin' way, thought Lucy, and covered her open mouth with her hand. Nancy's message continued, "Remember, this is in the vault. I just can't believe it. It's totally cliché when you think about it. Guy Has Sex with Someone New and Does a 180. But it worked. Or something worked. Maybe it was the blow job, I don't know. God, you know, we should go into business. Ha, ha. Yeah, right. We could totally—well, anyway, give me a call so that I know you're cool with everything and that you got the chili. I'm leaving it on the back stoop. Oh, and let me know if you need a new car, cheap. Loveyabye."

Lucy listened to the voice message one more time before erasing it, then lay down on the rug to think a minute. She couldn't help laughing. An hour later at church, when Lucy got to the part in the Lord's Prayer where she asked for forgiveness for her trespasses, she zoned out. Her list of trespasses had suddenly become very long.

The following Thursday, Lucy and Nancy sat down together in Lucy's living room after Gus had gone to bed and she'd finished prepping for the next day's classes. Nancy had asked to get together and Lucy felt she couldn't say no even though it was a busy week. She hoped it wasn't dire. Lucy opened a bottle of wine for Nancy and made sure there were fancy Belgian chocolate-dipped cookies on a plate in front of her.

Lucy said, "Thanks for coming to me. I tried to get a sitter."

Nancy said, "No prob. It was me who called you."

"The chili and cornbread you dropped off was delish."

"No sweat."

Lucy wanted to cut to the chase. "So, what's up? Are you freaking out?"

"Lucy. I trust you. I know you don't suddenly have feelings for Ted and Ted did not suddenly fall in love with you. I am not, nor do I plan to freak out. *Capiche?*"

"*Capiche.*"

Nancy continued, "This is about me revisiting my long-held ambition to be an entrepreneur. I was thinking we should start a business. Or, I'll start the business, but I thought with your connections to divorcées and me on the PTA and the board of the YMCA, and the Garden Club, and with Ted in the Rotary Club and my kids in two different schools, plus the ice hockey and soccer and piano people. I know so many women. And I know enough about their husbands. I thought maybe you could help me get the ball rolling. Or balls rolling, so to speak."

Lucy was floored. Amused but floored. "What the hell are you talking about?!"

Nancy said, "I was thinking of starting a business where I hook up my married friends with your divorced friends in a sort of barter system. Kind of a you-scratch-my-back thing."

Lucy just looked at Nancy. Looked and looked then cocked her head and sipped her wine, so Nancy kept talking. "Before you tell me I'm crazy, think about it: There are so many marriages that are floundering because of sex and so many divorcées who just want sex. Plus there are the wives who love their husbands but after fifteen, twenty years are a little over the sex, or at least don't want it as often. Or are too tired. It's such a stupid reason to get divorced, and I figure with my business plan, everyone would benefit and maybe more marriages would survive."

Lucy said, "You have a *business plan*?!"

Nancy said, "Shh, you'll wake Gus. Just listen. It really is a win-win-win if you think about it. The divorcées get to have sex with no risk of STDs or ending up with some sociopathic stranger because all the men are in monogamous relationships and we know them and they're decent guys. As long as the wives are in control, like I was, they can choose the divorcées and decide what they can do and how often and when. We can screen the divorcées to make sure they *only* want sex and are not out to find a husband . . . and you think I'm crazy." Nancy sunk into the couch. Lucy was staring at her, but she was also thinking—her mind was a whirr.

Finally, Lucy spoke. "No. Actually, I don't think you're crazy."

"You *don't*?!" Nancy's voice went up in pitch and her eyes flashed. She leaned forward on the edge of the couch.

Lucy said, "But I could lose my job. If anyone found out. I can't risk it. No way."

Nancy continued, "You wouldn't have to do anything but tell your divorced friends about it. I would handle the rest. Although, if you partnered with me," Nancy sipped her wine, "you would get the benefit of landscaping, hair and car maintenance, meals—there's no limit to the benefits, which could save you hundreds, maybe thousands in the long run." Nancy looked at Lucy with a renewed MBA intensity. Lucy could see it was all coming back to her now, Nancy's business brain. It had been very keen for a time before marriage and kids and it was still there, her business-major mind with an economics minor. Lucy knew she couldn't help out with the business, no way, but she was awfully curious. "Would people pay for services?"

Nancy said, "Nope, couldn't. That would be prostitution, which is illegal."

"Right."

"I was thinking that the wife would sign up her husband and then just tell the divorcée what she or her husband could offer to help her out. Single moms need more help, right?"

Lucy said, "Do we ever. But I could never. And if they're too busy to have sex, you can't ask them to make time for extra—"

"Not extra, just what they already have access to. Whatever's easy. Gift certificates at restaurants. Baked goods if they're baking anyway. Ted's hooking you up with a new used car for, like, forty bucks, right?"

"Were you serious about that? I'd love a new car, or a newer one," said Lucy.

"Talk to Ted, that's his department. But no rescheduling if you know what I mean. That'll be done through me," said Nancy.

"Wait, you want me to sleep with him again? I thought this was a one-time thing."

"Maybe down the road if we get into a slump again. Listen, there are accountants in town, and carpenters. There are wives who are attorneys. Others do hair or give piano lessons. It would be up to them to work it out, but we're talking about hundreds of dollars worth—"

"Are you thinking of *me* as one of the sex-giver people?" said Lucy.

"Why not? Just like how I arranged for you and Ted," said Nancy.

"Oh, my God. Seriously? Ha. That would sure solve my biweekly itch." Lucy laughed.

"Presto, problem solved. No strings. Make your own hours. Easy lays."

"Nancy, I could get *fired*!"

"Really? For what you do in your private life? That sounds like some major Supreme Court shit to me. Getting axed for not breaking any laws in the privacy of your own home, in your free time, with consenting adults? You could sue. Make millions."

"I don't want to sue anyone. And I don't need millions. I just want to keep my job."

"And what about the possibility of regular sex with safe, local, disease-free men? I thought you said you wanted that."

Just then, Gus appeared in the doorway to the living room at the bottom of the stair landing. He rubbed his eyes and squinted. His pajama top had a graphic of Lego Luke Skywalker battling to the death with a light saber, and his pajama bottoms displayed base-ball bats and footballs. Why didn't anyone make chess pajamas? Or ones covered in math or science?

Gus said, "Mom, you woke me up and now I can't get back to poop."

"I'm sorry, sweetie, we'll be quieter. Why don't you head back up and think about farts? I'll be up in a few minutes to check on you, okay?"

"Okay," said Gus, who turned around and headed back upstairs.

"Love you," called Lucy.

"Love you, too," Gus muttered to himself.

The women looked at each other and giggled.

Chapter 11

That Saturday, Lucy sat in the stands of a Li'l Ice Beasts hockey practice with Kit and Gina while their sons tripped over themselves and terrorized each other out on the ice like miniature vigilante Michelin men. The stands were packed with cliques of mothers sitting together, dressing and behaving like separate subspecies of the same errant culture.

There was one group of moms who all had pastel, puffy, down coats and wore lots of dark lip liner and gold jewelry with big, buggy sunglasses for headbands even though they were inside and wouldn't be seeing the sun for hours. They were the Snowbunny Moms. There were the Knitters. They were craftier looking, with hand-knit hats in bold colors like lime green and orange, and they wore mismatched scarves with little pom-poms. They often let their hair go gray, wore chunky glasses and even chunkier jewelry. The Knitters came in all shapes and sizes, unlike The Snowbunny Moms, who almost always had smooth, straight hair that they wore back in a single low ponytail and were fit and tan all year 'round. There were the Butchy Moms who never wore makeup or any accessories. They dressed dykey—in fact, some of them were dykes—and generally had very short hair. There were the Texters and the Multi-Moms with lots of little siblings to the hockey-playing kid that they carted around in giant, plastic-handled walnut shells, along with diaper bags and picnic bags. These moms took up about two extra seats per human, on average.

All these mom groups coexisted, orbiting around each other like moons whose paths never crossed but who tolerated each other's presence pleasantly. Lucy and her friends sat in the middle of them, elbow-to-elbow with the other cliques around them, undeclared and unintimidated, like Switzerland.

A scrimmage was just about to begin on the ice. Lucy turned her whole body towards Kit and Gina and said, "I have something to say."

Kit said, "You finally decided to let your grays grow out. I love that look. You'll rock it."

Gina said, "That reminds me, I need a reliable handyman if anyone has one, but not one that talks to you for forty-five minutes every frickin' time he comes over."

Kit said, "That don't exist. And how, exactly, did you get from grey hair to handymen?"

"My old handyman had gray roots," said Gina without looking up from her texting.

"She's *still* texting the penis-picture guy," said Kit. Lucy looked aghast at Gina.

Gina said defensively, "*What?* He's applying to law schools. I'm just proofreading his essays."

Lucy said, "May I please have the floor again? Let's focus, my ADHD friends."

Kit said, "You slept with Peter."

"No," said Lucy. "God, women with their interrupting. Makes me berzerkers. Did you know that interrupting is actually an aggressive act of verbal abuse?"

"You better not have slept with Peter," said Kit. "I thought you promised us that you wouldn't e-mail him."

"Well I think she should," said Gina. "Live a little. The woman's an elementary-school teacher for crying out loud. Let her have some adult fun."

"Jesus, just stop talking and listen to me, will ya?" said Lucy. "No more interrupting. Only nodding, okay? If you want to say something raise your hand, got it? Man, you guys. I'll send you all to the principal's office."

"Ooooooooh," they said. Kit raised her hand. Lucy called on her.

"Did you sleep with Peter?"

"Uhhhh," said Lucy.

Gina said, "She slept with Peter."

"No," said Lucy, then leaned in and whispered. "But I did sleep with a friend's husband, with her permission. Now will you two please zip it and listen? God." Lucy didn't have to do any more hushing after that. The girls were agape. They leaned in, too. Lucy continued, "After that lunch we had two weeks ago, remember? Nancy came up to me afterwards and asked me to sleep with Ted, and I did, and now Ted is happier, Nancy's happier, and I'm happier. Nancy is thinking of starting a business where horny divorcées take some of the sexual pressure off of local wives by being subcontracted *by the wives* to sleep with their husbands.

"There are two underserved populations in town—divorcées and married men—both horny, both not gettin' enough. We believe—er—she believes that putting them together to fulfill a common need could not only serve to help balance the inequality of desire in the respective marriages, but do so without any threat to the original marital foundation. We think that wives will take advantage of this opportunity to have some of their husbands' needs satisfied without giving up control or having to compromise. It's a win-win. Win."

Kit and Gina sat very still and looked at Lucy as the crowd of moms around them jumped up to cheer whatever had just happen on the ice. As the crowd sat down, Lucy's friends' hands shot into the air, straight as arrows. Lucy pointed at them individually, in turn.

"Question, Kit?" Lucy said.

"You really slept with Ted?" Lucy nodded. Kit cocked her head sideways.

"You're freaking kidding me," said Kit.

"I'm not."

"Get the fuck outta here," said Kit. She seemed to Lucy more irate than shocked. After a beat or two, she spoke again, in an unusually small voice, "Why didn't you tell me?"

Lucy leaned in again, "Kit, it's not the kind of thing you share, obviously. And for this to work, discretion will have to be everything. I'm only telling you about Ted because Nancy instructed me to, in order to drum up interest. All I'll say further on the subject is that it did the trick for everyone involved."

Kit said, "You sound demented." Lucy thought that was probably true. She also thought that perhaps Kit was jealous of her side project with Nancy. Either way, it was clear she was getting ticked off. Lucy said, "Kit, Nancy asked me not to say anything because there were too many variables. So I didn't. That's how this has to be if it's going to work. It's nothing personal. I still love you. Can we continue?" Kit crossed her arms and looked at the rink.

Lucy said, "Next question, Gina."

"Why isn't Nancy telling us about this if it's her idea?"

"She knew I'd see you all first and asked me to test the waters."

Gina continued, "So, the wives choose the divorcées?"

"Yup."

Gina said, "How often?"

"As often as they arrange for. Monthly, weekly, once and then never again. It's up to the wife."

Kit rejoined the conversation, though her vibe was skeptical and a bit icy.

"Next question, Kit?"

Kit said, "How do we know these women don't want to steal our husbands?"

"There will be a screening process wherein the divorcées or helpers will be vetted to make sure that they're fed up enough with the idea of marriage that there's no chance of that. Plus, they can be interviewed by the wife. I know it's hard for you to believe, ladies, but there are thousands, maybe millions, of divorcées out there who honestly wouldn't be caught dead being married again. And they sure as hell don't want your husbands—they're just ravenous. Most of these women have been ignored by their husbands for so long that by the time they get divorced, they're starving. It's part appetite and part need for validation that they're still worth touching. They just want sex, to feel that primal, carnal hunger sated. The wife will have full control. Maybe we'll even have a little portfolio with the divorcées photos."

Kit said, "We? I thought this was Nancy's idea. You'll get fired."

Gina said, "They can't fire her. It's not prostitution. Unless goods are exchanged. Did you get any goods from Ted?" Lucy froze. *Only a killer discount on a friggin' car.* "Um, what if I did, but it wasn't a condition up front? More like an elaborate unexpected thank-you note?"

Gina said, "Then you're fine, I think. I'll look into it. But they still might try to fire you. You could sue. It's not an offense. We're talking consensual adults, off school grounds, after school hours. Even if a jury found you technically guilty, the court could reverse it—jury nullification. You would walk. Make sure there's no e-mail trail. Nothing on paper."

"You're insane," said Kit to both of them.

Lucy ignored Kit. "Okay," she said.

Kit said, "And what happens if our husbands fall in love with these so-called helpers?"

"Oh, please, Duncan's not falling in love with anyone else. He's just hot for sex," Gina said, then went back to texting.

Lucy continued, "Maybe we'll tell the wives to explain to their husbands that any thoughts regarding falling in love will be met with abject rejection and ejection from The Program, and severe punishment by the management. I'll make a note of it." Lucy could be very organized. She was a teacher after all.

Kit said, "Is that what you're calling it? The Program?"

"So far. Maybe. Why, you got any better ideas?"

Gina said, "How about The Booty Boutique or The Whore Hut? You can call yourselves Prosti-Pals."

Lucy laughed and said, "You know what? Remind me not to hire you for branding."

Kit said, "Branding?! You planning to franchise? Why are you doing this, Luce? It's crazy talk. Have you really thought this through?"

Lucy had thought about it nonstop ever since Nancy proposed it. She knew it was risky but she also knew that she was one ovulation

away from having wanton sex with anyone who would have her—
the UPS guy, a random waiter—and felt that was way more risky.

"I have and I would rather sleep with harmless guys who are in
relationships, who have no diseases and who live locally than troll
the Internet for nitwitted strangers. It would be nice to be able to
get my rocks off—no strings attached—while I'm attempting to
date legitimate men. Might keep me from making rash decisions,
like bringing strangers back to my house or dating men who don't
get me just for sex."

Kit said, "You don't consider this a rash decision?"

"No. I've thought about it and, as Gina told you, I'm doing nothing wrong. Plus, if I can get discounts on doing my taxes or buying
a car, then why not? All my divorcée friends are single mothers raising kids. They can use all the help they can get."

"You'll be vilified by every woman in a tri-county radius," said
Kit.

"Or canonized," said Gina. "They'll erect a bust of you in the
town square."

"I wouldn't bet on it. She could lose her job," said Kit.

"Based on what?" said Gina. "She's a fantastic teacher with a
solid reputation for being terrific with the kids. She's not doing
anything illegal. She's not cheating on anyone. Besides, it's none of
their business."

"Yeah, but still," said Kit. Lucy felt she seemed to be groping
for excuses.

"But still, what?" said Lucy. "Didn't you say you could use a
jumpstart with Fwank?"

"Yeah, but I don't want Fwank sleeping with my best friend."

"So then choose someone else, choose someone neither of you
know. Or don't do it at all. *It's optional.*"

Gina said, "What about us wives? I could use someone new to have sex with, too."

Lucy said, "Based on the same model, that would entail finding divorced men who would rather sleep with married housewives than the twenty-eight-year-olds who are lining up to—"

Kit said, "Yeah, good luck with that."

Lucy continued, "And your husbands would have to be on board with your romp—fully complicit. Remember, this isn't about cheating. Some might go for it, but not enough to make it worth our while." Gina frowned like a circus clown.

Kit said, "I love you, but let the record show I think you're demented."

"Duly noted," said Lucy and blew Kit an air kiss. Kit blew her one back.

Kit said, "Will your friend Audra do it? I can see her doing it."

"Oh, she'll love it," said Gina. *"I'd sleep with Audra."* Kit squinted, picturing.

"That *can* be arranged," said Lucy with a smirk.

"I'm all over it," said Gina, "I could use a break."

"Just say you'll think about it," Lucy said to Kit. Kit just looked back blankly.

"I'm doing it," said Gina.

"You *are*?!" said Kit.

"Duncan's not leaving me for anyone, least of all, Lucy," Gina said.

"Thanks," said Lucy.

"Everyone knows that Duncan's a boob man, and hers are too small."

"Thanks again," said Lucy, "but really, you can stop right there."

Gina said, "Duncan ain't going *nowhere*. He loves me too much.

My grandmother told me to marry a man who's just a little bit more in love with me than I am with him, so I did. And she was right. It would be a shot of adrenaline for our sex life, and I know he'd love me for it. Are you kidding? Sanctioned adultery? Sign me up. He'd think he'd married a goddess. He'll be my man servant."

Lucy said, "Look, it's not meant to lord leverage over your husbands and it's not adultery if it's sanctioned. It's an 'arrangement.'" She used air quotes.

Kit said, "Well her husband will still be 'screwing another woman.'" Kit air quoted her right back.

"It's 'fine with me.' It's 'just sex,'" said Gina, also using air quotes.

Kit came back at both of them, irate, "There's no such thing as 'just sex.'"

"Oh, yeah?" said Gina, "Then what do you call what we've all been having for the last fourteen years?"

Lucy said, "Ooooo." Kit looked cut off at the knees. Lucy jumped in, "Okay ladies, break it up, break it up. This air-quote smack down is going to give me Little Bunny Foo-Foo nightmares. Gina, ease up. Kit, you can try it or not. I'll still love you. Just don't judge me."

"I'll try not to, but you make it hard."

Just then a text came through on Lucy's phone with Peter's name above it. She tried to cover it quickly, but Kit saw it and said, "Was that . . . did that say 'Peter'?"

"Nobody," said Lucy. She tried to suppress her smile. Her face turned pinkish red.

"You're blushing!" said Kit.

"It's Peter," said Gina.

"We're just friends," said Lucy, then turned a deeper shade of red.

"Ooooooooo," said Gina. "You slept with him."

"Is he married?" said Kit.

"I swear to God I didn't sleep with him, and I don't know. I didn't ask," said Lucy.

Kit gave her the evil eye.

"And down the slippery slope she goes, bye-bye," Gina said, and waved.

Lucy glanced up, exasperated, then swiveled back in her seat to watch the game. She was going to see this Peter thing through, dammit. She tried not to be pissed at Kit. She reminded herself that it was easy for married friends to judge her because they had someone to go out with at night and warm bodies to wake up next to in the morning. She knew that no matter what she said, they would never understand or support her decisions. But her divorced friends would. So she kept her mouth shut.

Chapter 12

Lucy's plan was to wait a day or two before returning Peter's text but he texted her again in the morning wanting to get together. Lucy hustled to find Gus an after-school playdate—furiously texting every one of Gus's friends' mothers, nannies and au pairs— and then, when she found someone, texted Peter to say, *Yes, c'mon over.* She would have exactly two hours before Gus was dropped off back home. *We can go for a walk*, she texted, trying to convince herself that sex was off-limits.

When she got home from school she put on some Django Reinhardt, raced upstairs and shaved pretty much everywhere. What did he look like again? It was funny how many times it could take Lucy to see someone in the flesh before she could recall their image.

She conjured a hazy likeness of his thick reddish-blond hair, but which side did he part it on, the left? His bangs sort of fell down, brushing his black plastic glasses frames, didn't they? She remembered liking his shoulders. She tried to imagine the shape of his ass and became turned on. He had great legs for a guy who probably never played a sport in his life—he was such a math nerd—though maybe he played soccer. His nose was a bit foggy in her memory and his eyebrows were forgettable, but his soft lower lip came into view. Was he Jewish? And that angular jaw. She smoothed cream on her legs and rubbed deodorant under her arms. His eyes were pretty, like a girl's, with long thick eyelashes. Green, no, hazel? Lucy spritzed herself with a hint of some ancient perfume she found in a drawer, recalling a little mole on his cheek she remembered thinking was cool—like a golden era movie star—and wondering if he had more on his body and where.

She swapped out her asexual teacher clothes for a tighter shirt with a plunging neckline, a full skirt and knee-high boots, applied mascara and blush, then flew down the stairs. The doorbell rang. *Shit.* "Coming!" she called out as she swiped a bit of tinted gloss from her purse across her lips. She unlocked the door and saw him standing there. He was even more beautiful than she remembered. *Act casual.*

"Hi, how are ya? C'mon in," she said, and then thought, *Damn he's hot.*

"Thanks," Peter said without smiling. He didn't look away from her as he moved into the living room but then broke his own gaze and began to look around. Lucy wished she'd fixed the crooked throw pillow on the couch. "Can I get you something to drink?" she said, leading him towards the kitchen. As she took two glasses from the cabinet she thought, *I wonder if we'll end up having sex today. I wonder if he'll think I'm too easy and not call me again if I do.* Then she thought, *Who cares?* and imagined what it must be like in hell. Hot, naturally. And the humidity, forget it. She'd hate it.

Lucy said, "I've got lemonade, water, ginger ale, Coke, vodka, milk, chocolate milk, whiskey, wine and beer."

"Is that all? I'll have lemonade, please," he said, and followed her voice into the tiny kitchen where he sat in a chair within an arm's length of her and watched her move between cabinets and counters. Lucy hoped he was checking out her ass. He said, "I don't drink before dinner, and then I rarely have more than one or two."

She handed him his lemonade and a bowl of peanut butter filled-pretzels and said, "No kidding. I don't either."

"Oh my God," he said picking up a pretzel-y nugget of heaven, "are these—"

"Yes," she said, and popped one in his mouth. He chewed slowly, closing his eyes and savoring the peanut butter/pretzel aphrodisiac. Then, making a yummy sound he put his hands on her waist and slowly brought her near. Lucy took a step towards him so that she was standing between his legs and swayed side to side a bit so that she knocked into his thighs with hers. Those astonishing electric shock waves zapped down her legs and up through her spine. She felt her ears heat up and her knees soften. She twisted her torso, moving her body back and forth a little so that it rubbed up against his jeans and found his hardness there, ready, but patient.

Lucy said quietly, "Can you explain to me the physics of what's happening inside my body right now?"

"You mean on a subatomic level?"

"Yeah," Lucy said.

"I could tell you, but then I'd have to kill you."

"Nice. High school physics teacher by day, assassin by night."

"Ninja by night."

"Excuse me. Ninja." Lucy put her glass down on the counter and lifted her hands to his forehead. Spreading her fingers, she scratched her nails up and over his ears and down the back of his neck and under his collar. Peter's shoulders dropped. He moaned softly. He bent his head forward and leaned it against her belly as she scratched parallel paths through his hair like cornrows, down his back and into his jeans. Slipping her fingers under the waistband of his boxers she made little sweeps with her nails at the top of his butt. She would have reached farther if her arms had been longer. His skin felt cool and smooth to her. It must have felt good to Peter, too, because he dropped his glass of lemonade and it broke in big pieces on the floor.

"I'm so sorry," he said, seeming genuinely contrite, and moved to clean it up himself. *That's good*, she thought, giving him points for apologizing.

"It's fine. It's just a juice glass. I have forty-seven more. Don't cut yourself. Here, give it a wipe with the floor sponge," she said, and tossed one down to him. "Don't worry about the glass. Step over it and follow me, you can clean it up later."

She pulled him up off the ground where he had already picked up all the glass pieces and pointed him toward the garbage can. Then she walked him backwards, holding his hand, leading him into . . . into—where should she lead him? Would it be too weird to sit him on the couch where she'd been with Ted a week ago? That's okay, right? It's just furniture. Peter doesn't know better, and the couch could be having the time of its life. As she looked over her shoulder to see where she should sit, he scooped her up by the waist and sat her down on the big chair next to the couch. *Mmm, strong.* He knelt in front of her and burrowed his face into her stomach like a pillow. Lucy's deepest, buried sexual longings cried out to her at his touch—she nearly had to shush them. Peter lifted her blouse and kissed her belly button, then undid the lowest button on her blouse and looked up at her for approval. Lucy smiled with closed lips. He undid each of the pearly buttons with care, then gently parted her blouse to reveal one of her fancy bras, a black, lacy demi-cup with a deep red underlay and a tiny black satin bow at its center. *Like expensive gift wrap*, she thought; she'd chosen that bra carefully. She understood that big or small or barely there, it didn't matter—breasts were, for most men, an undeniable trigger and a visual treat.

Peter swept his thumbs over her areolas, stopping at her nipples to pinch them awake. "We're up," they seemed to say as she stretched her arm out, closed her eyes and arched her back. *Mm-mmmm.* Every pore of Lucy's being was warming to attention as if awakening from a deep and leaden slumber. She couldn't believe Peter was here in her living room, seducing her. Wanting her. How many dips and turns had her life taken to lead her to this moment? Hundreds? Thousands? She had to stay present, had to thoroughly enjoy this. She knew that in an hour and a half she would be sitting with Gus, playing Legos, and the thought of having sex with Peter would be a distant dream. She snapped herself back to Peter's eyes, his mouth. This was no fantasy. This was really happening. Lucy's nipples stiffened.

Peter moved slowly up her body, leaning over her like a spaceship eclipsing the sky. She reached down and wordlessly lifted off his shirt. He had a nice, hairy chest—not too dense, but furry, which she liked—and gorgeous shoulders that damn near glistened. *Christ, he's hot*, she thought. *I hope he has a nice cock. I hope he makes me scream.* He pressed his lips to Lucy's with a hunger she hadn't anticipated. His mouth opened and his tongue caressed hers greedily, sucking her lips with a voracity she hadn't felt that night by the river. His kiss seemed laced with desperation and a teeny bit of anger, Lucy felt, but she knew it wasn't meant for her. Maybe there was a frigid girlfriend somewhere, or a wife who'd lost interest. But that wasn't Lucy's problem and she refused to waste time surmising. *Stay in the moment.*

Peter's heightened, raw energy made Lucy feel all the more desirous, which in turn made her voracious. The nexus of her thighs dampened as she returned his kisses deeply, wanting him, craving him, more, more. She slipped her hands into his pants, grabbed his buttocks and squeezed. How powerful it felt to have his warm flesh in her hands. She wished she could have driven him into her rigid walls right then. She sat up to wrap her arms around his neck and when she did, he smiled and gently pushed her back against the cushion. Lucy was confused, but as he receded from her, down her body, suckling her breasts and leaving her nipples erect in his wake, she understood. He kept his eyes locked on hers the entire time. Lucy was transfixed.

Peter said, "Do something about that, will ya?" pointing to her skirt. "It'll take me too long." Lucy grinned. "Got a plane to catch?" she said while unhooking and unzipping. He loosened the fabric down off her hips then said, "Not exactly." She took off her black thong and flung it across the room like a lasso. He threw her skirt over his shoulder in response and they giggled. Almost immediately his tongue was on her, tickling the insides of her thighs like eyelash kisses. He was going to begin minutely, she thought, then tease her into a frenzy. *Okay, pal,* she thought, *bring it.*

Lucy moved the pillow behind her to be more accommodating, then slumped down and closed her eyes. Peter's tongue circled the folds of her swelling labia with the grace and precision of a figure skater. She began to drift inward when he flicked the tip of his tongue against the top of her buzzing clitoris. *Oh my. Wow,* she thought, *the guy's got skillz.* He flitted his tongue inside her sideways and she twisted her head and moaned. Lucy furrowed her

eyebrows as electric pulses careened throughout her body, ping-
ing off her insides, and radiated out through her fingers and the
top of her head. How was her skin expected to contain all this energy? *I should be hooked up to a generator,* she thought. *I could
power a small village.* Another slow lick and her legs relaxed further. He flattened his tongue and its warmth blanketed her as she
exhaled. *He's showing off his best moves. He's trying to impress
me. I shall let him,* she thought, deriving immense satisfaction from
all the focused attention. It had been years since anyone had cared
this much to satisfy her—years. *Thank you,* she thought, then
moaned louder.

Her mind took her to happy-sexy places, even funny-sexy. Lucy
remembered the scene at the end of *Young Frankenstein* when Teri
Garr asks Gene Wilder what part of the monster he got in the trans-
fer and he makes that groaning sound. Lucy groaned like the
monster. What was his name? Peter Boyle! Genius. Another Peter.
Peter Falk, Peter Sellers, Peter Gabriel and Peter Max. Peter was a
good name. Solid, smart. "Oooooooh," she said when he hit a new
spot. Peter stepped it up a notch. He fluttered his tongue midway
inside her then spun it in tiny circles. He darted in and out and then
seemed to create different shapes, moving quickly back and forth,
flicking deeply then pulling gradually out to lick her surface. *Very
creative,* she thought. *He's got a good imagination.* And then, *My
God, what are you doing with your tongue? I've got to know,* she
thought and lifted her head to see if she could see, but all she saw
were his eyes looking back at her. Hazel! With green flecks! Now
she remembered.

The more Peter played inside her the more vocal she became.
Her back arched and she twisted occasionally, feeling like a mari-
onette, his tongue holding the strings. Sometimes she laughed and
sometimes the sounds she made were grunts and whines, moans

and squeaks. The subtle shifts Peter elicited in Lucy's body seemed more immediate somehow than penetration, and she liked that he wanted to please her. Peter was more creative than her college boyfriend, who eventually became an insurance adjuster. But that was college. No one really had their game yet. The four other long-term relationships she'd had before marrying were with mostly creative types, good in bed. But creative types could also be selfish and unwilling to please. Lucy's best friend from her first job always urged her to go for the nerds, the slightly pudgy, geeky dudes. "They're so desperate for action," she said, "that once they get you in a room alone, they'll do whatever you want. And they'll do it endlessly." She swore by it.

Lucy enjoyed dancing around this ecstatic precipice, but now she was ready, so she let herself fall. Her orgasm was profound in its length and depth as it caught her from below and lifted her up, up in a soundless explosion. She felt she'd lost her mind and voice to some hole in the stratosphere that had drawn her up through it with a teeny, yet very strong string. Weightless, she felt she'd flown beyond the moon to a place above the stars and hovered there a bit before touching back down in a modern dance of loose jerks and quiet convulsions. Then she laughed out loud and beckoned him to come inside and join her in her reverie.

Peter took off his pants quickly, slipped on a condom and lowered himself onto her. He moaned with a look of relieved delight. *Perfection*, she thought. *This is heaven*. Lucy didn't think she could feel any better, but she did. As he entered he fit snugly, her sides were wet and welcoming. It's like riding a bike, she thought, forgetting momentarily that she'd done this just last week with Ted. This felt different, though. It felt new. She thought she could really start to like this guy a lot and began to envision herself spending time with him. Weekend brunches and lazy mornings in bed. She hoped Peter liked her and felt that onerous feeling of auditioning that she remembered from dating years before. She tried to keep it at bay.

Their sex was very good for a first time and their rhythms aligned. Their tastes seemed well in tune. They took their time, eventually dragging the couch and chair cushions onto the floor to create a sort of flotilla for rolling about on. In the end, they came at the same time, a movie cliché she was happy to embrace. She slipped the condom off him, tied it in a knot and left it over on the coffee table amongst the Lego statues. They lay there and talked for the next hour, naked and glistening. They discussed fortunetellers and psychics, camping and Bill Gates. They talked about diets and smoking, architecture and eels. They agreed on the flawlessness of *Spinal Tap* and discovered their mutual love for arcane country music and Skee-Ball. They extolled the healing properties of toast and skinny-dipping, and learned they both disliked gyms. Then they made love again and slept lightly. She fell asleep tracing his moles.

Peter's cell phone alarm woke them out of their daze. He jumped up and, without ceremony, began dressing. "I like your bra," he said matter-of-factly. "Oh, do you? So do I, wherever it is," she said, and cased the room for wherever her bra might have ended up. The room looked as if a mischievous monkey had gotten into the clean laundry. Lucy watched Peter for a moment, taking in the last seconds of his bare body, then figured she might as well get dressed, too. Peter said, "Bras are pretty. Most men will probably never tell you that, and to be honest, they're not even thinking it consciously, but on some level, some Cro-Magnon I-like-shiny-things level, they appreciate the pretty ones. Just so you know. The Band-Aid-colored ones should be outlawed. Boobs deserve better than that."

"I remember driving behind a pickup truck once," Lucy said, "and there was a bumper sticker on the cab window that just said, *BOOBIES!* in all caps with an exclamation point. And it was italicized. I laughed so hard. It was very succinct."

"Yeah, no mincing words, there."

Lucy said, "I've always felt that it pretty much summed things up for most men."

Peter paused for just a moment while putting on his socks and looked up at Lucy. "Exactly. It does. You know, most women don't get that."

"It's taken me a while, but I think I get it now. Probably too late, but I get it."

"Never too late," Peter said. "There's always so much pabulum out there on sitcoms and in magazines and greeting cards about how men don't understand women. Well, I don't think women get men. We think about food, sex and sleep. The rest is filler. But women want to think there's more to us when there isn't. We are a very simple people."

"Yeah, I'm getting that from you now," Lucy said. "Where you heading off to?"

"Oh, I have to . . . um. Do you really want to know?" Peter was tying his shoelaces and looked up at her expectantly. She got it. She didn't know exactly what she got but she got something. Enough for her to stop questioning. "No," she said, "I don't want to know. It's none of my business. Don't tell me."

"Okay, I won't," he said, then grabbed his coat and headed for the door.

"Your shirt's on inside out." She caught a glimpse of the tag as he turned away from her.

"Christ. That's all I need," Peter said, and reversed his shirt.

"Hey," Lucy said. She pushed him over to the bottom stair, stood up on it and went in for a big bear hug. He dutifully wrapped his arms around her as she burrowed her head into his neck. He smelled good to her, but his hug was slack and pathetic. She kissed him on the mouth. His kiss was thin lipped and phoned in. Lucy said, "Wow, that was lame."

"Sorry, I'm just thinking of the time."

"Oh, right, go. Go."

"Okay, bye," he said, and headed towards the door. Lucy went to unlock it for him and the doorbell rang. It was Gus. A woman in a minivan was looking at the house.

"Back door!" Lucy whispered to Peter in a panic. He held his hands up as if to say, where? She pointed towards the kitchen, and Peter bolted.

"Just a sec, sweetie, let me unlock the door for you," Lucy said through the heavy front door, and waited until she heard the back door open and close. Gus ambled in, ducking under her arm, and Lucy waved at the driver. She asked Gus, "Did you say, 'Thank you for the hospitality'?"

Gus nodded and said, "Poop."

"And 'Thank you for the ride'?"

"Poop."

"Good. Did you have fun?"

"Yes, except that I hate Julian's little brother. He's always trying to menace us."

"Menace? Well, we have to live with little brothers, they're part of the package."

"I'm glad I don't have one, even though I guess Delphine's baby will be my part-brother."

Lucy froze and looked at her son, not quite sure she was hearing him correctly. Her head became hot and her skin tightened. She instinctively turned away so Gus wouldn't see her eyes well up. A baby. A new baby for her ex-husband and a stepsibling for Gus. *I don't fucking believe it,* Lucy screamed in her head. It took every ounce of her not to cry. "Well, I'm glad you're glad because we don't have a choice in the matter. And I'm sure you'll be a nice big brother so maybe your little brother or sister won't be such a menace." Lucy busied herself picking up so Gus wouldn't see her eyes and face redden. She remembered the condoms and surreptitiously palmed them. "You're just in time to help me put the living room back together. I pulled the cushions off the couch and chairs to vacuum underneath."

"Where's the vacuum farter?"

"I already put it away. Did Daddy or Delphine say when the baby was coming?"

"No. They said it was a secret and I can't tell anybody. But you aren't anybody, so I still kept the secret, right? Can I jump on the cushions?"

"Yes and of course."

"Awesome," said Gus. "Will you jump with me?"

"No, honey. I can't." Lucy was barely holding it together.

Gus slapped his arms down at his sides. "Now I wish I had a brother. He would jump with me."

"Well, you will soon," said Lucy, her breathing becoming labored. She inhaled deeply though her nose. Gus jettisoned himself into the middle of the pile of cushions and then bounced and rolled around in them. They seemed to be bringing as much joy to him as they had just brought to his mother. Before she felt her world closing in on her. Before she heard the news.

Chapter 13

- -

Three hours later, Lucy was still processing the remnants of her latest bombshell as she arrived on Audra's front porch. The imposing oak door swung open as if by magic to reveal Audra, standing there with a sympathetic smile and an overpoured glass of merlot. Wordlessly, she handed it to Lucy, who took it and said, "I'm sorry I'm early, I just thought I would cry when I saw you so I had to get it over with before anyone else came."

"It's fine. Dix texted me. You okay?"

"Yeah, I'm good. Well, not good. I'm passable. I put on a movie for Gus, screamed into my pillow then took a long hot shower. Don't I look clean?"

"I thought you looked different."

"And I'm here, because life marches on and, let's face it, we knew it would happen sooner or later."

"The cliché continues."

"Exactly. Need any help?"

"No, dahling, thank you, I'm set."

Forty-five minutes and two glasses of wine later, Lucy was in Audra's living room at a sex-toy party with Fran and Dix, plus Kit and Gina and a bunch of other women she didn't know but recognized from school—friends of Audra's. Her friends gave her big squeezes and looked deeply into her eyes with empathetic apologies. She waved them off telling them to stop or else she would lose it, with strict directives not to bring it up. Lucy was glad for the buffer of the other random women. They seemed cool enough. They were here weren't they? Sex-toy parties were the supposedly hip, happenin' nod to the Tupperware parties of days gone by. Oh, sure, instead of food storage containers they were selling battery-powered climax aides, but dress it up any way you like, it still boils down to some lady hawking her wares to make ends meet. Lucy knew it was a lame reason to get a sitter but Audra had asked that she come. Now she was glad she was among friends. She also wanted to test the waters of her "helper" idea, anything to get her mind off Matt's new and improved family.

The evening's emcee was Laura—pronounced Law-*rah*—a Jersey Italian-American self-proclaimed sex-goddess, resplendent in the latest rococo fashions, extra Jerz: big hair, lots of gold jewelry and an accent so thick as to make every product sound even more hilarious than one thought possible. Laura stood in the center of Audra's raspberry, salmon and forest green living room, amidst The Divorceés and The Marrieds who were wedged between overstuffed tasseled throw pillows, illuminated by lamps with silk-covered lampshades. Audra's twice-weekly maid, Rosie, kept her house looking spotless and unlived-in, almost like a spec home. No piles of mail or magazines, no coats or boots in sight. Flotsam was never left out and beds were always made. Lucy had heard the expression "hotel living," where women keep their houses so clean and free of any signs of regular occupancy that visitors feel like they're walking into a hotel. Audra's was a good example of this. Lucy couldn't imagine what it must feel like for a family to live in such a pristine environment for a home, but she supposed it was an attainable social goal that people could check off and so, good for them. Gus sure as hell wouldn't ever know hotel living.

Lucy did not exactly feel comfortable in this living room, but then again, neither did Audra, who'd been faking the suburban old-money façade for years, with the help of her sister-in-law, Cricket. Even though she'd won the house in the divorce, Audra still seemed a bit fish out of water in her own home. Hedge fund management had been very good to Audra's ex, Javier, but so had his personal assistant, Brandi. Audra bounced back quickly because the alimony was substantial and Cliff the carpenter had an impressive tool. (Audra broke him in first, then recommended him to Fran to do her cabinets, so to speak.) Cliff was there from the beginning of the end to smooth over the bumps, although Audra hardly needed smoothing. She had dates and offers within days of Javier moving out. What Lucy wouldn't have given for a Cliff. Now there's a business idea. The Randy Handyman; she could picture the business cards. *Some girls have all the luck*, Lucy thought. Audra was one of them.

"Does anyone want another dirty white mother?" Audra asked, holding a chartreuse and yellow zebra-striped enamel tray with a cluster of lowballs full of the yummy brandy, Kahlúa and cream concoction.

"I beg your pardon?" said Vivian—who was black—with a smirk. Laura interrupted, "Okay, okay, enough with the dirty muthahs, let's staht," and waved Audra off with her long, lacquered nails. Her stage was in front of the living room fireplace; the dildos were lined

up erect on the mantel like Greek obelisks. All the ladies—sitting
four to a couch and two to an ottoman—sat up a bit straighter and
redirected their attention to Laura. Fran was superfocused. Lucy,
Dix, Kit and Gina traded glances that said, clearly, they were in for
a real treat. Laura said, "Let's do an icebreaker, shall we, ladies?
Take the piece of tin foil I handed each of you and sculpt a penis
out of it. I'm gonna time ya. You got two minutes. Ready, go."

Fran said, "What the? . . ." and Dix busted out laughing. Lucy
was already hard at work. A sucker for any craft challenge, she
harbored dreams of *Project Runway* fame like any other self-
respecting former Girl Scout. Kit held her foil in her lap and leafed
through a magazine. The other ladies giggled and made typical
female disclaimers about being "so bad at this." Lucy wished women
weren't so quick to tell each other what they were "so bad at," a
holdover from high school, when if you were good at something,
the entire school turned on you with spears and stones. But that
was then and this is now and Lucy was proud of her crafting talents and not afraid to show it. Apparently sculpting a penis out of
tin foil was one of them.

Laura called time and then cased the room for a winner. She
walked towards Lucy, who had not only created a lifelike penis with
an anatomically correct Darthrim—penis heads looked a lot like
Darth Vader's helmet, or so Lucy thought—but had left enough foil
at the bottom to create complementary gonads.

"Well, now," said Laura grinning, "somebody has verrry good
penis recall. Have you had sex recently?"

"Um, no," said Lucy, but it was too late. She blushed and was
busted. Fran jumped to her feet and pointed as if she were in a
1950s courtroom drama. "You had sex!" she shouted. All the women
hooted and laughed. Gina grinned then waved bye-bye because she
knew Lucy was about to be busted. Lucy looked at her, broke up,

and gave herself away to the room. A memory of her and Peter laughing and naked in her living room crossed her mind, and there was nothing she could do to hide her smile.

"Was it Peter or?—" said Kit, then covered her mouth. Lucy shot her a look that said, *Mention Ted and I'll kill you.*

Gina said, "Peter's an old friend," to the room.

"Did you e-mail him?!" said Kit. To Lucy, she looked more hurt than disappointed.

"She wasn't going to. He might be married," said Gina mischievously.

"I'm glad she did," said Audra. "All's fair in love and war." The married ladies in the room stopped smiling as brightly. Now it was personal. Fran cut the tension, as usual, sensing Lucy's need of a rescue. "People, she's an elementary school teacher, which means she does crafts all day long, for cryin' out loud. If anyone can make a believable penis it's this woman. Doesn't mean a thing. Let's move on." Fran met Laura's stare and made a little circle in the air with her finger like, *let's go.* Lucy was relieved.

Refocused, The Marrieds hooted and raised eyebrows in mock shock as they passed around the panoply of sex toys molded into the anthropomorphic shapes of adorable dolphins, "frisky" flowers and purple puppies. Lucy figured the bright colors served to make women feel better about rubbing themselves with vibrating plastic to get off, but wondered why they would want a sex toy in the shape of a puppy. The product names were priceless, though, Lucy had to admit. Twiddle-Me-Dumb was a giant orange dildo; The Haymaker was shaped like an ear of corn; Jump for Joy had a constellation of bumps where the scrotum should have been at the base of a fruity pink-and-lime green-striped cock the size of a salami. *Jump for something, that's for sure*, thought Lucy. There was the MILFy Moaner, the Cunning Lingerer and the Humpty Dumpty

Humper. There was even the Anal Angel duo that came with its own spicy-cinnamon lube in its own cartoon angel/devil packaging. Lucy imagined passing by a tower of them at Costco, right between the tube socks and the breakfast bars, and tossing one in her cart unceremoniously.

She, Dix and the other divorcées maneuvered onto the same couch and whisper-chatted independently of Laura's married audience. They already had home-happiness arsenals and didn't need any more. They had really just come to be social and support Audra, who only offered to host because Laura had cornered her at a home jewelry sale. They passed around the Giddy Gal and the Peppy Pal with only feigned interest.

"And this is the Black Mamba," Laura said, and pulled a ginormous black rubber cock out of a pharmaceutical rep's traveling bag. "It's one of our best sellers. It's made of latex-free rubber and has five speeds."

"That's more than my bike," said Dix.

"It takes three triple-A batteries—" continued Laura.

"Per week," whispered Fran, "so stock up."

"—and works best with Slippity-doo-dah lubricant, which comes in pineapple, piña colada and fresh sage." Lucy mouthed the words *fresh sage* to Audra, who lifted her shoulders as if to say, *I know, I know.* Dildos and vibrators were still being passed around the room. The Marrieds were paying rapt attention and filling out little order forms, but The Divorcées had long since disengaged from the purpose of the party. Without looking down at the Hulk and the Bucking Bronco, Lucy, Dix, Audra and Fran slapped them into each other's hands and passed them on with the detached resignation of women passing out hot dogs at a picnic.

Lucy turned to Dix, Fran and Audra on the couch and said in a lowered voice, "Hey guys, my friend has a business idea I want to run past you and I figured this was the perfect place to do so. You know how we're all divorced and horny-as-hell and just want to have a little sex while we slog through dating? And how online dating has proven to be a huge time suck and a crapshoot at best, and at worst, is rife with whackos, illiterates, and STDs?" They all nodded. Audra knew where Lucy was going with this and began to grin. Lucy had their attention and paused dramatically. "We don't want to get remarried right now and yet we wish there was a way to get our rocks off every once in a while, no strings attached—but with a human and not an appliance. Am I correct?" The women all nodded. Lucy continued. "What if there was a way? What if I could get us all laid safely and regularly without having to worry about herpes or psychos or the legions of online grammar-challenged? And what if we didn't have to travel very far? And could have sex in our own homes safely, and then the men would leave so we're not left with some guy snoring in our beds all night?"

"Does this have something to do with foreign tradesmen?" said Fran.

"Or who you just had sex with?" said Dix.

"Did you find out if it's legal?" said Audra.

"It sounds immoral," said Dix, "which I have no problem with."

"It sounds like prostitution," said Fran. "I can't become a prostitute. Pretty sure."

"You wouldn't be putting this on your résumé, dahling," said Audra.

"Oh, okay," said Fran, dead serious. Lucy put her hand up. "Ladies, stop interrupting and I'll tell you." Just then Laura broke from her spiel and admonished the couch of divorcées huddled in a scrum of intrigue.

"I'm only gonna say this once," Laura said, "knock off the side chatter and get with the program." Lucy thought, *Hmmm, The Pro-*

gram. Laura continued, "Now, where were we? Oh, right. The Lumberjack, as you can see, is clearly one of our more popular items . . ."

Lucy leaned in. The others followed, completely sucked into Lucy's pitch. "Who's the friend?" Fran asked.

"Nancy. You know her from the Fall Fund-raiser, and I think one of her kids goes to that dance studio." They all nodded. "Nancy and I are thinking of starting a business where married ladies pick out divorcées to sleep with their husbands for them, when they don't want to, or, I should say, to take up the slack when they're too tired or busy." Her friends looked at her quizzically, as if waiting for a punch line they were pretty sure they wouldn't get. Lucy continued, "Their husbands aren't getting laid as much as they'd like to and neither are we, and the wives aren't as interested as the husbands but want to stay married. The husbands want to stay married, too, are disease-free because they've been in long-term monogamous relationships, and local. They're basically good guys, they're just underserved. And the wives are still interested in having sex, just not as often. And we don't want to break up any marriages, we're just underserved as well. It's a common problem and I think we have the solution."

Fran said, "Is this like when restaurants give their leftover food to feed the homeless?"

"Not really, no."

Dix said, "So you and No Fun Nancy are suggesting we become nonprofit hookers?"

Audra grinned and said, "Nancy's more fun than I give her credit for."

"No," said Lucy, "you wouldn't be hookers because you're not getting paid, so there's no chance of arrest. You're not doing anything illegal, you're just having sex with someone's husband, with permission. To save the marriage. Or help it along. You're a helper."

"A marriage sex helper," said Dix. "Can I make up business cards?"

Fran looked a little confused. "Like Florence Nightingale?"

Audra said, "Yes, just like Florence, but instead of giving out bandages we're giving out blow jobs."

Fran said, "I never gave Charles blow jobs. I think that's why he left me."

"I like to give blow jobs," said Dix.

Audra said, "You like a lot of things."

"I do indeed," said Dix. "Fran, this may not be for you."

Lucy said, "Look, it may not be for any of you. You have to decide for yourselves. Nancy asked me to sleep with Ted and I did, and now everyone's much happier."

Fran said, "See, I knew it."

Dix said, "No shit! Wow, I *really* underestimated Nancy."

"People aren't always what they seem. Think it over. There will be a screening process."

Audra said, "I want in. What's the screening process?"

"I haven't gotten that far, yet," said Lucy, "but I'll keep you posted."

Fran said, "'I'? I thought you said this was Nancy's idea."

Lucy shut her mouth. Why couldn't she stop thinking about this stupid idea? She stumbled. "It was. It is. I'm just. I'm the—I'm just going to hell."

"Well," said Audra, "we can be roommates, then."

Fran let out a loud laugh. "I'm in."

Lucy thought, *Well that's that, then. Damn the torpedoes.*

Leaving the party, Lucy was excited, nervous and anxious, all at once. Would this really work as seamlessly as it sounded? It couldn't possibly. But if everyone signed on, it could do all kinds of good for lots of people. And marriages. Maybe it would catch on and there would be a revolution. Maybe we'd finally bust out of our hobbling puritanical shells and start enjoying our bodies without condemnation and fear! And older divorced single women could finally enjoy the same carnal pleasures as older divorced men! And . . . *jeez. I am really nuts. This is a bad idea. It'll never work. I'll call Nancy in the morning and tell her I'm out.*

Driving home afterwards, Lucy was pleased to discover she wasn't crying over Matt's new baby, but instead focused on the positive aspects of her new life. She wound her way through her quiet little suburban town of Nohquee and fell in love with it all over again. Unexpected and exciting things were happening. She was coming to terms with the fact that she would never have a second child and refused to be sad about it. A sibling would be good for Gus. Her life was unfolding the way it should, and it was all fine, just fine. Too bad she'd be turning Nancy down on her entrepreneurial offer, but the stillness of the air and emptiness of the streets calmed and comforted her. If Nancy wanted to continue this harebrained scheme without her, she could. Lucy glanced beyond tree swings and gardens into the dining-room windows of modest-yet-comfortable homes as she drove by, thankful that the owners left the lights on so that she could peek in and imagine their lives. Her knee-jerk default was that there must be a loving husband and brood of kids in there, plus a dog—everyone getting along, reading by the fire, the husband's thumb gently grazing the back of the wife's neck as she enjoys the Arts & Leisure section of the *Times*. Then Lucy admonished herself and turned on the radio. No making up shit allowed. "Take the Long Way Home" came through the speakers and Lucy said, "Okay, Supertramp, I will."

Lucy sang out loud as she thought about how much she loved her home situation. She lived in a cozy little cottage with a wide front porch, stone columns, and a swing chair bolted into the ceiling. It sat on a bucolic tree-lined street in Nohquee, New Jersey, a midsized suburb of Manhattan named for the Lenni-Lenape derivative of *naxkohoman*: to sing. Or as Gus liked to tell his friends, "to fart." Whenever asked, Lucy described her hometown as "charming" to Californians and Europeans because they only knew the seedy underbelly of New Jersey from TV. But New-Jerseyans-in-the-know understood that there were hundreds, if not thousands, of beautiful towns in their great state, the kind where children's books were set and city folks ended up migrating to. Nohquee was the best of them as far as Lucy was concerned. It was her Shangri-la.

She loved its lively energy and collective sense of humor. The community was nicknamed Nookietown in the fifties by its randy teenage population. The town's merchant association worked overtime to eradicate it—with no luck. Once the seventies slinked into the eighties, the name finally lost its allusion to suburban swingers and became a peppy nineties name for a buzzing, friendly town, seducing young families away from Brooklyn and Manhattan in droves. The ice cream shop was the first to adopt it as its official moniker: Nookietown Sweets. The post office, however, was a stalwart holdout and refused to recognize any name other than Town of Nohquee on address labels. When correspondence marked "Nookietown" was dropped into the local slot it was promptly returned to sender.

Lucy stopped for gas. Thanks to New Jersey law, she had to stay in her warm car while an attendant pumped gas in the brittle, March-night air. This station attendant was a swarthy, probably foreign-born man in his midforties/early fifties. His skin was the color of maple syrup and his eyes were black-bear brown. He had unfortunate teeth, a mustache that neither added nor detracted from his face and wore a navy hooded jacket with the name "Phil" stitched on the front.

"Cash or credit?" he said in halting English at the driver's side window, then waited for Lucy's credit card. "Fill 'er up, Phil," she said with a slight grin but he didn't smile and it didn't matter. Lucy still imagined him taking her card, then slowly leaning in the window to kiss her, his eyes asking permission, but not waiting for an answer. Her thighs tightened and twinged at the thought as Lucy conjured their deep wet kiss, then closed her eyes. She imagined him opening the car door and taking her hand as if he were helping her out of a carriage, then lifting her onto the hood of her car where she'd lower her yoga pants just enough to give him access. Using the long sides of the puffy down coat she bought at Costco the week before, she would enclose them both in a quilted cocoon as he massaged her breast with one hand, and unzipped his pants and found her with the other. Her lower body stirred as she imagined the rhythmic bendy sounds the molded metal would make snapping back and forth in and out of shape while he rocked her world. Just as the ticking at the pump ended, Lucy would climax then flop back onto the hood and look up at the sky beyond the naked branches of tall oaks, dizzy and satisfied, her steaming breath obscuring the stars. Lucy shook her head slightly, reprimanding herself. It amazed her how she could go from zero to sex in such a short time.

She brought her gloved hands up to her face and rubbed the soft wool against her skin as if to smooth in the fantasy, or perhaps wipe it away. Sarah, a mom Lucy recognized from Gus's school, drove into the gas station, parked adjacent to her and waved. Lucy waved back, wondering why her kids were up so late on a school night, then felt like a judgmental ass considering what she'd just imagined. The attendant surprised Lucy at the driver's side window. She jumped, then groped for her window button, momentarily forgetting where it was. She gave him a small, weak smile and said, "Thanks, uh, Phil." Then to herself, "Oh, I get it. Phil. Fill . . ." but he was already onto the next car in line. Sarah signaled Lucy from her idling SUV then called over, "Don't you just *love* full-serve?"

Lucy hesitated then said, "You bet I do." Sarah added, "Sure beats self-serve," then rolled up her window. Lucy thought, *Self-serve's not so bad either,* then drove off into the dark, bitter-cold evening and back home to warm herself up.

Chapter 14

Lucy reversed her reversal the minute she finished masturbating. Self-served pleasure simply did not and would never come close to the feeling of actual sex. *Dammit*, she thought, *I have to try this cockamamie plan or I'll regret it the rest of my old, wrinkly, sexless life. I am not ready to give up sex, yet. Godammit. I'm just not.*

In the morning she still felt the same way. She was about to call Nancy when her phone rang. It was her mother.

"Hi, Mom."

"Hi." Lucy listened for the sound of Dottie dragging on a cigarette before continuing, "What's new?"

Lucy almost laughed out loud. *Well, let's see, I slept with my friend's husband because she asked me to, I slept with a man who's possibly married, I'm starting a little sex-share side business, and I'm fantasizing about schtupping pretty much anything in pants.*

"Nothing much," she said.

"Really? What's the much part? Tell me, there must be something."

"There's nothing, Mom. Really, we're good. Gus is good. We're busy. All good."

"Any dates?"

"No, Mom. No dates," Lucy said a little more insistently than perhaps she should have. "I've given up for now. On a little hiatus. Hey, Mom, do you miss sex?"

"You're joking, right?" Dottie said. Lucy shook her head in New Jersey and imagined her mother doing the same in Florida.

"Fine. I'm joking. I just thought maybe. But forget it."

"I sure as hell don't. What did you do last night?" Dottie could and was known to talk forever, but clearly not about sex.

"Last night?" Lucy recalled the vibrators and dildos. "Tupperware party."

"Oh, I didn't know they still—"

"They do. Hey, Ma, I've got a big week coming up and I need to get online and research some lesson plans. Is everything cool with you? Need anything down there?"

"Living the dream. I'll let you go."

"Thanks, Mom. Steer clear of those crocodiles. They're just squirrels with dentures."

"Oh, I'm very spry, don't you worry, dear. Call me every day."

"You know I won't."

"Okay, love you," Dottie said.

"Love you, too," said Lucy, and waited for her mom to hang up first.

Lucy called Nancy and gave her the news. A week or so later they were huddled over papers, clipboards, one of those new Polaroid-type mini cameras and a three-ring binder spread out on the coffee table of Nancy's well-appointed, perfectly bland, upper-middle class Pottery Barn/Crate and Barrel living room. They decided that Nancy's house should be used for interviews so that The Marrieds would have more trust in the concept. It screamed vanilla. This operation needed to feel safe, run-of-the-mill, and as mundane as possible. Nancy's house was perfect.

"Ready?" said Nancy.

"Ready," said Lucy. But she was anxious. She told Nancy she'd help out with the interview process and nothing more, but a little voice inside her wanted in. She knew the potential for career trouble if she were ever found out, but couldn't help herself. Her innate curiosity overwhelmed her. Plus she'd had a taste of excitement and wanted more. The danger part was also pretty compelling. And, of course, the wanton sex.

The first applicant was Audra, who looked predictably stunning in a rust-colored miniskirt and closed-toe wedges with a tight, dark brown, dotted Swiss cotton blouse under a tight, petal-pink rabbit fur, deep-V sweater—cinch-belted—which showcased her spectacular cleavage. Audra, not one to leave the house in sweatpants, wore everything as if it were leopard print.

Lucy began, "Thank you so much for coming. We here at the 'Audrey D. Marriage Maintenance Program' would like to spend a few moments with you to see if we think you're a good fit for us as one of our 'Helpers.'"

"I'm a good fit for most," said Audra, looking right at them.

"Yeah, yeah, I know, but just play along. We need the practice," said Lucy.

"Okay, got it. Who is Audrey D? Sounds a lot like my name."

"Just a coincidence. Audrey D is our code name for Audacious D." Then they both said in unison, "The D is for Discreet," like a homespun commercial for auto insurance.

"Cute," said Audra.

"Thanks. But we'll probably just call it The Program. Now, what is your current marital status and state of mind about it?" asked Lucy. Nancy sat poised with pen to clipboard, ready to record all of Audra's answers, which came fast, clipped and unwavering.

"Happily divorced for four years," Audra said.

"And would you like to get remarried?" asked Lucy.

"Never."

"Good. And do you have any children?"

"Yes, three."

"And do you want more?"

"No way in hell."

Lucy looked at Nancy who raised her eyebrows a bit. "Do your children have a father in their lives, or do you wish they had more of a father-figure presence?"

"Their father is around and he's fine. They seem to still like him, so, whatever."

"Good," said Lucy. "Do you have an income, and how secure are you about it?"

"I have alimony, child support, a secure job and my family is fabulously wealthy."

"Ideal. And do you own your own house and car?"

"I do."

"Okay," Lucy said, sitting back, a little relieved. She looked at Nancy, who smiled back at her. "You seem to be an excellent candidate so far. Do you understand that if you agree to our terms, you will be added to our roster of available Helpers and subcontracted out by local wives to sleep with their husbands?"

"Yes."

Lucy continued, "And do you understand that you will have to strictly adhere to the individual terms of the woman who requests you with regards to the services you provide for her husband, and if you disregard any of the limits set, even once, then you'll be asked to cease participation in our program?"

"Yes."

"No matter what the husband asks you for, you've been subcontracted by his wife. She's in charge."

"Got it," said Audra. "No one falling in love with me or late-hour booty calls. Just sex, no strings. This is exactly what I need. I have to get up early." She was unruffled, decisive and relaxed; she could have been talking about car-repair options with her garage mechanic. "And I assume that if I'm assigned to someone lazy in bed or sexually unproductive, or unattractive, I can request to be removed from his roster? I would tell you and you tell the wife?"

"Of course. He'll be reassigned elsewhere. This is equally for your benefit, remember."

Nancy added, smiling, "It's a win, win, win." Lucy nodded. Nancy said, "Okay, now, I see by our checklist that you filled out that there's pretty much nothing you won't do."

Audra said, "I used to live in Southern California."

Nancy continued, "I see here that you'll try any position; kiss or not kiss, talk or not talk; vocal or quiet; vaginal or anal; oral; blow jobs or hand jobs; you checked that your home is an available location when your kids are with their father every other week; and that you would be open to one-offs, weeklies or monthlies, but no more than twice a week with the same husband. Very good. You should be very popular with our participants."

Audra said, "I plan to be the most popular."

Lucy said, "Right. California. We get it."

Then Nancy leaned over and pointed something out to Lucy on her clipboard.

Lucy piped up, "Oh, right. It seems the only boxes you didn't check were 'I will listen to him talk about his wife' and 'I will listen to him talk about sports.'"

Audra responded with a pointer finger waved once perfunctorily in the air, "Yeah. Eh-eh. I will do most anything, but I have to draw the line somewhere. I will have sex with him but I will not listen to him drone on about inane drivel that I haven't had to listen to since I got divorced. Why do you think I got divorced? I'd rather they don't talk at all. I'm in it for the orgasm. And I won't cook for him. No food service."

"Oh, that's a good idea," said Lucy to Nancy. "You should add that to the checklist handout."

"Yes, I'll make a note of it," said Nancy. Lucy handed a pink sheet of paper to Audra. "Here's the 'Helper's Rules and Regulations' page. It covers the mandatory use of condoms, our anonymity policy against fraternizing on the street should you run into participants, etcetera," said Lucy, and then leaned forward and turned it over. "On the other side are the 'Guidelines for the Wives,' just so you know what they'll be adhering to."

"Okay."

"Please sign it and return it to me and I will give you a copy to take home."

Audra signed the paper and handed it to Lucy. "Thank you," said Lucy. "Now all we have to do is have you recite the Oath of Discretion. Raise your right hand, please."

"Seriously?" Audra was skeptical for the first time in the interview.

"Yes, seriously. Do you want women gossiping about you? How

helpful would that be to your kids and your job? This won't work if people start shooting off their mouths. There's got to be an element of self-policing when it comes to gossip. Besides, it's toxic and lazy. There are other ways to amass social currency besides gossip. Talk about books, for crying out loud, talk about current events."

"I got it, I got it," said Audra. "Enough with the lecture. I'm on board. What do I say?"

"Raise your right hand. We're all going to swear to put our sexual needs before our need to entertain others with gossip. Let's go. Hands." Audra, Lucy and Nancy all raised their right hands, looked at each other then repeated the little oath that Lucy had written out on a three-by-five card:

THE AUDREY D. MARRIAGE MAINTENANCE PROGRAM
OATH OF DISCRETION

I swear to be discreet and abstain from gossipy talk
If I change my mind at any point, I'm always free to walk
I swear to swap out judgment for a slice of happiness
What people think about me is none of my business

Lucy looked at her checklist. Their first interview had gone well. It was time to wrap things up. Nancy said, "Audra, we just need to take your photo for our file and then we're all set. You'll be getting your scheduling calls from me. Each wife is entitled to an optional ten-minute preinterview if she wants one at your house, at your convenience, just to meet you and tell you in person what she wants. Or I'll call you with the details once you've been contracted. If you want to have a copy of the wife's list of requirements, you can request a copy and I'll leave it in my milk drop box on the back porch in an envelope. No website, e-mail, or texting. We don't want any of this electronically traceable. The more we can do over the phone the better."

"Old school," said Lucy.

"Fine with me," said Audra.

Then Lucy took two little instant photos of Audra—a full body shot and a headshot—and handed them to Nancy who taped them onto the other side of her questionnaire. They shook Audra's hand, thanked her for coming in and ushered her to the door. Dix was next and her interview went similarly, except that she didn't mind listening to guys talk about sports. She was a true fan and had been way more into sports than her ex. Dix checked off all the boxes, including anal, which surprised the women. She said she'd always wanted to try it and now was as good a time as any. Her photos got taped to her questionnaire, too.

Fran passed her screening interview with flying colors. She recited the oath and then made a crack about the first rule of Fight Club. She said that her home was available, but not her bed, so Nancy made a note that she had a lot of nice couches, a guest room, and of course, the pool table in the basement. Fran checked all the boxes yes and in the little space provided wrote that she would wear any costume or do pretty much any role-playing within reason. She was adventurous in high school but married a man that her mother had always liked. Charles was smart and handsome but got caught up in what people thought and was expectant but narrow-minded in bed. Fran was such a free spirit that they'd butted heads from the start. It looked as though she was going to loosen him up and he was going to calm her a bit, but they grated on each other incessantly. Sometimes when opposites attract, they combust. Fran nearly killed him.

Nancy and Lucy thanked Fran for coming as they had thanked the other women, then broke for egg-salad sandwiches. So far, so good. Then they swapped out clipboards and got ready to meet the afternoon appointments of wives interested in The Program.

To their shock, all the married women Lucy and Nancy explained The Program to showed up. A couple of them even brought friends. The wives' screening process was a little different. Kit went first. She walked in with a sour puss. "I just want you to know that I'm only here because I want to support you both, even though I'm still pissed at Lucy for sleeping with Peter and Ted and not telling me." Nancy looked at Lucy, who shrugged.

Lucy said, "I'm sorry, Kit, I really am, I just didn't think you'd be supportive and I couldn't handle the judgment. But can we talk about it some other—"

"Well, it really hurt and I just wanted to put that out there. I'm here now being supportive aren't I?"

"You are, and thank you. I really am sorry." Lucy saw Kit warm slightly. She thought, *Man, I seem to be apologizing to Kit a lot lately. I'm always in trouble.*

Kit said, "Fine. We can talk about it some other time but I'm still not sure this is—"

"It's fine," said Lucy. "It'll be good to just have you in the system."

"What system?" said Kit.

"Our portfolio, that's all," said Nancy. "No data entry. Very old school. It's just one piece of paper in a binder. We can toss it out at any time."

Lucy said, "Do you understand how this works?"

"I think so," said Kit. She scanned the room. Lucy had never seen her look so uncomfortable. "I get other women to sleep with my husband."

"So you don't have to as often. That's right," said Lucy.

Nancy said, "I see that you checked off all weeknights except Friday night—"

"Soccer games. Oh, and Tuesday nights Fwank helps out the robotics club," said Kit.

"Fine. You also checked off weekday mornings for blow jobs and sex, but no kissing. Condoms always and never the same woman twice. That's fine."

Kit began, "I just think that for me, uh, for us, that maybe we—"

Nancy interrupted, "Kit, you don't have to explain yourself or have reasons for your choices. They're personal and they're between you and your husband. Here at The Program, our Helpers—I think that's what we decided to call them, right, Nance?"

"Yes," said Nancy.

"Our Helpers will stick to whatever you've ordered. Like checking off boxes on a Chinese takeout menu. We don't judge."

Kit shook her head with a chuckle. "You guys are unbelievable."

Nancy lowered her clipboard, squared her shoulders and said, "Kit, I did it. I asked Lucy to sleep with Ted two weeks ago, and Ted's a new man. Not because Lucy's such a dynamo in bed—"

"Thanks, Nance," said Lucy.

"—but because she wasn't me. Ted's happier. I'm happier. And I might do it again. I'm deciding whether or not to reserve Lucy or a different Helper this time. But it's helped. And it was my decision and my husband loves me for it. I'm just telling you it worked for me. Took the pressure off."

Kit said, "Duly noted."

Nancy said, "So, what will happen is, in the event that you should want to retain one of our Helpers for your husband, you call this number. It's an independent cell number that I will keep. You ask for a certain girl, or if you want to look at the binder, I'll leave it right inside the back door on the kitchen counter and you can look through it any time. Then we'll call the Helper, make the appointment, match your list of dos and don'ts with hers, and then call you back with a confirmation date and time. Here's your handout of The Program guidelines. It's got the oath, rules stating the forbiddance of Helper harassment, and an agreement stating that you accept full accountability for whatever emotional or marital fallout may happen between you and your husband and that your Helper will remain blameless."

Kit said, "In other words . . ."

"In other words, if your marriage takes a hit because of this, you have to accept that it's between you and your husband. Anything that might happen is just symptomatic of something else that was already there."

Lucy said, "It's never about the other woman. It's always about the marriage. It's between the husband and wife, if we're being honest."

Lucy, Nancy and Kit exchanged uncomfortable looks. They both knew she was talking from experience. Kit looked out the window and Nancy looked down.

Lucy continued, "On the other side are the guidelines for the Helpers, just so you know what we've asked them to adhere to."

"Okay, got it," said Kit. She was clearly ready for this to be over.

Nancy said, "Please sign it and return it to me. I'll give you a copy."

Kit signed the paper and handed it to Nancy. "Thanks," said Nancy. "Now then, let's see what you've put down in the compensation box. It looks like you can bake—"

Kit said, "You *know* I can bake."

Nancy said, "I know that you know that I know you can bake. I'm just practicing. I've got to be professional."

Kit said, "I haven't told anyone about this."

"That's fine. Your choice," Lucy said. "It's already spread by word of mouth. We have eleven more appointments after you today, and three more tomorrow morning. It's not just about you, Kit, and it's not just your marriage that needs this service. There are so many marriages in trouble." Kit looked at Lucy and Lucy thought for a split second that she might have seen something else in there—just a flash in Kit's eyes, but of what? Jealousy? Despair?

Lucy said, "Kit is an excellent baker. Everyone knows that. What else?"

Nancy said, "She put down that Fwank owns a landscaping business and could help out in that regard. And her brother-in-law's parents own a restaurant in Hoboken."

"Fantastic," said Lucy.

Kit said, "You know that no black woman alive will let her husband sleep with another woman. And most white women won't either. I can't speak for other ethnicities."

"Thanks for the odd insight," Lucy said.

Kit said sheepishly, "I did talk to my neighbor about it."

Lucy said, "Okay, then. It sounds like she won't bite, but you might."

"Fwank and I are different."

"All marriages are different and yet most of them are the same," Nancy said. "That's why you're here."

"This will never work," said Kit.

"That's what they said about MTV and FedEx."

"You're comparing yourselves to FedEx?"

Lucy said, "A girl's gotta dream. Now please raise your right hand."

At this point Kit looked too annoyed by the preposterous nature of the whole charade to care. She raised her right hand, mumbled the oath, then said, "All I know in this moment is that I want my

Fwank to be happy and my marriage to last." Then she left the room. Lucy managed to say a small, "I love you," in Kit's direction, but the door closed too fast.

Gina signed up without fanfare. She followed Kit with a "blow jobs and sex only" request, and said she wanted to find one Helper and stick with her. No kissing, no back rubs and definitely no cooking. Gina was a fabulous cook and knew deep down that men went where the food was and wanted to be Duncan's only source for nourishment. She was fairly certain that the administrative end of this business venture would break down within days, and told the girls that, point blank. Never blindly supportive for support's sake, Gina always had one eye squarely fixed on the cold harshness of reality, but she was attracted to this as a possible solution to her marriage's imbalance and found the business strategy intriguing, from an attorney's standpoint. She perused the binder and set up an appointment for Duncan to sleep with Audra the following Tuesday morning. His birthday was coming up and she hadn't known what to get him. Lucy assured her that Audra was a fine choice.

More women came and brought friends. Natasha picked Dix because she figured her sports-obsessed husband would like her ESPN banter, and her friend, Vashna, chose Fran because she was the most American to her and she wanted to prove to her husband that American women didn't know how to make love properly. *Whatever,* Lucy thought, *I'm not here to judge.* Then Nancy's friend Sarah came in. Lucy recognized her from her pack meetings and the gas-station fantasy. Sarah's marriage was on the skids and she wanted someone who would be good in bed, but not so sexy that her husband would fall in love with her. Nancy and Lucy showed her Fran's page and assured her that she was the best choice for her unique circumstance. What they didn't say was that there was nothing unique about her circumstance.

When Sarah left they packed up for the day and gave each other a high five and a hug.

"What on earth are we doing?" said Nancy.

"*We're* doing?! *You're* doing," said Lucy.

"Okay, *I'm* doing. But thanks for helping. I really appreciate your support."

"It's fine," said Lucy. "It's exciting. Now let's try not to get arrested."

Chapter 15

The following week Lucy had an appointment with Ted and a date with Peter. The Ted thing went well. Still no talking, which was fine by Lucy, and she still had plenty of time after he left to shower and research weather-system lesson plans online for her students. The sex cleared her head, realigned the molecules in her body, she felt, and reset her mind. The next day all the leaves were miraculously cleaned out of Lucy's garden beds to make room for her spring perennials, and her lawn was reseeded in patches left over from a muddy winter. Kit must have caved and sent Fwank to see Audra. He had sent his guys over to take care of Lucy's lawn; she could only imagine what he did to Audra's lawn. At the back door was a container of homemade chili, some three-bean salad with corn and avocados and a loaf of cranberry-walnut bread. Tied to the bread with red ribbon was a note that read, "You were right. xo, K." *Wow*, Lucy thought, *a girl could get used to this.*

The weather was finally warming enough for Lucy to wear a skirt without tights. She had just swapped out the crimson, eggplants and deep teals of her winter wardrobe for the tangerines and lavenders of early spring. The hydrangea in her backyard was starting to green, and she felt buoyant and pretty. She was also craving Peter. Lucy expected Peter to break off their date or not call, but he kept his word. She found a neighborhood kid to watch Gus and met Peter for a picnic in the park woods near the lake. She'd grown up near this lake and felt it had magical powers. She felt sexier near the water and freer under the canopy of leaves—looser, more relaxed. She also knew that Gus would be at the house and didn't know where else to go for privacy. Lucy and Peter took a long walk through the wooded path in the park and then sat at a picnic table by the stream. They shared a roast-beef sandwich, some grapes and a cream soda. As they ate, Lucy tried to get to know him better and explore his mind. She also figured that by doing so would help him realize how beguiling she was—but then she thought, *Silly girl, he just wants to sleep with you. It's all I want, why shouldn't he want it, too?* But a part of her still felt like she was auditioning for the role of girlfriend. She hadn't asked what his deal was and he hadn't volunteered the information. Instead, she chose not to think about it. *Denial, schlemial.*

"Tell me something about physics," she said.

"You mean like quantum effects and isotopes?" he said.

"Yeah, that stuff."

"Please don't do that. Don't pretend to be interested in what I do. It's interesting to me—doesn't have to be interesting to you. I already think you're smart and sexy. Don't pander."

"Really? Awesome." Lucy bit into a grape. "But what if I'm genuinely inter—"

"Then it's fine. Ask away."

"Got it." *Nice*, Lucy thought. *No pretending with this guy.*

"Have you always been hot?" Peter asked her, biting into his half of the sandwich.

"You mean like warm hot?" Lucy asked.

"No, sexy hot," he said.

Good Lord, no, Lucy wanted to say. *I had bad skin and bit my nails, bushy hair and was the opposite of chesty.* It had been so long since a man had called her hot—had complimented her at all—that she nearly swooned like a silent film star. *Play it cool,* she thought.

"Define 'hot,'" she said, totally fishing. She felt now, in her forties, that every compliment could be her last.

"C'mon, you know. The gorgeous face, the great ass and big boobs—you know you're hot."

Big boobs? she thought. *You think I have big boobs?!*

"I was a late bloomer. Hotness came late to me," she said, unaware until that very moment that hotness had, in fact, ever arrived at all. "I had to develop a personality. I had terrible hair."

"That's why you're funny. The hot girls in high school were rarely funny," he said, and took the soda bottle out of her hand for a swig.

"Thank you?" Lucy said flatly.

"It's a compliment, trust me," Peter said. Lucy put a grape in his mouth. She said, "It's a little harsh. But I suppose you're right. When I think back to high school, it *did* boil down to boobs and hair. You had to have one or the other. I had neither."

"But I bet you were always smart and had personality, right?" Peter said, and reached over to tuck an errant boi-yoing curl behind her ear. "Hot women rarely like science fiction and shooting pool. It's awesome that you're funny. It's been my experience that most women aren't. That's one of the reasons I like you."

So, he likes me. Verrry interesting.

Lucy said, "I know a lot of funny women. All my closest girl-friends are funny."

"But are they funny *and* hot?" Peter said.

Lucy did a mental scan of her girlfriends, "Actually, most of them are, yes."

"I bet they're all taken, aren't they?"

"Well, some of them are and some of them were. But we can be too intimidating for most men. That is, speaking as their fearless leader."

Peter got up off the bench to stretch.

"Man, if I ever met a funny, hot woman who loved the Coen brothers, I'd marry her." Lucy didn't say it, but she loved the Coen Brothers, the Wayan brothers, the Marx Brothers, the Wilson, Gershwin and Smothers Brothers. She loved all the brothers.

After they finished their picnic, and discussed which jobs they would want if they worked in a circus, Lucy stood up and slipped off her shoes. She waded ankle deep into the cold water at the edge of the stream and balanced on a rock in her bare feet. It was 4 P.M., just about the warmest part of the day, and the canopy of trees parted over the water to reveal what was left of a sunny, unseason-ably warm day. Lucy gathered the hair up off the back of her neck and peered down into the water at the moss, looking for signs of life. Peter kept his shoes on and followed her, balancing on bigger rocks. Gingerly, he bent down and scooped up the clear water in the cup of his hand and drizzled it against the faint perspiration that had formed at the base of her neck. "Mmmmm," Lucy said, and shivers ran down her back and straight to her thighs. She closed her eyes and felt the muscles deep inside her quake. Damn, that man could make her ache and tingle.

Lucy felt that the sounds of the birds and the rustling leaves, the woods themselves, gave her permission to put her hands on his body, so she turned and reached her arms up to his face and kissed him, warm and slow, her tongue grazing his teeth. She caressed his back, his shoulders, the round slope of his buttocks, she moved her hands to the front up under his shorts and found the tip of his cock. He backed away with a laugh then moved his hand under her blouse, found her left nipple and squeezed. It was as if the trees were egging them on, daring them to do it. This is right and natural, they were saying, the most natural thing you can do with one another. But she knew it was more likely the forest montage from *Dirty Dancing*, which had lodged itself in her brain when she was young and impressionable. She grabbed his butt with one hand and rubbed the other over the hardened bulge in his shorts. He lifted her skirt and moved a finger against her soft belly then down into her underpants where he found her moist and wanting, and set off a spark that caused her knees to bend and falter.

Peter tried to move his body closer to hers, but his footing slipped and one foot ended up ankle deep in the water. "Shit," he said, and was visibly annoyed for a moment. Lucy whispered, "I can put your sock and shoe in the dryer back at my house." Normally she would have told him that it's no big deal and maybe teased him a little about being uptight, but something stopped her. She took his hand and they stepping-stoned their way out of the stream, then walked briskly back to his car. Once inside, Lucy leaned over the gearshift, and nibbled his ear while stroking the prominent bulge in his shorts. How soon could he be inside her? Not soon enough, but his car was too small—and covered in pet hair.

"Your car is too small," she whispered in his ear. "And that dog hair—"

"Cats," Peter said. "Erdös and Schrödinger." He groaned softly. "The woods?"

"What about the woods?" she said, not getting his drift. But he was already getting out of the car again. He led her by the hand back into the brambles and off the beaten path—literally—to a more densely wooded area. She got it and began to help him search. "Here," she said, checking for poison ivy, then pulled him into an embrace behind a wide, grand oak. As soon as their lips locked, their hands hurried to loosen the necessary clothing. They plunged into each other, groping and stroking, searching for skin. Lucy stood up on a fallen stump to get higher and Peter entered her from just below. Immediately her brain flooded with mind-numbing chemicals, obliterating any sense of social responsibility or law-abiding decorum. *This is why people get caught having sex in stupid places*, she thought. *It's the damn chemicals, they're too powerful to override. Why weren't juries more understanding? Because people on juries have forgotten what it was like to want someone so badly that society and its rules can go to hell? Because it's too hard to recall when it's been so long?*

They pumped each other awkwardly against the tree, giggling and driving themselves into each other again and again until they climaxed, shuddering. As they finished Lucy let out a bright laugh, which Peter tried to muffle with his free hand while using the other to hold himself up against the tree. He smiled, panting and shaking his head. "Shhhhhh," he said, and laughed with her as she quivered, bright-eyed and flushed, weakened from their tryst, unable to move off the tree. Then her energy returned to her in a dizzying rush. After straining in silence so they wouldn't be discovered, Lucy finally had to let out a loud, cascading laugh. She couldn't believe what she'd just done. He shushed her and she giggled at their audacity and marveled at their stupidity. Then she smoothed her skirt. She looked at Peter, who shone with a thin veneer of sweat and thrill.

"That was super fun!" she said.

"That was incredibly stupid," he muttered.

"Yes, indeed, stupid as hell. But fun as all get out."

"I never said it wasn't fun, I just said we could be on the front page of the local paper."

"This is hardly news. Two consenting adults—"

"Arrest is news. Losing my job and jeopardizing my career is news to me."

"But we didn't, so can we please not rain on my sex parade? I just got laid in the woods, like Goldilocks," Lucy said with a note of triumph in her voice.

Peter said, "Okay, yeah. Sure. But I'm pretty sure Goldilocks didn't—"

"The porn version."

"Oh, right, the porn version. And that makes me . . ."

"Hung like Papa Bear," Lucy said. Peter laughed and Lucy was glad she'd been able to bring him back from the precipice of paranoia. She didn't want this memory ruined. They arranged themselves like guilty high school kids then she took Peter's hand and ambled back through the woods to his car. They walked in silence, but Lucy's mind was a whir. She felt high on the thrill and excitement of good, clean fun, though how good and clean this had been was debatable. There was a bounce in her step, though, more joie in her vivre. She hadn't imagined how much zing The Program would give her, and she certainly hadn't pictured herself screwing a physics teacher against a tree in the woods.

Chapter 16

By the end of the month, all the Helpers had called in and told Nancy that their dates had gone well, and all the wives reported back that they were happy with the results. Improbable? Yes. Unbelievable but true. Nancy was elated and shared her news with Lucy, who was outwardly cautiously happy, but inside concealed a little rush, a thrill. She was excited to be on the ground floor of this pioneering effort to reinvent the marital contract. Even though hers had failed, she still believed in the idea of marriage, and felt that right now, in history, marriage in America needed a few adjustments in order to be honest and healthy and actually work. Sure, she started The Program for the sex, first and foremost, but she liked the idea of being credited with Fixing Marriage. Her first one hadn't worked, but maybe if society changed and expectations shifted, she would consider getting remarried one day—or not. She thought she'd been so sure she wouldn't, but now, who knows? Lucy entertained the fantasy of being described as cofounder of the most subversive and groundbreaking psychosexual social experiment since the key party. She envisioned herself saving thousands of marriages and making that many divorcées happier. Wife swapping might work for married couples, but this was going to benefit divorcées. She'd be a hero. Or, she'd be vilified, like Kit said. *You know what? Fuck it*, Lucy thought. *As someone once said to Mel Brooks: If you're going to go up to the bell, you might as well ring it.*

That afternoon, Lucy bumped into Kit at the ATM in town and they went for a quick coffee. Kit apologized to Lucy and conceded that she'd been behaving poorly. Sitting across from each other at a teeny table, they hunched forward with their hands in a tangled heap.

Kit began, "I'm so sorry about Matt's new baby."

"Oh, it's fine. Thanks. I'm over it already. I promise. I'm good."

"You know I love you."

"I know you do," said Lucy. "I love you, too."

"I think I was just lashing out maybe because of Fwank." Kit and Fwank started dating in junior high school, when everyone teased him for having a lisp. Actually it was Kit who started calling him Fwank. They met up again at their five-year reunion and she got pregnant that night with Bertie. The twins followed right away by accident. Thankfully, Fwank's landscaping business took off almost immediately and never faltered. Kit always did the books and they always fought. It's just the way things were.

Lucy said, "Because he wants more sex? That's typical, Kit."

"No," said Kit. "Actually, the opposite. I've never told anyone this but—"

Kit stopped and looked down at the spoon in her hand. "But, what?" said Lucy.

"Before The Program, me and Fwank hadn't had sex in a while. Like, a long time."

"What's a long time?" asked Lucy. Kit looked over at a crying baby. "Kit?" said Lucy. She craned her neck to meet Kit's gaze.

Kit said, "A year. Maybe less. Maybe more. Maybe two."

"What?!" Lucy's huge eyes said it all. "You guys hadn't had sex in *two years*?"

Kit said, "Jesus, yes. Or less. Listen. I haven't told anyone. Please don't—we go through phases. It's hard to explain. He can't always get it, you know, up and refuses to take a pill, so after a while he stopped trying and I haven't minded 'cause I've been so busy and tired, so I let it go. Maybe he's depressed. I don't know. But I think that's why I was such a bitch about all this Program stuff. Please don't say a word to anyone." Lucy had never seen such a look of despondence on Kit's face and she couldn't get over the fact that her closest friend hadn't had sex for over a friggin' year. What was that all about? Lucy knew there were sexless marriages out there but she always assumed—unfairly—that it was the woman who didn't want it. But, the man? Was this endemic? A widespread thing that people just didn't talk about?

Lucy said, "Won't tell a soul. It's in the vault. How are you two doing now?"

"Much better. Fwank said his one appointment with The Program was good, whatever that means. I didn't ask. I'm assuming everything worked, which made me jealous at first, but then I was glad that maybe what wasn't working will now work again."

"So have you two—"

"Yes, and it's better. Things worked. And he seems much more connected to me and the kids, I think. At least it seems so."

"Why didn't you tell me? Does Gina know?" said Lucy. She knew she was being a hypocrite for keeping so much from Kit while poking around as to why she wasn't more forthcoming. Part of her was also realizing that this was how friendships slipped away.

Kit said, "It's embarrassing. And hard to talk about. So, no I didn't tell Gina—no one. And you're one to talk, after you didn't tell me about Ted, my hypocrite friend."

"I know, I know, but I couldn't because—"

"Yeah, yeah, discretion and all that b.s. I remember. Look, it's been hard to pretend with all the sex talk lately. We never used to talk this much about sex."

Lucy laughed. "Yeah, really. I'm sorry. It's what divorced women talk about. I mean, we also talk about kids, and refinancing mortgages, and our careers, but we usually lead with, 'Who's getting laid?' I mean, why bury the lead. I'm sorry if it's been too much."

Kit said, "My other married friends talk about sex, too, once in a while. I know they have sex once a week, every other, or in spurts and clusters and have for sixteen, twenty years." Kit sipped her coffee. "Sometimes it's hard to be friends with those women. Too much pressure."

Lucy chuckled. "I think it's great that people still turn each other on. You and Fwank used to turn each other on. Maybe it's just . . . have you tried counseling?"

"Counseling didn't work and he said he wasn't depressed. I've made a Program appointment for every other month. Thought I would try you next. I trust you. A screw and a blow job. So, we'll see." Kit perked up. "I'm done talking about it. What about you? Are you sleeping with every husband in town?"

"No, no, gosh, no," said Lucy. "Just Ted and one other. I'll probably just stick to them, or I may delegate one of them to Audra. I only need one appointment a week or every other week to be happy myself. That was my goal, so I'm getting everything I want. I also sub in at the last minute, as long as it's okay with the wife. There've been plenty of Helper applicants, so the appointments get spread around. It's all going very smoothly. Nancy's in charge."

"Oh, c'mon. You're the backbone of this operation and you know it."

"No, no," said Lucy, but she knew deep down that she was more invested than she would admit. Something about the experimental nature of it all. And the risk. Her life was unpredictable now, in a good way, and she liked it.

Kit said, "It shouldn't work, you know. No offense."

"I know, but there must be a frustration out there, some reason why people are trying it. I think they want to be married, but are struggling to keep it together."

"I think you're probably right. Which could also be why I was such a big bitch about all this. I hate it when you're right. I'm the one who's usually right." Kit smiled warmly and Lucy remembered why they'd been such good friends for so long.

Kit said, "Look, Luce, I want you to be happy more than anything, but I don't want to see you lose your job or head down the wrong—"

"You mean become a ho?"

"Exactly." Lucy was glad she was smiling. Kit continued, "I want to be supportive of you. You have so much to offer and you've been through hell. I get it. But you're a terrific teacher and I don't want to see you lose that. I'm not saying you wouldn't make a great ho."

"Thank you, and I'm pretty sure I can't lose my job over this. Consensual adults, nothing illegal. I asked Gina first. I'm not a total idiot."

"What you need is a boyfriend. Have you asked what's-his-bucket if he's married, yet?"

"Peter. And no. Shit, Kit, I'm starting to like him." Lucy was annoyed with herself.

"That's what I was afraid of. You know I don't want to see you get hurt."

Lucy grew defensive. Not entirely at Kit, but at society. "What's with the hurt? It's like the default rationale for everything these days. 'I don't want to see you get hur-urt.' Yeah, and I don't want to see you get run over by a bus. People get hurt and they move on, they push through it. Haven't I proven that? I survived a hideous divorce and I'm still standing."

"I know, but it almost destroyed you," said Kit, "and it was really hard on me and Gina."

Something about the way Kit said "me and Gina" stuck Lucy like a little pinprick. "I know," Lucy said, "and thanks again for standing by me. It couldn't have been easy for you guys, and I don't know how I could have gotten through it without you."

"It was hard on Fwank, too, he really liked Matt, and we couldn't find anyone else to split the lake house share with. But really, I became totally paranoid about my marriage."

"I know, Kit, I'm so sorry again. I really am. I don't know what else to say."

"It's fine. That's what friends are for," said Kit. Lucy was starting to get pissed but laughed it off to diffuse the anger. Divorce was not something you caught.

Lucy said, "Look, there is no magic bullet against hurt. It's part of life. You buy a puppy and you know it's gonna end badly. Should I not see Peter because it may end and I'll get hurt? Life hurts; love stinks. There's no way around it. I had little daggers plunged through my heart every day by Matt and lived to tell about it. I can *handle* the *hurt*. I will survive."

"I know, Gloria Gaynor, I know," said Kit, "and I'm proud of you for getting through your divorce without ending up in the police blotter. I would have killed him. I just don't know if I can handle you getting hurt again."

"Because it's all about you?"

"Always." Kit laughed.

"Well then, step back from it and don't get involved. Let *me* take *my* risks. I need to unleash the lady pirate in me once in a while or else I'll wither and die."

"Okay. Got it," said Kit. "Arrgh." Then she jumped a little, as if remembering something. "I have the name and number of a new sitter for you. She drives. I'll text you her deets."

"Oh my gawd, thank you so much," said Lucy and reached across the table for Kit's hand. "Not everyone is so generous. This is better than ill-gotten booty."

"Well," said Kit, "I am your lady-pirate friend for life."

"Good. Now please be happy for me that I met a nice guy who makes me laugh and brings me joy. Plus he's a physics geek. How hot is that?"

"So hot."

"Yeah, well, he's mine, so back off, sister."

"Just make sure he's not someone else's first. Nobody wants to be number two."

Lucy had given this some thought. She said, "Katharine Hepburn was number two."

"Lu-cy," Kit said with stern eyes, her chin down at her chest.

Lucy held up two fingers and whisper/chanted, "We're number two, we're number two."

Chapter 17

- -

Word of mouth spread fast. Lucy was eager to have a non-work-related project to occupy a little time when Gus was with Matt and liked the social aspect of having a partner in crime. Together, she and Nancy set up another screening day for Helpers and wives, created more blank pages for the portfolio, and added another binder for signed contracts, which they kept in alphabetical order by first name only. Lucy's coteacher, Gardenia, joined The Program, as did Laura, the fuckerware party hostess. Nancy's vast network of connections brought in six more applicants, and each of The Marrieds recommended at least one new friend, who interviewed and signed up. Some wives came to the initial interview, signed up, then chickened out of scheduling an appointment for their husbands, but that was okay. There were enough wives and husbands who were all in.

Finding Helpers for the husbands was a bit trickier. Lucy and Nancy had to be so discerning, so careful not to let a divorcée with an agenda sneak by. The success of The Program hung in the balance of the divorcées truly not wanting to remarry or break up any marriages. They couldn't just say the words, they had to radi-ate it. The guys had to get the signal, too—loud and clear—that these women wanted nothing to do with them aside from their dicks. If even one husband decided to leave his wife for a Helper, The Program would fall like a house of cards, and Lucy had grown to like her new life.

Once, as they were packing up after interviews, Nancy said to Lucy, "I'm really enjoying working with you." Lucy said, "Thanks, Nance, me, too." Lucy had always liked Nancy. Though they weren't superclose, she was easy to be around.

"Hey, Nancy. We know why I'm doing this, but why are you doing this?"

Nancy stopped straightening up for a moment and said, "I always wanted to work at a nonprofit, someplace where I could really help people and make a difference for the better. I think this is my own personal Peace Corps. My version of Habitat for Humanity."

Lucy laughed. "And yet nothing like either of those."

Nancy laughed, too. "True."

Within three weeks of starting up The Program, Lucy had a free haircut and color, plus coupons for free dinners at local Indian, Italian and Thai restaurants. She'd had her gutters cleaned, her lawn reseeded and two trees that had been dead for years taken down. She had a standing 20 percent discount at a cute gift shop in town, and a will that Duncan was drafting for free. One wife offered her a week at her beach house. She got a massage, three hours of child care, plus sex toys from Laura at cost. All told, she figured her new business venture would garner her thousands worth of thank-you presents by the end of the year, if you included the money she saved on her car. That was almost as much as she made teaching. She had a decent savings, and Matt would always have a steady income at a killer job and take good care of Gus—it was a point of fatherly pride for him—but still, it gave her pause for thought. The perks were amazing.

Nancy was doing well, too. She enjoyed similar perks and women smiled and nodded at them around town. Thank you, they mouthed to Lucy when she was having a pizza slice with Gus or dropping off dry cleaning. To each other, they smiled and said, "Are you in The Program?"

Soon they had twenty-eight wives and seventeen Helpers in The Program, with two lesbian divorcée Helpers available to satisfy the needs of bi-curious wives (with their husband's permission) who had missed their chance to explore their Sapphic side in college. Audra became a minor celebrity, as did Dix and Fran—all on the down low. Everyone was tight-lipped and took her oath seriously. Lucy couldn't believe how well it was working.

Lucy fantasized less about other men these days now that she was getting laid, though seeing more of Peter, oddly, led to more masturbation—about Peter. The instant she closed her eyes he was naked on top of her, making the faces he usually made when they slept together, his hair disheveled, his downy chest slippery with sweat. For some reason she never thought about the other guys in town she'd slept with through The Program. Easy come, easy go— whereas, her chemistry with Peter was maddeningly irrefutable. Even his soft, lazy voice made her smolder with lust. She responded to it like a Pavlovian research subject. The mere sound of his voice on the phone could make her moisten between her thighs. Some-times just the memory of his voice was enough to get her engine rumbling. The fact that he was tall and strong and could lift her up during sex was a bonus.

Occasionally she watched him sleep for the few minutes he al-lowed himself before jumping up and heading out the door. He

looked like a Rodin sculpture lying there—so relaxed, so beautiful. But more than anything it was their banter that drew her in
and kept her coming back. They got each other's jokes; they made
each other chuckle. She thought of Peter foremost as very funny.
The fact that he was physically beautiful to her was helpful, but not
germane to her interest in him. Or was it? Maybe it *all* had to be
there. Maybe women had to be as attracted to men as society was
always saying men needed to be to women. She had mulled over
this theory before, but now she understood.

Peter and Lucy fell into a nice rhythm of one weekday after
school every two weeks when their schedules dovetailed and Gus
had an after-school playdate. After all, she was a busy career gal
and single mother with a new start-up venture to help run and participants to coordinate. Peter ran two robotics clubs. It was just
often enough for both of them. At least that's what she told herself.
If she were truly honest, she would have asked for two or three
times a week with dinner and sleepovers, but that was unrealistic.
So, they had terrific sex in the middle of the afternoon. They fucked
on dining room chairs, couches, kitchen counters and floors. They
had sex in her shower and up against the stairs. Peter carried Lucy
from room to room like a gladiator in a big-budget movie and
they tried new positions and laughed a lot. Lucy rotated through
her pretty new lingerie and some that still fit from her honeymoon,
and unearthed the black lacy contraptions that snapped at the
crotch that she'd bought after college. Peter loved it all and told
her so. Once, when it was raining, Lucy met him at the door naked
under her raincoat. (His sense of humor egged her on.) But after
three months of after-school dalliances, she still hadn't asked him
what his deal was. There was too much that worked that she didn't
want to ruin.

They'd both been AIDS tested recently—Lucy through her

OB/GYN's office and Peter with his yearly physical—so they stopped using condoms. She explained that she couldn't get pregnant and chose to believe him when he said he wasn't sleeping with other women. It was wrong and stupid not to use a condom, but she did it anyway, the same way that her friends would split a bottle of wine then get behind the wheel. *Women meet strangers at bars and take online dates home with them, for heaven's sake.* She felt her judgment was sound. People made risky choices all the time—some were more socially acceptable than others. Lucy was no different.

One day, as things heated up, Peter pulled out a condom. Lucy took it from him and popped it in her mouth, then rolled it onto his stiff cock with her lips. She didn't mention it again until afterwards when she gingerly pulled it off him, tied it in a knot and left it resting on her bedside table. "Condom, eh?" she said as he stood up to get dressed.

"Yeah, well, things were feeling too good there for a while and the Jew in me felt I was due for some homespun guilt."

"You're Jewish? And blonde-ish?"

"Jews are like ice-cream cones. We come in many different flavors." Lucy imagined an ice-cream cone with a little black hat and curly *payot* hanging down on either side of the scoop.

"That would explain your ample *schwantz*," she said. "And the name Peter—"

"After my grandfather. There was some assimilation on my mother's side."

"Got it." Lucy smiled and stretched. She had nowhere to hurry off to so she stared at his beautiful ass as he got dressed.

"Besides," Peter said, "condoms feel soooo good."

"They do?!"

Peter gave Lucy a look. "No. They're awful. Every cliché you've ever heard about raincoats and wool socks are true."

"Then why the change of heart?"

"I don't know. Because I realized you're a hot divorcée and maybe you've got other—let's just say I still don't know you very well. And I just got to thinking about the risks involved, which turned me a little paranoid. But I want to keep seeing you. I didn't think it would be a problem if we were more safe. Is it?"

"Nope, not for me," Lucy said, then rolled over and took a sip of water. Peter was putting on his socks. She hated his socks and wished she could wave a wand and make them disappear. She wanted to reverse the time-space continuum, freeze the clock, anything to be able to make him stop, rip his clothes off, and throw him back down on the bed again—but she knew it was futile.

"Are you this honest with everyone?" Lucy said.

"No. But for some reason I am with you. It's weird. I can tell you anything and you understand. Or don't take it personally. I don't know why that is. I just know I can be totally aboveboard with you. It's bizarre." Lucy chose not to push that comment.

"Maybe because I'm not twenty-six. Or because I have no agenda. Other than sex."

"Ha. Yeah, maybe. How old are you anyway?"

"Not telling," said Lucy.

"Fine," he said, and shook his head and smiled at her. "Well, you have the body of a twenty-eight-year-old."

"Thanks, cowboy. Here's five dollars."

Peter said, "I'll try not to spend it all in one place." He leaned over and gave her one of his lame, thin-lipped kisses. It was perfunctory and bland, like a relative's.

"Your lame going-away kisses are award winning in their lameness. You could literally sweep the Lame Kiss Awards."

"Thanks. I'll work on my speech," Peter said, not looking at Lucy from the doorway.

"You do that," she said.

Swinging her legs over the side of the bed, Lucy caught a glimpse of the knotted condom on the nightstand out of the corner of her eye. Walking into her bathroom for her post-coital cleansing, Lucy stopped, looked at herself in the mirror and thought about how omnipresent the role sperm had played in her life all those years she was trying to conceive a second child. Matt's sperm had been collected and counted, analyzed and washed from here to kingdom come. Lucy had obsessed over his diet and exercise, mulled over boxers and briefs. Sperm was carted to and from labs nestled under armpits and lodged inside bra cups. There were long debates over the timing of sex and conflicting sperm properties and their ability to regenerate and do the *New York Times* crossword puzzle. The introduction of sperm as a supporting character in the Spanish soap opera that had become their lives eventually took on an *Invasion of the Body Snatchers* element of drama, turning Lucy and Matt into spermbots, until one day their quest ended along with their marriage. Matt would be able to have more kids at the snap of a finger. Clearly his fiancée was in her fertile prime.

Then there were the years that followed when Lucy fantasized about having a second child on her own. She imagined she would one day click through profiles, compare eye color and handwriting samples, then pick out some stellar sperm, which would hold the key to her happiness. That sperm would have been a balm for her wounded soul, would have given her a new lease on life and the chance at a "real" family. But first she had to get divorced, get her ESL certificate and a better job to make more money. Matt was sure as hell not going to support a stepsibling for Gus. She might have to move in with her mother.

Then Lucy was switched from fifth grade down to third, which meant a whole new curriculum and classroom library and here we were, three years later—her dreams of adopting or impregnating herself with random sperm dismissed the way one dismisses a vacation plan that's unaffordable folly. *What was I thinking,* she thought, as Gus turned six, then seven. *I'm too old/tired/single/ill-equipped to have another child.* And with that final assessment of her lot in life, the magical elixir of sperm—her Holy Grail—turned back into that sticky warm goo in the condom.

Warm.

Huh, Lucy thought. *Is Peter's sperm still warm?*

She walked back to the nightstand, picked up the condom and rolled the tip full of sperm between her fingers. It *was* still warm. She remembered that that was key. She looked at the volume. It filled the entire tip plus another half inch. *A nice, healthy shot,* she thought. *That's a good sign.* Then she wondered how its motility and anatomy measured up, and actually held the condom up to the overhead light. Maybe she would see the twinkling eyes of teeny wiggling sperm wrestling and jousting like sea monkeys in an aquarium. Could this be a sign? From God? Lucy didn't think she was anywhere near ovulating, but if there's one thing she'd learned about the female reproductive odyssey: There were exceptions to every rule and stories of women getting pregnant at nearly all phases of their cycle, not just ovulation.

What the hell am I thinking? was her next thought. *I can't be serious.* Then she tossed the condom into the wastepaper basket, where it landed on top of a soap wrapper. *That's hundreds of dollars worth of grade-A sperm I just threw away. The sperm of a man who is healthy, smart and funny. And can recite the periodic table of elements. Is it technically my sperm?* she wondered. *He didn't want it. If he'd wanted it, he would have taken it with him. Or thrown it away. But he left it on the nightstand. My nightstand. So, now it's mine, right? Am I delusional? Is this how criminals think? Is this because Delphine's pregnant? No, this is fortuitous happenstance. A happy accident on top of an already good life. It's a cosmic reward!* Lucy knew that the lobe of her brain that conjures rationalizations was nearly steam-whistling with denial, it was working so hard. How could she even be having these thoughts?

How could she not.

Oh, for heaven's sake, she thought, *lesbians impregnate themselves with turkey basters all the time. No one would have to know it's Peter's child, and by the time the baby is old enough to look like him we would either be a couple or friends or no longer dating, in which case, what's the diff if he knows or not? If I'm going to raise a baby on my own either way, and sperm is sperm whether it comes from a computer profile or a random hook-up then . . . holy shit*—Lucy stopped herself. *I've gone off the deep end. I have lost my rational mind.*

Lucy switched off her brain and went downstairs to the kitchen—too much chatter. This sperm was liquid gold and she'd been conditioned to not squander it. She rummaged in a drawer for a turkey baster then went back up to her bedroom. Having annexed all rational thought, she could now concentrate on the DIY science experiment-y angle of her project. She knew it would never work, so why not give it a go? Lucy found herself suctioning up the contents of the condom as best she could. Lying on her bed, she spread her legs, inserted the baster gently into her vagina then squeezed the rubber ball at its end. It didn't make much of a sound and she felt nothing, but she propped her torso up into a shoulder stand and rested on her elbows for good measure.

Up in that shoulder stand Lucy thought about how she would explain this to her daughter. Other folks she could evade—it was none of their business—but she knew she couldn't look her seven, twelve, thirty-year-old daughter in the eye and lie. One day she would have to tell her that she didn't make love to her bio-dad, but confiscated his sperm without his permission. Like a well-meaning sociopath. Then impregnated herself with a kitchen utensil. Her daughter would be horrified then devastated, and probably chuck her moral compass out the window as well. Straight to the pole. Or meth addiction. If there ever were a more direct road to ruin, Lucy didn't know of one. Plus she would never be able to make a Thanksgiving turkey. This had been a very bad idea. A person can enjoy only so much risk before she runs out of luck. Lucy was thinking that maybe deep down she believed luck was finite; there was only so much of it—so like wild cards in a deck she would have to choose her acts of anarchy wisely. Or there was a time limit on luck, so she had to binge while she could. What started out as an adventure, Lucy was realizing, could also be seen as a heinous act of immorality. Possibly even a crime. On so many levels. Affecting numerous innocent people. She felt terrible. And very wrong.

Lucy rolled off the bed and jumped up and down a few times so that whatever sperm was on its way up the vaginal canal would be bounced and shaken back down to the entrance like dizzy kids after a carnival ride. Then she knelt down on the ground at the side of her bed and begged God for forgiveness. *I'm sorry, so sorry, so very, very sorry. It was a bad, dumb idea and I take full responsibility. Never again, I promise. It was unacceptable, inexcusable, wrong, and I'm sorry.*

Then Lucy got up and turned on the shower, swatting away thoughts that she secretly hoped it had worked.

Chapter 18

Lucy was a little more tired than usual at work but that was okay, she rallied. Her students kept her on her toes, and they were heading into testing season, so the curriculum was pretty much preset. She didn't get the chance to do laundry as often, either, now that she had a side business, and a semiboyfriend, but that was okay, too. She just bought more underwear for Gus—five pairs for twenty bucks at the mall. When one of Lucy's Program wives heard her joke about it to Nancy at a hockey game, all her laundry was washed and folded within the week by her nanny. Lucy's fridge and freezer were stocked with delicious homemade foods, and one of her Program wives sent her maid over to clean her house. She was loving her new car and her new haircut and highlights and marveled at how quickly she'd acclimated to the good life.

The next divorcée dinner they had was at Audra's *Architectural Digest* house of perfection, where their evening's takeout containers on the dining room table always made it look like Gypsies had broken in and were squatting there illegally. Lucy checked in with her friends, going around the table clockwise. Dix, Fran and Audra were all much happier lately as a result of The Program; they were getting laid and having fun. Everyone was adamant about not gossiping or comparing notes on husbands. Audra tried at one point, but Fran cut her off and reminded her that she was still under oath. Fran took oaths very seriously, probably as a result of all the courtroom dramas she watched on TV.

Having said that, The Divorcées could confide if it was important. Lucy and Nancy had told The Helpers that if they ever felt unsafe or compromised in any way, they should tell one of them and further action would be taken, which would result in a stern talking-to and, if necessary, expulsion. So far, all the husbands had behaved themselves beautifully, were enthusiastic pleasers and generous lovers. No one wanted to risk expulsion, and Nohquee was still a very small town. One husband was a closeted gay man whose wife thought that he just wasn't attracted to her. When he got together with Audra twice a week, they talked about fashion and looked through her closet. Audra told Nancy and Lucy, who of course kept mum, but Lucy started thinking. She decided to gauge the crowd. Lucy said, "What about the husbands who don't want to have sex with their wives, for whatever reason? Would it be impossible to get divorced guys to be available for the sex-starved wives?"

Audra was the first to speak. "That's another business. Someone else's problem."

Dix said, "I'll do what I can," with her trademark smirk. Two wives had tried out Dix in the sack, with their husbands' permission. One never did it again; the other made Dix her regular.

Lucy said, "Guy helpers, Dix, not bi-helpers. You're already that. I'm just saying that there may be women out there who aren't necessarily tired of sex—they're just tired of sex with their husbands. Or perhaps aren't getting any from their husbands and want some." She was thinking about Kit.

Fran said, "Are there straight men out there who don't want sex?"

Dix said, "More than you know, but no one talks about it."

Audra said, "They might be depressed, or on antidepressants, or alcoholics, drug addicts or addicted to porn."

Dix said, "Or were abused as kids, or Catholic. Or a combo of any of those. I knew someone—"

Audra said, "Everyone knows someone. It's the last big secret out there."

Lucy said, "So why don't we—"

Audra said, "Because it would never work. The Program works because everyone's in on it; all parties grant permission. We don't want to condone women sneaking around on their husbands and few husbands are going to condone their wives sleeping with another man even if he doesn't want to—"

Dix said, "Some will."

Audra said, "Not enough to support a small town program. Few enough wives admit to the issue as is. Then we would have to find a stable of divorced men who'll have sex with women their own age—"

Lucy said, "An infinitesimal subset. I get it."

Audra continued, "It's not for us. That's another program for someone else to run."

Lucy said, "Fine, you're right. I told The Marrieds almost the same thing when they asked me about guys for them to sleep with. Can anyone see their way around this?" No one said boo. "Case closed." The room nodded. Lucy decided to pose another hypothetical to the crowd. "Here's another one: What if someone were to use the sperm in a leftover condom to get herself pregnant?"

"Without his knowledge? You mean after he's left the building?" said Audra.

"Yeah. They have sex, he leaves, then she empties the sperm into her vagina."

"Is this a new business model?" said Dix.

"No, just a hypothetical," said Lucy. "Off topic."

"Are you *deranged*?!" said Fran. "No *way* is that cool!"

Lucy clarified that she wasn't talking about any of the husbands in The Program. They all groaned. "We know," they overlapped.

"I'm not talking about *Peter* either! *Or me*! It's just a hypothetical," said Lucy.

"Yeah, right," said Dix.

"No one should do that," said Fran. "It's bad karma."

"I don't know," said Audra. "Men donate sperm. My brother, Federico, did it in college. What's the difference if she chooses Peter's number in a clinic or grabs it off the nightstand?"

"Permission!" said Fran. "Permission is the difference! Have you gone morally AWOL?"

"Is this because Delphine's pregnant?" said Audra.

"No, it's just a thought I had, jeez," Lucy said. "I would be pretty pathetic if I made all my biggest life choices in reaction to Matt's." Lucy still worried in her deepest core that that's why she did it, but pushed the thought away. She didn't give a rat's ass what he did with his life anymore. Thank God for that. "I was just trying to stir up some lively debate. You can all relax. I was just wondering if anyone had ever heard of someone getting pregnant that way and what you all thought about it. We can't talk about our sex lives and I don't want to start talking about our lame health issues like The Marrieds do. Or our kids."

Fran said, "Agreed. I don't care about any of your kids, and you don't have to care about mine. That's my job. Unless you have a real issue or want help. But if it's just to tell me about their sports schedules, I swear, the next time a playdate mom recounts for me *each* of her children's *entire* schedules in crippling detail, I'm going to vomit into her mouth."

"That'll win you friends on the PTA," said Audra.

"These mothers and their fucking kids' schedules. There ought to be a law."

Dix said, "We *have* a law," then counted them off on her fingers, "No kids, carpools, scheduling or sports. No health issues, nanny issues, zoning laws or in-laws. No car or house repair complaints, tedious workout stories or lice monologues. We have e-mail for genuine questions. Or a dollar goes in the jar."

"What jar?" said Audra.

"The jar," Fran pointed to her temple, "in my head."

Dix straightened and in a boardroom voice said, "Are everyone's kids basically fine?"

They all responded, "Yes!" in unison.

Dix said, "Fantastic. Next topic."

Fran said, "How about that teacher scandal?"

Dix said, "Yawn. They were both off school grounds and adults. How about current events or travel? Music or famous fascist leaders? What's the Supreme Court up to, Fran? C'mon, Audra, you had a brain before you had kids? What did you used to talk about?"

"Food and sex."

Lucy said, "All right then. Who's got a tasty recipe for crème brûlée or how 'bout an international trade embargo story they'd like to share? Who's read what lately?"

But Audra wanted to keep talking about the sperm. She and Dix eventually said that they thought it was fine, but that Lucy would kill herself to start over at this age with a newborn—and *diapers*! Fran was horrified at the thought and admonished Lucy severely. Lucy reminded them that it was just a hypothetical and quickly changed to a new subject, which should have been easy but was still harder now that they no longer talked about sex. There was a heated discussion over the latest shooting scandal and whether to have an indoor or outdoor cat, and there was a robust discussion about art forgery, the bee problem, and what books they were all reading—fiction, natch. Things always got lively over books.

When Lucy got home, Ted was lurking in her backyard, sitting in one of the swings on the swing set in his work clothes.

"Ted, what are you doing here? You know we're not scheduled to—"

"I know. I just . . ." He couldn't finish his sentence, yet something told Lucy this was serious.

"Wait here while I pay the babysitter, then we can talk."

Lucy paid the sitter and checked on Gus. She grabbed a big comfy fleece and zipped it all the way up to her chin, then headed outside. She sat on the bouncy swing next to Ted. "Have you been here long?" she asked.

"No," he said.

"Are you and Nancy okay?"

"Um, yes. Actually, it's better, but it's still . . . I don't know . . . I was thinking . . ."

Lucy spoke with an admonishing tone. "Ted, does Nancy know you're here?"

"No."

"Well then why are you—have you seen a doctor about something?"

"No."

"Oh, thank goodness. Is it—did you tell someone you shouldn't have?"

"No, it's not that."

"Ted, please don't make me guess. I'm too cold for this. Wait."

Then Lucy got it.

"Ted, are you here because you think you have feelings for me?" He said nothing.

"Ted, you're going to have to talk to me with your mouth, not your invisible mind rays."

"Yes," he said.

"Yes, what?"

"Yes, I've been thinking about you a lot." Ted looked up at Lucy when he said this.

"Oh, Jesus," Lucy said, and shook her head. Then she rubbed her face in her hands. *Think, think, think. Oh, shit.* "Have you told Nancy?!" She tried to ratchet down the volume.

"No."

"Where does she think you are?" Lucy said. She was in full panic.

"Working late."

"Ughhhh. Godammit, Ted, you are *this close* to fucking everything up. Now, listen to me. We are *not* having an affair. We are *just* having sex. It's like a root canal only it feels better. That's all it is, get it?"

"But me and Nance . . . I don't feel . . ." He was muttering, barely audible. Ted looked down at his shiny workingman shoes as he spoke. He looked like a big, sad kid playing dress up in his father's suit.

Lucy went off. "Feel *schmeel*! You feel exactly like you're supposed to about someone you've been married to for eighteen years. You're bored and underserved sexually. Well, no duh. Take it up with the church, or our ludicrous, puritanical, North American mores. But do *not* take it out on Nancy. *Talk* to Nancy. She loves you—and you love her—and you are *damn* lucky to have her. And you're uber lucky that she's arranged for you to have sex with me. *What an amazing woman!* You should be thanking your lucky stars!" Lucy rubbed her arms and began to pace. "Honestly? I can't believe this is happening. You think you're going to give up your marriage because you're falling in love with me? Sex is not love. You don't love me. I'm no different than your wife. One day you'll walk in on me bleaching my mustache in filthy sweats and I'll say, 'When are you gonna call the guy to fix the thing?' and you'll realize what all men realize three years into their second marriages with their trophy wives: same shit, different face. And what makes you think I even want you? Why do all men assume a single woman wants them? Why do all married women assume a single woman wants her husband? Believe you me, I'm *not* living through another man spending all weekend on the couch watching sports when there's housework to be done and a child to play with. Been there, done that. So you stick with your wife and have sex with me, and I'll stick with my life and have sex with you. Got it? I won't kick you out of The Program, because then Nancy will have to know why, but I will if you don't knock it off."

Ted didn't say anything. Lucy stopped pacing and looked directly at him. "It's only sex. Can you say that?"

Ted stared down and kicked a filthy tennis ball out of the oval of dirt worn bare beneath him.

Lucy said, "Love is listening and caring and supporting each other and 'how was your day?' and—are you with me, here? Okay, on second thought—no more sex with me."

Ted looked up. "Aww, c'mon," he pleaded.

"Oh, so you speak, do you? I'm going to tell Nancy that she's got to choose another Helper because my plate is full with school and Peter and running interviews. And don't you act all hurt puppy dog. Better yet, tell her you're getting bored with me, that I'm lousy in the sack."

"But you suck my—"

"Other women will suck your precious dick, don't worry. Jeez.

You men and your dicks. You've been brainwashed by your own anatomy. It's like the *Manchurian Candidate* around here. Is there anything you wouldn't do for a blow job?"

Ted looked at her blankly. She figured either the *Manchurian Candidate* reference threw him, or he was honestly racking his brain to see if he could come up with something he wouldn't do for a blow job and couldn't think of anything.

"Have we got a deal, Ted?" He said nothing. "Ted, tell your brain to move your mouth in the 'yes' formation."

"Yes," he said.

"Now go home and do *not* tell Nancy you were here or that we had this conversation. Your sex life depends on it. Got it? She will *freak out*. Do you read me?"

Ted nodded then said, "Who's Peter?"

"*He's my boyfriend!* I have a boyfriend, Ted! You're just a business arrangement. Go home and don't come back here again. You're in strict violation. I should kick you out of The Program for this."

"Lucy, please—"

"Yeah, yeah, I know, I know. Good night. Go home."

Lucy went inside and shut and locked the back door, but as mad as she was at him, she still left the backyard light on. Ted sat on the swing set for another long minute looking dazed, then left. Lucy watched him go. *Poor guys,* she thought, *they really do love their wives. They just need more sex. With different vaginas. It's not even that they need it so much as they don't know how to not need it. And it's not with every man, but it is with lots of them. And women for that matter. It's the way we were designed in order to propagate the species. It's reflexive. It's coded. It sucks.*

Lucy listened to her voice-mail messages. There was one from Nancy. One of the husbands, Antonio, thought he was in love with Audra. Apparently three weeks of new sex after fifteen or so years

of monogamy was all these dorks needed to think they were falling in love. Idiots. Antonio's wife, Akiko, was pulling Antonio from
The Program effective immediately. Fantastic, Lucy thought, and
called Audra. She said, "I just left your house, like, an hour ago,
why didn't you say anything to me about Antonio."

"What's to say?" Audra said. "He has a big cock. I thought we
weren't supposed to talk about—"

"Are you aware that Antonio thinks he's in love with you and
Akiko is pulling him from The Program?" asked Lucy.

"I don't speak Italian. I don't know what he's saying when I have
my mouth on—"

"Well, apparently he's been waxing rhapsodic about leaving his
wife for you."

"I just assumed he was saying that he liked what I was doing to
him. He talks *a lot.*"

Lucy said, "What were you doing to him?"

"This thing I read in *Cosmo* about rubbing the perineum—you
know that little space between the ball sack and the anus—while
he comes. He was mad for it. You can learn a lot about sex from
Cosmo. It's a shame that just when we can finally use all that sex
information with some degree of competency, we're too old for
the magazine. If it weren't for my monthly pedicures, I'd never
read about sex. *The New Yorker* needs to have more articles about
sex ed."

Lucy said, "I don't think that's gonna happen. Look, you can
keep rubbing all the perineums you want, but make sure these guys
know that you're not running away with them and that they're not
leaving their wives. Learn how to say it in every language, all right?"

"*Certo,*" said Audra.

"Yeah, *ciao bella,* yourself," Lucy said, and hung up.

Chapter 19

- -

The Program was growing, but there were fires that needed to be put out, which was making Lucy cranky. She had to convince Akiko to let Audra call and convince Antonio that he was not in love with her and that under no circumstance was he to leave his wife. Audra learned some Italian so that she could tell him, *"Non lasciare tua moglie per me. Io non ti amo."* (Do not leave your wife for me. I do not love you.) But he didn't care. It only made him want her more. Once he heard her speak his native language he shot back in rapid-fire Italian that she was the most breathtaking creature he had ever seen since Botticelli's angels. Audra just told him she was hanging up. Akiko didn't speak Italian, but picked up on his sentiment and allegedly pulled him from The Program with an irate phone call to Lucy only seconds later. Lucy had not anticipated an emotional outburst directed at her in Japanese, but figured she would have done the same thing, too, if she were in the same pickle. It had been quite the international night of drama.

Laura, Vashna and Kit followed suit. They had various reasons for pulling out. For all of Laura's open-minded sex-toy-capades, she was too conservative to let her husband "stick it to other women," as she put it. The old-world Italian in her said *basta* and that was that. Vashna's husband's experience with Fran did exactly what it was supposed to do and snapped him out of his penchant for American women. Vashna was so pleased that she promised to send homemade curry chicken and naan to Lucy and Nancy for a month and with no more use for The Program, quit. Kit dropped out soon thereafter. She was skittish around Lucy and made condescending jokes about The Program. (Because of Lucy's popularity? To downplay her sexual issues with Fwank? Lucy wasn't entirely sure.) Lucy overlooked the comments and hoped that in doing so their friendship would rebound to its original groove, not to mention Kit's marriage, as long as they didn't talk about either. Kit was a big part of her life and nothing was worth losing her friendship over.

There were still plenty of satisfied participants in The Program, and a few more joined every few weeks. Lucy started to notice that the good marriages, the ones where the husband and wife were best friends, could navigate the tricky emotional landscape with fun and relative ease. Those were usually the wives with a sense of humor and an even greater sense of self, they were just superbusy or wanted to liven things up, try something new. That's why Gina was still in The Program. She knew that she and Duncan were fated, solid and good. She also understood his needs and her capacity to service him and didn't take their sexual discord personally. Having him in The Program gave them something to talk about on date night and spiced up their sex life. She even broached the subject of finding a boy toy for her, which she informed the girls Duncan was supposedly "possibly open to." Nancy said that having Ted in The Program was good for her sex life, too. She said it made them more creative and that they tried harder. Nancy never asked him to divulge anything he didn't want to, and as long as his Helper didn't cook for him, she was fine. Though she did scale back from two nights a month to one.

The Helpers were happy as well. Fran amassed a trunk full of props and costumes, so Lucy and Nancy sent all the role-players to her. Often upon meeting Fran, they hesitated at her large, boxy form and tough countenance, but by the time she got through with them as Wonder Woman or Nurse Ratched, they couldn't get enough. Dix had a similar effect on her participants with her athleticism and hijinks, and Audra continued to bathe in her own luster. Her constant demand freed her up to drop Howard and a few other ne'er-do-wells from her personal stable. Tarrique, she kept around. Lucy took on another guy, Morris, who was the husband of the local prosecuting attorney, Jill. Jill was a tough broad and not someone to be trifled with in any way, so Lucy was glad when Jill chose her to work with her husband, since she didn't want this one in the hands of anyone else. When Morris followed up his extreme performance anxiety by preferring to chat about moisturizers and toile wallpaper patterns, she pretty much figured he was gay.

Birthday treats, dry-patch jumpstarts, last-ditch attempts; everyone had their own reasons for trying out The Program, and the reactions Lucy received in town from the results were mostly good. Gus started to ask why so many grown-ups were winking and mouthing "Thank you" to Lucy in the supermarket, so she told him that she was sometimes what's known as a baby whisperer who helped mommies and daddies get their babies to sleep at night. They were just showing their appreciation for all the peace that she had brought to the household, which she felt was what she and

Nancy had done, in their own way. Lucy was just happy to be getting laid.

At the end of the week, Nancy stopped by to borrow Lucy's hedge trimmer just as Peter was due to arrive. She had her youngest in the car and the motor was still running, but ignored all that to discuss Ted. Lucy rummaged in the garage for the trimmer so she wouldn't have to make eye contact. She knew exactly where the trimmer was kept.

Nancy followed her. "Ted wants a new Helper."

Lucy said, "Fine, no problem."

"Your feelings aren't hurt?"

"No, I don't take it personally. It's just sex."

"Are you sure there's nothing going on between you and Ted?"

Lucy was slightly panicked. "No. Absolutely not. Why, did he say there was?"

Nancy pressed, "Is there?"

"No!" said Lucy, maybe a little too loudly. Maybe not loudly enough. "Nancy, what's going on? And make it quick, I have an appointment." Lucy downplayed the concern, hoping to dissolve it.

"It's just that he was happy with you, and I trust you the most, and now he says he wants to switch to someone else and he won't tell me why."

"I'll tell you why: He wasn't holding his hard-on with me and he's probably embarrassed to tell you. It's no biggie. It's just because he's conflicted, which is a good thing. Means he loves you. Now, amscray."

Peter pulled up in his car and waited. Nancy noticed and then looked accusingly at Lucy. Peter stayed in his car. Nancy gave Lucy the once-over and said, "You look awfully dressy for a Wednesday afternoon. Who's that?"

"He's not in The Program," Lucy said, and then realized that was the wrong thing to say.

"It's Peter, isn't it?" said Nancy.

"No, now go away. I only have a little time."

"Because he's married, you fool. Why else won't he get out of his car? A-doy."

"Just go," Lucy said, and Nancy bugged her eyes at Lucy as she took the trimmer. Lucy chose to ignore Nancy as she watched her pull out of the driveway with a screaming child in the back seat and awful plinkety-plunkety music at full volume. *That's probably why he's crying*, she thought to herself. *Kiddie music sucks!* She imagined his little baby mind wailing. *You want soothing? Try The Mills Brothers.*

"You're an id-i-ot," Nancy sang back over her shoulder as she pulled away.

"I know you are but what am I?" Lucy sang back from the front stoop, then ducked inside to text Peter to come in.

Peter got out of his car and sauntered up to the house. Lucy was wearing a strappy flowered sundress and a push-up bra that worked miracles. She was also having a good hair day, but something was off with her mood. Her conscience was getting in the way, which she knew was because of what Nancy said. Lucy stood blocking Peter in the doorway, but he ducked under her arm to get inside the house. She turned as he walked towards her. "Mmm," he said, and put his hands on her hips, pulling her into him for a steamy kiss, but she pulled away. Lucy had been put on the defensive by Nancy and was pissed at Ted for being such a shitty actor, pissed that Nancy almost found out about Ted and had busted her with Peter. She was pissed at Kit for not supporting her and pissed at Peter for probably being married. The upshot of all of this pissed-offed-ness was that she spoke without thinking.

"Are you married?" Lucy said, looking straight at him, hands on hips.

"What?"

"Are. You. Married," she said. Her stern face said it all.

"Do you really want to know?"

"Well, now I know, don't I? I knew it," Lucy said, and began to pace. "Actually, my friends knew it before I did. How about them apples?"

"You told them about me?" he said.

"Yeah, it's what women do with their girlfriends when they start dating a nice, funny, handsome, available guy. They *tell* them."

"You *told* them?" he said.

"Hey, jerky, this is about me for the time being. We'll get to you in a minute."

Peter clearly wanted to disappear but sat down on the couch with a sigh of resignation. Lucy's voice jumped half an octave, and the speed with which she spoke neared that of a sports radio announcer covering the Preakness. "I knew it that day in the woods when your sneaker got wet. I thought, why would a guy flip out over a dumb wet shoe unless he doesn't want anyone to know or have to explain? And we never met at your house and you were never available for dinner and then that day you used a condom—how long have you been married? No, don't tell me. No, do tell me. Dammit, tell me everything. And then tell me why you didn't tell me."

Peter spoke. His voice was small. "You said you didn't want to know."

"I did say that, didn't I? You should have told me anyway. No, you're right. I asked you not to tell me. But now I want to know. How long have you been married?"

"Six years."

"*Six years?!* Do you have any kids? Please say you don't have any kids."

"Three."

"*Three kids?!*"

"Twin five-year-olds and a three-year-old."

"Peter what the hell! Why the fuck?!"

"Because they sleep in the same bed with us every night!"

"So man up and kick them out of your bed!" Lucy was pissed.

"I've tried, but my wife won't." Peter was pissed, too.

"Try harder. Jesus, Peter."

"You don't understand. We are *never* alone."

"So get a babysitter!"

"We don't get babysitters because my wife doesn't trust anyone— not even my mom, who's a retired nurse and raised six kids—and we almost never have sex anymore. Ever. And if we do it's lame and fast and I have to beg for it. It takes my wife an hour to put them to bed."

Lucy said, "I cannot believe I'm hearing you say the words, 'my wife.'"

"Then she lies down with them and falls asleep!"

"Sounds like she's avoiding you. What time do the kids go upstairs to bed?"

"Nine, nine-thirty," he said.

"That's too late! Your kids' bedtimes are killing your marriage. That's why she's too tired for sex. And they need more sleep. Google it, for crying out loud. This is an easy fix."

"I've tried. She says they can't fall asleep without her."

"That's bull and they need to learn. Maybe you're not a good lover. Are you generous? Do you try to please her? Every time? Do you get hard?"

"Yes! I try! I do! I love my wife, or I think I still do, but I hate my life. Not my kids, I love my kids but I hate . . . I don't know. Everything. But when I saw you at that convention . . ."

"You must have been married by then."

"Yes."

"But you flirted with me!"

"Because I thought I was dying inside."

"You were *dying*?!"

"No, I'm not dying. You don't understand. For a guy, being married is like going through the seven stages of death. Denial, anger, depression, denial . . ."

"Oh, *for chrissakes*," said Lucy, "that's horseshit. Grow up. Get it together."

"*It's true!* But most guys won't tell you that. They're not allowed. And then I saw you and I'm always happy when I see you. And you're always happy to see me. And you smell good and look pretty and I used to think of you, did you know that? When I masturbated. And sometimes just when I saw something funny I thought of you and then when you e-mailed me I was so excited, and I hadn't been excited about anything in a long time."

Lucy felt her head start to buzz and her teeth chatter ever so slightly. She was so mad at him, so angry with herself and enraged at the universe for putting her in this position. Dammit, why couldn't he be single? Why was she being tortured? She kept listening but it was as if she were hearing everything through a large, glass tube. She thought she might be having some kind of old-fashioned fit. Would she actually faint? It was hard to breathe.

Peter paced. His voice jumped a pitch and got louder. "One of the main reasons guys get married is so that they can have sex whenever they want. Then the *one* woman they want to have the *most* sex with *stops* having sex with them. It's torture. And I don't even get to sleep next to her because the kids are in the way, and the *friggin' cats*! And my balls are so blue that I want to shoot them off. *Who the fuck invented cosleeping?!* I want to *kill* that bastard!"

"Shhh, you're shouting," Lucy whispered.

"I know, I'm sorry. I just. I'm sorry." Peter held his hands up to his face. Lucy and Peter were standing now at opposite ends of the room. They took a moment to look at each other. She was so mad at him for deceiving her but knew she was complicit and accountable, which made her even more livid at herself. She hated him but was still attracted to him. It was that damn hair. And those stupid blue eyes with the green flecks, and the little gap between his teeth. She still wanted him, the jackass. She groped for solutions. For excuses.

"Isn't your wife funny and sexy?" she said.

"Sort of. Not really. She can be, though. She was before we had kids. I don't know. She's in toxicology research for a pharmaceutical—really smart. She's got things that you don't have and you've got things that she doesn't have."

Lucy wanted to slug him. "Sounds like we make a good team, your wife and I. Should we all become Mormon?"

Peter said, "You don't understand. Men settle. I did it. Most men do. I sized myself up and said, 'I'm about a solid six. What's the best woman I can get for the job I have and the money I make and my looks and personality?' Then I looked around to see who was out there in the six range and I settled. Hell, I think I even nabbed a seven, but I'll always want a ten."

"That's horrible. It sounds like you're shoe shopping."

"More like outdoor-grill shopping. You know you can't afford the best, so you make do with one of the lesser models. But it's a good grill. It's a great grill. It does what it needs to do and you're happy with it. But you never stop wanting the top of the line. You never stop comparing your grill to your neighbor's."

"Okay, stop. This is absurd and it's cliché. And now your wife is an outdoor grill. Christ," said Lucy. She'd already found the loophole in their marriage—the cosleeping, the late bedtimes and no sitters—all that was left was to explain to the voice inside her that was screaming, *Get out! Get away from him! He's awful and you're a monster!*

Peter said, "But it's okay, really. I love my wife. And we make a good team. I'm just not in love with her. I don't think I ever was."

"Then why did you marry her?"

"Because it was time. Because she's a good person and I didn't think I could do any better. Because I don't want to grow old alone. Because I thought that she'd make a good mother. Because she doesn't mind that I don't drive a BMW and never will. I sure as shit didn't know she'd want to have our kids sleeping in the same bed with us, between us, every friggin' night of our lives. Wish I'd known *that* ahead of time, would have been useful information. And she was pretty but not gorgeous, which was good because a man shouldn't marry a woman who's too sexy because then he'll spend his life expecting her to leave him for a more successful guy. Because men are basically insecure and pathetic, and want to be taken care of."

Lucy looked at him. "That is insecure and pathetic. And the worst advice. How can a smart guy with so much self-awareness have so little confidence? How can you be such a douche bag? I trusted you." But Lucy knew that deep down she hadn't completely. He looked insecure and pathetic to her for the first time. She said, "I hate you. Who do you think you are? You don't have that much control. *She could still leave you for someone else.* It's all a crapshoot. You married the wrong woman for the wrong reasons and you think that gives you license to cheat?"

"My point is, people marry for love all the time and end up getting divorced. So I married for practical reasons and we'll see if it works. I met you too late. I wish I hadn't."

Lucy was incredulous. "So it's all one grand experiment to you?"

"Yeah. But isn't it for everyone?" Peter asked. He was serious.

"Sure, but in most cases *the wife is in on the experiment*! I can't believe the conversation we're having. I can't believe this is my life. You're an asshole."

"Yeah," Peter said, and sighed heavily.

Lucy slumped to the floor in front of her couch. "And I'm an asshole," she said quietly. She hated everyone and everything in that moment, especially herself. She felt rejected by normalcy and love while aching for it immensely. She felt punished by the world and deeply, deeply alone. She wanted to be held and rocked while she cried; she wanted to curl up and die.

Peter sat against the cabinet across from her. Lucy's throat tightened and her stomach began to revolt. She wanted to run and scream and punch him and fuck him, all at the same time, but all she could do was sit there and look at him. He had such nice hands for an asshole. And she was no better. Deep down she'd known all along he was married. Couple of assholes, they were. Peter spoke tentatively. "Do you remember in *Groundhog Day* when Bill Murray says, 'I had a day once—it was in Acapulco. I went swimming and ate lobster, then made love to a beautiful woman on the beach. Why couldn't that be the day that I have over and over?' But instead he has to relive that shitty, cold day in that stupid town with all those idiots he's stuck with. Do you remember that line?"

Lucy mustered, "No."

"Well," Peter said, "you're my Acapulco."

Lucy looked at him as tears welled in her eyes. She thought it was one of the loveliest things anyone had said about her in a long time, even if it was a stolen line from a movie. She'd never been anyone's Acapulco. She doubted if Matt had ever felt that way about her. Maybe a long time ago, when they first began dating, when he told her that he missed her when he slept. But perhaps never. Now that she knew that men sized women up and settled for what they thought they could get, maybe she had been Matt's consolation prize all along. Maybe he had been hers.

"We have to stop seeing each other," she said.

"Okay," Peter said.

"*Okay!?!*" she snapped. Lucy was indignant. Conflicting emotions vied for dominion.

Peter said, "Well, what do you want me to say? I get it! *I'm a dirtbag!*"

"The douchiest bag of them all," said Lucy.

"Okay, the dirtiest."

"I said, douchiest."

"Okay," said Peter, "I'm the dirtiest douchiest. Look, I'm just trying to be understanding."

"Well, *stop*! Jesus. I don't buy it now. *How* can you love two people at once?"

"I don't know what to tell you, Lucy. People are complicated."

"Men are *not* complicated," Lucy said, and kicked him in the shin as hard as she could, just to hurt him. "That is *bullcrap*."

"Ow. Okay, okay. Look, I never said that I loved you."

Lucy kicked him again harder.

"Ow!" The statement stung. Lucy knew that she was just his escape and nothing more. She was crushed and knew she would have to pull herself out of denial into Grown-up Land, fast. *Somebody throw me a line*, she thought. But there was no one there.

Peter said, "People have more than one child and they love them all. So, it's doable. We're designed to love more than one person."

Lucy thought a moment. "Do you think you could tell your wife about me?"

Peter looked at her like she was the mayor of Crazyville. "Uh, no."

Lucy pleaded. "Can't you just say, 'Look, sweetie, I love you and the kids and want to grow old with you but there's this other woman—just a friend—and I'd like to have sex with her from time to time.'"

Peter said, "I don't think she'll go for it. And it doesn't sound like you could handle it either."

Lucy supposed he was right. It was crazy talk and she was clearly flailing. "The desperate ravings of a madwoman," Lucy said. She had finally run out of ideas.

"Marriage is so fucked up," she said. "We have to stop seeing each other. I'm not *that girl*. I'm not anybody's mistress—" here Lucy made a distinction in her mind between being a sanctioned Helper, and an unsanctioned lover, "—and I have too much respect for marriage," which, she felt she did. "I was married, too, and I *never* cheated on my husband. It's nonnegotiable, we have to break up."

"Okay," Peter said, this time with more empathy. They sat there on the floor for a bit. Lucy took off her shoes and Peter ran his hand through his Hollywood hair.

He said, "Starting now?"

"Yes, starting now," Lucy said. "And yes, breakup sex is out of the question! Jeez."

"Okay, then I'm going."

"Okay," she said.

"Okay." They both got up slowly. Lucy watched Peter head towards the door.

"Wait," she said, "come back." Peter stopped in his tracks. "Come over here," she said. He walked over to where she was standing. Lucy knew he was hoping he might still get laid. He had joked once that men were like Russian nesting dolls and inside each man, after uncovering layers of dolls—regardless of how chivalrous and kind he is—is a teensy little jerk doll. Some guys have many layers of good stuff and some have just a few, but they all start out with a teensy little wooden jerk inside. The two of them got a big laugh out of that one. At the time Lucy thought it was brutally hilarious. "I need a hug," she said. "A hug from a dirtbag."

"Well, you've come to the right place," said Peter.

She reached up and put her arms around his neck. She liked his smell and thought the pink button-down shirt he'd worn that day looked beautiful on him. He wrapped his arms around Lucy's small body and even leaned his head on top of hers. She closed her eyes to stave off the tears. Above all, Lucy didn't want to cry. She wasn't ten and going to sleepaway camp.

"G'bye. And thanks," she said. "I had a really nice time. You brought me a lot of joy, and I needed that, pal."

"No problem," he said. Lucy waited, cozy and warm in his arms. Peter said nothing.

Lucy looked up and said, "And didn't I bring you joy, too?" then pulled away and punched him again. This time in the shoulder. *He's such an ass.*

"Yes, ow. Thank you for the joy," he said, rubbing his arm.

"Okay. Christ. Now, go," she said, and this time let him leave. She couldn't bear to walk him out.

The moment the door shut Lucy broke into heaving, gasping sobs. She realized she'd been stupid enough to let herself fall in love with him. And that he hadn't, and wouldn't. And she felt stupid and pathetic and sad and lonely. And desperate, let's not forget desperate. Who in their right mind asks a man to ask his wife if it's okay if he has a mistress? The Program had clearly skewed her perception of reality. Lucy felt embarrassed and asked for forgiveness. She cried laps around the dining room table as if she were in mourning, circling, unable to stop moving. *Dammit,* she thought as she grasped the backs of chairs to keep from falling. *Damn, damn, damn. I could have really loved him. And he was perfect for me.* But of course he wasn't, because he was unavailable, in every way conceivable. Lucy slowed down, got a handle on her breathing then flopped onto her couch, getting wet mascara on the upholstery. She couldn't be *that girl* to anyone else's husband, no way. Lucy would have to let him go.

Chapter 20

Everyone arrived seven minutes late to the next married-ladies luncheon at the new restaurant in town. The raspberry brocade drapes and deep-plum carpeting did little to soothe Lucy's dark, anxious mood. Even the comfy upholstered semicircular banquet covered in peach velvet seemed annoying instead of sumptuously plush. Maybe it wasn't exactly anxiety she was feeling, it was more of a low-grade perturbation—if that was even a word—an irkedness, which Lucy knew was definitely not a word. People loved to say, "Oh, you'll meet someone," as if it were some foregone conclusion, but Lucy knew statisticswise her chances were slim. She'd given up this really terrific thing in her life, which worked on a bunch of levels, and now she was alone again. Lucy snapped at the waitress then apologized profusely. Kit noticed.

"Is Matt being a jackass?" asked Kit. She really could be empathetic.

"Yes. Always. But it's not—" said Lucy. Then, "How was the zoning hearing?"

"Nice try," said Kit. "Now why don't you tell me what you were really going to say." Lucy inhaled then looked up at the heavens. *Here goes nuthin'*, she thought. "It's Peter. He's married." They all reacted as if Lucy had missed a free throw at the buzzer in the fourth quarter of the final. Hands flailing, name-calling.

Lucy said, "Okay, knock it off. I don't want to hear it. I broke up with him." Her friends let loose a collective, "Awww. " Kit reached across the table and touched Lucy's arm.

"Douche bag," said Kit.

"You did the right thing," said Gina. "Did you sleep with him?"

Nancy said, "Yeah. You did the right thing. Did you?"

Lucy made a snap decision in that moment to lie. She was mad at her friends for judging her and didn't think they deserved—or could handle—the truth. She said, "No, I didn't sleep with him and I feel miserable, thank you. And I'm alone again. But as long as you're all proud of me for doing the right thing, that's all that matters." Sarcasm dripped from Lucy's every pore.

Gina said, "I didn't ask you to stop seeing him. Don't do it for me."

Nancy said, "Yeah, I think it's fine. I mean it's not *fine*. I think you'd be happier if you were dating someone who's *available*, but if this makes you happy, go for it."

Kit said to Nancy, "How can you say that? How can you condone that behavior when you're a married woman yourself? I want her happy, too, but—"

Gina said, "Fortune sides with she who dares."

Kit, "What nut job said that?"

"Virgil."

"Virgil who? From the pool?"

Nancy said, "Look, obviously I'm all for the 'unexamined life' get-out-of-an-ethical-dilemma-free card, as long as it doesn't lead to a life of crime."

Kit said, "Yeah, hello slippery slope."

Gina said, "Sleeping with a married person is not breaking the law."

Kit said, "But it is sleazy and morally wrong if the wife doesn't know. No offense, Luce, but it is. Too bad you can't get her to join your Program."

"Yeah, ha," said Lucy.

"Did you tell Peter about The Program?"

"Are you kidding? No."

Gina said, "I would consider having an affair if Duncan let himself go. Thank gawd I'm still attracted to him. It's a miracle, I know."

Lucy said, "And you still like each other's company."

"Oh, we do. I like him. I mean, I hate him, too. But we're best friends. I love him."

Lucy said, "See? I think that's key! You like his company and want to sleep with him. You're not just going through the motions."

Gina said, "Oh, we're going through the motions all right. But it's fine. It's fun!"

Kit said, "God, my marriage is like a three-legged race, but we're shackled, not tied. By our kids. It's grueling. And there's no end in sight." Kit laughed weakly.

"Yikes, Kit," said Gina. "Really?"

"I don't know. Sometimes."

Nancy said, "You guys don't cosleep, do you?"

Kit said, "God, no. Are you kidding? No."

Nancy said, "I think that cosleeping jackass who wrote that book should be blamed for most of the infidelity in this country."

"And the divorce," said Kit.

Gina said, "I think the nitwits who accepted his premise that what works in remote preindustrialized African villages works for postindustrialized America are to blame. Shoehorning cosleeping into our modern concept of childrearing—without taking into account the physical needs of modern parents—is shortsighted and naïve. Obviously if a man has to share the marital bed with kids and dogs, and rarely gets laid, infidelity is eventually . . ."

Kit said, "I think cosleeping is one big fat excuse for women to avoid having sex with their husbands and has nothing to do with what's best for their kids. I think there are a lot of men out there who suck in bed and that's why their wives avoid sex. Men should take classes."

Nancy, "Yeah, and porn is not the solution."

Lucy said, "Matt and I never coslept. That wasn't one of our problems. Matt and I were never best friends, though. He didn't believe your spouse was supposed to be your best friend."

Nancy said, "That's because Delphine was his best friend."

Lucy said, "That's true. But, look, Delphine wasn't the problem, my marriage was, and I take full responsibility. Delphine could have been anything: addiction, porn, gambling, whatev. I'm fully accountable. I tried to fix it. I tried to change. It wasn't enough."

Nancy said, "It wasn't all yours to fix, Lucy. Matt had to want to fix it, too."

"Now that you're divorced," Gina paused, "do you still believe in marriage?"

Lucy said, "God, yes! I think it's great when it works. I love being around good marriages—reinforces that I was right to kick Matt out. Ours was not good, for many reasons."

Kit said, "We've got to find you someone available. We need to see you happy."

Lucy said, "I was happy with Peter. Aren't we only responsible for ourselves? I'm not cheating on anyone and I'm not in charge of Peter's wife's happiness. If he wants to sleep with me it's between him and her, right? I'm not accountable for her happiness, am I?"

"Ughh!" Kit said. "Of course you *are*. Karmically, religiously, morally, socially . . ."

Gina said, "I disagree. There's something that Peter's wife needs to learn about herself by being married to a man who sleeps with another woman. The same way Lucy learned a lot about herself by being married to Matt."

Lucy said, "That's true. But what's morality? Why was it invented? Everything had a purpose in biblical times. Was it to keep the serfs in line? Church control? What?"

Gina took a sip of wine then said, "Moral codes arose spontaneously in social systems because there are certain things that we have a personal incentive to do—like drive on the right side of the road, which keeps us alive—but we needed codes to reinforce the incentives for things we didn't want to do, like pay our taxes. Church dogma posits that God laid down the law, but some philosopher bigwigs have suggested that we have a naturally occurring moral instinct. Although we may have since ascribed it to God, the moral instinct came first. 'Do unto others' is a very old concept. It's in place to see to it that we don't hurt those around us because we don't want those same pains visited upon us. The bulk of moral doctrine really is in our best interest if taken to its logical extreme, but we live in a world of complexity and spiritual warfare. There are opposing forces always at odds in all of us that are left to us to navigate."

"Use the force, Luke," said Nancy to no one in particular.

Kit said, "But in this case, right is right and wrong is wrong, right?"

Gina said, "It's rarely that simple, Kit."

Lucy said, "Let's say a man can have what society perceives to be great character. He keeps his word and pays his debts, never cheats on his wife or parks in spots reserved for the disabled. But let's say he never hugs his wife or asks about her day. He spends all his free time online or watching sports and never ever talks or listens to his wife or takes her out to dinner. On the weekends, he ignores his kids. But he never cheats. Is he still a good man? Is that a good marriage?"

"No," they all said in unison.

Lucy said, "So, across town there's another guy who fully participates in his marriage and the raising of his children. He gives to charities and coaches Little League. He builds birdhouses with his kids and goes camping and attends church with his family. He tells his wife that he appreciates her and they laugh and make love. He wants more sex than she does so he takes care of the deficit on his own time. Maybe he never tells her because who really wants to know? Especially if everything else is working. He never spends a dime on his lover or forsakes his family for her timewise. Does that wife have a good marriage? Can he still be a good man?"

No one spoke up right away. Kit ran her finger around the rim of her glass while Nancy refolded her napkin into the shape of a cootie catcher. Nancy said, "Sounds like an ad for us."

Kit said, "I think he sounds like a douche and I don't care about him. And honestly, Lucy, it sounds like you're pissed that your marriage failed so you're looking for excuses to wreck someone else's."

Lucy said, "I know I'm all over the place, but one thing's for sure, I don't want to wreck his marriage. I don't want him for myself. I mean, I did, when I thought he was single. But he's not. I'm just trying to figure out a way . . . what a mess."

Nancy said, "Life is messy."

Gina said, "Did Peter tell his wife about you?"

"No!" Lucy said, then put her head in her hands. "But maybe he should have. Who knows? Kit's right. Karmically I'm dead meat, but hanging out with Peter brought me sublime levity and pleasure, how can that be wrong?"

Kit said, "We've been over this."

Nancy said, "You're floundering. It really is a shame she doesn't know about The Program. Might solve everything."

Gina said, "As long as you don't fall in love with him and want him for yourself, I think it's fine if you sleep with him."

Lucy thought of the sperm in the condom. Was she trying to trap him? No. That was separate. Screwy, but separate. She said, "I swear I don't want him for myself. What if she never found out? What if the whole reason their marriage survives and he sticks it out for forty years with hardly any sex, and fixes the gutters and takes his kids to games and financially supports his family is because he has me on the side every two weeks. What if she gets the whole enchilada *because* of me?"

Kit said, "Please. You think she should thank you for screwing her husband?!"

Lucy said, "Maybe! *She's* not sleeping with him!"

The women inhaled collectively. Their eyes opened wide. So did their mouths.

Kit said, "Now *that's* fucked up. You are deep down the rabbit hole of justification, my friend."

"I know," Lucy said, and slumped back into her chair.

Gina said, "Is that how you felt about Delphine? Did you want to thank her for sleeping with Matt? Write her a little thank-you note?"

"No, of course not, but I *was* sleeping with Matt. We were trying to get pregnant, remember?"

"There's a recipe for disaster," said Nancy.

Kit said, "Lucy, you have to be able to live your life in the sun. No shadows. You need to feel good about yourself."

Lucy spoke in a small voice. "Peter made me feel good about myself."

Gina said, "I say you do what you want. There's no order in the universe unless you believe there is. No piano's going to fall on you. Life is mostly full of struggle with a few bright moments, then you die. Savor the bright moments."

Nancy said, "Yikes. Who brought Good-Time Charlie over here?"

"You're on your path and his wife's on hers. Her experience is none of your business and vice versa. We're all responsible for our own happiness. Isn't that in your Program oath?"

Lucy said, "So my Program question is this: Because *you arranged* for your husbands' infidelity, does that make it morally hunky-dory?"

Nancy said, "It makes it *not* infidelity."

"So, I can sleep with Ted because you know about it but I can't sleep with Peter because his wife doesn't? That boils infidelity down to knowledge and not the act, yes?"

Nancy said, "Right, because knowledge and trust are the foundation of a healthy marriage."

Gina added, "And regular sex."

Lucy, "So, when you go shopping, do you always tell your husbands what you bought? Or do you squirrel away a little cash for yard sales—"

Kit said, "Yeah, but he doesn't have to know about that. It'll just make him mad and as long as it's just once in a while and I don't plunge us into debt, it's fine."

"But he could say the same thing about his extra sex. *So could you*, if *you* wanted extra."

"But that's different."

"But why? It's just sex."

"There's no such thing as 'just sex.'"

Nancy said, "And, full circle."

There was a pause in the conversation as everyone leaned back from the table and adjusted in their seats. Nancy put on a sweater and Kit opened her menu. Lucy said, "And what about the marriage pact? What about your vows, Kit? How did The Program factor in to 'forsaking all others'?"

Kit said, "I've been married twelve years and we were together for five before that. We do what works and that worked. For a time."

Gina said, "I think our vows have to evolve with us. They have to be fluid and malleable as our relationships ebb and mature."

"I agree," said Nancy. They all nodded in agreement—on that much, at least.

Lucy said, "I read something in a magazine that I still think about to this day. Some ancient broad who had been married sixty-two years was asked the secret to a successful marriage. And do you know what she said?"

"Enjoying sex?" said Gina.

"No, she said, 'Don't take it personally.' And the reporter said, 'Take what personally?' and the old lady said, 'Everything.' I think that's the key. I think if we could all stop taking everything so damn personally, it might open us up to enjoy our freedoms and each other, and our marriages a little bit more."

Kit said, "But at the very root of it, there has to be trust."

Lucy said, "I agree. So, why can't we trust each other to do what we have to do to keep us coming home and going to trumpet recitals and standing around at each other's mind-numbing work functions? Why can't that marital trust extend to extramarital relationships, like the work wife and the tennis pro? Who decided that fidelity is the barometer of a successful marriage? Why couldn't friendship or humor or a shared sense of adventure be the most sacred element of marriage? Why couldn't infidelities be dismissed with the same wave of a hand as hours of fanatical sports watching or flirting with a sexy waiter or waitress? We could *choose* to see things differently. We could choose to see infidelity differently, to recast it."

Kit said, "But we can't."

Lucy said, "Why, because we get naked?"

Nancy said, "Because it's too intimate."

Lucy said, "But not always. Not when the kids are interrupting. What if we had sex with our clothes on, would that make a difference? And no kissing? What if you were just screwing up against a tree in the woods with your clothes on?"

Kit said, "Oh, for heaven's sake, people don't really do that, do they?"

Nancy said, "Sounds splintery."

"I think it should be allowed," Gina said. "Then everyone wouldn't have to work so hard to not feel so confined. I think it's worth exploring. For generations women tolerated men's indiscretions. In the seventies, women demanded equal pay. They could have also demanded equal marital freedoms, but instead they insisted that their husbands endure the same life of monogamy. It was a golden opportunity for sexual liberation within marriage, blown. Some took it and ran with it—agreed on open marriages—but most didn't and they feel trapped. We weren't designed to be monogamous, men or women. And we sure as hell didn't start out that way as a species or we never would have made it this far."

Lucy said, "I think the rules need to be rewritten."

Nancy said, "Beginning with what?"

Kit said, "Beginning with lunch. I'm hungry. Let's order. Gina, can you flag down the waiter? Hey, you're not texting!"

They all looked at Gina, whose phone was not in her hands, nor on the table.

Nancy said, "Did you and penis-photo guy break up?"

Gina took a moment to respond. Her usual grin was gone and she tapped her fingers back and forth on the tines of her fork as she answered.

"He's good. He's fine. He's studying for the GRE."

Nancy said, "And . . ."

"And Duncan checked the call history on my phone and went a little ballistic, but we're okay, we're fine. We're still in The Program. He likes his Helper, Goldie." Gina looked down then back up at each of her friends. She tried to smile but only the corners of her mouth turned up a little, her teeth were still hidden. "We're fine, really. It's no big deal. He just asked me to stop and so I stopped. We're good. Let's keep going. Movin' on. Where were we?"

They all looked down at their menus. Kit was the first to close hers and look up. "I'm having the western omelet."

Nancy said, "I'm having the ham and cheese crêpe."

"Fine, eggs benedict," Lucy said, and closed her menu, but little had changed. Her dilemma was still between her moral compass, her churning hormones and her aching need to be desired.

Chapter 21

The weeks passed slowly as the ground finally thawed. Spring had arrived with a Bollywood flourish, but Lucy coasted through it in a haze of malaise. School was busy but fine. Gus was busy but fine. Even Matt hadn't bothered her lately. Lucy was gearing up to direct the elementary school's Spring Concert, which kept her busy after school most afternoons and her mind occupied, but her body was another matter. She was subbing in for The Program every once and a while, but missed Peter, missed feeling emotionally and physically connected to him and felt frustrated she couldn't sate her craving for him. This made her slightly depressed and she slept a lot.

Lucy's students noticed her crankiness. One of her more feisty kids, Stella, put her hand on her hip before recess and said, "Miss Larken, what's *up* with *you*?" Lucy had to smile. *What's up with me?* she thought. *I'm not getting' any, that's what's up,* she wanted to say, but instead she looked at Stella and sassed back, "The *sky* is what's *up*."

Sebastian, one of her quiet ones, raised his hand during class and said, "Mrs. Larken, would you like a joke to be in a better mood?"

Ouch. Lucy said, "Sure, Sebastian, shoot."

"Where do you find a dog with no legs?"

"I don't know, my friend, where?"

"Right where you left him." Sebastian's eyes twinkled.

"Good one," she said. And it was. She smiled but didn't laugh, figuring she was probably getting her period. Lucy told her students a joke: "What did the zero say to the eight? Nice belt." She hoped it would help to mask her pain but it only served to remind her how much she and Peter used to laugh together. Lucy gave her class two minutes to turn and talk to a neighbor and tell each other a joke. Then she shook Peter out of her mind and held it together for the rest of the day until she got home, poured herself a beer, and cried.

Lucy had underestimated how much she would miss Peter's friendship. Sure, she missed the sex, but also came to realize how much of a friend he'd become. She missed his honesty—with her, at least, she thought—and his companionship. They had no legitimate investment in each other, therefore no risk of saying the wrong thing for fear of offending the other. They used to share intimate details of how their bodies worked and what they liked and disliked about sex, and gleaned quite a bit of new information from one another. They discussed the politics of everything from swallowing to holding hands and as a result, Lucy felt their conversations made her a better lover. She believed she'd unlocked some secrets to men—things she never could have asked another man, not even Matt—which made her feel informed and powerful.

And yet, if she were really honest with herself, Lucy had to accept that Peter was wrong for her in the long term. Sure, he hated mayonnaise and old movies, and talked about losing his house keys and forgetting to pay parking tickets—all stuff that would have driven her to the brink. But at the root of everything, Lucy rejected his grand-experiment theory and found it repugnant. She resented that he felt entitled to have it all, a wife and a mistress, and knew he would have likely cheated on her someday, too. For these reasons, she wasn't jealous of Peter's wife. If she felt envy at all it was towards Peter, because he was in a relationship that meant something to him, in a twisted way. He was invested in his wife and their kids, however fucked up the marriage might be. Peter and his wife were still, in spite of the lies and deception, building a life together. Ultimately Lucy was building bupkes.

As gloomy as she was, Lucy held it together during school hours and poured even more into her teaching. The Program was coasting along; the Helpers were satisfied, wives relieved, and the husbands were over the moon. Nancy put together a second Helper portfolio and the last screening for new Helpers had gone well. A few more of Lucy's coworkers at school signed up, which meant more winks in the hallways, and Nancy's friends kept joining, too. Ted ended up really liking Dix and also tried out the new girl, Goldie, who had the name of a stripper but the body of a Wisconsin hospice nurse. She looked the most like a mall mom, but word got around that she gave masterful blow jobs and had a nice, tight vagina, so her dance card was usually full.

Gina and Duncan had a rough ride for a little while—he was thrown by Dick-Photo Guy and apparently kept referring to it as her *relationship*. Gina waved him off with a wide smile saying, "Don't be ridiculous," but Nancy recommended she pull Duncan from The Program and give him extra personal lovin' for a while. Nancy counseled that even though it may not have been a big deal to her, the Dick-Photo Guy incident had been a big deal to Duncan, and that she should focus on her marriage.

"Love bomb him," Nancy said, "women get a bad rap for being needy, but men are superneedy."

Lucy was assigned to sleep with Felix, the popular crepe shop owner once, which was weird but fine. She also subbed in for Audra, who had been invited by a one-time appointment to take a steamy helicopter ride over Manhattan as part of his fiftieth birthday present—some bucket-list bullshit. Lucy had to admit that was exciting. She was also scheduled to sleep with Morris again, who really just wanted to try on a few things from her closet. Her mom's loud polyester zip-up pantsuit from the seventies stretched to fit his burly body and she giggled as Morris vamped in front of her full-length mirror. They put on the Gap Band and boogied around the room, and the magic of funk helped to wrench her out of her funk.

Chapter 22

One night Lucy put Gus to bed at 7:30 P.M., went over her lesson plans, then decided to check out the profiles that were unceremoniously shoved at her inbox once a week by the dating sites she'd joined then lost faith in. She poured herself a glass of tequila, squeezed a little bit of lime, added a heaping teaspoon of honey, then dropped two ice cubes into the glass. Shuddering at the first and second sips, she cracked a window, took in the cool evening air, and nestled into her wumfy chair with her laptop. These Internet dating browsing blocks always felt like the lesser version of a movie montage to Lucy, wherein the single woman sits home alone in her pastel cashmere lounging pajamas, clicking away as she listens to Sam Cooke by the fire. Lucy's lounging pajamas consisted of layers of old, pilly sweaters, grubby slippers and clashing sweatpants. She loved Sam Cooke, but it was more likely that *Antiques Roadshow* was on mute. In the movie-montage scene there is never piles of folded laundry dotting the living-room landscape; there's never an opened box of Mallomars next to the remote and an empty bowl of reheated penne al vodka crusting over on the coffee table. But there it was, her glamorous life.

For Lucy, looking at profiles was a surgical affair. She wanted to give them a chance, wanted to find a couple of message-worthy guys out there, but the prospects were dismal and her expectations were low. She began talking to the computer screen the way disappointed fans talk to athletes on television during the game. "No smile? Get a clue, dude. How am I supposed to know you have all your teeth? Next." She skipped any that had no photo—clearly married—or where the guy was wearing sunglasses—too douche-y. If his user name included the word "Gentleman," it was usually a harbinger of smarminess. If Lucy got as far along as reading a guy's profile, there was a very good chance his grammar and/or punctuation would take him down. *How did these guys land jobs? Didn't they proofread their résumés? Could their friends have glanced at their profiles before they posted them? Why the hell don't any of these dating sites have a grammar filter?!* It made Lucy nuts.

Lucy spoke to her laptop screen, "Hey dorks, put down your beer bottles and wineglasses and take off your stinkin' hat and sunglasses." Click, next. "It's not that I don't drink or disapprove, it's just that a profile photo is like a driver's license and ladies are like cops—we want to see your eyeballs." *Oh man, I'm buzzed.* Click, next. "Let's see. Okay, hello, 'magnum', 'duwayne' and 'brad.' Please, dears, put on a shirt. Anything you got, really. Pull something out of the hamper, even if it has a small stain. And if every friggin' shirt you own is at the laundromat and you can't borrow one and you have to take your profile photo this instant up against a cinder block wall, grab a flag off a pole, a floor mat from your car, a dish towel— anything, really. It's not that we aren't intrigued by your comely physique; we just want to be assured that you own a shirt. And know how to separate the lights from the darks. At this point in my life, not having to do your laundry beats out a nice chest, hands down."

So, click, click, click Lucy skipped, skipped, skipped. It's too bad, too, she thought, because it's such a good idea, this Internet-dating business. Lucy was all for it and used to egg on her single friends to jump in and explore it, back when she was married. She knew at least twenty couples who'd met online and felt that it had successfully filled the void that church socials and town dances had left behind after the *Little House on the Prairie* era ended and the sixties ruined everything—as her father used to say. But she was perpetually striking out.

"If you tell me you're funny and then spend a good six paragraphs not saying anything remotely funny—I hate to break it to ya— *you're not funny*, but keep on hiking, NatureBoy11. Hikers are notoriously hilarious," Lucy said, then took another sip of her drink. "And if you say you have a sarcastic sense of humor, that's code for 'I'm a charming, verbally abusive bully' because sarcasm is rarely funny to the person it's directed at. And if you are funny, but your user name is 'drugster,' there's a pretty good chance I'm not going to take comfort in that. Don't you have any other hobbies?" Ugh. Lucy took a big swig this time. "To 'sirgotalot' and 'damimgood,' I like your user names, I do. They're confident, optimistic and your appreciation for life's bounty is infectious. I just wish your joie de vivre extended to grammar. And kerning! Always with the no-spacesbetweenwords. Can you not see that? Can none of you see that? Do I alone have some superpower? We learned to separate words in kindergarten and not to put a space before a period in second grade. Christ." Click, next.

On the rare occasions when Lucy did come across a profile that looked friendly and intelligent, she would e-mail the guy and never hear back. She was forty-two, and most guys her age set their cut off age at thirty-five—forty if they were feeling magnanimous. She figured that by being honest about her age, Lucy pretty much obliterated any chance of meeting men her own age. Lucy read some more, then sipped and clicked some more. "To 'juancarlos' and 'benny,' why the tiled room, boys? It smacks of *Silence of the Lambs*. And why no smile? So hard and so cold—like my coffee."

Lucy was on a roll. "Hello, 'mr.sustainable,'" she said, "is your love sustainable or will I be reduced, reused and recycled the first chance you get, know what I'm sayin'? And to 'firmfox.' Really? Am I supposed to read an IM from you tomorrow at eight A.M. and get excited about that? I don't neet to be navigating the drivel of your sexual innuendo while I'm trying to get out of the house for work. Please think of a user name a little more daytime friendly. Speaking of eight A.M.: I remember you, 'mistergentleman,' and I beg to differ. Didn't you ask me if I was wearing panty hose or thigh highs at ten of eight in the morning a while back?! Honestly, shouldn't you be keeping an eye on the toaster at that hour? Your toast is gonna burn. Focus on not missing your bus, then you can worry about what I'm wearing. Breakfast is the most important meal of the day, for cryin' out loud."

Lucy took another sip, then laughed, dribbling a little on her pajamas. "Why, hello, 'FriendlyGentleman.' So many gentlemen and yet so few, but you intrigue me. Why is your profile photo a picture of you sitting in a hospital chair, holding a newborn infant? Is it yours? Why is it that in your profile under 'Wants kids?' you've answered, 'Not sure.' A gentleman and an enigma? I should say. Speaking of which, 'zendust,' 'kineticarcade' and 'b4stillness,' you're all so slender, so cryptic. Is there more to life than yoga, fellas? Why don't you tell me? Or allude to it in hushed tones on your yoga mat, all sweaty-like. It'll never work between us. I can't keep a straight face for that long. But journey on, wandering souls, journey on."

Lucy was ready to pack it in. It was getting late and her head was fuzzy. She felt futility talking to these guys and even stupider for spending money joining dating sites. If their staff programmers couldn't write the code to, at the very least, filter out the difference between your/you're and there/their, or capitalizing the first word of a new sentence, then it was useless. *Give me a dating site with a grammar and punctuation filter and I'm yours for life.*

"Oh, my dears." Lucy was losing steam and growing empathetic towards her dating compadres. "Misters 'italianNJ,' 'jerzital,' 'italygumba,' 'ItalianGuy,' 'ItalianFunnyGuy,' 'SicilyPaisan,' 'tigerSal' and 'BigTony.' My father was full Italian and I was raised in New Jersey, and yet something tells me I'll never be Italian enough or Jerz enough for you. But I applaud your righteous pride and wish you well. All a yous."

With that, Lucy clicked back to the home page. She thanked the dating site for reminding her that there were droves of guys out there who were aching to "go to restaurants," be "good listeners," and who "like to travel." She acknowledged that they were safely and reliably there, within reach and right inside her computer—humorless, unsmiling and putting spaces after the last words in their sentences and before the period. Then she thanked them all and thought, *Good luck.* "If it weren't for your profiles, fellas, I might be lonelier, but when I realize who I could be stuck with, I'm actually relieved," she said. Then she sighed and closed her laptop.

With her online prospects going nowhere, Lucy's sexual fantasies returned with a vengeance. She seemed to have no control over them and no scenario was too outlandish or inappropriate. Chaperoning a field trip to a nearby ice cream-cone factory, Lucy sat on a school bus full of amped-up third graders one early morning, diesel exhaust wafting through the cracked windows. At a long stop light, Lucy found herself staring at the day laborers lined up at the edge of a White Castle parking lot, waiting wordlessly for roofers and landscapers to pull their vans over and offer them a day's work. They were placid, serene men, neat and clean. *Dark and sexy*, Lucy thought. She rarely saw them speak to one another and never saw them smile. They struck her as confident, capable men, then she realized how patronizing that was. She wondered if they were good in bed. Dix, who'd been in charge of bully oversight at the back of the bus, slid into the seat next to Lucy and whispered in her ear, "Hot little tamales, aren't they?"

"You're going straight to hell," Lucy said.

"Not if I see you there, first," Dix replied, and elbowed Lucy. "Do you think anyone ever picks them up for you-know-what?"

"No!" Lucy said. "*That* would be the lowest. And illegal."

"But fun for them, maybe," said Dix. "Beats landscaping."

Lucy pictured herself slowly driving by one morning. She imagined herself sizing them up, like Madeline Kahn did with her male escorts in that scene from *History of the World: Part I*. Of course, she wouldn't be able to get out of the car for inspection and they would have to keep their pants on, so Lucy would just drive slowly by, pretending to be looking for muscle, when really she was looking for lips, shoulders and that special je ne sais quoi. One guy might be a little taller and smolderingly hot. His soft, maroon T-shirt would look good next to his butterscotch skin and his Levi's would be well worn and a little loose, fitting him like an indie rock star's. Maybe he would meet Lucy's gaze. Then she could circle the block again, this time stopping in front of him and beckoning him over with a come-hither look. She daydreamed him ambling over and bending down to look into her car, his long, shiny, black hair held in a low ponytail down his back. *Mmm, sexy*, Lucy thought, as she pictured his almond eyes and beautiful skin. *Cuarenta dólares por dos horas?* Lucy thought. *That's enough, right?*

Dix whispered to Lucy, "How much do gigolos get for sex these days?" Had Dix read her mind? "I was thinking forty dollars for two hours."

Lucy laughed. "First of all, that's racist. Secondly, that's more than I pay my babysitters. But somehow, I don't think enough."

"I'm thinkin' he's welcome to take a shower then I can drop him back off, but he'd miss a full day's wage, so I could give him some yard work then pay him for a full day."

The Program had taken care of Lucy's yard. *I could ask him to fold laundry with me when we're done.*

Lucy snapped to. She scolded herself along with Dix, "Day laborers are not gigolos, Dix, and my goal is to not have to pay for it. Plus I'm pretty sure we would go straight to hell for paying day laborers for sex."

"Some of them are very cute. Too short for me, but good for you."

"Dix, I mean it."

"Yeah. That's the lowest," Dix said with final mock judgment. Lucy changed her tone. She knew that Dix knew she was being preposterous.

Lucy said, "Do you suppose everyone is going to hell for one reason or another? Is there anyone left *not* going to hell?"

"Not that I can think of," said Dix. Then, "Oh, Marybeth. I bet she's not." Marybeth was a coworker of theirs and the chorus teacher. She had never married and as far as anyone knew, never dated. She lived with her ailing mom and never gossiped or said an unkind word towards anyone. She had no sense of humor and was very conservative, but she radiated goodness, like Melanie in *Gone with the Wind*. Lucy thought about what it would be like to be that selfless and kind. She figured that access to heaven was a cumulative thing, like earning the perfect attendance award, and she'd already blown it.

"Yeah, Marybeth, for sure. I bet she goes to heaven," said Lucy. The two of them paused the conversation and craned their necks for one last look as the bus drove off and left the day laborers behind.

Lucy said, "Do you think I'll go to hell for just thinking these thoughts? Do you think we're the first women to have considered it?"

Dix said, "Nope. I don't think we're the first women to have any of the thoughts we have. I think our thoughts are as old and mundane as the hills."

Lucy shook her head. Dix said, "I'm not kidding, Luce."

The two friends rode in silence for the next few moments, thinking about sex and Mexican men, heaven and hell. They drove into a tunnel and the students squealed with mock terror as the bus rumbled into temporary darkness. It was a tunnel that many of them drove through every day, but the novelty of screaming alongside your best friend never seemed to wear off.

"I'd rather be in hell," said Dix, and affectionately nudged her friend's shoulder.

"Me, too," said Lucy. She was pretty sure she'd rather be in hell, but not entirely convinced. She would have a hard time with the heat. And the humidity. The squeals lasted until the bus emerged from the other side of the tunnel. Dix returned to her seat in the back and Lucy's life returned to organized chaos as usual.

Later that day, after school, Gus had a Lego Challenge class and a friend's nanny would be dropping him off afterwards, so Lucy went home, peeled off her clothes and headed straight upstairs for a short nap and to release the day's tension. But when Lucy lay down, she realized she had no will. The thought of Peter was too depressing and the images of her Program guys weren't doing it for her. She felt no connection to them and realized she was slipping back to that place again: an apathy towards passion, the languishing desolation of feeling unwanted. As she drifted off to sleep, the image of shutting down her body like so many layers of clanking metal doors stung Lucy.

When she woke up, she experienced a bolt of clarity. She reached over towards the nightstand and felt for her phone.

"Hello?" Peter said.

"Hi," Lucy said. "It's me, Lucy."

"I know who it is."

"I just . . . I've been thinking." Lucy sat upright and hopped off the bed. She started pacing her room, making a horseshoe back and forth around her bed.

She said, "I want to keep sleeping with you."

Peter said nothing. Lucy kept talking.

"I know it's wrong but it's the only bad thing I will ever do, I hope, unless I really do start robbing banks, which I'm pretty sure I won't, but, shit, who knows now, at the rate I'm going. But I'm calling because . . . because I want to keep going. I know it's one of the more repugnant moral infractions you can make against another person—especially another woman—and I get that it's a sin against the sisterhood. And breaking a commandment. I get it. But I help old people across the street and I pick up other people's garbage on the ground. I'm forgiving of my ex-husband who literally and figuratively robbed me, and I always use my blinker. I stay after school to tutor ESL students even though I'm not getting paid, and, and I'm a public school teacher, for chrissake—the most overworked, underpaid, under-respected, lambasted profession in America—because I love it and I'm good at it and the kids love me.

I'm teaching them respect and how to be good citizens and I call my mother at least three times a week and never take up two parking spaces. I married the wrong man and there's no do-over. I blew it. I get that. And I've accepted it. But now I just want to do this thing for me. This one thing. I want to have sex with you because it makes me feel good and nothing more. I don't want you to leave your wife or spend any money on me or love her any less. I just want your sex. And your friendship. And some laughs, I guess, is all."

There was silence on the other end of the line. Lucy had been monologuing for so long that she had a momentary panic that Peter's wife had answered the phone in a really deep voice because maybe she had the croup and that this whole inane speech had been recited to her, in which case she should probably just take Gus and move to North Dakota.

"Hello?" she said.

"I'm here," Peter said.

"So, what do you think?"

"I think let's have us some more sex."

"Really?" said Lucy.

"Really," said Peter.

Lucy threw herself onto her bed and kicked her feet in the air, giddy like a game-show winner. She rolled onto her stomach and said, "Okay, good. Gotta go, bye," then hung up the phone and felt like shouting, *Weeeeeee!*

Chapter 23

It was Book Fair Day at school and Lucy was humming and whistling as she snapped the cardboard book displays together. Sex with Peter was predictably amazing and she couldn't imagine a more promising prospect on the horizon. Kit arrived to help her unpack the boxes of books and arrange them in stacks by genre on long tables, for the early morning before-school shift in Gus's elementary school gymnasium. Gina had taken off the morning to volunteer, as had Fran and Audra. Nancy and Dix were there somewhere, too. Everyone had at least one child at the school or worked at the school and Lucy liked looking around and seeing so many familiar faces, though something was off. While everyone busied herself stocking and shelving, Lucy felt an undercurrent of unease, which she couldn't quite put her finger on until she scanned the room again and it hit her. *They're all here.* Wives and Helpers. Together in the same room. *Oh shit.*

It didn't occur to Lucy when she imagined The Program that

this would happen, as she had always thought of them as two distinctly separate groups of friends. But the book fair changed that. Damn books. The tension in the room was palpable, like the Sharks and Jets gymnasium dance scene. Good thing the walls were padded with hanging mats.

Kit spoke quietly as she sidled up to Lucy. "I always bitch and moan about signing up for the book fair, then once I'm here I'm really glad."

Lucy said, "Me, too. I love seeing what books the kids gravitate to. It's like a portal to their futures—the science geeks, the lit majors, the *People* magazine devourers. They're all here."

"We called them the jocks and the freaks growing up," Kit said, then stopped shelving and looked over at Lucy. "Hey, I'm really sorry about Peter. You seem like you're doing okay, though." Lucy realized she needed to rein in her excitement and act more bummed or else no one would believe that she'd ended it. "Yeah," Lucy said, attempting to act. "It's been hard, but I'm glad I broke it off." She hoped she'd done a thorough job lying. She knew that Kit would never be able to wrap her head around such a breach of morality. Ninety percent of Lucy's married friends would never fully understand her choice, as depraved as it was. Besides, husbands and wives didn't tell each other everything and Kit had lied about Fwank, so she didn't feel full disclosure was mandatory. Plus, the voice that had been telling her lately that Kit's friendship was conditional was getting louder, and as much as she purported to love and support Lucy, that voice suggested that Kit's own moral code trumped her best friend's happiness. *Boundaries are good,* Lucy had read in a pamphlet somewhere. Now was as good a time as ever to try put that theory into practice.

"Well I'm proud of you," Kit said. Lucy knew that Kit meant well in spite of her patronizing tone, but it still irked her.

"Good," said Lucy. "I'm getting tremendous satisfaction out of knowing that you approve of my behavior. It's almost as satisfying as hot sex."

"It is?"

"No. I'm being facetious."

Kit's warmth chilled like a flipped switch. "So sleep with him. I don't care."

Lucy felt contrarian. She had switches, too. "Yes you do. You care very much."

"So what if I do?" said Kit. "Some people have standards. Would you be my friend if you knew I was a serial killer?"

"No, but I don't want to die, nor do I want others to die. And yet you get into a car after our long lunches and drive—after you've had two, three glasses of wine—and that's potential negligent homicide. So you could be a murderer. And it's illegal, so you're breaking the law."

Kit interrupted. "I don't drive drunk." She was indignant.

"Fine, tipsy. You drive tipsy. Potentially murderous and illegal. And yet I still love you and count you as my friend. Because I don't judge you."

"Apparently you do," said Kit.

"I'm just saying that I think it sucks that you wouldn't be my friend if you disapproved of one of my behaviors. It's conditional and judgmental. And hypocritical, quite frankly."

"You should talk."

The other women were starting to notice the conversation slicing through their corner of the room like sabers. Lucy knew she should lower her voice. She tilted her head at Kit chin down as if to say, let's not go there now, and Kit knew exactly what she meant.

Lucy whispered, "I stopped seeing Peter. It's moot."

"Fine," Kit whispered back.

Lucy wondered a lot lately what kept their friendship moving forward. Was it a shared history? Years logged side by side in the trenches of early motherhood? Was that enough? She sighed and switched tones. "How are things with Fwank?"

"Fine," said Kit, unconvincingly.

"Okay, we don't have to talk about it now. I have a bunch of *Nate the Great* books that Gus doesn't read any more if you want them."

Kit said, "Fine. I mean, thank you." She was thawing.

Lucy said, "I'm sorry. I'm just a little tired." They smiled weakly at one another.

Gina walked up with a stack of book-genre cards and a roll of wide tape. She said, "Tired of what? Screwing my husband?"

Kit said, "Wooooah."

Gina said, "I'm kidding."

Lucy said, "Are ya? Besides, I'm no longer screwing your husband. I think Audra is."

"Why, because Duncan isn't good enough in bed for you? I thought you liked sleeping with married men."

"Woooahh," Kit and Lucy both said, and looked at Gina with big eyes and raised eyebrows. Even Fran stopped shelving, turned towards the floor show and said, "Dudes."

"I'm sorry. Sorry," Gina said as if to a crowd at a fender bender, "I'm PMS-ing big-time."

"So am I," said Kit.

"No kidding," said Lucy.

Kit scowled, then laughed, saying, "God, I can be such a bitch."

"Ya think?" said Nancy who was shelving nearby. Fran, who had just set down a box of books, leaned in and said in a stage whisper, "Gotta love being postmenopause. Those homeopathic herbs kick ass. No PMS and no risk of pregnancy, so I can sleep with your husbands without a condom and I'll never get pregnant. It's pretty awesome. No muss, no fuss. And your husbands love it." Then she bounced off. Fran's comments often defied and confounded convention and this was one of those times. There was no patented lady-look to follow this comment. Gina's mouth fell open and she forgot to close it. Kit thwapped a *Captain Underpants* book on the table. "That could very well be the last straw for me."

Lucy said, "Simmer down, ladies, the kids are due to arrive any minute."

"I can't believe I let you people sleep with Fwank."

Gina said, "And Duncan."

"Lucy's right," said Nancy. "Let's finish up. New subject. What's everybody reading these days? I'm on book two of the trilogy by that Canadian chick who writes those sexy mystery things."

Fran said, "I'm rereading Jane Austen."

Gina said, "You *are*?" in a voice that sounded almost angry, which induced half chuckles among the women and dismissed what was left of the tension. Gina said, "I mean, that's great, Fran." Lucy broke up. Gina continued, "I'm reading a sonnet cycle so dense that I want to throw it against the wall. And just finished, *West with the Night* on my commute. Beautiful."

Lucy said, "I'm rereading an old textbook on classroom management skills. And David Sedaris and Melissa Bank. I'm a vacillator."

Audra sashayed up, looking more like she was going to a Hampton's polo match than a public school book fair. Clack, clack, clack went her shoes, which were as outstanding as her cleavage and both antithetical to 7:45 A.M. She arrived at the table at the same time as Dix, who was carrying in extra copies of Rick Riordan books.

"Hey, guys, can I unload this here?" Dix said, and lowered a box onto the table.

Gina said, "Sure, I can help." Then, "You missed the fireworks."

Before Dix could respond, Fran bounded back over and, reaching for a new stack of books, said brightly, "So, who's enjoying The Program these days? Everybody happy?" She said it without guile, as if inquiring about who would be in the dunking booth at the school fair. Gina turned and looked at Nancy and then at the group with knit eyebrows. No one spoke. Dix said, "What exactly *did* I miss?"

Kit said, "Lucy broke it off with Peter."

"I'm sorry, Luce," Audra said with genuine compassion. Lucy looked over at Kit, who looked up at a helium balloon stuck in the gymnasium rafters. Nancy just shook her head.

Gina said, "Also, we're all reading, Kit and I are PMS-ing, and Fran's been screwing our husbands without a condom."

"Excuse me?" said Nancy.

Gina answered that bit of information with another of the pantheon of wordless lady-looks, but this one was emphasized with hands on hips, which is lady-look for an exclamation point.

Nancy said, "Fran, I will need to meet with you about your Helper status in The Program as soon as possible. In private."

"No problemo," said Fran, totally oblivious to any wrongdoing she might have committed. Then she walked away to shelve the last stack of books.

Lucy shook her head and said, "We'll deal with her later. I'm going to go meet the students at the door. Dix, ladies, are you with me? Let's stick a pin in this. We're here for the kids."

Tensions crisscrossed the room like a field of laser trip wires. Lucy felt those who had left The Program were amazed that they'd ever considered it at all, and worried that those still in The Program might be considering for the first time getting out. Somehow, what seemed to make sense in theory, for a time—sanctioned infidelity in a small community—felt more and more weird and uncomfortable now that everyone was in the same room together, picturing each other—or, rather, trying not to picture anything.

The first thing Lucy thought to do while tempers were short and talons were coming out was to get Audra the hell away from everyone. "Audra, why don't you go relieve Goldie as cashier, she could use a break." Audra gave a look as if to say "fine" then said, "Lassen sie ihre frau für mich. *Ich liebe dich nicht"* ("Do not leave your wife for me. I do not love you," in German), turned and clacked off. The women looked at her blankly, then over to Lucy as if to say "What the? . . ." and Lucy said, "Don't worry about it."

As Audra walked away, the rest found themselves drawn in by her girl-from-Ipanema sway. She had enviable posture and a spectacular ass, and they were mesmerized. No one else's ass even came close.

Kit broke the silence. "Wait a minute, did you just say, Goldie? Where is she? I've heard so much about her."

"Yeah, no kidding," said Gina. "Isn't she the blow job queen?"

"Yes, she is, ladies. Over there," Nancy said, and pointed to the large, boxy woman with big Midwestern arms and short cafeteria-lady hair. Goldie nodded as she stepped out from behind the cash box to let Audra in. She had a wide, sparkly smile.

"*That's* Goldie?!" Gina said, nonplussed.

Gina, Kit and Nancy stared at Goldie, and Lucy could tell they were imagining her mouth on their husbands' dicks. They'd been through a lot as friends, but this took the cake. Lucy watched them picturing The Helpers going at it with their husbands, and the looks on their husbands' faces, looks that they knew all too well but perhaps hadn't seen in a while. At that unfortunate moment, a gradual influx of little kids began filling up the empty space in the gymnasium—first two or three, then twenty and forty. As the students excitedly buzzed from book to book, the volunteer moms still glanced at Goldie. Lucy figured if they left The Program they'd have to put out more, go down on their husbands more—back to square one. It had been nice having some of the pressure taken off, but it was beyond awkward, and what was novel and exciting for a while wasn't sitting right. Their husbands would be crushed—devastated might be more like it. The fallout might leave everyone worse off than before. Lucy sensed that this might be the beginning of the end, the way she sensed her marriage was collapsing or the way her friendship with Kit was fading. There was rumbling beneath the foundation and like old milk, things were turning. She realized that she'd have to say good-bye to the good life—to the landscaping and lawn mowing, the pedicures and highlights. She'd come to enjoy the Indian food, the cranberry bread, and the easy-breezy no-strings-attached sex. Easy come, easy go.

One by one, students came over to ask the moms questions, snapping them out of their thoughts and dropping them squarely back in an elementary-school gymnasium book fair.

"Where are the books about horses?" Fiona asked Lucy. And "Do you have *Miss Daisy Is Crazy*?" asked Joshua. "What?" the women kept saying, and the children had to repeat themselves. Other students couldn't wait to show Lucy what they had found and gathered around her, three deep, to get a little piece of her. She offered an enthusiastic perusal of each bound treasure, then handed it back with an approving smile. More than anything, she loved to see her students excited about new things, whether checking out a dead dragonfly on the blacktop or listening to a dad visiting the classroom play banjo. It lit her up to see them excited. Eyes bright and minds whirring, Lucy wanted them to become addicted to knowledge; to have a lust for learning.

"You're going to love this book, Daphne," she said, and, "Oh, Luke, this is right up your alley. Good choice." The other moms noticed how the kids beamed when they saw Lucy—even older kids she'd had years ago drifted over—and they marveled at the gift she'd always had with kids, even theirs. What a shame, they sometimes told her, that she'd only been able to have one.

Etienne, a little boy who had recently been adopted from Haiti, brought a book about race cars up to Audra at the cash box. *"Avez-vous d'autres livres sur les voitures de course?"* he asked her. Audra looked at him warmly. She bent her knees and leaned over a little to get down to his level, then sweetly replied the only phrase in French she knew, *"Ne laissez pas votre femme pour moi. Je ne t'aime pas."* ("Do not leave your wife for me. I do not love you.")

Etienne nodded because he understood, shrugged, and bought the book anyway.

Chapter 24

It was the weekend and Lucy was gardening. The stars of scheduling had not aligned yet and now Peter was away with his family. She tried not to think of him but it was challenging. She listened to podcasts to fill up her brain so there'd be no empty room. Dix stopped by to borrow folding chairs for her neighbor Miguel. It was his partner's fiftieth birthday party and Dix was helping them set up.

"Come to the party," she said. "You've got to meet new people. We'll get you laid."

"I'm getting laid," Lucy said, passing chairs to Dix from the back of the garage.

"I'm not talking about random sex with other women's husbands—not that there's anything wrong with that—but it's getting you nowhere."

"I like nowhere. I'm very comfortable there. I have a Snuggie blanket and tv and—"

Dix said, "I'm talking boyfriend sex. I'm talking dinner and movies, foreplay and naps. I'm talking moonlight walks and skinny-dips. Birthday presents and weekend plans."

"You think I'm going to find all that at Randall and Miguel's? It'll be a sausage fest."

"Not entirely. Gay men have straight friends, too, you know."

"Single straight male friends?" Lucy gave Dix a look. "Please."

"Please-schmease," said Dix, "you're coming. Wear something sexy. And clean up your act." Lucy was gardening in baggy shorts and a T-shirt covered in paint. She had dirt on her knees and under her nails from weeding, and her hair had mostly fallen out of a ponytail.

"What do you mean? I think this is a good look," Lucy said as she vogued.

"For a lady hobo, maybe."

"A *sexy* lady hobo," Lucy said, and touched her finger to her tongue then butt and said, "*Tsssssssss.*"

"You just keep telling yourself that, ya fruitcake. I'll swing by at seven."

It was a gorgeous night for an outdoor birthday bash; the gods of party planning had been kind. Lucy wore a mint-green-and-lilac sundress that made her eyes pop with a cinch waist and full skirt that flattered her figure. The cork wedge sandals she hoped made her look taller and svelte were actually comfortable—bonus. When she climbed out of Dix's car, Dix appraised her and said, "Good work—A for effort, but fix the twins, ya got crab-eye." Lucy laughed and leaned forward to reposition her uneven nipples. "Much better," Dix said, and they entered the party through the back patio gate. A clear, cloudless sky soon filled with stars, and the aqua glow from Randall and Miguel's pool lit up the underside of everyone's chins, heralding the onset of summer. *Wow,* Lucy thought, *what a fabulous sight*: strings of flamingo lights hung under a white tent with scalloped flaps; gorgeous people chatted on orange, glowing couches set in klatches on the lawn; real gardenias floated in the pool. There were tall cocktail tables with magenta-and-orange tablecloths that skirted the dance floor, napkins printed with "Randall—still randy after all these years," and buttons imprinted with Randall's eighties high school graduation photo, replete with his Flock of Seagulls hairdo. Excellent.

The band was pretty great. It was led by a female singer about Lucy's age with an affable bunch of incredibly good musicians backing her: guitar, upright bass, keyboards and drums. Lucy usually referred to these types of bands as "dad bands." The musicians were often in their forties or fifties, had families and regular day jobs. They'd played instruments in the jazz or marching band in high school, or had rock bands of their own in college. They loved playing music and still wanted to rock out and saw no reason why they shouldn't—if Mick can, anyone can. So they rehearsed once or twice a month, came up with a name and presto: dad band.

But this band seemed a bit different, less predictable and was fronted by a woman. Their music was catchy and put Lucy in an upbeat mood—that, and the margarita she was sipping. She bopped her head and hips—swaying the skirt of her dress back and forth like Kim Novak in *Picnic*. Then Lucy zeroed in on the bass player. He was cute, fit. Kind of hot. He had rhythm—a big turn-on for Lucy. And some hair. Not much of it, and gray, but enough. At least he hadn't shaved it all off. Good man. Lucy sipped and watched and swayed and sipped. She didn't know anyone at the party except for Dix, who had already introduced her to everyone—all couples—and she had said "Happy birthday" to Randall in passing. Lucy was content to listen to the band by herself because it meant she could watch the bass player. She liked what he was wearing: loose jeans and a collared shirt that fit him properly in the shoulders, like an adult. He smiled broadly when he looked at the other musicians. She liked the crinkles around his eyes and the way his body moved to the music. He seemed relaxed, happy and somehow kind. Dix floated by and asked Lucy how she was doing.

"I'm doing great," she said. "I really like the band."

"Yeah, it's all their own stuff, no covers. Did you hear the one called 'Mister Match.com'? And the one about her ninja boyfriend?"

"Uh-huh. And I liked the one about losing her car in the parking lot at Target. And the one about her mom being an anarchist because she still smokes—very funny."

"I like their jazzy-bluegrass-pop hybrid thing. I think they're called Tori Erstwhile and The Montys or something like that. I can get you a business card."

"It's okay," Lucy said looking away from Dix and towards the band. "Maybe I'll get one from the bass player." Dix looked in the direction Lucy was staring.

"Oh, him," she said. "I forgot about him! You'd like him. His name is Topher. Divorced, two kids. I thought he had a girlfriend, but I'll find out because we know you can't be trusted in that department. He's a copyright attorney, I think. Makes a boatload. I'm pretty sure he's funny, too. Let me see if he's taken and I'll get back to you." Dix took off. Lucy hadn't had to say a word, which was nice because then she didn't have to take her mouth off her margarita straw. *They sure put a lot of sugar in this batch. And fresh lime juice, yummy.*

Towards the end of one song, the bass player looked up and caught Lucy looking at him. *What would Audra do?* she thought. Lucy smiled slowly. He smiled back. She looked demurely away then glanced back to see if he was still looking. He was. He had good teeth and a bright smile. Lucy wished she had shaved her legs—it was only one day's growth, but still. Dix swung back around and told her he'd broken up with his girlfriend recently, that he was apparently well hung, and that if Lucy didn't hit that tonight she would never speak to her again. Then Dix darted off. Lucy just listened and smiled, swayed and sipped. During a break, Topher walked up and said, "Hi."

"Hi," said Lucy.

"I'm Topher Hackman."

"I'm Lucy Larken."

"Pleased to meet you, Lucy Larken," Topher said, and reached out his hand.

"Pleased to meet you," Lucy said, shaking his hand and smiling. She liked that he looked her in the eye and wasn't wearing a baseball cap. He had warm eyes and dark, articulate eyebrows, and was only about two inches taller than Lucy, which was nice. She waited for him to steer the conversation.

"How do you know—" Topher hesitated.

"I don't," Lucy said. "His neighbor's my friend and she dragged me here."

"Kicking and screaming?"

"Less kicking, more screaming."

"Well, you don't seem to be doing either right now."

Lucy looked at him, still smiling. She wanted to say something provocative like, "Well, I could be if you play your cards right," but she decided against it. She liked him and wanted to do this like normal people. Two normal, unattached, age-appropriate adults.

She said, "I'm kicking and screaming on the inside."

"Got it," he said. He looked a little nervous and she thought for sure that he would make up some excuse to walk away, but he didn't. He stayed. He had a friendly little tuft of curly gray chest hair peeking out from his collar. She liked his calm baritone voice.

Topher said, "You're one of the few people actually listening to us tonight."

"I like your music," Lucy said. "It's fun to watch you play. You seem to be enjoying yourself."

"I am."

"That's good. And rare."

"Well, I figure, if you get to be my age and don't know what makes you happy . . ."

"Agreed," said Lucy. His eyes were dark chocolate brown and he had wide, full lips that Lucy imagined herself biting ever so slightly. He had little upside down triangles for nostrils and a sculpted chin, like an old-time movie actor. She was drunk and wanted to make out with him. *Thank God he's not the lead singer. So cliché.* The margarita had made her frisky—bad, bad, tequila.

Topher said, "Would you have any interest in taking a stroll around the block when we're done, after I pack up? You would have to wait a bit, but I'll hurry as best as I can."

"Sure," she said. She didn't care what he was proposing, she was game. She liked his hands. Then she remembered to play harder to catch.

"If I'm still here. Come find me."

"Okay," he said, "I'll find you."

After the band packed up, Topher found Lucy with little effort and they left the dregs of revelers and went for a stroll around Dix's neighborhood. Lucy was tipsy but not drunk. She could walk and talk just fine, it was her rice-paper wall of defense that usually failed her. She took in Topher's tan skin and fine dental work lit by street lamps and started to tingle. Topher talked to her about music and how the band formed, and how much they laugh and all about the lead singer's songwriting process. Lucy half listened, half looked for a place where she could lead him. She wanted to push him up against something solid and kiss him, squeeze his butt and see if he was hard. Then she remembered the Jamesons. They were older neighbors of Dix's who spent six months out of the year in Florida. They had a nice, wide back patio, she remembered, and a glider couch that she'd spent the afternoon of a fund-raiser gently gliding back and forth on. Trees and tall shrubs separated the backyard from their neighbors, and the cushions had been thick and plastic, so maybe, just maybe there was a chance that they left them out year round.

Lucy steered Topher over towards the Jamesons' and up their driveway. "They're in Florida," she said when he asked where they were going. He stopped for a moment in protest, so she decided right then to kiss him. He seemed surprised but hardly resisted. Wrapping his arms around Lucy's back he returned her kiss with sudden purpose. Their tongues slid easily between each other's lips and Lucy's body sparked as Topher pulled her against him closer. Lucy arched her back and pressed herself into him gently. His tongue responded with more urgency; his right hand made its way to Lucy's ass. They stood there in the driveway, making out for a few minutes until a car passed, its headlights breaking them apart. Lucy and Topher instinctively turned away from the light the way teenagers might from a passing cop, then she grabbed his hand and pulled him up the driveway towards the Jamesons' backyard. "C'mon," Lucy said, and Topher didn't resist. In fact, that was the last word that either of them uttered for a very long time.

Lucy led Topher over to the long, wide, glider couch and un-tucked the tarp. She sat him down then straddled him, hiking up her dress a little and slipping off her shoes. Pickled in margarita, she felt beautiful, alluring. There was no one sexier in the universe right now; Lucy was irresistible. Topher spread his fingers around her waist—good, strong bass-player hands. He kissed her again. When they broke apart she caught him stealing a look at the shadow between her breasts. Lucy nibbled his ear and Topher's body went limp with the heat and sound of her breath, then feeling for her dress, he found the zipper. Leaning back to meet her eyes, Topher paused after an inch and watched for any sign of stop, but Lucy smiled so he continued easing the zipper down the small of her back. The straps of her sundress fell away from her shoulders and revealed a lacy pink bra. Lucy felt good in her skin. She wanted this and was high on the thrill of being outdoors under the moon and stars. And tequila. The air was perfectly still.

Lucy leaned back a little as Topher surveyed her shoulders and neck, moving his hands to cup her breasts while she mapped the curly gray hairs on his chest with her fingers. She leaned in to kiss him as he kneaded her nipples then expertly unsnapped her bra. Lucy laughed. Topher raised his eyebrows, which she knew was his way of saying, "That's right, don't mess with me." She let out a single chuckle then dove back into him. The moment reminded her of college. The whole night did. In fact, she felt permanently nineteen when she was making out and wondered if other people did, too. Laying on trampolines, talking under the stars, making out on cool nights, skinny-dipping in the dark—these were physical acts that felt ageless to her, happy years spent in the glorious, endless hours of nighttime, unaccountable, lost. Foreplay was one of these acts that melted away all sense of time and past. Maybe that's why she liked sex so much, because it was a way to lasso her youth and deliver her back to a place where her whole life was still up for grabs. Anything was possible—even love.

Topher moved his hands over Lucy, peeling her bra straps off with the evident appreciation of peeling a perfect banana. She unbuttoned his shirt. Lucy's insides tightened as he took her naked breasts into his mouth, drawing one out, then the other, sucking, flicking his tongue over the nipples as he squeezed. She felt twinges begin to rise between her legs, and glistening tingles grazed her cheeks and shoulders like pixie dust. She shook her head back and forth to keep the energy moving, as if it were she who was solely responsible for stirring the air around them. Then she slid away from him and felt for his hardness. It was there, firm and ready. Lucy moved her hand over it, slowly. Satisfied, she unzipped his pants. His ample penis sprang to life with cartoon conviviality. Topher opened his palms and shrugged his shoulders as if to say, "Hey, what can I tell ya?" Lucy cracked up.

Licking the palm of her hand, Lucy wet the head of Topher's cock with her fingers, smoothing her slippery saliva over its surface before brushing it against her own dampening thighs. She felt powerful. Topher reached under the pleated skirt of Lucy's sundress and found her wet and ready. Lucy moaned quietly with the thrill of another man's fingers in her, exploring the moist folds between her legs. She squealed the tiniest bit as Topher lifted her up then lay her down on the couch, removing her matching lace panties like an old pro. "Oh, my," she said.

Lucy liked that he was strong; she liked that he was in control. She'd found the location and led them there, now it was his turn to take the lead and he was. Lucy surveyed the tall wall of shrubs one more time then, lifting her sundress over her head, felt Topher's skin against hers. She felt the night air move over her as she caressed his thighs—they were soccer-player thighs. When he entered her he dipped in just the tip, then pulled out. Lucy arched her back with an aching want and dug into his ass with her hands. He dipped a little further, then slowly withdrew. *Not in any rush, eh? And not put off by the risk of getting caught, either? Nice.*

Topher slipped on a condom, putting the wrapper in the pocket of his pants—not a litterbug, she liked that, too.

Topher was very hard and his cock was impressive, longer and thicker than Peter's, which Lucy welcomed. "I want all of you," she said, and he plunged into her this time, pushing himself all the way until his pelvic cradle met hers, filling her up completely. Lucy moaned louder than she meant to. The feeling of fullness was incredible, almost shocking. She wanted to growl but stopped herself, then wondered which cultures made the most noise during sex. Warm-weather people out in the middle of deserts and plains? Or cold weather folks holed up in caves and igloos? For Lucy noise was integral to sex the way whooping during a roller-coaster ride was expected and couldn't be helped. She wondered if one could tell how much noise a person made during sex by how loudly they sneezed.

As Topher eased himself out of her again, Lucy begged him to stay inside. He shook his head, sitting back on his haunches, then bent his head down and used his tongue to make her squirm. She reached back with her arms, searching for anything to grab on to and found the back of the glider with one hand and the leg of the coffee table with the other. Lucy became gripped in sudden frenzy and whipped her head from side to side as she arched her back, trying not to squeal. It was maddening that she couldn't make any sounds. Her energy had to go somewhere, but where? As her orgasm approached, Lucy allowed herself the tiniest muffled squeak, as if air was slowly being let out of a balloon. Topher slowed down his pace so that she could enjoy floating back to earth, then entered her once again with a hearty slam. Lucy gasped with delight. He moved in her only long enough to come himself, the driving rhythm of which made her orgasm a second time. *Oh, my God, here it comes again,* she thought, ignoring the squeaks of the ancient glider. Lucy's mind disengaged from her body as she climaxed. Then she quietly caught her breath as she quaked.

Moments later Lucy listened as they panted together, layers of breath weaving through the gently rustling leaves in the maple canopy high above them. Lucy thought, *Those margaritas—two was one too many. Oh, my head. That was fantastic. I hardly felt the condom. What brand does he use?* They collapsed next to each other laying side by side on the couch. Lucy rested her head on Topher's arm as he gingerly lifted a thick strand of hair off her face, then reached down to grab her sundress off the patio, covering her with the full skirt. *Who cares. Don't want to talk. Just rest.* And with that Lucy closed her eyes, saying to herself, *must . . . not . . . fall . . . asleep.*

Song sparrows echoed in the distance and a dog barked somewhere, waking Lucy as the sky was just beginning to lighten through the trees. She was damp from the dew, but realized immediately where she was and was impressed that she'd been able to sleep so long in one position, wrapped up in Topher's arms. Was that her sundress they were using as a sheet? Ha. *Spooning's the best,* she thought and snuggled into him more deeply. Topher slept soundly, his shirt unbuttoned, his breathing low. Thunder rumbled in the distance. Lucy was sad that they would have to be getting up soon but glad that Topher had taken the trouble of tucking things back in before falling asleep—although she couldn't remember him doing it. *Ow, my head hurts.* The inside of her mouth felt woolen, and she was grateful that she didn't smoke, but boy was she thirsty. Her secondary concern was the mascara under her lower lashes. She didn't want to look like a raccoon with Topher. She knew that his first sight of her the morning after would be important—a seminal image seared into his mind forever—and she wanted to look ravishing, or at least as ravishing as possible given the circumstances. But who was kidding who? Lucy was supposed to play hard to get last night. Clearly she forgot. Wups.

Topher stirred as Lucy began to maneuver her arm in order to lick her finger and wipe under her eyes. Then she farted. *Oh. My. God*, Lucy thought. *I hope to hell he's still sleeping.* It was a medium loud fart of short duration and way stinky. Not terrible, but devastatingly embarrassing, nonetheless. Damn, she thought. Damn, damn.

"Mmm," Topher said into the back of her head, "smells like victory."

Lucy squinched her face. Busted. "Really?" she said with a tiny shred of hope.

"No," said Topher. "Smells like a fart." His delivery was very dry.

"Aw, c'mon," said Lucy, "you were supposed to pretend you didn't smell it."

"Or hear it? Sounded like a dime-store whoopee cushion."

"Did not," Lucy said.

"Did, too."

"Did not." In her mind, Lucy packed it in. There would be no rebounding from this. She sat up and slipped her sundress on over her head. "Hey, turn around," Topher said, and Lucy slowly swiveled around. He lifted her chin until their eyes met. "Are we having our first fight?" he said. Lucy still found him gorgeous. "Yes," she said, "and our last, I suppose."

"A one-night stand, eh? I didn't figure you for the type."

"I've never done this," Lucy said. Or exactly this.

"What, sleep with someone on the first date?" he asked.

"No, sleep with a lawyer." Topher chuckled. Lucy said, "But

seriously, you can't possibly want to stick around, I just farted and I'm pretty sure the women you date don't fart. Plus, guys like you who make a ton of money never go for me. You're probably conservative, which is fine, nothing wrong with that, but I'm not fancy enough for you. And I'm too, um, outspoken. Too controversial."

Topher said, "Maybe I like controversy."

"And what about farts? Do you like farts? Because for most guys it's the death knell of a relationship less than eight weeks old, much less eight hours old."

"Well, maybe I'm not like most guys. You women. You love to generalize. You don't think you do, but you do."

"You just generalized." Topher gave up a small smile. Lucy said, "Look, just tell me straight up that the fart was the end of this for you. Don't torture me."

Topher gently led Lucy back down next to him so that they were laying nose to nose.

"I already tortured you," he said, "last night." His voice lowered. "And if you're very lucky, I may do it again." Then he kissed her. Warm and slow. With his eyes closed. Lucy sunk into the kiss. Her body began to awaken again. When they pulled away from each other she said, "Regardless of the fart?"

"Because of it."

"Ha," she said. "Weirdo. Now it's *me* who might not want to see *you* again."

"That's up to you," he said, and licked his finger. Then he ran it under her lower lashes to wipe away the raccoon mascara. "But you'll never know what you're missing."

Gulp, she thought. *Oh my. That might have been the sexiest, most tender . . .* If Lucy had known how to swoon she would have done so right there in his arms. This guy was not like any other. *Wow, wow*, she thought, *I like this guy*. She grinned and nuzzled in for another kiss, but it was interrupted by the sound of that damn dog barking again, then car doors shutting nearby.

"Holy shit, quick!" Lucy said. The sound of hard shoes walking briskly on a brick driveway drew nearer. She bent down and swiped her shoes from the ground as Topher grabbed his. They sprang up and instinctively ran towards the back of the house, the glider couch squeaking behind them. Lucy's sundress was still unzipped and her heart was pounding. She tried not to giggle. Barefoot, they ran around the far side of the house and squeezed through a small break in the hedge and into the neighbor's backyard then kept running. Lucy liked the feeling of Topher's hand resting on her lower back as she wedged through the next hedge. She was good at running in bare feet and felt fast in the wet morning grass. The barking finally stopped; the dogs must have been penned in somewhere. Lucy and Topher crossed behind two more backyards, swerving around playhouses and pools, then emerged onto the road, where they stopped to put on their shoes. They downshifted to a saunter so as not to draw attention. Their walk-of-shame countenance and disheveled dress at 6:30 A.M. on a Sunday morning was bad enough, they didn't need to be running, too. *Play it cool. We're just out for a walk.*

"Looking for our lost dog," Topher suggested while zipping up Lucy without needing to be asked. He could think on his feet. This guy was creative *and* a good kisser. *Don't get your hopes up.*

At Lucy's car, Topher closed her car door for her, stepped back and looked at her with his warm, crinkly eyes. He said, "I'll be calling." Lucy said, "If you say so," then drove off with a big smile and a small wave.

Chapter 25

Goldie needed a sub for an appointment—something about her twins' Girl Scout fly-up ceremony. Audra had a regular appointment and couldn't make it and the wife, Sandy, was pretty sure the other Helpers weren't her husband's type. So Nancy asked Lucy to jump in, even though her duties with The Program had been mostly administrative for a while now. Lucy felt she had to say yes so that no one would suspect she was getting her needs met somewhere else— i.e., Peter—plus she was feeling phenomenally sexy and turbo-charged after meeting Topher.

Topher had said he would be traveling for a week or so and their first date for dinner couldn't be until the night he returned. Lucy tried not to think about Topher and just lived her life. She told friends she was cautiously hopeful, but really she was ecstatic. Subbing for Audra's client Bill would be a welcome distraction.

Bill had been married for nineteen years to Sandy, a friend of Nancy's from their sons' chess club. Sandy told Nancy she was interested in The Program right off the bat and presented Bill with a gift certificate for the program the way a child presents a gift certificate to his daddy for a hug on Father's Day. "Good for 1 Roll in the Hay with Another Woman," it said. It was signed, "Love, Your Wife." She drew hearts and little penises with balls in the corners and put it in an envelope labeled, "Hon." Luckily the kids weren't around when she presented it to him. He'd laughed so hard he had a coughing fit. The story went that Sandy had to convince Bill that it was for real. She told him, "It's because I love you and I trust you and I know you're not going anywhere. You're always getting neckties and radial sanders and I figured this time I'd get you something you really want. Now," Sandy had said, "do you want the sex or don't you? Because I can get you a putter." Bill apparently answered, "It's a tough call but I'll take the sex."

Bill was very prompt for his appointment with Lucy. She opened the door in her patented scoop-neck shirt/miniskirt, and opened-toe sandals and said, "Hello there."

Bill said, "Am I at the right place?" Lucy always wanted to answer with a "Does a bear shit in the woods?" because she got this question a lot, but never felt it was appropriate.

"You bet you are," Lucy said, ushering him in.

"How do we—" he began and Lucy nudged him over and pushed him gently down onto the overstuffed chair in the living room.

"Wow, okay," said Bill. "We're not going to—"

"Nope, we're not," she said, cutting him off and putting her hands on his knees.

He flinched. "Wait a minute," he said. "This is all going a little fast for me."

"I'm sorry. I'll slow down. Most guys usually want to—"

"Well, I'm not most guys," he said with nervous laughter, then he got up out of the chair and walked a few paces away from Lucy.

Bill looked at her nervously. She smiled; he was adorable. Lucy hadn't counted on this reaction. This was something new. He wasn't exactly angry, he just seemed—conflicted. She went for humor to ease the tension. Lucy said, "I would wine and dine you, first, but it wasn't on the work order. Would you like something to drink? I have cheap Scotch, vodka—"

"Work order? Jeez. I feel like a Buick on an assembly line. Do you have lemonade?"

"Uh, sure. Lemme check. And work order does make it sound a little like work, but it's not. It's fun. Helluva lot more fun than assembling Buicks, I think you'll agree."

Lucy flashed a wide, toothy smile when she handed Bill his lemonade. She looked into his eyes as he gulped it down, searching for—for what she wasn't quite sure—but there was something in there that intrigued her. She thought she recognized him from somewhere, but where? All the guys were local, so it was common for Lucy to recognize a face. Plus she was a teacher, so she knew loads of folks in her district.

Bill said "Thank you," then noticed the large abstract painting on Lucy's living-room wall, painted by her grandmother. "I like it, too," she said, then in a sexy voice, "What else do you like?"

Bill said, "Oh, you mean like blow jobs? Yes, I like blow jobs. Is that your segue? Very smooth." He had a dry wit. Lucy liked that.

"Not so subtle, eh?" she said.

"You're clearly not a professional."

"Nah, I'm more the DIY type."

"Crafty," Bill said, and drained his lemonade.

Lucy said, "Would you like to? . . ."

"Oh, sure, right. Let's get down to business. Not that it's business. . . ."

"I get it. I don't mean to rush us, but I have to pick up my son from piano in two hours."

"Got it," said Bill. "Let's do this," he said, and clapped once.

"Okay," Lucy said, and backed him over to the chair again. Bill sat. She leaned over and took off his glasses, folded them and put them on the end table. Then she sat back down in front of him, kneeling like a Japanese geisha about to perform a tea ceremony. Lucy was looking forward to seducing Bill and welcomed the challenge. She gently put her hands on his knees again. "Is this okay?" she said.

Bill closed his eyes. "Yes," he said, then opened them. "Oh, are you talking to me?"

"I am."

"Of course you are."

Lucy slowly slid her hands up his knees in a straight line to his hip bone, then she spread her fingers out and brought her hands back down to his knees again, digging in this time a little deeper. There was ample flesh there to work with. *He must have a desk job and a short commute*, she thought. He didn't work out, she surmised, but he had a kind face that any woman would want to kiss. She didn't, though. The work order she received from Goldie had "no kissing" checked off. Lucy reached down and picked up a foot. Placing his shoe on her thigh she began to unlace his shoes. Bill said, "Oh, I can do that."

"I know you can, but I'm happy to do it for you."

"Oh, okay," he said, then sat forward. "Do you want me to do the other one?"

"No," she said. "Sit back, will ya?" She looked at him and tried to transmit calm with her eyes, the way yoga teachers did. It worked, and he leaned back in his chair again. Lucy moved her hands back up his legs from his ankles, then inwards to where he was beginning to show the rumor of a hard-on. Bill sank into his chair a little and let out a soft sigh. She moved her hands over his bulge and he groaned a little, then let his head fall onto the back of the chair and closed his eyes. Lucy reached for his belt buckle. She was easing the leather strap through when Bill gripped the arms of the chair. She stopped and pulled her hands away.

"You okay?"

"Yeah, I'm good," he said, "keep going."

Lucy went back for the buckle and pulled it through quicker, giving him less time to react. Bill turned his head to the side and squinched his eyes tight like a child on an amusement park ride he's not exactly enjoying. Lucy unbuckled his pants. Then she took the zipper in her hand as if it were a fallen eyelash and began to unzip. She'd never heard a zipper make so much noise. Spreading his fly open gingerly with both hands, she moved one finger across the waistband of his boxers and then with the other—

"Ahhhhh, dammit," he said, and jumped up out of his chair. He paced the room.

"Dammit, I can't. I can't," he said, "God dammit. I can't. Why can't I? Because I love my wife, that's why. But why does this change anything? I'll still love my wife. It's just a blow job, for chrissakes, and cunnilingus, and sex. Why can't I do this?" Bill was exasperated.

"Are you Catholic?" Lucy asked.

"Yeah, but shouldn't matter. A ton of my friends are Catholic and some cheat on their wives with no problem. It's practically an amendment to the commandments at this point. Thou shalt not . . . well, unless she's stopped putting out and your balls are so blue that you think they're going to atrophy and fall off, then, go for it. But never on Sunday."

"And never at dusk," Lucy said.

"Steve Martin?"

"Correct." She nodded, pleased.

"Nice," Bill said, then slowed his pacing and looked down at his front. He'd tucked in his shirt and rebuckled his pants without realizing it. Bill rolled his eyes at himself. "Sorry that I undid all the work you've done undoing."

"Oh, it's no biggie," she said, "I can always redo the undoing."

Lucy sat still. She'd learned from Peter that guys start out in their heads and need to get their minds empty and into the game before they can switch over to autopilot—when their big brain shuts off and their little brain takes over. Peter explained that there's more mind control that goes on with guys during sex than most women realize. Sure, the outside world vanishes for a time, but getting hard, staying hard, then coming at the right time requires a series of well-timed intellectual hurdles. A guy has to manage his dick like one might a moody dilettante. And the older men get, Peter said, the more delicate the negotiation. Lucy decided the less she said the better, so she kept quiet and let Bill work things out, get back into his zone—his batter's box or whatever precipice he spearfished from in his mind. But he wasn't moving towards the chair. He was still standing in the middle of the living room. Lucy looked towards the clock over the living-room mantel.

Finally Bill spoke. "Is this what you do do?" Lucy blurted out a laugh. Bill did as well. They had grown up with Beavis and Butt-Head and the comment clubbed them both with a silly stick. Bill said, "Heh, heh, I said doo-doo."

"Yeah, ya did. Hey, listen, are you stalling? Because we—"

"No," he said, "I want to do this. More than you'll ever know. But I don't know if . . . I just can't. But I want to try. Dammit. I'm doing this for me. It was Sandy's idea for God's sake. So I'm going for it. Let's do this." He clapped again once.

Bill walked over to the chair again, unbuckled his pants, thrust them down to the ground with a flourish then sat. Lucy straightened her shoulders and knelt again. She was getting a huge kick out of Bill. And the challenge. They both let out a good long exhale. Then Lucy whispered, "Ready?" Bill whispered back, "Bring it." Lucy put her hand on top of his flaccid penis and kneaded it gently. She brought her other hand up to the waistband of his boxers and began to tug them down and . . .

"Nope," Bill said, and leapt up. Forgetting that his pants were down around his ankles, he reached out to balance himself by palming Lucy's head like a basketball. Lucy couldn't hold his weight and Bill never found his balance so they both went down like a pile of bricks—Lucy onto her back with her boots in the air and Bill just off to the side of her, facedown in the deep pile carpet. Lucy laughed at their vaudeville moment, but when she looked over she saw Bill pounding the floor with his fist like an exhausted wrestler, too spent to say "Uncle." She felt badly for him. He seemed like a really nice guy. She would have been happy to give Bill a little blow job and have some quick, breezy sex—he seemed like he'd be fun in bed—but thought *this aint happenin'*.

Lucy rolled onto her stomach and inched over to him on her elbows. She crossed her arms and rested her head on them, waiting for him to come around. Bill kept his face turned away from her, knocking his forehead repeatedly into the carpet. "Are you upset?" she asked.

"No," Bill said, muffled by carpet.

"We don't have to do this, you know," said Lucy. She felt terrible. She tried her look-on-the-bright-side voice that she used on herself and her students. "It was a *really, really* nice present from your wife. Amazing! In this case it *is* the thought that counts."

Bill lifted his head. "With all due respect, the *thought* of sex or *almost* sex with a hot stranger doesn't hold a candle to *actual* sex with a hot stranger."

"Well, thank you. And I agree one hundred percent. But it doesn't look like—" Lucy cut herself off. "Just don't beat yourself up about it, okay?"

"I'm such a chicken. I don't get it . . . I was *so* excited, like a kid on Christmas morning. And I love my wife. I mean, I want to kill her pretty regularly, don't get me wrong. She makes me unhinged, but she's the best. And the sex is great. I mean, nineteen years with the same person, don't get me wrong . . . it's . . . you know . . . the same deal, but great."

"I think it's wonderful that you love your wife."

"Do you think she knew I wouldn't go through with it? And that's why she gave it to me? Do you think it was a test of my love?"

"Is she calculating?"

"No. She's a prankster, but she's not calculating, not mean."

Lucy said, "Then I think she loves you enough to give you the best present she could think of. Actually, Goldie's the best available, but she had a thing, so I'm filling in."

"So you're the second best?"

"Actually Audra's the best but she has a regular at this time."

"You're *third* best?" Bill said with mock affront.

Lucy deadpanned, "At your service." Bill broke a smile.

"I've seen you around, too."

"Yeah, I'm a teacher at Margaret Dumont."

"Dumont Elementary? My kids went there."

Lucy said, "Well then that's where—no, I got it, Little League! Are you a coach?"

"Yes."

"My son's team played your team once last year, that day with the unbelievable rain. You were so good with the kids."

"Thanks," he said. "That day was insane. I can't believe you're a schoolteacher. What if you were my kids'—ah, it's moot now. What would we have done, though? It's a little—"

"We're both adults," Lucy said. "We would have compartmentalized, I suppose. Or had you reschedule with Goldie. But your wife would have known and wouldn't have scheduled me in the first place. Teachers have sex lives, you know, just like ministers, librarians and Little League coaches."

"I know, I was just thinking—"

Lucy chided him gently, "Thinking or judging? You want to neuter us, like everyone else? You think that by exorcising all sexuality from us that somehow we'll make better teachers? Please. It's archaic, hypocritical and not very practical. Teachers screw, you know, just like parents. How do you think baby teachers are made?"

"I know," he said, letting her chastise him. He was a good sport.

"You just go back to thinking of us as asexual good Samaritans with hearts of gold."

Bill said, "Like giant Barbie and Ken dolls with brains."

"Exactly." They both laughed. "Gus switched to soccer, so you won't run into me."

"Oh, I wouldn't mind. I think you've been great." She could tell he meant it, too.

"Well, I think you're pretty great, too. Your wife's a lucky woman."

"Thanks, but I'm the lucky bastard," Bill said. "She's my world. She's my whole universe." *What a prince,* Lucy thought. Fully recovered, Bill rolled onto his back, rocked onto his feet and said, "Look at me here with my pants down around my ankles. I'll never become a titan of industry this way."

"Oh, you'd be surprised," Lucy said, and raised her eyebrows. Bill laughed and pulled up and buckled his pants. Lucy said, "Hey, we still have some time left. Would you mind taking a look at my bike? It's in the garage." Lucy knew that the quickest way to re-store a man's dignity and self-confidence was to give him a chore he could master successfully. It was manipulative, but she meant well. She said, "There's something up with the brakes or the chain and I can't figure it out and want to start riding it again. Would you mind?"

Bill said, "Pants on or off?"

"Pants on."

"You got it. Where is it? I'll find it," he said, and walked off.

Bill headed out to the garage, dignity restored, and Lucy got up, straightened the chair and picked up his lemonade glass. Holding the glass, she felt a bolt of something, a flash of deep sadness, and started to choke up a little. The way Bill spoke about his wife with such warmth and camaraderie, the fact that he couldn't accept a blow job, even though he *had her permission*—Lucy fell apart. Sure, maybe their marriage was codependent. Maybe Bill was passing on the sex for a host of dysfunctional reasons, fear and repercussion among them. Lucy knew she shouldn't be envious because she didn't really know what was going on in his marriage and for all she knew they were miserable. But that wasn't it. She could tell they had a good marriage and figured it had a lot to do with Bill's character. The man had integrity. Sandy had found and mar-ried a wonderful guy and it killed Lucy that Sandy got to him first. Plus he seemed nice and funny, was terrific with kids, and still loved his wife after nineteen years. None of the men in Lucy's close prox-imity were that aboveboard, maybe that's why she'd been able to ra-tionalize her poor choices lately. But she couldn't blame her lack of moral code on those around her. Not accepting full accountability was almost worse than what she'd been up to. No, it was all on her.

But maybe that wasn't it, either. Lucy decided she was crying—nearly sobbing at this point—because she would never be that loved by anyone so dear. Matt had been a disaster. Lucy simply wasn't one of the lucky ones. Or maybe it was bravery. Or street smarts or tenacity. What did other women have or do that she hadn't? No one would ever adore her with such sincerity and deep connection, and she would never feel cherished. She would have to be content just knowing those marriages existed and be happy for other folks. Radical acceptance. Look on the bright side.

Lucy forced a grin through tear-stained cheeks, splashed her face, patted it dry and hopped up and down like a fighter, shaking it off. Bill would be finished with her bicycle soon.

Lucy went out to the garage and Bill beamed when he saw her, proud of his workmanship. He pushed the pedal and made the wheel spin; the calm of the ticking sound filled the air between them. Lucy thanked Bill and handed him his briefcase. They shook hands awkwardly and said good-bye, chuckling. As Bill headed to his car, Lucy hopped on her bike and rode it to the end of the street. She still had a few minutes to kill before leaving to pick up Gus and the laundry could wait. Lucy waved to Bill as he drove past her. The wind felt good on her face, daring her to go faster. Lucy sat up straight and found her balance. When she was ready, she lifted her fingers off the handlebars—no hands.

After a brief ride around the block Lucy went inside and discovered a text from Topher. *I'm asking you out to dinner. But only to prove you wrong,* it said. There was no winky-face emoticon. Lucy knew it was implied.

Chapter 26

Peter reached out and grazed Lucy's butt as she passed him to and from the refrigerator, making them egg salad sandwiches. She allowed it because she knew he never could have done this in his own kitchen. His wife would have probably swatted his hand away and admonished him for being inappropriate in front of the kids. Apparently, his wife was always admonishing him for something. Lucy understood; Matt had admonished, too. Six years of marriage and Peter already felt beaten down. Lucy had felt that way after five. But who ever knew if Peter was telling the truth about his wife? She might be a doll. Lucy had no way of knowing, plus it was easier on her to believe him—made it harder to cast herself as a monster.

Peter loved Lucy's breasts and told her so—he loved his wife's butt and Lucy's boobs and said that he wished he could combine them to make a hybrid wife, but "Ah, well."

"That was a jerky thing to say," Lucy said. She knew he sometimes said asinine things to push her away and stave off the crushing wall of guilt that bore down on him when he was with her—guilt that threatened to rob him of his hard-on. But fuck him.

"I met a guy at a party. He asked me out." Lucy wanted to make Peter jealous.

"What's his name?"

"What does it matter?" Lucy said then told him. Peter called him Gopher and asked how long he'd worked on *The Love Boat*. Lucy rolled her eyes and handed Peter his sandwich. He took a bite and said, "The minute you start sleeping with someone else you have to stop sleeping with me." He was also chewing and talking with his mouth open—another reason why Lucy knew she could never be married to Peter. But, wait, *what the hell did he just say?*

"Back up, mister. You get to sleep with your wife *and* me but I don't get to sleep with you and another guy? *Are you joking!?* What a prick thing to say. I thought the whole boon for me in this scenario was that I get to sleep with you while dating. Then if there's overlap, good for me. Your whole life is overlap."

Peter said, "Yeah, but if you ever gave me anything, how would I explain it?"

"Gave you anything? Like what?"

"Herpes, the clap."

"The clap? What is this, 1944? I'm not giving anyone the clap."

"It's out there. And I'm not talking about anyone, I'm talking about you and me. If you're sleeping around, I can't take any chances."

He wasn't kidding. What a prick.

Lucy said, "Well, that's pretty controlling of you."

"Of course it's controlling," Peter said. "I'm trying to control my life from imploding. I'm trying to make smart choices to preserve my marriage, which means not sleeping with someone who has sex without a condom."

"So then stop sleeping with me," Lucy said.

"I'm trying to. I can't help it."

"Well that's convenient. And completely lacking accountability. What are you, twelve?"

"Twelve and a half," Peter said, and kept chewing. He appeared unrepentant and unfazed. Lucy realized she would have to lie to Peter—the one guy she felt she could say anything to—but he was being an ass so it was easy. How could he possibly demand the pristine truth from her when he lived such a lie to so many others? They were both playing a liar's game now. The thought made her angry.

"First of all, I'm not sleeping with him, yet. And I do use condoms. You're the one who doesn't." But she didn't need to, except for STDs. Knowing she couldn't get pregnant anymore, her adherence to condoms had waned with Program guys in monogamous marriages.

Lucy continued, "You know, none of this has ever stopped you from sleeping with me before."

"I didn't think you were dating anyone before. Were you?"

"No." Lucy got up to clear so he wouldn't see her face. "Are you jealous? I thought I wasn't your girlfriend."

"You're not. And I think it's great you found someone. In fact, I'm a little relieved."

"Ouch," Lucy said. This was not fun. She folded her arms. What a complete stinker.

"C'mon," he said, "you know what I mean. I mean that I'm just glad that you're happy."

"You're trying to break up with me," Lucy said.

Peter said, "Of course I am! Every time I see you I want to break up with you. I'm *not* your boyfriend!"

"I know that! But where else are you going to find a replacement mistress who's available in the afternoon, who won't drain your bank account, and who isn't going to show up on your lawn, drunk at 2 A.M. in a peignoir set?"

Peter said, *"Craigslist!"*

"Oh, screw you," Lucy said, and meant it.

He said, "Hey, if you're not using a condom with me, there's no telling what you're planning to do or not do with Gopher—"

"It's Topher. And fuck you. I'm not sleeping with skeevos or junkies. Topher is a respectable guy with a career, an ex-wife, and teenage kids. He's not *cheating* on anyone."

Peter said, "You sound like a poster on an AIDS-clinic wall. 'He looked like a decent guy . . .' Jesus, Luce, don't be so goddamn naïve. Besides, it's not you I don't trust. It's him."

"No. I think it's *everyone* you don't trust. How can you trust anyone if you're always lying? You must assume everyone's always lying to you."

"I trust my wife," Peter said.

"A lot of good it's doing her," said Lucy.

"Hey, let's not talk about my wife, okay?" Peter pushed away from the table and crossed his arms. Now they were both pissed.

Lucy said, "I think you're a hypocrite and a stinker and I can't believe you're trying to impose a different set of standards on me. It's controlling and lame and you're starting to remind me of my ex-husband."

"And I think you're being—"

Lucy whipped around and cut him off, *"Don't.* Say it. You don't want to regret—"

"But you're—"

"Zzt. Don't do it," Lucy said, pinching the air. "I have a memory like an elephant."

Peter said, "No you don't. You have a memory like an eggplant."

"For where I parked my car maybe, but cruel things that people have said to me are burned into my memory forever."

"Or maybe that burning sensation is an STD."

"Hardy-har. Look, are we going to have sex or not, because the longer we argue, the less I want anything to do with you." Lucy knew Peter would want her, had no idea when he would get to have sex with his wife again—it could be weeks, months. She was also thinking that this was a sure thing, Topher was not. And yes, Peter was being a jackass today, but her greed for orgasm trumped her need to kick him out of her house. It wasn't her job to educate him—he knew he could be an ass. She just wanted to lose herself, and as long as he stopped talking, she would. Lucy stood in the middle of the kitchen and looked at Peter. She unbuttoned a single button on her blouse then let her fingers linger on the next.

"No talking," said Lucy. She unbuttoned the next button. Peter's eyes narrowed.

"Fine," he said, and got up, put his plate on the counter and brushed past her.

"Fine," Lucy said, and followed him as he marched upstairs to her bed.

Chapter 27

- -

A few days later Lucy, was seated across from Topher at a little sidewalk café a few towns over. They'd decided to meet in the middle; Lucy was shocked they were meeting at all. She kept thinking she never should have slept with him on the first night she'd met him. Duh. What was she thinking? She felt certain she'd blown it, but he'd stood and kissed Lucy warmly on the cheek when she'd arrived.

"Is this a date?" Lucy asked Topher.

"It is," he said.

"Just making sure."

"Of what?"

"Of what. Where I am in the scope of things. In the time and space continuum, I don't know. I'm talking sideways out my ass."

"Another talent of yours?" he said, and grinned. His shirt cuffs were unbuttoned; he seemed completely relaxed. Topher looked right at Lucy with his big brown eyes, so handsome in his pink linen button-down. All men looked good in pink, but not all of them had the confidence to wear it. Topher wasn't fidgeting or looking past her at all the prettier, younger women walking by, just at Lucy while calmly holding the stem of his wineglass against a pale melon tablecloth. A magenta peony sat in a milk-glass vase. Lucy thought she'd died and gone to date heaven.

"And you," Lucy said, "what are your talents? Aside, of course, from the ones I already know about." She felt pretty relaxed. She liked the sundress she'd chosen, then hadn't given it another thought since leaving the house. She hoped he was funny.

Topher said, "My talents? Gardening, heavy lifting. Parking karma, model rockets."

Bingo, Lucy thought. "That's quite a skill set. I can see why you went into law."

"And pies," Topher said. "You'd be amazed at how far strawberry rhubarb pies have gotten me."

"I'm not surprised in the least. And where is the ex-Mrs. Rhubarb these days?"

"Three blocks away. The kids walk back and forth. We're civil. Borderline friends."

"Sounds idyllic."

"It is," he said.

"And there's no one else, um, special at the moment?" Lucy said.

"No. How about you?"

"Well, there's me, I'm special. I mean, no. No one special." She wasn't technically lying. But she squirmed on the inside because she was. Lies of omission were the worst.

"And where is the ex-Mr. Special?" Topher said.

"He and his fiancée bought a brownstone in Harlem."

"To be near his son?"

"Ha. Yeah," Lucy said, "Gus adores him. We're borderline civil."

Lucy took a sip of wine. Talking about Matt made her fidget. She was becoming self-conscious so she picked up the menu to reorient herself. *Be in the now*, she thought. *Get it together. Breathe.* Just then a woman walked into the café wearing the very jacket Kit had lost months ago. She was being seated a table away. "Oh, my God," said Lucy and a hearty laugh escaped her.

"What?" said Topher.

"You're not going to believe this. But that woman who just sat down—don't look now, wait, I'll tell you when—the tan leather blazer she's wearing with the birds and flowers hand-painted on the pockets and lapel . . . it's vintage, from Mexico, and it belonged to my best friend, who thinks she left it on the train a few months ago. We saw her walk by once and tried to ask her about it but we lost her in the crowd and now she's sitting right here. Bizarre. Okay, you can look." Topher glanced over his shoulder as he took a sip of his wine. He was cucumber cool. "Nice jacket," he said to Lucy, still appraising the woman.

"Kit loved it. She was crushed to lose it. It was her favorite. A real one-of-a-kind."

Topher thought a moment then looked at Lucy and said, "This is your *best* friend?"

"Yes," said Lucy, although now she wasn't so sure. Topher got up from the table with his wineglass, and before Lucy realized what he was doing, approached the woman in the jacket. Nonplussed, Lucy slumped in her chair, hid behind her wineglass and eavesdropped on the exchange. "Excuse me," Topher said to the woman. "Please forgive me for interrupting but that's a very unique jacket. Beautiful detail. May I ask where you got it?" The woman smiled up at Topher then looked around and spotted Lucy looking at them. Lucy thought she detected a trace of disappointment after the woman's initial efforts to dazzle.

"Uh," she said, "thank you. I love it, too. My brother gave it to me for my birthday."

"In the last three months?"

"Yes. Why do you—"

Topher took his time. "My friend over there is pretty sure it belonged to her best friend who mistakenly left her favorite jacket on the train—"

The woman's smile fell away. "That would be just like my brother. He told me he 'procured' it." She shook her head in disappointment then looked at Topher. "It's mine now."

Topher was quick to respond. "Of course it is. No doubt." He took a lazy sip of wine. "Tell you what," he said, "we've all lost something that we cherished—left something behind that we might kick ourselves about to this very day. Everyone has a story like that. I know I do. I just thought in this case that it was worth trying to reunite the person with the object—facilitating the universe and all that. Imagine the thrill that it would bring the original owner. This rarely happens, so I thought I'd try. And I'd be more than happy to pick up your dinner check and throw in a bottle of wine. For your birthday."

The woman looked over at Lucy then back up at Topher and said, "My birthday was last month and I appreciate your offer, but I like the jacket, so . . ."

Topher jumped in, "I get it. I get it. It's always worth a try. Thanks for your time. No hard feelings." He lifted his wineglass to her, smiled broadly and backed away. Lucy was dumbfounded. When he returned to their table she didn't know what to say—"Wow" was all she could muster.

"Wow, nothing. I failed," Topher said, calmly sitting back down.

"You were incredible," Lucy said. "You were charming and reasonable, not pushy or manipulative. You didn't mention guilt or whip out your wallet. You were gracious and . . . just . . . you handled that beautifully."

"Well, it never hurts to ask. And straightforward is generally the best direction."

"Well, thank you for trying. You don't even know my friend whose jacket it is."

"Was. But I know you. And I like a challenge. Shall we order?"

Lucy opened her menu, then thought a minute, closed it and leaned forward. "Why are you . . ." she lowered her voice, ". . . I mean, obviously you could have whomever you wanted. Someone younger, taller, fancier. Why are you?—"

Topher cut her off, "Because you have good grammar. You're beautiful *and* funny. And you'll have sex with me outdoors. Women like you are not a dime a dozen."

"Oh. Okay." Lucy tried to suppress a smile. She said, "I suppose all of that's true," but wanted to say, *you have no idea.* Her confidence returned. She leaned back again.

Topher said, "What do you say we just get to know each other for a while and not get ahead of ourselves? It means giving up control, though. Think you can do that?"

"Are you kidding? No. But there's always a first time."

"Well, I'd like to be your first time."

"Ha. That train left the station ages ago. But sure, let's give it a whirl," Lucy said, and bit into a skinny garlic breadstick. From there they shared two appetizers, an entrée and everything but secrets. Their conversation meandered and converged, slipstreams of information leading to new questions then jokes. They connected on levels both obvious and obscure, but more importantly, they laughed.

"Last meal," Lucy said. "Haggis or tripe?"

"Can I use condiments?" asked Topher.

"There are no condiments on death row."

"What did I do to get there?"

"You killed a man for flamenco dancing with your wife. No pardons. The governor's at his niece's wedding in Cabo. Haggis or tripe?"

"There must be a few duck sauce packets laying around. Or soy sauce. I'll use those. In this scenario, am I a good flamenco dancer?"

"You're the best, but not as good as the man you murdered."

"A crime of passion. I see. In that case, I'll go with the haggis."

Topher knew about global economics and stealth robotics, Jonathan Winters and stew.

They sat for hours, discussing David Lynch, impressionist painters, vaudeville and puns, and Lucy's mind was awake and on heightened alert the entire time. *I can learn from this guy*, she thought, *and laugh with this guy. Don't blow it*. They were there for so long and ate so slowly that all the tables, which had been seated after they arrived, began to empty. Finally, their waiter put the check down on the table. In his other hand he was holding the leather jacket. He said, "The lady at the other table said you left your jacket." He held it out. Lucy's mouth dropped open. Topher handed the waiter a credit card and said matter-of-factly, "Thank you very much. Lucy, take your jacket."

Lucy reached out and took the jacket.

Chapter 28

Two weekday mornings, Lucy arranged for a small group of ESL students to get dropped off thirty minutes before the school bell to work on English reading strategies. She didn't get paid for her time and knew that it wouldn't be forthcoming—the administration wasn't happy with the liability—but knew they were bright and able and the sooner they caught up to grade level the better. It broke Lucy's heart to see kids slip behind. She wished she could meet with them three mornings a week, but knew she couldn't pawn Gus off on neighbors that often. Besides, Lucy knew she had to have boundaries. They were every teacher's secret weapon against burnout, and their biggest challenge.

Just before the bell, Lucy told her ESL kids that they were doing very well and urged them to read at home before they met again next week. She made sure to smile warmly at each of them and make eye contact as she said good-bye, then straightened the chairs for her homeroom kids' madcap arrival. She loved the immediate challenge of trying to assess everyone's mood. There were the tell-tale signs of various home situations, which she had to decode, sleuthlike. Lucy hoped to hell that all her students had dry shoes on their feet, a balanced breakfast in their tummies, and at least ten hours of sleep under their belts, but knew that was unlikely.

She greeted them without having to harangue them about what to do, having trained them well by this point in the year. It was an efficient and organized classroom with consistent systems and attainable goals. Students put their folders and lunches in the proper bins, hung their windbreakers and hooded sweatshirts on their hooks, then sat quietly to copy that night's homework assignments into their daily planners.

At exactly 8:07 A.M., Lucy rang a gently tinkling bell and the kids pushed in their chairs and met her on the rug in front of the big calendar for Morning Meeting. She believed wholeheartedly in fostering independence and the ability to stand in front of one's peers and present information, so she allowed her students to take turns leading Morning Meeting: recording the weather, lost teeth, counting days of school, etc. But first, Lucy led the Greeting Circle and Calendar Time before turning it over to her students. After everyone said their hellos—using eye contact and their neighbor's name—Lucy stood in front of the big calendar with a wand in her hand that had a green, glittery star on its end. First, she asked what yesterday's date was and the children recited it in unison. Then she asked what today's date was and they repeated it in kind. Then she took the wand and counted out how many weeks there were in the month of May, tapping the star on each Sunday as she went down the calendar. Then Lucy froze.

Oh, no, she thought. She flipped the giant page of the calendar back to the month of April and counted those weeks. Oh, no, she thought again, then flipped back to May and tapped the green, glittery star quickly down and back up the Sundays, then flipped back to March and froze again. The math came at Lucy fast, pelting her with subtraction. *Remember, remember,* she said to herself and tapped the wand against her forehead. The children giggled. Lucy looked over at them, smiled nervously and drew a blank. Her heart was pounding out of her chest and her hands were beginning to perspire.

Joshua asked, "Miss Larken, are you okay?"

"What?" Lucy said, stalling for time.

"Are you okay?" Fiona asked.

"Huh?" she said, staring out over their heads at the fire alarm. She wondered briefly what would happen if she pulled it. She needed time, just some time to think and that would buy her about thirty minutes of quiet out on the playground field. Her students would stand silently according to fire alarm protocol, the softly chirping birds would sooth her. But it would also get her fired. And arrested. *No, Lucy, don't pull the alarm,* another voice told her. She hoped that that voice would tell her what to do next and next and for all the nexts in her brain that lined up, single file like her students, waiting to be told what to do. But the voice was still.

Lucy's students looked at each other, laughed louder and began conferring with one another. They thought their teacher was baiting them, goading them to say it in unison, so they recited, loudly, "ARE. YOU. OH. KAY?!" Lucy snapped out of it. "Yes, children, yes, boys and girls, I am o-kay," Lucy said, and forced a big wide smile. "I was just thinking that after Morning Meeting, just for today, we should switch around Ready Readers and Math Attack and give you all a chance to read silently for thirty minutes first, *before* we do math."

"Yay!" they all said.

"Yay," she echoed back at them, but her voice was decidedly weaker.

Once the children were all reading back at their desks, or on the floor, or in beanbag chairs in Calm Corner, Lucy took out a big social studies textbook and opened it on her desk so that it wouldn't appear to her students that she was staring into space. She held her head in both hands to keep it from spinning off her spine and anchored it there for the full thirty minutes. Her knee bounced like a rabbit's heartbeat as she instructed herself to breathe through her nose. While she was thinking, a low rumbling in her stomach grew in pitch and strength. She felt hungry again even though she had just eaten. And just the teensiest bit nauseous.

Lucy had a forty-five minute prep period that backed up to her lunch break—which bought her another thirty—so she hopped in her car and zipped over to Audra's, even though the principal discouraged leaving the grounds unless it was unavoidable. Lucy figured that keeping her head from exploding and her heart from pumping out of her chest and splattering all over the walls of the teacher's lounge was a valid reason to leave. She parked her car on the access road behind Audra's house and ran through the hedges, in the back door, and flew up the stairs calling Audra's name as she skipped steps. She figured she'd find Audra in her home office on a conference call, but that was not the case. She found her lying in bed, bare-shouldered, with an adult-sized blobby lump under the covers between her legs. Lucy said, "Hey, I need to—oh, sorry." Then she mouthed, "Who's that?"

"Who's who?" Audra asked wearing only a smirk.

"I'm sorry," said Lucy realizing, "I should go, I just thought . . . I'm sorry."

But Audra was still smiling. What was so funny? Did she have a lunchtime appointment? Lucy was pretty sure that most of The Program husbands in town commuted into the city. Maybe one of them worked from home today. Lucy scraped some composure together and whispered, "I'm sorry to interrupt. I have to talk to you. It's very important and I only have another fifty-five, so, when you finish up, please—"

"You can talk now," said Audra. She sat up and knit her hands together in her lap. Her bed sheet slid down—exposing her left, perfectly round, C-cup of a bosom with the prettiest, pinkest areola you've ever seen—but Audra didn't care. Clothes and bed sheets were incidental and she was just as comfortable wrapped in them as not.

Lucy said, "Aren't you? Why don't you—who's under there?" Lucy was impatient. She had a balsa-wood dam keeping her emotions at bay and this little game Audra was playing was more annoyance than intrigue.

Lucy said, "Godammit! I need to—" then she was interrupted by a sneeze the size of Texas. It was a lady sneeze, but loud. As if it had come from a big woman. Under the covers.

Lucy bellowed, "*DIX!* Audra, is that—for chrissake, is there anything you won't fuck?!"

"Not really," said Audra, with a dopey grin.

"Want to join us?" the lump said with a muffled, poorly disguised man's voice. Audra raised her fist and brought it down hard on the lump.

"*Ow!*" Dix said, and came out from under the sheet. "That hurt! What the hell?!"

Audra said to Dix, "Our friend needs to talk to us. The fucking must cease."

"Cease fuck?" said Dix, and she sat up straight. Another stupid grin to contend with.

"Cease fuck," said Audra.

Dix said, "Oh, is this about Topher? Did he call you?"

Lucy stammered. "Yes, we had dinner. He's amazing. But this isn't about that."

Audra said to Dix, "Is that the bass player you were telling me about?"

Dix said, "He's way dreamy. I saw them leave together."

Lucy said, "This isn't about Topher. It's more important." She took a moment to gear up for the big reveal. Her eyes began to well. Audra and Dix glanced once at each other and then looked back at Lucy.

"You're pregnant," they said, pretty much in unison. Lucy stared at them, her mouth slightly open. They looked excited, expectant, hoping.

"But I just—"

Audra said, "We were just talking about it. You've been tired and cranky—"

Dix said, "—and eating like a refugee. You always complain when you have your period and you haven't mentioned it in ages. It just occurred to both of us and we were going to ask."

Audra said, "Your boobs are plumper."

"Juicier," said Dix. Lucy couldn't decide if she was more shocked by her news or the fact that they came to the same conclusion on the same day. And were sleeping together.

"I need to pee on a stick," Lucy said in a whimpering lilt.

"Yes, you do, darlin'," said Dix, "but you know the answer."

"Congratulations!" Audra shouted and raised her arms in victory. Her other naked breast bounced out from under the sheet to join the party. "When are you due?"

"Who says I'm keeping it?" said Lucy.

"Oh, sweetie, you've wanted this more than anything," said Dix.

Lucy said, "I know, but I—"

Audra snapped, "Of course you are, don't be foolish. That's the end of it."

Lucy snapped back, "That's not the end of it! How can you just say that like it's some proclamation?! You're not the queen! How would I support another kid? How would Gus handle it? And I don't know whose it is! I can't even begin to guess." With the last statement, Lucy burst into gasping sobs dotted with intermittent squeaks. "I, I, I, I've had s-so much s-sex and I . . . it could be a-a-any-one's. I-I was s-sub-bing and I can't e-e-ven. I, I—"

"Woah, girl. Hold on, hon, deep breaths," Dix said, and crawled out naked from under the sheet and over to Lucy, where she took her by the hand and set her down on a turn-of-the-century French velvet settee under a salmon-pink silk-fringed lampshade. Dix sat next to her and rubbed her back while Audra sauntered away to fill a glass of water.

Dix said, "Could it be Peter's?"

"Y-Yes," said Lucy. She didn't go into details. She still felt horrible about the turkey baster.

"Could it be Ted's?"

"Yeh-huh. Nancy told me not to use a condom."

"How about Topher?"

"Uh-huh," Lucy said, then, "No. Well, maybe, I gue-ess. He did a li-ittle dipping, you know, with his . . . before he put the condom on."

Dix brightened. "How was he?"

Audra said, "Not now," to Dix, and put the glass in Lucy's hand. She drank the water in big sloppy gulps. Audra asked, "How about Ted or Fwank? Or Duncan?" Lucy nodded yes from behind the glasses rim. Their eyes popped. Dix said, "Whaaaaat?"

Lucy defended herself, "I always used one if they brought one!

I was diligent, but if it broke or fell off, I didn't panic. It's not a perfect system. I didn't think it mattered because I can't get pregnant!"

"Even Fwank? Yikes. What about Jill's husband, the girly-man?" Lucy shook her head.

"Well that's something," Dix said. Lucy choked on her water.

"I'm telling you, I've been pronounced infertile by numerous doctors!"

Dix said, "No, it's cool. It's cool. Don't panic," and looked at Audra with a jump-in-here-please look.

Audra said, "What about Goldie's guy—the birthday boy with the coupon?" Lucy shook her head, no. Dix and Audra celebrated. "All right! Not him, either! Yay!" Lucy almost did a spit take. It was funny in a pathetic, impossible, awful way. Then her eyes grew wide and she gasped and put her hand to her mouth.

"Another one?" said Dix sympathetically. Lucy slowly nodded, yes.

"Shit, darling," said Audra, "you make us look like a couple of nunnery lezbos."

Lucy threw what little water was left in the bottom of her glass at Audra.

"Okay!" Audra said. "Stop!"

"You stop!" said Lucy.

"We have to help her," Dix said to Audra. "She's turned to us in her moment of crisis. Let's find our clothes and head back down to the kitchen. We need to talk this through."

They all went downstairs to a trail of clothes strewn about—apparently Audra and Dix had disrobed each other over chopped chicken salad. Huddled in the kitchen around the island, they picked at the food that was left on the two plates before them. Audra brought out additional containers of sliced fruit, bruschetta, olive tapenade and half a loaf of garlic bread. They ate with their fingers.

"How can *you* be here?" Lucy asked Dix, jabbing in her direction with a snap pea.

Dix said, "My schedule was switched around with Reilly's and I have prep now before lunch. We don't have much time. Do you want another baby?"

Lucy said, "Yes, but—"

"That's enough. No 'buts.' It's a good start. Remember that when this all starts to get away from you. That's your home base. 'Yes, I want another baby.' Say it."

"What about Gus?" Lucy asked, ignoring her.

Audra said, "Gus will adapt. It's your choice not Gus's, dear. You are the parent and he will roll with whatever you toss at him."

"My mom will freak."

"Your mom is irrelevant," Audra said. "We're too old to be making life's grand decisions based on how our parents might react."

Audra looked at Lucy. "Please tell me you're beyond that."

"I'm beyond that."

Dix said, "Are we ever really beyond that?"

Audra said, "As of today we are. Yes. What else?"

"How do I figure out who the father is? It's going to be like a game show with contestants. So many contestants." Lucy's eyes started to glaze over.

Audra said, "Why does it matter?"

Lucy snapped back. "Why does it *matter*?! Because it *does*! Because I have to discuss it with the father and, maybe, his wife, who *also might be my friend*, or not—I don't know which is worse— and, oh my God, no one's going to let me keep their husband's baby. I can't have this baby." Lucy shook her head back and forth and raised her hands up to cover her face.

Dix reached over, took her hands down and said, "No, sweetie, hang on," then she put Lucy's hands in hers and pinched the little web of skin between her thumb and pointer finger in an effort to stop her from crying.

Dix spoke again, her voice rich with compassion. "Why do you need anyone's permission to have this baby? We're all adults and everyone knew the game they were playing. There are risks involved with every choice we make, and this was one of them. All the husbands and their wives are just as accountable."

Lucy whimpered, "I could lose my friends. Everyone would hate me. I'd have to move."

Audra said, "You could do worse, moving out of this flea-bitten town."

Dix glared at Audra. "Shut it, Bette Davis. Lucy, what you're thinking of doing isn't going to be easy. We've established that. But I will stay your friend and so will Audra. I'm sure Fran will, and certainly Kit and Gina. They're your closest friends. They won't abandon you in your time of crisis. True friends don't do that."

Lucy said, "Oh, I don't know, I'm starting to wonder."

Audra said, "Well, don't. There's too much to do. You'll just have to take each reaction as it comes, like anything else in this world. Keep swinging. You've got tenure?"

"Not yet, but on day one of next year. In September."

"Good, so health benefits are secure. And we know the day care in this town is terrific. So don't worry your pretty little head about that for one minute. This baby will be the luckiest child in the world to have you for a mother and Gus for a big brother, and nothing else matters."

"But that's not true. *Everything else matters.*"

Dix said, "Only if you let it. You'll see. Your friends will rise to the occasion. Who wouldn't want your child as a half brother or sister? They'll be so happy for you. You're going to have a baby!"

Dix and Audra smiled at Lucy, but Lucy had a very difficult time smiling back.

Lucy peed on a stick after work. Two pink lines. Now she really had to tell Kit and Gina. They knew she'd wanted this for so long. Eight years. Actually, her whole life. Kit would be thrilled for her, wouldn't she? Even if it were Fwank's? Maybe not, she thought. A year ago, she might be open to the idea, but now—*not so much*. They'd practically raised their kids from babyhood as siblings already—so close, like brothers. They may not play together as much anymore, but, that's okay. Friendships ebb and flow, right?

Gina she wasn't as sure of, but she was an open-minded cosmopolitan woman who could handle anything. Lucy would make a date to see Kit and Gina for lunch first, then she'd tell the others. She texted them and waited to hear back. A feeling of low-grade dread crept in.

In the meantime, Lucy was buzzing, literally vibrating with excitement over being pregnant. Gus was at Matt's for the night and she had no plans, so she decided to go bra shopping. Her boobs were already growing. Target was open until, what, 10 P.M.? Plenty of time. Lucy glanced at the maternity department first but knew better than to try anything on—too soon. She knew damn well that the chances of this pregnancy reaching full term were slim. She was older now—mid-forties—and had lost other pregnancies. Two that she knew of and Lord knew how many others that she didn't. None of those so-called perfect zygotes had implanted in her uterine wall after they'd been escorted right up to the doorstep of her ovaries after multiple IVF implantations, so this baby would probably not hold. Lucy decided right then and there to not buy a single piece of maternity clothing until she absolutely needed to, or accept any baby gifts until the baby was born. It would be hard—she had loved shopping the first time around—but she'd stick to her guns. Her old heartbreak was still loitering nearby.

But she needed a bigger bra. Crossing the aisle from the maternity department to ladies underthings, she noticed Ted walking up the aisle. It was too late to hide from him—he'd spotted her. What the heck was he doing here on a Friday night?

"What the heck are you doing here on a Friday night?" Lucy said. Ted was wearing a T-shirt, khakis and a windbreaker. His white sneakers looked brand new. He looked dorky, seemed lost. Not literally—there wasn't a soul alive for miles that didn't know this Target like the back of his or her hand—she meant more metaphysically. He was wearing his loneliness like an accessory.

Lucy said, "If you're stalking me, you're terrible at it." It was a weak attempt at humor.

"No," he said seriously, "Nancy's having some friends over for dinner and I just wanted to get out of the house. You know how it is."

Huh, Lucy thought. *I wonder which friends?* Nancy had so many groups of friends from all those kids in different grades and schools and teams. She hoped Nance hadn't had her group over and not invited her. *Don't be paranoid,* she thought. *Why would she do that?* No one knows she's pregnant, yet. "So, who was at the house?" Lucy asked anyway. Ted said, "Oh, I don't know. I left before they arrived." "Huh," Lucy said. But her mind was racing. *Stop being so insecure*, she told herself. *Hormones*, she thought. They've already got her in their grip. *Settle down,* Lucy nearly said aloud.

Ted finally spoke. More like sputtered, "Hey, um. I was wondering . . ."

"Oh, jeez," Lucy said. "What? Do you still think you're in love with me?"

"No, not you, but . . ."

"Oh, no. Who? C'mon, out with it."

"Dixie."

Lucy blurted out a comic book laugh, one of those big giant *HA-HA-HA*'s that take up all the leftover space on the panel next to the cartoon character's head.

"Dix? *Our* Dix?" Lucy said, and the image of Dix under the covers, going down on Audra, came to mind. Poor Ted. He still looked like a big, sweet Labrador retriever.

Lucy said, "Okay, you know what? No. You're *not* in love with Dix, Ted. Why are you so hot to be in love? Is it the falling in love you miss? The chemical rush? The serotonin release?"

"I don't know," he mumbled.

"Is it the hot sex with someone new, Ted? Reminds you of high school, doesn't it—all those steamy nights on basement couches, before you had to worry about buried oil tanks and when to repave the driveway?"

"I don't know," Ted said, and stared off again over her shoulder. Lucy turned around to see what he was looking at. He was gawking at the big hanging sign of skinny young models having a pillow fight in their cute bra-and-panty sets. He was listening, though.

Lucy said, "I know you don't know. Ted, look at me." Ted refocused his gaze at Lucy. It seemed to take everything he had. "If you want to leave Nancy, then leave her. But you have to know why you're leaving her or else you're doomed." Then something occurred to Lucy and she inhaled through her mouth. "There's no other woman, is there, not really? It's the life, isn't it? It's this—Target on a Friday night. And Home Depot and Costco on Saturday morning. They try to design the stores so you won't feel castrated, but you do anyway. It's sapping the life force out of you, isn't it?"

"I don't know," said Ted. He appeared hollow. Lucy could practically see his soul leaking out of his body, puddling on the linoleum. She hadn't thought him capable of such a look, but there it was in his eyes—despair. Lucy should have been sweeter with him, more compassionate, but she was cranky for her own reasons and didn't make room for him in her heart at that moment. But she softened her tone. "Where would you rather be, Ted? Building fences? Riding the range? What would it take for you to feel like a man in control of his life? Barn raising? Bull riding?"

"I don't know, I—"

"There are lots of women out there, Ted. And they'll line up for a nice, clean-smelling employed man like you, but you've got to know what it really is you want, and what it is about your life that you're running away from. Then tell Nancy and give her a chance to fix it. Let her try to help you. 'Cause you will be lost without her, my friend. Do you know that? Lost."

"Yeah, I know," he said, and looked back at the models in their underwear.

"Okay," Lucy said, "you've got a lot to think about. Go over to the automotive aisle and buy something you don't need for your car. Then try to figure out your life. I gotta buy a new bra, Ted. I gotta figure out *my* life." Lucy patted him on the back twice and then headed off into the bra racks. She left Ted standing there, staring at the pillow fight.

Lucy was in a changing room stall trying on bras, her least favorite pastime next to bathing-suit shopping. *I should be slightly buzzed,* she thought, *but now I can't drink.* She wished she weren't by herself, but this was one of those quests that a woman had to do alone, her version of riding the range to bring back the herd. Sure, it would be fun to be bra shopping with a friend. Why not dinner, drinks, then bra shopping together? She could start a trend. But the truth was that being divorced, she had more free time than her friends. Everyone loved to say, "Oh, you're so lucky to be alone in your house without a husband or kids around. It must be heaven. I can't imagine what that's like." To which she would smile thinly and reply, "You should get divorced and find out." Some women laughed while others considered the idea. No one realized that Lucy would have traded places with them in a minute.

Taking a closer look in the mirror, Lucy noticed a big white underarm deodorant stain on the black bra she thought fit pretty well and said, "Oh, great," out loud. A voice in the next stall said, "Lucy? Is that you?" It was Kit. She came out of her stall and they met in the hallway wearing only jeans and bras. They laughed and hugged but then Lucy's delight abruptly ended. Following Kit out of the same stall was Gina in a skirt and bra. She was happy to see Gina but a little hurt that she hadn't been invited to join them. *No biggie*, she thought. *This is a coincidence. Be positive.*

"How funny is this," said Lucy. They were all standing there in shiny new bras with tags hanging from their armpits.

Kit said, "What a bunch of losers, right?"

Gina said, "Yeah, dinner, wine, then bra shopping at Target on a Friday night. Pathetic." She and Kit giggled. They seemed buzzed. Lucy felt a lump in the pit in her stomach begin to rise into her throat, but pushed it down and shook it off. She had news to share and needed to find a segue. She felt like she was inching onto the high dive.

Lucy took a breath. "I don't know about you, but I come here for the ambiance."

Gina added, "I come here for the lighting."

Lucy tried to stay positive. "Are you guys getting anything?" Kit held up a bra with leopard cups and a tiny ruffle of red lace peeking out from along the rim. Gina said, "It looks really good on her."

"Oh, it's totally vetoed," said Kit, and she and Gina laughed like sorority sisters.

"Yeah," said Lucy making a squinchy face. "Hey, ladies, I have something to tell you."

"Okay," they said, and Lucy looked around for the right place.

"Come in here," Gina said, "We're in the 'Differently-Abled' together."

"Cozy," Lucy said, and felt the corners of her smile working against her. Kit and Gina squeezed together on the little bench in the changing room and looked up at Lucy. Lucy stood in front of them like she was about to perform a magic trick. She didn't know where to begin. She watched their bra tags swing back and forth and then still themselves. Then she inhaled.

"Looks like I'm pregnant," Lucy said with clear eyes and a hopeful smile.

Kit and Gina gasped. "*Ohmygod*, that's great! No way! That's *amazing*! Holy *shit*!" followed by little country-club golf claps. Lucy curtsied then watched them watch her. She folded her arms and scratched at her elbows, waiting for what she knew was coming next.

"Who's the father?" asked Kit with big, expectant eyes. Lucy started rocking back and forth; her scratching became more intense. Her friends waited for an answer, assuming it would arrive bundled into one word. "Well, that's just the thing," began Lucy, "I'm not exactly sure."

"Well, how pregnant are you?" asked Gina. Kit looked skeptical. "I'm not sure about that either—anywhere between eight and twelve weeks, I think—maybe more." She thought about Topher; he was pretty recent. "Maybe less. I peed on the stick and it said 'pregnant' right away. Practically leapt up and congratulated me. I have an appointment with my ob-gyn on Thursday." Lucy could feel her big, dopey smile forced onto them. They weren't so thrilled.

"Wait," Gina said a little sternly, "you could be through your first trimester?"

Lucy said, "Yeah, isn't that great? I mean, it's a little Guinness book-y and all that—not realizing until now—but it's pretty good when you think about it. No morning sickness, just tired. I thought I was a little depressed. Turns out I was pregnant. Same diff. Just kidding."

The math started to tug at Kit.

"So," she said, "does that mean that it could be Fwank's?"

"No," said Lucy. "Well, there's always a slight possibility, but probably not. To be honest, there are a bunch of guys that . . . um . . . We always used condoms but sometimes things happen . . ." she trailed off, deciding not to tell them about Peter.

She continued, "Realistically, I'm like sixty-two in fertility years with a long history of miscarriages, but I'm *hopeful*. And you've both been amazing over the years. I know you know how much I've dreamt about this and I hope I have your support, even though . . ."

"Even though it could be *Fwank's*, you thought I'd be *excited for you*?" said Kit, a little heated. Gina placed a hand on Kit's knee to calm her. "Hold it together, Kit."

"Really?" Kit spat at Gina. "*Hold it together?!*"

Lucy said, "Kit, I don't get it. We raised our boys like brothers. What's the difference?"

Kit pointed a stern finger at Lucy's tummy. "Because *that* baby would *not* be partially mine. It would be *yours and my husband's!*"

Gina turned to Kit and said, "Keep your voice down."

Kit whipped her head around and shot darts at Gina with her eyes. "Don't patternize me!"

Lucy corrected, "Patronize," and then almost immediately covered her mouth. She hadn't meant to correct her; it slipped out. Force of habit. Oh, shit.

"Fuck. *YOU!*" Kit said, and stood up. Lucy instinctively opened the latch of the stall door. She stepped out backwards, feeling like a clown had just hit her over the head with a rubber mallet. What on earth made her think Kit would be happy for her for even a second? Because she was her best friend? *Was* she her best friend?

Kit was still freaking. "I can't believe you're fucking *pregnant* and it could be my *husband's* and you thought I would be *happy for you*! Are you out of your *fucking mind*?! How arrogant can you get? And now you're keeping this baby just because Matt's wife is pregnant? I can't fucking *believe this*!"

Lucy was speechless.

Gina said, "Kit, shhhh!"

"Gina, shut *up!*"

"Don't tell me to shut up!" Gina said as both women groped at the tangle of plastic hangers looking for their own bras. Lucy called out from down the hall, "Kit, I'm so sorry . . . I . . . ya know . . . Matt has nothing to do—" She decided to get dressed, then she'd go back and explain her position again. Differently this time, so that they would understand. As Lucy fumbled with the bra hanger she started to shake. Her heart was pounding, her stomach tightened and her ears grew hot. She thought she could hear the blood rushing in her brain; it made a high, hissing sound, like a snake. Where was her own bra? Where was the damn plastic number-five thingy? Lucy needed to get away as quickly as possible. She realized now her initial reaction was correct: *No way in hell does a married woman want her husband fathering another woman's child, even if that*

woman is a close friend. Duh. She saw that she had to be supremely
self-absorbed to think this would fly, and not a little stupid. She
realized that she had made a naïve mistake the way a felon realizes
too late. *Fuck*, Lucy thought. *Fuck, fuck, fuck.* The blood-rushing,
heart-pounding sound in Lucy's head obscured the words that flew
back and forth between Kit and Gina in the corner stall at the end
of the dressing room, but the tone was clear—and it wasn't forgiving or compassionate. It was nearly hysterical with vitriol.

Gina appeared in the doorway to Lucy's stall. She was back in
her street clothes and had her hands on her hips like an angry
schoolmarm.

"This entire situation is *very uncool*," said Gina.

"Thanks, *friend*," said Lucy, slipping her shoes on and snatch-
ing the plastic number from the bench. She couldn't stop her body
from shaking; her jaw was beginning to lock. "I gathered that
much," she said, and walked out of the changing area towards the
shoe racks. Gina followed.

"Quite frankly, I'm a little shocked that you thought that we
would be happy for you."

Lucy spun around in front of the summer sandals. "*We?!* Are
you two a *we*, now?"

"In this case we are, yes." Lucy hadn't ever disliked Gina before
this moment.

"Huh. Interesting," said Lucy, "Well, once I talk to Kit and apologize, we'll figure this out. I'm sorry I was insensitive but it wasn't
all me, you know. She can't foist all the blame . . . I'm just ecstatic
to be pregnant and foolishly thought that you would be happy for
me, but I can see I was woefully misguided." A pregnant woman
pushing a cart in the maternity section slowed to catch whatever
pieces she could of their argument. Gina walked a few steps away
and lowered her voice, "I don't think you get it, Lucy. Kit is fed up

and can't take any more. I'm doing what I can to keep her from killing you right now."

"Fed up?" Lucy said. "Can't take any more what?"

Gina said, "Your Program and your immorality. Your superior
attitude, judging all of our marriages ever since yours failed."

Lucy was no longer in her body. "I don't . . ." She was so livid
she couldn't even answer. She turned on her heel from Gina and
walked off. Gina raised her voice, "Do you expect us to drop everything again to help you? Kit's over your neediness. It's exhausting,
you know."

Lucy stopped in her tracks and spun back around. "Whoa. I'm
sorry if my infertility and divorce was a buzzkill for Kit but I got
her over a few humps, too, you know. *Has she forgotten all that?!*"

Gina spoke with the steely intensity of a movie villain. "Lucy, she's
had it."

At those words, Lucy reached out for a pair of sandals in a shoe-
box. They were attached with those stupid department store elas-
tic bands that make them impossible to try on. She gripped them
in her hand, "When did you become—" and threw them nunchuck-
style, "—such a *bitch!*" at Gina. The sandals flew awkwardly but
managed to clip Gina in the shins.

"Ow!" said Gina, with more surprise than legitimate pain.

Lucy grabbed another pair of sandals—wedges this time—and
continued, "Did you *remind her that I drove Fwank to AA meetings when his alcoholism got ugly and he had those DUIs? So she
could stay home with the kids because they couldn't afford a sitter, because he got laid off?*" Lucy whipped the wedges at Gina,
who sidestepped them.

"Lucy, stop it," Gina said, but Lucy did not stop. She was hell-
bent on hitting something.

"And when she had that *stalker at work?* And her *father's*

Alzheimer's?!" Gladiator sandals with flowers appliquéd across the toes nearly caught Gina's shoulder but instead landed behind her on a rack of socks. *My aim is getting better,* Lucy thought.

"What the hell, Lucy," was all Gina could say, then she picked up a pair by one shoe and threw it back at Lucy. The shoe hanging from the rubber band pulled the other one right to the ground way short of her intended target.

She needs to throw them as a pair, Lucy thought, *obviously.* She picked up another pair and aimed. "Did you remind her of all the times I took her kids when she was *too depressed to get out of bed in the morning during her biopsies?*" Woosh-thud. Ninja shoes flew at Gina like colorful projectiles at a carnival booth. "The biopsies *I dropped everything for and drove her to because you were at work!?*" Lucy was on a tear. She would have thought the whole scene campy-funny if she weren't so pissed—and focused. She grabbed a pair of faux-leather ankle-strap numbers and aimed higher this time. "*Can't believe she has the gall to call me needy!*"

"*Ow,*" Gina said, and took cover behind a rack of cardigan sweaters.

"No," said Gina, her voice was pleading, resigned. "She hasn't forgotten. Jesus. *Stop,* for chrissakes. Okay, you guys are even. She just needs some space. This is a lot to digest. I'm sure we're all sorry and we'll work this out. Clearly this is not the place or the time."

Lucy looked at Gina crouched by the rack. She thought they were friends. In fact, she'd always felt that Gina was the rational one, the one to see things from every perspective. Lucy shook her head. What a scene. Pairs of sandals lay askew, checkering the floor like piñata detritus. Kit came out of the dressing room and stopped in her tracks when she saw Gina hunched down and what looked like the Normandy invasion of shoes.

"What the hell?" said Kit.

"You guys are lame," said Lucy. "You're shitty-ass friends and you can have each other."

A small Indian woman in a red Target-team shirt and name tag marched out from the changing area, wielding a hanger like a light-saber. "What is going on here? I have complaints of a fight. And shoe throwing. There is no throwing shoes in my store. Who is going to pick these up?" Gina and Kit looked at each other.

Lucy said, "They are," and pointed at Kit and Gina before making a beeline for the exit.

The woman continued, "Take your fights outside to the parking lot. No fighting in my store. Go, *go!*" she said making a little "shoo" movement with her hands.

Lucy heard Gina say to Kit, "This is on you," and Kit reply, "*On me?*" She knew Kit would react defensively to Gina's comment and that her famous hair-trigger temper would erupt loudly, so she speed walked her way to the exit—her heart beating violently—and shook as she walked, grateful for the wide aisles leading towards the main doors. She felt as if a small, spirited child had punched her squarely in the stomach as she blinked away big Keane-painting tears. Whatever judgments Kit had made about Lucy, she'd made without giving her a chance to apologize, consider or correct her behavior. And with no room for forgiveness. *This is how marriages end*, Lucy thought. Even Matt had been given a second chance. Lucy had had no idea her friendship with Kit had been on probation, and she wondered for how long. *What jerks*, she thought. *Screw them.*

Lucy's teeth chattered as she made it through the big sliding doors and out into the warm night. It was just starting to drizzle, and folks were picking up the pace as they headed towards the store. Trying to find her car, Lucy broke down. She felt rejected and betrayed, her heart pummeled. A zaftig black lady with braids that twisted and wound skywards into a diagonal peak stopped to ask if she was okay. She was a Target employee collecting shopping carts. Lucy found a break in her sobs just long enough to answer, "My best f-friend just broke up with me and my o-other friend is gone, too-oo, I think, and I can't find my car-ar-ar."

"Oh, baby, that's a hard thing," the lady said, her voice soothing like warm honey. "I can't help you with your friend but let me help you find your car. What color is it?"

"Gr-ay-ay," Lucy stammered, holding her face in her hands. The lady's voice was so patient, so serene, Lucy didn't feel worthy to be its benefactor.

"So many gray cars in the world. Let's see if we can find yours." Lucy and the woman looked for her car while the woman continued to monologue in a soft, meandering lilt. "We-all children of the seventies grew up wearing bright colors. Why don't they give us more colors to choose from? I had bright green clogs with orange daisies. Why are all the cars black and white and gray?" Lucy was afraid to leave the company of this woman, she was so calm. But no one person had all the answers. No one person could give her that much love, not even Gus. Maybe Matt had been right. Maybe no one can love anyone enough. Lucy wished she could be in her car by now, on her way home, but she knew it would be dangerous for her to drive so upset.

"Now, baby, stop your crying," the woman said. "A friend like that doesn't deserve to take up space in your heart and mind rent free." With that she put her arm around Lucy, who buried her head in the woman's ample bosom. She would have stayed there all night, crying, but it started to rain, and Kit and Gina would be coming out of the store any second. Lucy broke away from the woman, calmed down long enough to wipe her nose on her own sleeve and thank her. "I'm okay, I'll find it. Thank you so much. You should run inside." The rain was coming down now in big splattering glops. It landed on their arms and the ground around them like teeny water balloons. The lady said, "Okay, baby, good luck," and scooted towards the store. Lucy began to cry again at the sound of someone calling her baby and ran towards the shopping cart return. She seemed to remember glancing up at the samba line of red shopping carts out of her rearview mirror while she was parking. *Maybe it's there*, she thought. Lucy hoped and prayed that she would find what she was looking for when she got closer to it.

Chapter 29

Lucy knew she didn't have much time. Word would spread around town and possibly to other towns, and her life would change drastically, of this she was certain. Topher was away on business so she would leave that for now, but she texted Peter first thing in the morning, *You need to get here today for an hour before noon. Run an errand. Make it happen.* Peter did. When Lucy opened her front door at 10:30 A.M., Peter was already in midsentence, as if they'd started their conversation telepathically while he was still in the driveway.

". . . it's not that I don't appreciate Einstein—I do—but there were others, you know, far more groundbreaking thinkers who don't get bobble-head dolls made in their likeness. Einstein didn't single-handedly—"

Lucy grabbed Peter and pushed him up against the coat closet. She pulled his face down into her mouth and engaged his tongue greedily, then reached down and grabbed his cock. Peter pulled away from her briefly. He looked incredulous.

"Um . . . hi?" he said.

"Yeah, whatever," Lucy said, and unbuckled his pants. He laughed.

"Look who's got a plane to catch. And why was this so important? It wasn't easy to—"

"*Sh*, stop talking," she said curtly, and reached down to discover his warm cock, which had clearly been caught unawares, sad and small. With her other hand she took his palm and moved it under her skirt. Dragging his hand up her thigh, she surprised him with a bare ass and no underwear.

He said, "Mmmm, this must be my lucky—"

"No talking. C'mere," she said, and shuffled him backwards into the television room, where she had already drawn all the curtains and closed the blinds. She pushed him down onto the large, orange-sherbet velvet couch. He looked surprised but welcoming. Without hesitation, she straddled him and unbuttoned his shirt. He took the hint and unbuttoned hers. He smiled when he saw Lucy's bra, a black lacy thing worn by spider-women and film-noir temptresses. Moving her hands across his chest, she noticed her fingers disappearing into the tunnels of his curly hairs. *When will I finger Peter's chest hair again?* she thought. *When will any man sleep with me again once everyone finds out, once I'm branded with a scarlet* A. *Probably never.*

Lucy was lost in these thoughts. There was something crazed and preoccupied about her eyes. "What's on your mi—" he said, but Lucy interrupted him by sucking his lips into her mouth. She wanted more of him, needed to devour him, and bit into his neck.

"Quit it," he said, and pulled back. "I could never explain that to my wife."

"I don't give a crap about your wife."

"I mean it."

"So do I," she said, and thrust her hands back into his pants.

Peter said, "What's up with—"

"Shut up and fuck me," Lucy said, then brought his hardened penis into the open air, raised up on her knees and, sitting astride Peter, guided him into her, moist and ready. "Ohhhhhhhh," they both said in unison. He closed his eyes as she settled down onto him slowly. Lucy didn't close her eyes. She wanted to watch him, imprint his face on her mind. Peter's beautiful lips parted and his head tilted back showing that gap between his front teeth. His throat was long and fair. *This is why people take videos*, she thought. Peter took Lucy's lead and picked her up, moving her into different positions against the furniture. She screwed him sitting in his lap on a dining room chair; he screwed her up against the fridge. Sometimes they laughed, and sometimes Lucy slammed him so hard she thought she might hurt him. She wanted to. She pounded into Peter, slapping his skin, trying to shatter him with her pelvis and ass. She also slammed into him to save her from herself. She knew he'd hate her after today and wanted to hate him first.

They ended up having sex on the stairs, in her bed and in front of her full-length mirror. Lucy watched Peter pull her hips onto him as she arched her back and shook her hair. She liked his gorgeous cock and the way he looked under, over and behind her and wondered if she would be able to recall these images the next time she masturbated. They wound up on a big pile of blankets and pillows on her bedroom floor. Slowing down, panting and sweating, their breathing became syncopated and layered one another. Peter's eyes warmed and held Lucy's gaze for longer than usual. She again let herself toy with the idea that he was falling in love with her. Then she picked up the pace slightly, looked away from him and triggered a deep orgasm for herself, loud and long.

Unraveled, Lucy splintered into a billion incandescent bits. Peter moaned loudly, pounding the floor with his fist, then wondered aloud if his eyes would ever return from the backs of their sockets. Lucy laughed once as she shuddered, her body convulsing inside electrified skin. She realized, returning from corporal abandonment, that she could never truly hate Peter and would probably always love him the way you love someone that you hope is faring well. But she knew this would be the last time, once she told him, and this made her hate him for now.

Their sex had been fast and rough—a rousing slamfest. When they finished, they lay there panting, looking up at the ceiling, saying nothing. A dog barked down the road; a train rumbled by a few blocks away. She wondered if he would notice the redness of her chest or the pink in her cheeks. Lucy felt radiant and wanted him to see her flushed and alive. As if willing him to, Peter turned his head and looked at her. He stared first at her eyes then scanned her glowing body. She felt zaftig and powerful, all flesh and strength. He reached out in slow motion, took a dark curly tendril from behind her ear and pinched it gently between his thumb and forefinger. He pulled it taught until it stretched straight, then let it snap back into a tight ringlet. Then Peter combed his fingers through Lucy's hair, tenderly. "Your hair gets curlier after sex," he said. "From humidity? From our perspiration?"

"I prefer to think it's magic," she said. She went back to deciding not to hate him. She rolled over onto her side and looked at Peter, choosing not to care about her side-sloping breasts, or that his juices were running out of her onto the comforter. Laundry was incidental. Life was incidental. Right now, nothing else mattered.

"Hey," Lucy said, and traced his profile with her finger, "thank you for never calling me a cougar. I truly loathe that term."

"Don't mention it. But what's wrong with cougar? It means you're still attractive, sexy."

"The word 'still' is the problem. Plus it's humiliating and demoralizing, placing women in the role of predator and men as their unwilling victims, and I appreciate that you never used it to describe me, at least not to my face. Especially since you kissed me first, remember that."

"Well, you're welcome, and I do remember. I remember everything about that night." Lucy saw questions in Peter's eyes. He said, "Are you going on a long trip or something? I feel like I'm in a Lifetime special and tomorrow I'll learn that you killed yourself tonight, just after I left."

Lucy's face clouded over. She guessed that now was the time. She stood up, put on a bathrobe, then began to toss the pillows back onto the bed.

Peter said, "Because if you're going to try to foist all your worldly possessions onto me, I don't want them."

"Fine," said Lucy, "you don't deserve my comedy record collection and my stuffed squirrel smoking a cigarette anyway."

"Yes, I don't."

Lucy tugged at the blanket and comforter under Peter. He grabbed her ankle. She flicked it away from him then headed into the master bathroom to brush her teeth. "Hey, what is it? You're acting weirder than usual," Peter said. Lucy had a mouth full of toothpaste but she turned and paused in the doorway anyway, just long enough to say it.

"Te, fregnit," is what came out.

"What?" he said. "I don't understand." But Lucy thought the cadence sounded plenty close enough to "I'm pregnant," even though they both knew that Lucy couldn't get pregnant. The air seemed to sharpen; the sweetness between them fell away. Lucy spit, turned off the water, then walked back into the bedroom and sat on the mattress.

"You might want to get dressed."

"Why?" Peter said, sitting up. She knew he knew what he'd heard and was just stalling, attempting to block the words from entering his brain. Lucy looked him square in the eyes.

"I'm pregnant. And it could be yours. But not necessarily. And I'm pretty sure I'm going to keep it regardless, even though the baby probably won't make it because I'm old. And now you'll want to get dressed, maybe yell at me, then walk out of here and never speak to me again. I promise never to tell if it's yours. I won't even tell you unless you ask. I plan to raise it on my own as if the sperm came from an anonymous donor, which it sort of did, in a way. I want you to know it's been wonderful being your friend and I wish you all the luck in the world."

"What?" Peter said.

Lucy continued, "I'm sorry if you hate me. I hope someday you'll feel differently. Your world really doesn't have to change at all. Life is long and there's always forgiveness. And acceptance, I suppose. Or not. It's up to you. Please call if you ever . . ."

Lucy trailed off. Peter stared at the painting on the wall of a pitcher of lilacs, which Gus had drawn in second grade. He didn't move. His eyes appeared frozen to that one spot, but she saw whirring behind them at a million miles per hour. He reminded Lucy of playing freeze tag as a kid.

Lucy said, "I'm sorry, Peter, because I probably love you. But I love you the way people love each other who want the best for each other. I don't want you for myself—I get that that's not an option and never was. I promise not to contact you. I hope you have a good, happy life. That's about it. Oh, and I—"

"Shut up," said Peter. Ordinarily, Lucy didn't allow anyone to say "shut up" to her. It was a no-no in her household growing up and she'd always taken it to be the most crass and ugly form of disrespect, but this time she made an allowance. Peter got up off the ground then froze, looking at her. Lucy found him beautiful, even as his disdain for her began to move across his face and alter its expression, even though his anger extinguished the flicker of light in his eyes. He was receding from her without moving. She hoped she wouldn't dream about Peter for too long—his thick, sandy reddish-blond hair, exquisite shoulders and ridiculous pale eyes. Lucy was lucky to have had him at all. She hoped the baby would look like Peter, have his long legs and eyelashes. But maybe that wasn't a prudent wish to have.

Peter glanced around the room. Lucy knew he was in pain, yet knew not to reach for him. She maintained her distance. It had been calculating to sleep with him before telling him—even cruel—but her life was about to implode over the next twelve hours and she wanted a parting gift. Yes, he was a willing player, but he was also a casualty. Where did her brutality come from? It suddenly made her feel ugly. Bewilderment and panic surfaced in Peter's eyes. Lucy wondered if he was looking for a weapon, some blunt object with which to strike her. Her hair dryer was too light, but she supposed a lamp would do. Lucy wondered if it was really as messy and cumbersome to clean up a bashed-in body as it was in the movies. But she wasn't really worried. Just imagining.

She said, "You're not going to kill me are you?"

"How long have you known?" Peter asked. His voice carried little air.

"Since yesterday," Lucy said. "And like I said, it may not be yours, I just thought—"

"Because you've slept with someone else without telling me?"

"Yes," Lucy said.

"So, you lied to me."

"I did."

"Because I'm a liar and so you thought it was okay."

"Yup," she said, and then realized that saying "yup" at a time like this sounded flip. "I'll help you look for your clothes." She shook the sheets and blankets for loose clothing items.

"So you knew *while* we were having sex? And you had sex with me anyway?"

"Yes," said Lucy. "I figured it might be my last chance, maybe with anyone. I'm truly sorry about all of this. But I'm not sorry about the sex. It was really good—phenomenal—sex. God, can you blame me? You would have done it, too. What am I saying . . . you cheat on your wife." Peter looked dumbfounded. Lucy continued, "You told me once how sometimes guys have sex right before breaking up with their girlfriends—to get in one more. You told me *you've* even done it. *You gave me the idea . . .*" Lucy stopped. It was monstrous. Peter had said at the time that he'd never known a chick to do it. Certainly not to him. And not while pregnant with his possible child.

Peter spoke evenly, "I don't think I've ever hated anyone more than I hate you right now . . . maybe myself. My life is over."

"Your life is not over. Anything could happen or not happen," Lucy said. "Here's your other sock." She figured Peter should leave as soon as he could, before he punched something. She didn't think he'd ever punched anything in his life, but there was a first time for everything. She imagined he felt betrayed the way a double agent might upon finding out his contact is a triple agent. Peter and

Lucy had shared a huge secret together, which meant to him in a fucked-up way, he explained to her once, that their mutual dishonesty was more honest than his marriage. Until now.

Lucy threw on a robe and scanned the upstairs rooms they'd been in, gathering his jetsam of clothing and placing the pile on her bed. She turned to leave him alone, but then added from the doorway, "I just wanted to say, um, one last time: I've really enjoyed the way, hmm, the way we . . ." Lucy's throat tightened. "You know what? I'm going to stop talking now. I'm just really grateful. And I'm really, really sorry."

And with that, she went downstairs with the understanding that there was nothing left to say, and that even if there was and she said it, Peter probably wouldn't be able to hear her. She figured his head was spinning or maybe his ears were ringing. He could be in some sort of shock.

Down in the living room, Lucy gathered the rest of his stuff and placed the pile at the bottom of the stairs. Then she went down to the basement to switch over the loads of laundry and be out of his way when he left. Standing in front of the washing machine, Lucy completely forgot why she was there. She crumbled into sobs on the cold cement floor and cried, "Oh, shoot, oh, shoot, oh, shoot," over and over, like a child's shattered toy. She missed Peter already, missed him like mad and felt terrible for what she'd done. She pictured him standing naked and alone in her bedroom, immobilized, trying to remember what to tell his brain in order to move his feet. She knew what that felt like. She'd been there, too.

When Lucy finally got up from the basement floor, she texted Gina. *Please, please I need to see you. Please agree to meet me. I promise not to throw anything. Please.* Gina texted back an hour later. *I have a pedi appt. Meet me at the nail place in 10 min.* Lucy texted back, *Crying all day. Eyes red, face puffy. Big mess. Your place?* Gina replied, *Not my problem. Splash face, Hester Prynne.*

Lucy found Gina already sitting in a nail chair, placidly leafing through a well-worn *Cosmo* from last winter. Lucy climbed up onto the open seat next to her and melted into the Naugahyde throne like she was easing into a hot tub, slowly and with care. Gina did not look up and continued to turn the pages of her magazine. Lucy set a bottle of dark navy polish she'd swiped off the shelf on the low table between them. The morbidity of the color was fitting; she didn't feel the occasion called for anything brighter.

Lucy began, "I am so, so sorry I threw shoes at you. I was out of my mind."

"Clearly. We'll deal with that later. For now you're forgiven. You're lucky I'm Catholic."

"Oh my God, thank you. Most Christians I know aren't forgive— You're not really joined at the hip with Kit, are you? Do you feel the same way about all those things she—"

"Not all. Some of the things she said pissed me off, too. But I'm not going to speak for her. That's separate. Deal with her on your own time."

"Okay, okay. Good point. Thank you for meeting with me."

Gina switched to a *Vanity Fair* but still didn't look at Lucy. "Everyone knows."

Lucy's stomach dropped. "Shit, really? Are you kidding me?"

"This is Nookietown. News travels fast. It's a miracle The Program was never found out."

"Yeah, no joke. Do you think Nancy's heard?"

"Didn't mention it. She told me this morning that she was headed to her mother's, first thing, for the night and doesn't talk to anyone while she's driving—"

"So, how many hours do I have?"

"About three more. Twenty if she left her car charger at home and her phone runs out."

"And what about—"

"I think it's safe to say that everyone else with a pulse knows."

Lucy said "fuuuuuuuck," long and drawn out, losing steam before she reached the *K*. She put her hands up to her face and rubbed, wishing she could rub it off and stomp on it. The Korean woman slated to do her pedicure turned off the tap and placed Lucy's feet, one at a time, into the steaming tub of scalding water. "Ow!" said Lucy and yanked her foot out of the bath.

"That's what you get," said Gina coolly. "Boiled alive at the stake."

Lucy whispered, "Do you think that all the Korean women are mad at me, too? I'm certain I didn't have any Korean appointments." The Korean woman grabbed her feet and plunged them back into the water. Lucy smiled wanly and asked for a bit more cold water to be added. They all sat in silence for a moment, then Gina spoke in a calm, sober tone.

"You can't get out of this one."

"I know," said Lucy.

"You're normally not a reckless person."

"I know."

"What were you thinking?"

"I *know*! I honestly didn't think I could get pregnant. I swear. "

"I believe you. Congratulations, by the way."

"Thanks," Lucy said. "Are you going to vilify me, too? I think the public stoning is set for high noon in the town square."

"Don't be so dramatic."

"Too late for that."

"No kidding," Gina said, and cracked a smile.

Lucy asked, "Did Duncan get a vasectomy? Is that why you're

still speaking to me?" Gina looked up from her magazine for the first time and turned her body to face Lucy.

"No. He didn't."

Lucy began slowly, "Then how can you—"

Gina interrupted, "I knew what I was doing when I signed Duncan up for The Program. Knew that he was responsible for using condoms and that you might be subbing in for other Helpers. I knew that you've always wanted a second child, still get your period, and that I would have to give up a level of control if I was going to go forward with this experiment. I did so of my own free will. Having said that, I would be lying to you if I didn't say that this is one possible outcome that I didn't think likely. I considered it briefly then dismissed it. But if this is what happens, I have no choice but to accept it. You're keeping the baby, aren't you?"

Lucy's eyes welled up at the thought of a baby for her and a sibling in the house for Gus. Her throat tightened against her will. "I really want to," she said, "and not because Delphine's pregnant. Please tell me you know I wouldn't make such a life-altering decision based on—"

"I know. I know you wouldn't. Well, then, there you have it. It would be foolish of me to rage against reality. It would be wasted energy."

"You could hate me for it," said Lucy. She was testing Gina, looking for holes.

Gina said, "I could. Do you want me to? Interested in fueling some victim fantasy?"

"No. I just hope . . . I'm wondering—"

"I'll stay your friend. And I'll stay Kit's friend. You're funny and you make me laugh. And you appreciate my mind and I appreciate yours. You enrich my life and I mostly love you."

"Really? Can I get that in writing?" Lucy chuckled. Gina didn't.

"There are no guarantees. But for this week, yes. I don't know the rest. I try not to dwell on the future. But you should take what you can get. Beggars can't be choosers. And you my friend are a—"

"Yeah, no kidding," Lucy said. She stared at her toes, hoping that if she stared hard enough at them they would sprout little cartoon-balloon answers from their tops, give her instruction, then explode with confetti.

Gina said, "People aren't going to have any empathy for you. They'll conveniently forget that the husbands were accountable, that they themselves are not perfect and have made mistakes, too. And this is not a culture of forgiveness, my friend. The era of 'live and let live' is long past. We are living in times of harsh judgment. It will take a very long while, but it will finally blow over. It'll become Nookietown lore. You'll have to explain it to Gus probably sooner than you would have liked. Unless you move."

"How far?"

"How's Lapland strike you?"

"Sounds cold."

Gina shot a look at Lucy. "Things are about to get pretty icy here, pal."

"Yeah, well . . . I don't want to move. I just had the gutters cleaned." Lucy loved her house, her job and her town. But she'd also never been under such public scrutiny before.

Gina said, "Then you'll have to dig in your heels. It's going to be a long fight. I can be there for you as much as possible, but I can't be there all the time. You're going to have to do this on your own. And it's going to get ugly before it gets pretty. At least school's almost over. Summer vacation will work in your favor."

Lucy marveled at Gina. "You sound like a campaign crisis-control expert crossed with a Zen Buddhist priest."

Gina said, "Well, you're in my life for a reason. Everyone's a teacher. It's my job to figure out why and what I can gain from all of this."

"Thank you," said Lucy.

"It has very little to do with you. No offense, but your life is none of my business except for what I can learn from it."

"None taken."

Lucy looked down at the Korean woman snipping off little pieces of irrelevant skin around her toenails with what looked like miniature hedge clippers. It felt consoling to have her feet cleaned and scraped. The dark polish she'd chosen took on an air of war paint, and she considered herself a warrior gearing up for the big fight. Lucy thought of that passage in the Bible where Jesus washes Judas's feet, which was odd, because she rarely thought of the Bible. It made her Judas in this scenario. She didn't feel deserving—though she did feel like Judas—and thought she should be washing the Korean woman's feet. And yet, Jesus knew what he was doing. He wore a permanent sandwich board of forgiveness. Lucy considered the baby, the innocent object of future derision. She didn't have high hopes for the little zygote.

"You know this baby probably won't stick. The chances of it lasting to term are pretty slim."

"I know," said Gina with a measure of empathy. All her friends knew Lucy's medical history had been challenging; the forecast wasn't bright.

"And you realize there's an eensy chance it could be Duncan's. I mean, we used a condom, but hell, they slip off and break, and I don't know."

"Did it slip off?"

"No."

"Did it break?"

"No."

"Then the baby's probably not Duncan's."

"Yeah."

Gina said, "But if it were, we'd know when he starts to look like Duncan and then we'll deal with it. Okay?"

"Okay." Lucy looked at Gina, trying to read her face. She couldn't quite believe her reaction. Lucy said, "Am I on a hidden camera show? Are you visiting from another planet?"

Gina smiled. "No. I just think life's too short and there are much bigger issues than if my kids end up with a half sibling with my good friend as the child's mother. Hell, I like you more than I like my own sister. I'm just not looking for stuff to be angry about. I feel fortunate to live in relative peace, health and safety compared with most of the world. The rest is what we choose to make of it. Mountains or molehills, it's all up to us. We are in total control of our perception. In fact, it's the only thing we do have control of."

"You're amazing. How come you never talk about this stuff at our ladies' lunches?"

"When? Before or after the discussions about hammertoe?"

"Yeah, I guess you're right. Ha."

Just then Jill—the scary attorney with the possibly-gay husband—walked in and spied them. "Oh, shit," said Lucy. Gina saw her, too. "Damn straight, 'Oh, shit,'" she said. Jill marched over and planted herself at the foot of Lucy's lounge chair, bumping into the Korean woman who was scraping Lucy's feet.

"You are *lucky as hell* that Morris had a vasectomy, you know that?!"

Lucy said "yes" as seriously as she could, but the sensation of getting the bottom of her foot scrapped was maddeningly ticklish and it was challenging to keep a straight face. She also wanted to laugh because Morris hadn't had sex with any of the Helpers and you couldn't impregnate someone by trying on a little black dress.

Jill said, "If that baby was my husband's I would make your life so miserable you would wish you and the baby'd never been born. In fact, I'm considering a class-action suit against you."

Lucy blurted out a hearty guffaw. It was the foot scraper thingy, she couldn't help it. It was bad timing, she knew, and she had every right to be terrified of Jill, but she couldn't believe how nonsensical the idea of a class-action suit sounded to her, and she was still giddy and felt fortified by the news that Gina would stay her friend.

Jill said, "I don't know what you're laughing about. There are women in this town who want you dead."

Lucy gently pulled her foot out of the Korean woman's hands. It was the only way she could keep a straight face. "I know. It's not funny. Do you think there's going to be a hit put out on me? Seriously?" She turned to Gina. "Do I need to worry about that?"

Gina slapped her magazine closed and looked directly at Jill. "Look, this is *not* Long Island and the Sopranos aren't real. We don't put out hits on people here, okay? Jill, do you really think that you can get enough women to commit to a suit saying that they would take the stand if your case went to trial, and testify publicly that they willingly and knowingly engaged divorcées to schtup their husbands because they weren't putting out enough? Good luck with that. Now please walk away. We're having a moment."

Jill looked at Gina, looked back at Lucy, considered her next move, then turned on her heel in a huff. Lucy sank down into her chair, shaking with muffled giggles. When Jill was about seven paces away, Gina said, "Oh, and your husband is gay."

Jill whipped around. "What did you say?"

Gina held her ground. "I said have a pleasant day."

Lucy used a *People* magazine to cover the gaping-mouthed look she couldn't control.

"No. Way," she said.

"Way," said Gina.

"But where did you hear that?"

"Please. It's well-known among local lawyers."

Lucy gasped then doubled over laughing, and the Korean woman holding the scraper grabbed her foot back as if she were its rightful owner.

Gina said, "I don't like Jill."

"Ya think?"

"Her son bullies Charlie all the time at lunch."

"Why am I not surprised?" Lucy clasped her hands together. "I just can't believe this day, this week! It's totally surreal! And I've never seen you in action. You're a friggin' *force*!"

"Yeah, well, be grateful I'm on your team," said Gina. "For now."

"No shit," said Lucy. And she meant it.

Her brief moment of laughter with Gina ended. They read their magazines for a while in silence then hugged for slightly longer than usual as they parted. Lucy arrived at her car with the little foam-wedge fences still stuck between her toes and discovered that it had been keyed. It looked like someone had started to scratch "whore" in the driver's side door, then gave up and just dragged the key across both doors. *No imagination*, she thought. *No follow-through.* And technically not accurate, since Lucy had never been paid to have sex. Well, not cash, anyway. This was going to be awful, she thought. She was going to have to move away from Nohquee. How could she have done this to Gus? How could she be so dumb? She wasn't dumb. She was book smart *and* street smart. But this was really thoughtless—shortsighted and negligent, to be precise. Could she have orchestrated this outcome because she wanted another child so badly? Why was adoption so damn expensive? Her thoughts thrashed about in her mind. *The devil made me do it. The dog ate my homework.* None of her piss-poor excuses held water. She had to own what was coming to her.

Lucy fished for her keys in the outside pocket of her purse. She took the sharpest edged key she had and decided to finish the job. Next to the word *who* etched into the driver's side door, Lucy carved, *wants a cookie?* Then, at the far end of the long, trailing horizontal scratch, she added, *I do.*

Lucy's phone rang as she was making dinner for Gus that night. She kept her back turned from him so that he couldn't see she'd been crying again. Nancy's photo popped up on her phone. In the picture, she's laughing, wearing a bonnet. Lucy remembered that day, when they were at their church rummage sale with Kit and Nancy tried the bonnet on. Lucy interviewed Nancy as if she were Laura Ingalls Wilder all grown up. Nancy went on about having to spend all day in the wagon, dropping one kid off at her butter-churning class and then having to go all the way across town to take the others to whittling lessons and blindman's bluff tournaments. She deadpanned that her pioneer kids were overscheduled and that they should just be let loose to hunt possum after school, and that that would solve her hemorrhoid issues. Lucy nearly died laughing. Kit almost peed.

Lucy watched her phone go to message and Nancy's photo in the bonnet disappeared. She couldn't imagine deleting Nancy's number from her phone and never seeing that bonnet photo again. She hoped that Kit wasn't gone from her life. It would be so weird if she was—almost as if she had died in a car accident. Lucy couldn't go there now; she had other priorities. She had to compartmentalize, so she left their numbers in and listened to Nancy's message, bracing herself for the worst.

"Lucy, so unbelievably psyched for you, holy cow. I wanted to wait 'til I got back from my mom's so I could hug you but had to leave a message. I'm assuming it's Topher's. Good genes. Did you tell him? Are you going to? So many questions. He seems like a really good guy, stand up and all that, but that's your call, of course. You could always coparent together. What am I saying . . . totally ahead of myself. Well, I've got boys' clothes up in the attic; so whenever you're ready, let me know. Gotta go, bye."

Lucy thought about her own attic full of baby-boy clothes and how embarrassed she'd been to tell anyone they were still up there, just in case, for the last eight years. Lucy also thought about the chances that the baby was Ted's. Pretty slim, but still. She'd call Nancy tomorrow. They weren't superclose and never had been, but Lucy liked having Nancy in her life and found her a solid hang and reliable friend—very easy to be around. She was pretty sure Nancy would oust her from her life once she found out it could be Ted's. Sure, people can surprise you—Gina had—but honestly, this would be a tough one for most folks. Lucy would also have to tell Nancy she couldn't continue with the Helper or business side of The Program for much longer. She could blame it on the baby, but really, she knew it was time she got out. Lucy's risk taking had gotten out of hand and it was time to dial it down. Nancy could ask someone else to step up and run it with her—maybe Dix or Fran—that is, if there were any clients left after Nohquee imploded.

Lucy deleted the message from Nancy and called Gus to the dinner table. They sat down together to a meal of steamed broccoli, corkscrew pasta and chicken in various states of crispiness. Lucy lit a candle and lifted her glass for a toast. She felt brave and terrified all at once. What mattered most was this—her family. She counted her blessings knowing it would be increasingly important to keep that in sight.

"What should we toast to, tonight, Gus? Napkin in your lap." She would wait until she was showing to tell Gus.

"We're toasting to napkins in our laps?"

"No, and we're not toasting farts or Minecraft, either. What are you really grateful for? Raise your milk so that we can clink glasses."

"Poop?" said Gus.

"C'mon, sweetie, seriously."

Gus said, "You're no fun tonight."

"You're right. I'm no fun tonight. But some nights aren't as much fun as others." Lucy was starting to spiral downward; she could feel the hitch in her throat returning. She tried never to cry in front of Gus unless it absolutely couldn't be helped, but she was tanking fast. She needed an emergency dose of Carol Burnett or Kristen Wiig, *The Onion* or therealblabbermouse.com. Later she'd Youtube all the Amys: Schumer, Sedaris and Poehler.

Gus nibbled his chicken nugget into a *G* shape and said, "*Our* nights are *always* fun." And with that Lucy was saved. Thank God for Gus. His blithe comment yanked her back from the ledge.

Lucy's home life with Gus was a constant good—evenings relaxed and harmonious with reading, board games and Marx Brothers DVDs. It was a wonderful life ever since the divorce. Is that why Lucy had groped for excitement? Risked sabotaging her serenity? Too peaceful? *That's a damn shame.* Lucy said, "You are right, Gus. Our nights *are* always fun. Let's toast to our nights, shall we? And our days and weekends. And let's say how grateful we are for this food and our health and the house and—*"

"Our friends and family?" said Gus. Lucy took a deep breath.

Who knew how many friends she had left. Her brother Tim was in San Francisco. Her mother would be horrified once she found out Lucy was pregnant and might not speak to her for a while. Or years. Friends and family—*which friends and family?* Things were about to get so very ugly. Yet possibly wonderfully thrilling. Lucy patted her tummy—*Baby, hang on.* She looked at Gus and said, "Yes, to our friends and family. To Uncle Timmy and your cousins who are so far away, and Mom-mom in Florida, and Pop-pop who's in heaven. And everyone in your daddy's family."

"Even though you don't like Daddy?"

"I like him for being nice to you."

"Even though he's not nice to you?" said Gus.

Lucy hid her surprise. Had Gus already started to notice how Matt treated her? "Well, all that matters is that he's nice to *you.*"

"It would be nice if he were nice to *you, too.*" Lucy paused to consider this carefully.

"Yes, Gus, it would. You're right about that. But then I wouldn't have divorced him, right? This way you get to see why it made sense for Mommy to get divorced. Get it?"

"Poop," he said matter-of-factly. Lucy clinked his glass.

"I hate broccoli," Gus said. "How about a joke?"

"Of course you do. No self-respecting eight-year-old doesn't. I want to see you take at least four farts or else no dessert. And yes to the joke. Let's hear it."

Gus said, "Why did Sally fall off the swing?"

"Why?"

"Because she had no arms."

Lucy smirked then said, "C'mon, honey, I told you not to—"

"Oh, Mom, don't be such a buzzkill."

"Buzzkill? Where did you learn—"

"Mom! I'm not done."

"Okay," Lucy said.

Gus said, "Knock-knock."

"Who's there?"

"Not Sally."

Lucy laughed. Then she guffawed. Then her laughter snowballed into inane chortles and snorts.

"Oh-kay," Gus sighed. "It's not *that* funny."

"It is," Lucy said, and pictured herself armless, bumping up against a door with her shoulder like the armless knights in *Monty Python and the Holy Grail*. How much worse off her life could be. What's a little unplanned pregnancy compared to losing your arms? Lucy braced herself for the coming onslaught. *Bring it,* she thought, *I can handle this town. With Gus and my sick sense of humor, I can handle anything.*

Gus said, "Are those laughing tears or do you feel bad for Sally?" Lucy could only squeak "ly" in order to correct his grammar. She couldn't have stopped laugh-crying in that moment if her life had depended upon it. Gus rolled his eyes and said, "Oh, brother." Lucy held up three fingers, which Gus knew to be the international sign for Three More Bites. He blew her a big Harpo Marx raspberry, then braced himself for his fate.

Chapter 30

- - - - - - - - - - - - - - - - - - - -

After Lucy put Gus to bed, she got a text from Topher. *Back from London. Heard rumor. True? Need space. Will get in touch.* Lucy typed, *I get it. But I hope you'll give me the chance to explain. I really . . .* then she paused. Had he heard about The Program or the baby? Did it matter which? Lucy had a weak defense for both actions—midlife boredom? Reckless horniness?—and he'd probably heard an irreversible earful by now. How could she expect anyone to understand? Or forgive her? Topher barely knew her—nothing invested, nothing to fight for. He was cutting his losses. She got it. Lucy erased everything but *I get it* and hit send. Then she ate a sleeve of Mallomars at the kitchen table and cried. With that accomplished, she figured she may as well call Nancy.

"I'm hearing the baby could be anyone's," Nancy said. Her voice was even, careful.

"That's true," said Lucy. "There are some more likely than others."

"Where does Ted fall?"

"Less likely. We're thinking this pregnancy is more recent."

"Well, that's something."

"Nancy," Lucy broke in, "I'm really, really sorry, first of all. Truly and deeply sorry—"

"But you're keeping the baby."

"I am," said Lucy. She hoped she came off compassionate as opposed to defiant. "And regarding The Program, I don't think I should—"

"I agree. It would be better for all involved, if we want The Program to survive."

"I guess that will be up to you now."

"Seems so." There was a pause in the conversation. Lucy waited respectfully for Nancy to continue. "Lucy, I want you to know that I'm extremely angry and frustrated and a host of other things, but this is a longer conversation and we have a science fair project due tomorrow."

"I understand. I hope that you and I—"

"We'll see," Nancy said, and hung up. Lucy felt stung to be hung up on but understood in this case. She had no idea how Nancy would process all of this and what the outcome would be.

With no choice, Lucy fortified herself against whatever else was coming. She hung two small, plastic dolls—Mr. Bill and Xena, Warrior Princess—from her rearview mirror to remind her to maintain fierce tenacity. She read "McSweeny's Internet Tendency" and watched Monty Python YouTube clips before bed every night. She tied a single orange thread around her wrist to remind her to count her blessings and not let the stinkers get her down. Whenever the thread caught her eye she murmured two or three things she was grateful for and said a makeshift prayer of thanks to the sense-of-humor gods to please let her keep hers and give her strength to carry on. Lucy instituted a Joke-of-the-Day series with her students during Morning Meeting (after first explaining the difference between an appropriate and inappropriate joke). She figured that would start her day off on the right foot while teaching her kids timing, editing and "know your audience"—a useful life skill. Lucy also tried not to engage in catastrophic thinking. She could always move in with her mom if push came to shove—it wouldn't *actually* kill her. Come close, sure. Now, more than ever, she needed to stay in the moment and not freak out about the unforeseeable future. Gina had the right attitude: don't sweat the small stuff. She needed to be more like Gina and get her hands on some Buddhism pamphlets. She needed to stretch and meditate, read the Dalai Lama. *I'll train my mind to take it all in stride, dammit. Fuck it. Shit.* Wups.

But Lucy's life became increasingly complicated—from alternately glum and zanily hopeful, to exhilaratingly happy and occasionally miserable. The baby was healthy, but Lucy got dirty looks from people who didn't know her and more than a few lectures on morality from people who did.

Old woman in supermarket: "I've heard about you. You have no shame."

Lucy: "Must have run out. I'll add that to my list. Milk, eggs, shame. Got it."

And there was this from Mrs. Vygotski, who taught fourth grade: "I've always thought very highly of you, Lucy. Until now."

Lucy: "Well, I'm sorry to disappoint you, Meredith. Up until now I'd been living my life to impress you and clearly I zigged when I should have zagged."

Like a well-practiced improv comic, Lucy took whatever toxic dreck came at her and turned it into snappy banter. Unless she was hormonal, in which case it did exactly the damage that was intended, and Lucy was an uncontrollable mess—cue big salty tears. She tried to remind herself that most of the lectures and dirty looks were from people who hadn't joined The Program and were using her situation to work out their own internal morality squabbles, marriage issues or fisticuffs with God. She did her best to not take it personally. Lucy figured she'd triggered so much anxiety about sex and guilt, monogamy and the modern family that she should just smile thinly, nod and keep walking. She knew that in other countries reactions would have been downright blasé, and she'd lived long enough to know that people eventually forget or get bored, accept and move on. The folks who were or had been in The Program were easily divided into "Had a Vasectomy" and "Not Had a Vasectomy" camps, but regardless, both camps gave her a wide berth physically and psychically. A few Program wives shot Lucy dirty looks but most others kept mum. Possibly they were angrier with their husbands. And themselves. The "Had a Vasectomy" camp was the least conflicted and kept The Program hobbling along.

Lucy's professional life took a turn when her principal, Mrs. Jenkinson, called her into her office. *Uh-oh,* Lucy thought.

"Lucy, do you have anything to tell me?" she said. Lucy had so much she could have told her that she knew enough not to guess which "something" she was referring to. She put her hand on her belly reflexively then pulled it off and rested it on her knee.

"I don't know what you mean," Lucy said, adjusting in her chair.

"I'm hearing things, Ms. Larken. Things that don't befit an elementary school teacher."

"Complaints about my teaching? The children are doing very well, testing well."

"Not your teaching," said Mrs. Jenkinson. She glanced down at Lucy's stomach.

"Is it the Joke-of-the-Day thing?" Lucy said. "I'm keeping the Borscht Belt stuff off the table. And nothing blue, of course. Just kidding."

"It's not a joking matter," Mrs. Jenkinson said as her desk phone rang. Lucy's palms were sweaty and she felt as if she might throw up in the waste paper basket. Mrs. Jenkinson said a few curt words into the phone then stood up abruptly. "I have to go. Please make sure that the decisions you're making in your personal life are reflecting well on this school and your profession." She briefly softened. "You know I've always liked you, Lucy, but I don't like what I'm hearing."

"I understand," Lucy said, and stood to watch her go. Once Principal Jenkinson had closed the door behind her, Lucy dry heaved into her wastepaper basket, then returned to class.

Narrow escape, now what? The warrior/zen priestess razor's edge was tricky to navigate ever since the siege of crazy-lady pregnancy hormones had hijacked her brain; she was barely able to hold it together in public. Barely. Some days she cried rivers, other days she cackled herself silly. Sometimes the crying was accompanied by gasping and hiccupping, but always a runny nose and stinging eyes that made her think she must look unhinged to her students' parents and high to strangers. But who was she kidding? Even strangers knew. Small town *Peyton Place* bullshit. And now her job. She wanted to make up a T-shirt that said, *I had your permission* or *Condoms are not a perfect system*.

If Lucy were younger, she might not have had the strength to follow through with keeping the baby, but being older and more seasoned—notice she didn't think wiser—she knew that once people got to know the baby, and once the baby was a kid with a personality and a winning smile, then all that who's-your-daddy stuff would be incidental. She knew this baby would grow up among other kids who had sperm donors for daddies and donor eggs for moms, and that at the end of the day—at soccer practice or marching band—no one gives two shits. *What matters is that you are kind and courteous and you brush your teeth and finish your homework. Everybody's got hurdles to jump, and yet they all make it through somehow.* Lucy's kids sure as hell would. She'd see to that.

Lucy waited for Kit to reach out but it never happened. Every day Lucy thought to call her but had so much other b.s. to deal with, she couldn't imagine adding Angry-Judgmental Friend to her plate. Throw in losing Peter and Topher and now the possibility of losing her job, and she was peering into the abyss of some very, very dark days. At those times Lucy felt as if she were mourning a busload of family members who'd been run off a cliff after a picnic. But she kept it together for Gus's sake. She had to. And there might be a baby coming—maybe, hopefully, things were looking good—which made her want to kick up her heels like the happiest gal in an MGM musical. The baby was growing nicely and her checkups were normal. Astounded, Lucy glanced at the orange thread on her wrist and thanked her lucky stars, God, Buddha, the universe and Mother Nature for the cells dividing inside her. *Thank God for the baby. Thank God for Gus.* Thank God for her awesome students whom she loved and who clearly adored her. How else she was going to muddle through this shit show? Lucy was glad she'd found her lost list of gratefuls in a pile on her kitchen's mission-control desk and taped it to the inside of the mugs-and-glasses cabinet.

The "Gratefuls List" was messy and the corners were curled, but Lucy paused to read it every so often when setting the breakfast table. This was one of those mornings. At the top of the list was her health and Gus's health, her "f&f" (friends and family), and home, then included things like Madeline Kahn and penicillin,

Gary Larson and thumbs, ukuleles, Alan Arkin, banjos and indoor plumbing, birdsongs, kind crossing guards, paved roads and pie, then a jumble of writers, musicians, comedians, websites, movies and flowers she couldn't live without. The last entry was scrawled, *poop*, and decidedly not in Lucy's hand, but she added an exclamation point then reread the list aloud as if reciting her rosary. She also gave thanks for a job she couldn't possibly lose because of a dubious pregnancy, could she? She closed the cabinet and set her sights on the Spring Concert. She would dazzle everyone, especially Principal Jenkinson. Yessiree, she would blow them all away.

But first, she had to tell Gus. She was starting to show.

Chapter 31

- -

Within minutes of arriving home from the Spring Concert rehearsal, Gus was on the carpet building spaceships with Legos and humming to himself. Lucy thought now was as good a time as any.

"Hi, honey," she said.

"Hi, Mom," said Gus.

"Step into my office, will ya?" What she meant was come join her for a family meeting wherever she deemed was her office—could be the bottom step of the stair landing, the back seat of the car, or the edge of the bathtub. Her office was more a state of mind than anything else, and Gus knew that a serious family discussion was imminent. Gus stood up and walked towards her.

"Can your office be outside in the tree?"

"Sure, honey," Lucy said, and they headed outside to the backyard where Gus had a climbing tree. He spent hours in it. He and his friends had built a hammock, stocked a Nerf pellet arsenal, and added many important traps with pulleys, hula hoops, horseshoes and butterfly nets in order to catch bad guys. It looked like Rube Goldberg meets *The Swiss Family Robinson* and was cherished by all the kids on the block. Gus climbed up into the tree and cozied into his bespoke hammock. Lucy sat on the swing she made for him out of an aluminum baseball bat and some old nylon lawn-chair webbing. It was one of those perfectly warm-but-not-summer-yet days. The air was clean and clear and the sky was blue jay blue. Lucy swung back and forth a little then said, "Gus, I have some news. I'm pregnant."

"With a baby?" he said.

"With a baby."

"Is Daddy the daddy?"

"No, honey, Daddy's not the daddy. Daddy's with Delphine."

"They're having their own baby."

"Yes. Yes they are. And I'm having a different, separate baby and there is no daddy because this baby is going to be part of our family and there's no daddy in our family. This baby will have a mommy and a big brother."

"But what about the sperm?"

"I beg your pardon?" she said.

"You told me babies need sperm and eggs, or ham and eggs or something, and ladies have eggs and daddies have the sperm. Who gave you the sperm?"

"Well, I was thinking that I wouldn't tell anyone. Even grown-ups."

"But you would tell me."

"No, honey, I would keep it a secret. It would be a secret just for me."

Gus was quiet. Lucy assumed it was because of the rift between he and his mother he hadn't seen coming. Maybe he was sad, as if he thought his mother were somehow going away. Lucy gave him a respectful moment of silence before continuing, but instinctively reached up to grab hold of his ankle. She hadn't really thought this conversation all the way through and was making it up as she went along, so she was grateful for the pause.

She spoke again, a little more upbeat this time, but not cloyingly so. "Are you excited to have a baby brother or sister? Two?"

"I guess," he mumbled.

"Well, may I ask why you aren't excited?"

"Because you said that if we had a baby that I would have to share you with the baby and I changed my mind and now I don't want to share you."

"But the baby might grow up to play four square with you. And Daddy's baby, too."

"But what if your baby doesn't like four square? I live with you."

"Honey, I'm having this baby because I would like to have a baby and I hope you'll decide to love the baby as much as you love me. Or almost as much. This won't change how much I love you. This just means I'll have one more person to love, besides you and Mommom and Uncle Tim and my friends. I will always love you, you know. Whether you love me or not. You can't stop me from loving you. It's just a fact."

"Why won't you tell me who the daddy sperm is?"

"How about I will tell you when you're sixteen."

Gus said, "You'll forget."

"I probably won't," Lucy said. "And if I do, I bet you'll remind me. But if you badger me about it every day until you're sixteen, I will push it back to seventeen, then eighteen. And then you won't know until you're thirty-three."

"By that time you'll be dead."

"Thanks, kid. I hope not. How about I'll write the answer on a piece of paper and hide it for you to find just in case I die."

"Okay, but how will you die?" said Gus. This interested him immensely.

"How about spiders and worms will eat my guts."

"And piranhas," Gus added, thoughtfully.

"And piranhas," Lucy agreed.

Lucy sent Gus inside to practice his guitar, then she sat cross-legged on the slate stones of her back patio, dialed her mother and began to weed. She pictured Dottie padding through her Vero Beach condo in her stuffed flamingo house slippers following the ring to the other end of the phone in the kitchen. Her mom still didn't have call waiting, so Lucy's visual was fairly accurate.

"Hello?" Dottie said.

"Hey, Mom, what's up?"

"Why?"

"I don't know, why not?"

"Ha. What is it? Tell me now or I'll fear the worst."

"It's nothing bad. When are you coming back?"

"A week from Sunday. You're already divorced. What else is there?"

"Thanks, Mom." Lucy yanked at the tenacious carpetweed roots that had become the bane of her patio existence. Her mother continued, "Is it Gus? Is he all right?"

"He's fine. It's not Gus."

"Is it your job? Did you lose your job? You need money. Do you need money?"

"It's not my job. They still love me, Mom. The students, parents, everybody loves me."

"What about the principal?" Dottie said.

"Stop worrying about my job. The Spring Concert's next week. You coming?"

"I told you, I have my bridge cruise with the girls."

"Oh, right." Lucy paused. "Bermuda in June."

"It's cheaper."

"Right," Lucy said, and inched over to another part of the patio. Damn weeds.

Dottie said, "Gus isn't in this one, is he? Am I missing Gus play the clarinet?"

"No, and it's a recorder, not a clarinet. He's singing, but he can give you your own show."

"Oh, thank goodness. So, what is it?" Dottie said. Lucy could tell her mom was smoking on the other end of the line. And that she wasn't going to budge. Lucy was glad that Dottie was forcing her hand now, on the phone. That way she'd win points for trying to tell her in person, yet would be able to escape the conversation just by hanging up when things got rough.

Lucy said, "I don't know, I'm thinking of maybe tutoring on the side. Make a little extra money. You can make a lot of money tutoring."

"You would make a great tutor. Need help? I could be on your staff. I could toot."

"You'd be an awesome tutor, Mom. What would you toot? Hospital corners?"

"Very funny."

"Or smoking. Why don't you tutor smoking, Mom? Or martyrdom?"

"Why don't you get to the point?" Dottie said.

Lucy stopped weeding and sat up straight. She took a deep breath and threw a clump of carpetweed onto the growing pile. Gus came to the window and made a hand gesture, flipping his thumbs up and down. Lucy knew this to be the international sign language for "May I play video games?" and nodded yes. That would buy her at least forty more minutes.

Dottie said, "Spill it."

Lucy said, "Fine. Kit broke up with me. It's over. Probably for good."

Dottie jumped in. "I'm not surprised one bit. Kit was never a very good friend to you."

"Mom, she was my best friend for nine years."

"But she didn't treat you very well. You refused to see it but I did. And you never felt good about yourself around her. I can't say I'm surprised. What happened? Why now?"

Lucy went for it. A cannonball. "I'm pregnant," she said, then thought she'd better not let too much time go by, so she let loose with all the details in one mad torrent. "And I'm not telling any-one who the father is, and it's due in late November, but it may not make it with my history of infertility so don't get your hopes up, and don't try to stop me because I'm having this baby if it will have me. End of discussion."

This time there was a pause on the other end. A long pause.

"Oh, Christ," Dottie said, exhaling. "You're kidding."

"No, Mom. No joke."

"Well, I don't believe this," Dottie said as if it were happening to her. "Who's the father?"

"I told you, I'm not telling."

"That's hooey. Who's the father?"

"Mom, I love you, but I am *not telling*. It's not important. He's not in the picture. You can harangue me until you're blue in the face, but I'm not telling. Next question."

"How did this happen? I thought you couldn't get pregnant."

"It's a miracle. Next question."

"Does Matt know?"

"No. *No!*" said Lucy. "Totally incidental. Why do you even?!— *Uhh!* What else?"

"Does your brother—"

"I'm calling him next."

"Well, what am I going to tell my friends?" said Dottie.

"Perfect. It's all about *your* friends. Hey, Mom, why don't you begin by congratulating me? Then you can ask me, 'How do you feel?' and, 'Do you need anything?' Let's start there."

"Well, what should I tell them?"

"Mother, your friends do not define you. Society doesn't define you. This has no bearing on you. I'm telling you as a courtesy."

"Oh, well thanks for not making me read about it in the papers."

"Mom, this isn't 1951. No one will be reading about this in the papers."

"Your father would have gone ballistic."

"Yeah, well, Dad's dead and who knows, he may have actually been happy for me."

"He would have thought it was irrespons—"

"Whoa, okay, you know what? I'm going to get off the phone now. I'm going to give you some time to think of one or two positive things to say, work out the right wording, and then you can call me back when you're ready. Or e-mail me. But I have to go now. So that I don't kill you. Loveyabye."

Lucy hung up the phone. Her heart was racing and her ears were hot. *That went well*, she thought. Then she realized that only a week ago, she would have called Kit to decompress. Matt always had something funny to say about Dottie when Lucy got off the phone with her and was exasperated. She thought about calling Gina or Audra or Dix, but became paranoid, worried that they might be getting fed up with her problems, too. She couldn't take any chances.

She would need Audra and Dix's friendship in the future. *I better handle this myself*, she thought. *Damn, I miss Peter.*

Lucy remained on the patio. She sat there and stared into space. Thankfully, Gus was content inside. *May as well call Tim*, she thought. *Get it all over with at once.* He picked up on the second ring.

"Hello?" Tim said. It was her big brother all right.

"Hi, it's me," was all she could get out before she burst into tears.

"Goose, what is it?" he said, and she told him right off the bat she was pregnant. Then she told him about how her best friend broke up with her right after she told her, and how she's scared but knows she can do this, and how she just wants someone to be happy for her. He listened as compassionately as he could for someone who rarely did that sort of thing and who really didn't know her as an adult, then asked her if there was anything she needed.

"No," she said, "but thanks for asking." Then she said, "Well, there is one thing." She blew her nose into her sleeve.

"What?" Tim said.

"You could be happy for me," Lucy said in a tiny whimper. Tim's voice was calm and reasoned. "I *am* happy for you. And I want you to be happy. You can do this. If anyone can do this, Goose, you can. Bigger idiots have done this."

"Right," Lucy squeaked. That made her laugh. "Thank you."

"Congratulations," said Tim. He actually sounded like he meant it.

"Thanks," said Lucy. They commiserated over how Dottie made them cuckoo, briefly caught up on their families and jobs, then said their good-byes and hung up. For a moment she wished that Tim lived closer, but knew that the reality was that he wouldn't be that much of a help to her. And his wife, Ursula, would be useless. Lucy wanted to call Peter so badly. He'd been a great advice giver, would have made her laugh. For a moment she had this rogue thought of, *Fuck it. If I'm going down, I'm taking everyone with me. So what if I call Peter and his wife finds out? Not my problem. No one's my problem. Fuck the world.* But her destructive thoughts stopped abruptly. Lucy cried for forgiveness. She never wanted to hurt anyone or break up any marriages. She'd done it for herself, not against anyone's wife. That's what made this so awful. Lucy wasn't mean. If she were meaner, she could probably shrug the whole thing off, flip everyone the bird, hop on her Harley and peel out. But that wasn't her. She simply coveted what her friends had, though clearly what they had was far from perfect. Still, she ached to love and be loved and remained carelessly open to the possibility—even if it was highly unlikely—cautiously hopeful, quietly yearning.

Lucy rolled down her spine, and lay on the warm slate, letting a day's worth of heat seep into her skin. It felt good on her back and shoulders and she stretched. Closing her eyes she took three deep breaths. The sun felt pleasing on her face and arms. She could count on the sun, at least. That much she knew. "It's just you and me, sun," Lucy said, "just you and me." She let the warmth of its rays bake the salt from her tears back into her skin and claimed the thin hope for herself that everything would work out just fine.

Chapter 32

- -

A couple of times in the last month Lucy had returned from gro-
cery shopping to find that a cart had been rolled into her car.
Maybe on purpose. Maybe not. Just in case, she began shopping in
a neighboring town, and using their post office and ATMs as well.
The day before the Spring Concert, Lucy was loading groceries into
her car when she heard a familiar voice.

"I like cookies, too," the voice said. It was Topher's. He was reading the keyed scratch job on the driver's-side door.

"Yeah, well, necessity is the mother of invention," Lucy said, and
grunted as she lifted the laundry detergent from the bottom rack
of her shopping cart. She felt pathetically weak and exhausted
over the littlest things.

"Speaking of mothers," Topher said.

Lucy forced a smile and said, "You got that right."

"Can I help you load the rest?" Topher seemed sincere. Lucy
softened.

"I thought chivalry was dead." She meant for him to take it a few different ways.

"Depends," said Topher. He picked up the last of the heaviest bags and placed them in the way back of her car.

Lucy said, "Speaking of fathers."

"Yeah, I heard," he said, and looked at the ground. His brow furrowed. Lucy shut the hatch, not meaning to slam it.

Lucy said, "It's probably not—"

Topher said, "It's none of my business."

Lucy looked away, thinking she understood, then looked directly back at him, as if seeing him for the first time—as if seeing him as the father of her child. He looked at her squarely in return. The seconds stretched the outer limits of time.

Lucy spoke first. "I never took money for—"

"I know," he said. "I got the whole story." He seemed to have other things to say on the subject, so Lucy waited for him to speak again.

"Interesting business model," he said.

"Yeah, well." Lucy gave an empty chuckle then fished in her purse for her car keys. She was pretty sure he was just being polite and didn't want to linger. It was torture for her; she figured it must be for him, too.

"Okay, then," she said.

"Okay, then," said Topher.

Lucy gave him a brief low wave from her hip and moved towards the driver's-side door. As she put the key into the lock Topher spoke again.

"Maybe we can—" then he stopped himself. Lucy froze, then waited a beat before speaking, believing that the careful timing of her next word could tip the balance in her favor.

"Really?" she said, and looked into his eyes.

"Maybe . . . maybe," Topher said, quieter this time, then added, "I don't know." He looked away and scratched the back of his neck.

"Fair enough," Lucy said, and smiled a closed-mouth smile. She was lucky to get that at all—to get anything. She opened the door to her car, climbed in and turned on the ignition. When she looked back over her shoulder to grab the seat belt, Topher was gone. She found him in her rearview mirror. He was putting her shopping cart away for her.

Lucy had paused to glance over the Gratefuls List while grabbing two juice glasses from the cabinet when the phone rang.

"Hello, Dix."

"You're in a good mood, considering."

"Considering what?" Lucy said, and turned her attention to the frying pan—three eggs to scramble, toast in the toaster. Gus would be downstairs in a few. Her timing was perfect.

Dix continued, "They're having to combine all the concerts into one today. Something about the bus unions and the district calendar and snow days. I don't know, some b.s."

"Okay, well. That's cool," said Lucy. "No biggie. I can combine the songs and have the older kids stand in the back. You can help me with that, right, oldest to youngest?" Two slices of toast popped up and Lucy pushed down the lever again.

"Of course. Whatever you need," said Dix. "I'm not saying I don't think you can handle it. I just thought you'd be freaking out about . . . you know."

"About what? Get to the point, I'm trying to get out of here."

Dix said, "A combined concert means that basically the entire student body and their parents will be in the same room with you in an hour and a half, with you at the center of attention. You, your baby bump, the whole town and all the possible baby daddies in one big room together. I just figured. I don't know, that you'd need some moral support."

"Well, I hadn't thought of it that way, Dix, until you just laid it out for me in crippling detail." The fork Lucy was scrambling eggs with slipped out of her hand and clanged in the sink.

"Honey, I'm sorry, really. I called to tell you good luck and not to let anyone get to you. Just look up, don't focus on the faces and you'll do fine."

"Shit, when were they going to tell me?!" said Lucy. The kettle began to whistle.

"Jo Ellen was supposed to leave a message with you yesterday."

"Dammit. I've told her a thousand friggin' times that I never check my home machine."

"Okay, look," said Dix. "You'll do great, you always do. Eye on the prize. The concert's going to be fabulous. The kids love you. That school loves you. Ignore the parents."

"Dix, the parents *are* the school."

"No, the *kids* are the school. And the kids love you, so hang tough. Whatever you need."

"Thank goodness," Lucy said. "That helps." The toast popped up. It was smoking.

"Don't think about it," said Dix.

"I wouldn't have if you hadn't—"

"I know, I know, I'm sorry. Kill me later. Loveyabye," said Dix.

"Yeah, you and Jo Ellen. Loveyabye," Lucy said, and hung up. The eggs were dry but she plated them anyway and set them down on the island counter. She swung open the kitchen back door and pitched the smoking burnt toast where all of the other pieces of smoking burnt toast had gone before them—onto the patio, so as not to set off the fire alarm. She zipped over to the bottom of the stairs and shouted "Breakfast!"

Later that morning, Lucy and Dix were lining up two hundred and forty students—grades two through five—on stage risers in the auditorium. Parents were settling into their seats as folding chairs were being brought in to accommodate the unexpected overflow. The room was bursting at the seams, but Lucy had hosted full concerts before and knew the drill. The audience was usually forgiving.

"Knock 'em dead, sister," Dix said to Lucy, then she disappeared into the crowd.

Principal Jenkinson took the stage and made what Lucy thought was a warm welcome and tepid introduction; she'd gushed about Lucy in previous years. Lucy walked forward to the center-stage apron and took the microphone. "Thank you, Principal Jenkinson. Welcome to the last week of school," Lucy said, slow-and-steady like a circus ringmaster. The kids erupted into a rousing cheer. Lucy continued, "I know you kids are thinking, 'I'm really going to miss school this summer,' so why don't we all keep going to school until August?" The kids erupted again into a thunderous laughing response: "*Noooooo!*" They knew this routine; she did it verbatim every year. Lucy said, "Oh, so you'd rather stay in school until September?" The hollering laughter swelled. "*NOOOOO!*"

"All right," she said once they quieted, "then one more week it is."

"*YAAAAYYYYYY!*" The kids went bananas.

"But only . . ." she interrupted, ". . . only if you behave professionally and respectfully for the entirety of this concert. Beginning . . ." her voice dipped to a whisper, ". . . now." The kids became still and quiet. Some of the older kids even corrected their posture and took their hands out of their pockets without Lucy having to remind them.

"Much better," Lucy said. "Let's get this show on the road." Addressing the audience, she brightened her intro banter. "How is everyone? I'm having a good day. I'm having a sunshine day—"

A kindergartener on a front-row lap shouted, "And you're having a *ba-by*!"

Lucy looked temporarily struck. She scanned the audience, even though Dix had told her not to, and realized that she could put a name to every face and most of them were Program faces. Dix had been right. There were some titters from the kids, but the parents didn't crack a smile, instead she saw heads crane and knowing looks exchanged. Lucy caught Nancy's face, which was unusually neutral. And Kit and Fwank's faces were—oh, God, the stink eye. Rough crowd. *Okay, get it together.* Lucy caught sight of Fran, who gave her a toothy smile and a hearty thumbs-up. Dix circled her fingers around each other as if to say, keep it moving. In seconds Lucy regrouped and decided not to validate the kindergartener's comment but move on.

"So, let's get this show rolling with the Brady Bunch's 'Sunshine Day'!" Lucy climbed down into the pit, turned her back to the audience and counted off the kids.

The children really knocked it out of the park. Even the second graders kept up with the lyrics and enthusiasm. Following robust applause, Lucy launched them directly into a kids' version of "Vacation" by the Go-Go's, whose lyrics Lucy had changed to celebrate going to the town pool, playing outside after dinner and sleeping in. After "Vacation" they sang, "When You Wish Upon a Star"; "I Want Candy" with additional verses about recess, four square and movies; and "I Want to Hold Your Hand" with the two-one beat clapping and yelling part in the middle—always a crowd pleaser. Lucy was particularly proud of how well the children conducted themselves between songs. They beamed, and their parents ate it up, taking endless photos with smart phones and giant, distracting iPads.

At the end of the concert, Lucy returned to the front of the stage and faced the audience.

"Thank you so much, moms and dads, for coming in this morning for our Spring Concert. The kids worked so hard and I think they did a fantastic job, don't you?" The audience responded with a hearty applause. One of the fifth graders—their class president, Lily—walked to the front of the stage and asked Lucy if she could say a few words into the microphone. As Lucy knew Lily to be responsible, she allowed it. Lily said, "Ms. Larken, we just want to say thank you for all you've done for us over the years. The fifth graders who are leaving to go to the big school are really going to miss you and want you to know that you're one of our favorite teachers."

The kids applauded. The parents did not, which was a bit awkward, but Lucy focused on the children. She found Gus's face in the crowd; it helped to see him smiling. Lily gestured for Dante, her vice president, to join her at the front of the stage, and he stepped forward from the back row, holding flowers and an oversized homemade card. He handed Lucy the card and flowers, then Lily handed him the microphone. Dante cleared his throat then spoke slowly and clearly into the mic, "And we just want to say now—since we're not going to be here next year—good luck with your baby and we think it's cool that there's no daddy."

This time no one clapped. No one giggled or nodded and no one moved. Lucy looked at Gus and smiled plaintively; he rolled his eyes. Lucy looked back at Dante and with a weak grin, gently took the mic back, turned it off and tucked it under her arm so that she could shake his and Lily's hands. Dix started to clap from the side of the auditorium where she had been leaning against the wall, but no one joined in, which made things even worse. Audra and Gina were too stunned to know what to do and hadn't reacted quickly enough to join in the clapping, and Fran clapped twice before stopping then shouted out a single, "Yeah!" which was left hanging in the quiet for an uncomfortably long time. No one was prepared. Thank goodness Principal Jenkinson was out of the room. Then it happened.

Could someone in the audience have coughed and said "whore" at the same time? Like in the mock trial scene from *Animal House*? Lucy cocked her head in the direction it came from and knit her eyebrows. She couldn't possibly have heard what she thought she just heard, but then it happened again. "Huh-ore," this time from the other side of the auditorium. Then again from a woman's voice. *Shit*, Lucy thought, *I guess plenty of women saw* Animal House. *Unbelievable. And in front of the children, for chrissakes.* Lucy thought fast. She turned to her students and spoke briskly as the coughing grew to epidemic proportions behind her.

"Children, some of the grown-ups aren't feeling well and I don't want you to get their germs. As you leave the auditorium, please sing, 'Fly Me to the Moon' three times, followed by our school song. Ms. Kirnbaum will help you file out quickly, then head back to class. A-one, a-two, *Fly me to the moon . . .*" sang Lucy as Dix leapt up on stage and got to work herding the students out the two stage-exit doors. Their teachers met them in the hallway. Lucy whipped back around to the audience, raised her eyebrows and shook her head back and forth as if scolding a class of rambunctious teens. "Seriously?" she said to the crowd of coughers. Then her blood started to boil. Lucy switched on the mic and said, "Ladies and gentlemen, I don't think it's appropriate—" but was interrupted by a woman who shouted, "What do you know about being appropriate?" Lucy was agape. She shot a look at Dix and circled her fingers in the air. Dix told the kids to hustle. Another voice called out, "I don't think it's appropriate that you're teaching our kids!" Sounded like Rebecca Shanker.

"Really, Rebecca?" Lucy said with steely reserve. "Are we going to do this now?" She looked at Gina who shook her head no, even Nancy dragged a finger across her neck, but Lucy's mind was made up, if she was in her right mind at all, which was questionable. She spun around to the thirty or so students, who were still waiting to file off stage and said to them, "Children, plug your ears as you sing. It'll be more fun that way. Go ahead, put your fingers in your ears and sing while I talk to your mommies and daddies. I bet you can't do it." The children put their fingers in their ears and kept singing. They were on the second verse and already mumbling through the words they weren't sure of. They thought the fingers-in-the-ears thing was hilarious.

Lucy turned back to the crowd of parents, gently smoothed her blouse over her stomach and spoke in a clear, stern, teacher voice. "How I conduct my private life has absolutely no bearing on my effectiveness as an educator and you know it. This baby and the manner in which it was conceived is my business and my business alone. I'm entitled to the same level of privacy when I'm away from my job as you all are."

"Who's the father?" Mike Lo's voice called out from the back. All the children were off the stage and out of the auditorium at this point.

Lucy scanned the audience. "None of you," she said. Akiko and Antonio—the man single-handedly responsible for Audra becoming multilingual—remained stony, but she saw relief on Fwank's face. "Or one of you, possibly, but highly unlikely," she said, feeling honesty was the best policy at this point. The crowd murmured like in a TV courtroom drama. "Look, people, it's not your problem. I'm having this baby so you may as well let it go. Why are you itching for a fight? You've got better things to do with your energy: run for the board of ed, tutor a kid. Don't take it out on this baby, that's just unnecessarily cruel, and you're better than that. Choose not to care about my private life." The auditorium was cleared of students. The noise level fell but the tension in the air dipped and swirled.

Fwank yelled out, "That's bullshit!"

Lucy said, "Which part? This is my life, pal, like it or lump it." She looked around the room and saw a few confused faces—Margaret and Ben's, Dina and Boris's—but mostly ticked-off ones. Rachel Neuman, a former class mother, called out, "I don't want a prostitute teaching my children!" Lucy retorted with steeliness, "And I don't want an emotionally abusive or depressed addict parenting my students." People gasped. Lucy inhaled, switched off her mic and stepped towards the crowd. Dix would have stopped her, but she was still in the hallway with the kids. Gina tried again to shake her head no, but Lucy ignored her and assumed her this-is-just-a-big-misunderstanding tone. "Not that you're an alcoholic or depressed, Rachel, I know you're not, but some of you are—a teacher knows. I'm not going to name names, even though the situation practically begs for it, but I'm also not going to play your game, am I, Audra?"

"You know it," said Audra. She was enjoying the smack down immensely.

Lucy continued in her reasoned tone, "I've got better things to do with my time."

Kit shouted, "Like not buy condoms?"

Lucy said, "Look, condoms are 98 percent effective. They are. Yay for condoms. But 2 percent of them can slip off and break. *You* should know that better than anyone." Some women in the audience—including Gina—emitted a low level, "Ooooo." It was common knowledge that Kit's last two children were mistakes. Lucy said, "Don't push me. The other Helpers and I, we know things now. Private things. So I would back off if I were you."

Kit said, "Are you threatening us?"

"No, Kit. Frankly, I'm too busy to wage some kind of invented war. I'm too busy teaching *your* kids."

Someone said, "Not at this school anymore, you're not." Sounded like Rita Aquino.

Lucy ignored the comment—more like blacked it out. She found Rachel again in the crowd, smiled and said, "Rachel, you know me—I'm not a prostitute. None of The Program's Helpers are. We're just helping each other out. It's all aboveboard. Besides, if we were prostitutes, that would make you wives our pimps." Audra snorted as Lucy gestured to the wives in the audience, of which there were many. Lucy wore a slight grin, but the wives were dully horrified by the comment. A couple of men chuckled. Lucy continued, "You thought it would help your marriage, so you subcontracted some of the work that you didn't want to do that needed to get done, to the underserved population in town, who also got what they needed. Just a bunch of consenting adults getting their needs met." Lucy saw Goldie near the center aisle and caught her eye.

"My marriage is none of your *damn business!*" another woman's voice called out. Lucy was pretty sure it belonged to Jill.

Lucy said, "Who is that, Jill? Jill, you *made* it my business! You *put* me in business!"

Jill said, "Don't flatter yourself."

Lucy snapped. All the calm and understanding flew out of her in a whoosh and what was left was self-righteous rage. Not good.

"Thankfully, your husband is not my problem, Jill, he's still yours." Lucy wound up. "You are all educated people! If you made

time for each other, if you weren't so tired, The Program wouldn't
be in business. Put your kids to bed earlier or get babysitters. This
town is crawling with teenagers dying to earn some cash and yet
none of you hire them. That, alone, will end your marriage. Get a
friggin' babysitter! In fact, get *five*! They're everywhere. No excuses.
Then you can go out and remember what drew you to your husbands in the first place. It'll help you to be attracted to them again
so you'll want to do those things *to* them and *with* them. You have
to *want* to be with him, ladies, or be willing to fake it forever,
because they're not going to stop wanting it any time soon. Are you,
fellas?" Lucy saw Ted shake his head imperceptibly. "Either way you
should be putting your kids to bed earlier. Your kids are supposed
to be getting ten to twelve hours of sleep a night. Every night! And
don't give me any of that 'my kid's not a sleeper' malarkey. Children need sleep. Google it! They're overtired and not learning up
to their potential. Give yourselves some adult time. We're talking
biology, here. His desire isn't going away just because you're too
tired. You're in it for the long haul, ladies, *'til you die*!" The women
looked slightly stricken. The men looked smug—in fact, a little too
self-satisfied for Lucy. Some guy in the back—possibly Hector
Forsythe—started to clap but was hushed by his wife.

Lucy pounced. "And you *men*." She changed her tone and
began pacing the apron of the stage. She felt like a TV-celebrity life
coach at a marriage retreat. Dix returned from getting the littler
kids to their classrooms and was trying to get Lucy's attention, but
it was too late, the damage was done. Lucy was on fire. She had
completely lost track of the fact that it was 9:15 in the morning
and she was at work—which also happened to be an elementary
school—and she was telling off the parents of her students, which
was like telling off seven hundred bosses.

"If you men want more action—Mike, Hector, Steve and the rest of you—if you want your wives to *want* you? Get off your butts and lose twenty to forty pounds. Sit up straight and stop chewing with your mouth open, for Pete's sake. You want more attention? Treat her like your girlfriend, Steve, not your mom. Take your wife to dinner, look her in the eyes, and ask her about her goddamn day!"

Lucy saw a few women smile and a few others elbow their girlfriends and husbands. "Stop acting so entitled," Lucy said. "Get it together, men. It's that simple. If you want her to desire you, you need to look and act desirable, so get healthy. And if she likes a bigger man, or you're already healthy and your wife still isn't interested, then maybe you're *doing it wrong*! Maybe you're *lousy in bed*. Did you ever ask yourself that, gentlemen? *Make an effort!*" This time about ten or twelve women applauded—mostly ex-wives. Audra jumped to her feet and hooted. Fran, who had learned how to finger whistle as a child, whistled good and loud. Nancy laughed and clapped, and Gina slapped a hand over her eyes. Unfortunately, Lucy's performance high was short-lived. She caught sight of Principal Jenkinson returning through the double doors at the back of the auditorium, then noticed Marybeth, the choir teacher, whispering in her ear. Lucy knew she was out of time—probably in more ways than one.

"Look," Lucy said, and to quiet the crowd then she spoke softly, with a near-pained empathy. "I know marriage is hard. Really, really hard." From the audience, hollow souls looked up at her, whom she knew loved and respected their marriages deeply and desperately. "And I know you're all trying your best to make it work because you value each other so very dearly." A few men and women reached for their spouse's hands. "Clearly I don't have the answers because I couldn't make my own marriage work. The Program was an idea, not a solution, truth be told, for either husbands, wives, or

Helpers. It's a quick fix, a scratch for an itch. And you were brave to try it, those of you who did. It's optional—always was. Kind of like . . . marriage."

"Ms. Larken," Principal Jenkinson said sharply as she marched down the center aisle.

"I know," Lucy said.

"*Right now,*" she said, walking up the steps and onto the stage. What Lucy had done—talking to the student-body parents in *this* fashion, about *this* topic, in such a public way—had clearly been a deal breaker. "Right now-right now?" asked Lucy. The gravity of the situation and scope of her stupidity hit her all at once. The audience seemed to be a few moments ahead of her and was already whispering feverishly.

"Right this instant," said Principal Jenkinson, "I don't want to say the words here but I will if I have to."

"Okay," said Lucy. She felt horrible. Mrs. Jenkinson had been a good administrator and a real cheerleader, backing her after-school arts programs and looking the other way during her early morning literacy lessons. It would be about lunchtime before Lucy really came to understand that she'd been fired, permanently, and that meant no tenure, no benefits, and if she ever wanted to teach again, she'd have to teach out of district. Way out of district. Like, Upper-Mongolia-out-of-district.

For now, Lucy just wanted to appear graceful under fire. She turned on the mic. "Sorry, everyone! Thanks for coming to the show! Your kids did a fabulous job and I'll miss them!" Lucy smiled and handed the mic to Principal Jenkinson. Backing off stage, she hugged her flowers and card to her chest and waved as if she were a Miss America runner-up trying to put on a brave face after bungling the pageant. She caught Audra, Dix and Fran's faces, smiling supportively, waving as if she were an astronaut going into space. *What the fuck have I done*, Lucy thought, walking backwards and smiling her weird frozen smile. *Why couldn't I stop myself? I must have a screw loose. Thank God Dad's dead. That's what Mom would say. What the hell happens next? I'm sunk. So very, very sunk.*

Chapter 33

- -

Lucy spent her last few days at school in a puffy-eyed haze, her
life resembling the very definition of the phrase "shit show." Word
got around that she'd been fired, which made some parents very
happy and others so incensed that there was a petition circulated
to keep her employed, and local labor-rights lawyers slipped her
their cards. She was alternately ignored and congratulated by her
colleagues, which gave her emotional whiplash, but thankfully the
district let her finish out the week so she wouldn't have to abandon
her students so close to the year's end. Principal Jenkinson point-
edly avoided Lucy, but the kids were blissfully unaware of what
had gone down and gave her homemade gifts and huge, envelop-
ing bear hugs, and rubbed her tummy on the last day of school.
Lucy would be back in a few days to pack up her personal stuff,
but for now she carefully removed the piece of butcher paper that
hung above the pencil sharpener. It contained the word wall of
potential baby names that the kids had created and added to

throughout the last few weeks. Lucy's favorite names were Shark-lord, Pokemonlego, Prettycute, and Supercalifragilisticexpialido-cious. She decided she would frame it and hang it in the baby's room—but not 'til the baby came, which was looking likely. Lucy's morning sickness had disappeared and she'd even gained a few pounds, which made her ob-gyn very pleased and Lucy ecstatic.

Lucy's friendships were limping along, equally erratic. She was all over the place with her married friends: Gina was tentatively still friendly but busy; Kit and she were still not speaking, which was made easier by Kit's decamping to her brother's lake house in the Catskills for the summer; and Nancy put The Program on a summer hiatus and kept a frosty but civil distance; their second phone conversation was shorter than their first. When Lucy picked up, Nancy spoke right away, "I only have thirty seconds. Here's my deal: I've always liked you, I don't blame you, and I plan to keep you as a friend, just give me the summer to regroup. It's been a tax-ing spring and my home life has taken a hit."

Lucy said, "I totally get it."

"I'm sorry I won't be there for you but I have to put my family first for a little while. Plus I'm still a little pissed at you for taking down The Program after we worked so hard to build it. But if it wasn't you, it probably would have been something else eventually, let's face it."

"I understand."

"Let's get back in touch in September." Then Nancy paused. "I'm truly sorry about your job and I'm really happy for you and your baby. I know this is huge for you. Bigger probably than any of us can imagine."

"It is," Lucy said. Her voice tightened, her eyes moistened. "It's huge. Thanks, Nance. I love you and I'm sorry for everything." Nancy said okay then hung up.

Lucy ended up spending more time hanging around Fran, Dix and Audra until Audra cleared out for July to her family's place in Aix-en-Provence, the South of France. Fran gave Lucy free gentle prenatal kickboxing lessons to help get her aggression out, give her more energy and "tire her ass"—as Fran said—so that Lucy would sleep better. Even so, she was still up at odd hours of the night, combing the Internet and mulling over small incidentals, like where would she and Gus live, and the ever-popular what would she do for money? Folks at the town pool gave her a mixed response, especially in her advanced stage of maternity bathing-suited-ness, so she and Gus stuck to Audra's pool. The larger Nookietown community went about their business the way a small town would with a celebrity in their midst, bending over backwards to suggest cool detachment. Lucy's brother was predictably absent from the whole sticky mess, but said he would wire money so she wouldn't have to move back in with their mom, and Dottie finally came to grips with the inevitable, and said she would fly up for the baby's birth and stay a week to cook and clean.

Out of the blue, Topher texted. He wanted to get together for lunch and said he would meet Lucy in her town. She was baffled but intrigued, shoring herself against the sting that would undoubtedly follow their encounter. She figured he probably wanted some closure and perhaps the chance to air grievances. But she also thought that for him to take the trouble to meet up with her in person, maybe she'd made a bigger impression on him than she thought—maybe she still had a chance. And lunch was better than coffee. Lunch was promising.

The day before their lunch date, Lucy rehearsed her apology and created a playlist. She thought she might even burn him a CD— wasn't that the way to a musician's heart? Years of mixed tapes given to her by old boyfriends had worked their magic on her. Lucy would decide whether or not to give it to Topher when she saw him— depending on how things went. She noodled obsessively over the order and even included her own brief liner notes.

"I'm Sorry" - Brenda Lee
"Sorry Seems to Be the Hardest Word" - Elton John
"My Fault" - Imagine Dragons
"Please Forgive Me" - David Gray
"One Is the Loneliest Number" - Three Dog Night
"I Want You Back" - Jackson 5
"Baby Come Back" - Player
"Take a Chance on Me" - Abba
"Give Me Just a Little More Time" - Chairmen of the Board
"Without You" - Harry Nilsson
"Call Me Maybe" - Carly Rae Jepson

Lucy and Topher met out in front of The Nookie Nosh, Nohquee's local diner.

"Hi," Topher said. Same soothing voice and handsome face. She was blown away that he'd made the effort.

"Hi," said Lucy. Her heart was actually thudding a bit. Then she remembered she was pregnant—stupidly pregnant—and her heart rate slowed. She had nothing to lose here, may as well relax.

"You hungry?" he said, and smiled—closed-mouthed and small, but a smile nonetheless.

"Always," she said. "But, would you mind—I don't feel like eating lunch-lunch. Would you mind if we had some ice cream? I'd really like an ice cream cone for lunch."

"Sounds good," Topher said, and waited for her to turn in the direction they would walk. Lucy remained quiet and tried not to bump into him. She wasn't sure who should start.

Topher said, "So, how are you?"

Lucy let slip a "Ha!" Then a, "Hmm." Another pause. "Well . . ."

"That grim, eh?"

"Ohmygod, so grim. But also good. Amazing." Lucy glanced down at her belly.

"You look good," Topher said.

"Smoke and mirrors, smoke and mirrors," Lucy said, then caught her reflection in the window of the dry cleaners. She looked as if she was smuggling a large ham under her blouse. Her hair was good, though. "It's the elastic-waist pants. They're very slimming."

"I see," Topher said. "And your job?"

"I'm between jobs at the moment. All the best people are. But you've probably heard that. I imagine you've heard it all."

"I've heard a lot, but I wanted to hear it from you." He wasn't accusatory in his tone, just matter-of-fact, but Lucy wanted to get it over with now. She stopped walking and looked Topher in the eyes for the first time since she'd said hello. They were gentle, not hard, she thought, perhaps, even possibly . . . forgiving.

"What do you want to know?" she said. "I'll tell you everything, though I don't know what good it would do or why you would even want to know. I had been beaten down for so long in my marriage— my ego was the size of a pea—and was looking to connect, physically, but not emotionally. I couldn't handle emotionally. Plus it was exciting as hell and I felt desirable and wanted for the first time in years. And I love to orgasm and the way a man feels inside of me and the perks were great. And, it turns out, I'm totally capable of corunning my own side business, which is good to know. It was lot of fun and a great confidence builder. But it got me pregnant and cost me my job. And that's pretty much it in a nutshell. Questions?"

Topher looked at Lucy for an uncomfortable minute, which was interrupted by a loud, gurgling, hungry noise emitting from Lucy's stomach.

Topher said, "The baby has a question."

Lucy said, "The baby doesn't get an answer until it finishes its homework." Topher gave Lucy another thin smile and turned to continue walking in the direction of ice cream. Lucy stopped and said to herself aloud, "Wait a minute. I'm blowing it," then dragged Topher a few steps around the corner to a bench surrounded by potted palms in a little public-seating area, where they would be alone. She sat down and patted the bench next to her, then held her own hand in her lap. Topher sat.

"I want to be completely honest with you because I respect the hell out of you and want you to be able to make an informed decision about me. And because it's time I started owning up to my shit and making myself available for an adult relationship, i.e., you."

Topher said, "Okay," turned his body towards Lucy and settled in.

Lucy took a deep breath and began, "I married the wrong man for the right reasons, which was my fault. Then I couldn't have a second child, which was not my fault. But I think I blamed the universe for rejecting me, even though I felt I was to blame, even though I know blame has no emotional usefulness. I think I wanted some kind of cosmic compensation in return, maybe felt I was entitled to it, which is terrible and wrong. I wanted to feel close but I couldn't imagine the emotional rejection again, so I went after the physical connection. With a vengeance. The end result was The Program. I also had a brief affair with a married man, not while I was married, but still, unforgiveable, and used his sperm in a half-baked bid to get pregnant, unbeknownst to him, and also unforgiveable. I was careless with condoms because I was certain I couldn't get pregnant and everyone I was with was in a monogamous relationship, except for you, and we used a condom. But this baby could be yours. It's a slim chance. But there are others in that boat as well."

"How big is the boat?"

"Bigger than a bread box."

"I see," said Topher.

Lucy waited.

He said, "Do you think this is who you are? Do you think this is some sort of pathology, which cannot easily be altered or fixed? Like an addiction?"

"I've thought about that," Lucy said, "and no. I think it's been a phase of my life, a complicated chapter, like a psychoemotional wilding or an Amish rumspringa for recent divorcées. I think it was a reaction to a dark, painful time that lasted years and mangled my ability to see myself as valuable, so I groped, recklessly, at everyone's expense, for that feeling, in whatever way I could manifest it. And sex felt the best. But no, I don't think that's intrinsically who I am. Other things make me feel good. And valuable. I'm very good at being a mom and a teacher. And hula hooping. Or I was. I'm also excellent at badminton and shooting pool."

"You are?"

"I am, actually. Shot a lot of pool in East Village bars in my twenties. Paid my way through college. Just kidding." Lucy realized she was deflecting with humor and stopped. Instead she allowed for the truth to hang there awkwardly, and felt an odd, calm relief.

Topher said, "I value you."

Lucy paused. She spoke softly. "I was wondering."

"I think there might be more good in you than bad. It's just a feeling I have."

Lucy thought, *Go with that feeling. Run with it!*

Topher continued, "And I'm willing to see where this goes. But slowly, and only because you told me the truth." Relief shone in Lucy's eyes. "And because you're great in the sack," he said.

Lucy went for it. "That's what they all say." But Topher balked a little so she quickly added. "Kidding. Okay, not funny. Not even a little bit. But you gave me a lob."

Topher laughed. "I did. You earned it."

"That was a close one. Oh, hey, speaking of earning something. I have something for you." Lucy smiled, reached into her purse and handed Topher the CD. He smiled as he turned it over and skimmed the handwritten track titles. "I love mix tapes," he said.

Lucy said, "And ice cream's on me."

"Okay," said Topher. They stood up and Topher put his hands squarely on Lucy's shoulders, a magical touch that made Lucy's knees weak. He paused there for a moment and looked into her eyes, then leaned in and kissed her slowly and faintly on the lips. With purpose. Lucy buzzed so much from the inside out that she thought her eyeballs might catch fire. Topher pulled away and said, "But after this, from here on out, everything else is on me." Lucy knew she would have to give up control and let go if this was going to work. She would have to be very real and very honest with this man. And herself.

Chapter 34

- -

The seasons passed the way seasons do, and Lucy's scandal was replaced by a predictable parade of others. By the time her birthday luncheon rolled around, she had managed to condense the previous year's hard-boiled odyssey into an easily relatable story for the one guest who didn't know the nitty-gritty—Dix's oldest sister, Di, visiting from Nashville. Lucy was celebrating at her kitchen table with the ladies who'd ridden out the shitstorm with her: Audra, Fran, Dix, Gina and Nancy. Five friends plus a random houseguest. Not bad for the town pariah.

Lucy had moved into a smaller house with no yard, but it was cozy, near a park, and had that happily-ever-after look. Sunlight poured in through the windows and bathed the kitchen in a warm glow. The room itself was sparkling clean and Stevie Wonder grooved in the background. A centerpiece of blue hydrangea and lavender snapdragons draped over the lip of a tarnished flea-market vase in the center of the table, and gaily printed aquamarine linens graced each setting. Cooking-magazine-beautiful food was arranged on matching chunky white plates, and water glasses sparkled with wedges of lemon. All of Lucy's guests were freshly showered and wearing clean clothes, and everyone was having a good hair day.

Lucy's story of her previous year's woes sounded as if she was recounting the lyrics of an unimaginably hack, old-school country song, and all Dix's sister Di could do was repeat, "Noooo, noooo," with wide eyes and that family grin. Lucy's friends jumped in to tell their favorite parts—fudging the story to leave out The Program—and Lucy just smiled as she ate her breaded chicken cutlet over fresh spinach, drizzled in balsamic vinaigrette and cracked pepper. She related how she'd cried at least once every day for about ten months, gained ten pounds, then lost double that. She explained to Di how she withdrew, barely cobbling her sanity together every day in time to pick Gus up from school, then collapsed every night into bed.

"But we were there," said Audra.

Nancy said, "Well, most of us," and smiled, embarrassed. Lucy squeezed her hand.

"You were there," Lucy said, and lifted her glass to them in toast. "To my friends—those who toughed it out with me, who were able to withstand the wicked social lashing that followed my bastard pregnancy and infamous hormone-induced rant at the school concert, I salute you!"

Dix explained to Di how they brought her meat loafs and Mallomars, washed her hair and rubbed her hands. Gina added that they sent her subversive videos on YouTube and trashy magazines. Di was very impressed. Audra added that thankfully Gus was unaware of Lucy's summer status as unemployed social kryptonite and by the time he was in school again, his friends either forgot or never knew in the first place. Then Fran told in gory detail how Lucy's baby came, how Lucy named him Ernie, and said he was healthy and a bruiser.

Finally, Lucy recalled how she turned a corner in the same way that an interminably long winter slowly but surely gives way to spring. One night, when Ernie was six months old, sleeping through the night and rolling over like a champ, Lucy climbed into bed and realized that she hadn't cried at all that day. Not once.

Dix said, "And that's when she knew she'd be fine."

Gina raised her glass to toast Lucy, adding, "And she is."

The other ladies followed suit, lifting their wineglasses with red-wine smiles.

Di-from-Nashville, said, "What a story."

Audra said, "If only it were a story, darling."

Dix said, "She was a mess."

"A hot mess," said Gina.

Di asked, "And how many days short from tenure were you?" They all looked at each other and chuckled, then they each held up one finger.

"Nooooo wayyyy," said Di, looking for confirmation from her sister.

"Yes way," said Dix.

Lucy started to laugh at the absurdity of it. How could she not? To lose her job a day short of tenure with a baby on the way was so awful, Lucy cracked up, which invited everybody to crack up.

Di said, "How can you all laugh? It doesn't seem funny."

"It's not," Lucy said, laughing,

Fran said, "Did you say snot?" They all broke up further.

Di asked Lucy, "So what are you doing now?"

Gina said, "She has her own tutoring business."

Di said, "Really? Can you make money doing that?"

Fran said, "Are you shitting me?"

Lucy said, "It's going well after a bumpy start. I'm grateful as hell. I finally have a steady, loyal base and they're very good to me."

Dix said, "She gets a decent amount of recommendations."

Fran said, "And it's totally legal."

"Legal?" said Di.

"Who wants dessert?" said Audra, who glared at Fran then started clearing. Fran said, "I do!" Audra didn't know if Lucy wanted to go there on her birthday. Gina joined Audra. They carried the dishes over to the kitchen counter, got the champagne ready, and put candles in a strawberry rhubarb pie.

Nancy said, "So, is anyone dating?"

Fran said, "I am."

Dix said, "I had a blind date. A setup by a neighbor. And then it turned out that Audra had met him online already."

Audra said to Dix, "You can have him."

Dix said, "No, that's fine, he's all yours. Add him to your stable."

"But he's more your type. You take him."

"I don't want him."

Gina said, "It sounds like you two are talking about the last sweater on a rack at the mall."

Fran pitched her voice high to sound girly and said, "*You* take it, *I* already have one just like it. Well, it looks better on *you*. No, *you!*" Everyone nodded and laughed.

Audra said to Dix, "He talked to me about his hair, did he do that with you?"

"Yes" said Dix, "he gave me the 'I still have thick hair' speech."

"He talked about his *hair*?" said Gina.

"You mean, in case you didn't notice it sitting there on top of his head?" said Nancy.

"He was proud that he still had a bunch and wanted to make sure we noticed."

"This stuff really happens on blind dates?" Nancy said, and looked at Audra.

"You have no idea," said Audra, then, "Stay married, dahling."

"I'm trying." Nancy grinned.

Lucy said to Dix, "So, did you make sure he knew you appreciated his hair?"

"I did," Dix said. "Then I asked him for a lock as a souvenir. Too much?"

Gina said, "Nah."

"Jeez, you know," Audra said with a pronounced sigh, "men are so . . ."

"Don't say it," a voice said flatly from the next room. It was Topher's.

Lucy and Topher hadn't moved in together and they weren't exclusive, but they ended up being monogamous without meaning to be. They seldom discussed their relationship and just happened to prefer each other's company. They laughed a lot together, he was terrific with the baby and he was rarely, if ever, critical of her. Sure they got into it occasionally about generic stuff, but for the most part—easy. So when Topher spoke up from the other room he was mostly joking. But Lucy knew he was right. She had two sons now that she had to raise to feel good about themselves. Dumping on men was counterproductive to her long-range mission of releasing two reasonable teenagers and future good boyfriends and husbands into the world. So generalizing about the lameness of men was verboten, even when Topher wasn't around.

Gina and Audra turned to face the table with the candles on the pie lit, singing the Beatles birthday song. Fran's enthusiastic air guitar part woke up the baby, who had been asleep in his pack 'n' play around the corner. The ladies kept singing as Lucy walked over, picked up Baby Ernest and brought him back over to the table, nestling him onto her lap as she made a wish. He was hearty, beautiful and smelled like heaven. Ernie stopped crying the second he saw the candles. He was entranced and held everyone's gaze as Lucy gave him an extra moment to watch the glow. Lucy hadn't required any time to think of a wish. She had everything she needed and couldn't have been happier. She'd learned to value herself and that the riskiest thing she could do now was be honest with someone. Her life was perfect, she decided, as perfect as it might ever get—perfect enough for today, that's for sure. So she blew out the candles, not making a wish *for* anything, but in gratitude. Lucy closed her eyes and thought, *Thank you. Thank you for forgiveness, too.*

When Lucy blew out the candles, Ernie began to cry and all the ladies let out a reflexive, "Awwww." Lucy called over her shoulder into the next room, "Topher, hon?"

"Yup. Got it," a man's voice called out. Everyone dug into the pie.

Dix said, "Okay Fran, your turn. Go."

"My new guy's a mime," said Fran. She was still chewing.

Lucy said, "What about Cliff? Did he ever finish your cabinets?"

"Nope."

Nancy said, "Contractors and carpenters. Gotta love 'em."

Gina said, "Many married women do. I think it's the tool belt and the can-do attitude."

"It's the way their jeans fit," said Nancy.

Audra said, "And because they're actually doing something around the house without having to be asked a hundred times."

Topher called out from the other room, "Audra, put a nickel in the jar!"

"Sorry, dahling! Back to Fran. Did you say mime?"

Dix said, "I thought you told me ex-mime?"

"Mime. Ex-mime. Whatever," said Fran.

"Once a mime, always a mime," Gina said under her breath.

"Now he's a textbook editor. He's got good grammar and we have great sex."

Nancy said, "Wait a minute, back up. He really was a mime?"

"Someone had to be the first mime," said Lucy.

"Yeah," said Gina. "There must have been an original mime."

Lucy said, "Who begat the second mime."

Fran continued, "This guy was a total mime. He left a good New England college his sophomore year to go to mime school. It was the eighties." Fran gave the last bit of info by way of explanation.

"Smart move," said Gina. "His parents must have been proud."

Lucy asked, "Did he joke about it?"

"No. What's so funny about mime school?" said Fran without irony.

"Nothing," Lucy said. "Nothing is funny about mime school. Especially in hindsight."

Fran said, "You guys are getting it confused with clown school. Different discipline."

"He sounds perfect for you," said Dix with mock sobriety. Audra kicked her.

Topher walked in with a warm bottle for the baby and handed it to Lucy saying, "Just a bunch of hot women sitting around talking about mimes." Lucy smiled up at him and said, "Thank you very much for bringing this in. And thanks for the pie. It's delish." All the women thanked Topher and complimented him as well. They liked his pie, but they really liked the way he treated their friend.

Lucy batted her eyes up at Topher like a cartoon showgirl. She still liked his face and his voice, and yes, his gray thinning hair.

She appreciated the fact that he was fit and healthy and made awe-some fart noises under his armpit. He showed Gus how to build and set off model rockets and always kept Lucy thinking. She didn't know where it was going or how long it would last, but she was content. What they had together was respectful, relaxed and uncomplicated. She thanked her lucky stars for him every single day, all day long. Topher rubbed Ernie on the head then smiled back at Lucy. "I am here to serve you, birthday girl," he said with a wry smile, and gave Lucy's shoulder a light squeezed before pad-ding back towards the TV room. Over his shoulder, Topher dead-panned, "A mime is a terrible thing to waste."

Fran pounded the table, "Don't I know it, sweet heaven above!" Dix mimed a man trapped in a box, feeling up Fran's boobs and the women became giddy all over again.

Gus came into the room and rolled his eyes at the table full of whack-a-doo women. "Hi, Gus," they overlapped. Gina had tears in her eyes from laughing. "Hi," Gus mumbled. Audra held her arms out to get a hug, and he walked right by her, knowing that he would be assaulted by kisses if he went anywhere near her side of the table, which just re-energized the laughter. Gus went over to baby Ernie, rubbed his little brother on the back and said, "Mom, why is Aunt Gina crying?"

Lucy said, "Because someone told a funny joke."

"The rabbi joke?"

"No, dear, it wasn't the rabbi joke."

"Then can I hear it?"

"No, you may not. It's a grown-up joke. This is grown-up time and you are standing in a Grown-Ups-Only zone. But you may take your brother in to Topher for a kiss and then upstairs for a nap. Please read him a book."

"Oh-kay," Gus said. Then Lucy pointed to her cheek and Gus acquiesced, leaning over to give her a quick peck. Gus lifted Ernie up gently and with seriousness of purpose. He cradled the baby into his arms thoughtfully and walked him into the next room.

"That's really sweet," said Di.

"I've been very lucky," said Lucy.

"What about you?" Nancy said to Di. "Tell us a little bit about you."

Di exhaled and said, "Not much to tell. I've been married forever, if you know what I mean." Audra slipped in, "Oh, yes, we know what you mean." The others nodded then stole glances from behind sips of champagne.

Dix jumped in, "But you do have dating issues of sorts these days, right, Di? Tell them."

"What do you mean?" Di said.

"Robbie," Dix said, then smiled. Di just shook her head, let out a sigh and looked to the heavens as she leaned in with her elbows on the table. The other women sensed a juicy revelation coming and leaned forward, too.

"I have this son, Robbie," Di said. "He's my oldest. He's twenty and he's home from college this summer. He's only been home for two weeks and already he's driving me insane."

"No job?" asked Fran.

"No, no, he has a job, a good one," said Di, "but he's climbing the walls and a real bear to be around. I think he just needs to get laid. He's a good-looking kid and I'm sure marinating in hormones, but he doesn't seem to be connecting with the girls out there his age. Honestly, he doesn't want to deal with the demands of a girlfriend. He doesn't get home from work 'til after ten. And he's trying to save money. He just wants sex. Sometimes I wish that there was some service out there for mothers of cranky, horny sons. Some way we could get them laid by nice, attractive, disease-free women without having to send them to hookers. I know it sounds loony."

Di had been looking at the centerpiece as she spoke, but now she looked up at the faces at the table. All the ladies were staring at her, agape. Then they looked at Lucy, who reached for her champagne and took a huge gulp. It was Nancy who managed to speak, "No, Di, it doesn't sound loony."

Di said, "And I know what you're all thinking."

"Oh, no," said Gina, "you can't possibly know what we're thinking." Her dry delivery made Lucy cough just as she swallowed, spraying a little champagne on her pie, which pushed everyone else over the edge into peals of teary laughter. Audra emitted an unladylike snort, Fran fell onto the floor for comic effect and Di just watched them all unravel, dumbfounded, chuckling along with them without knowing why.

"What did I say?"